# Mistresses:
# Passionate
# Revenge

### TRISH MOREY

### CHANTELLE SHAW

### MELANIE MILBURNE

MIX
Paper from
responsible sources
FSC
FSC C007454

This book is produced from independently certified FSC paper
to ensure responsible forest management

For more information visit: www.harpercollins.co.uk

Printed and bound in Spain
by CPI, Barcelona

# MILLS & BOON

First Published in Great Britain 2020
By Mills & Boon, an imprint of HarperCollins*Publishers*
1 London Bridge Street, London, SE1 9GF

Mistresses: Passionate Revenge© 2020 Harlequin Books S.A.

*His Mistress for a Million* © 2009 Trish Morey
*Proud Greek, Ruthless Revenge* © 2009 Chantelle Shaw
*Castellano's Mistress of Revenge* © 2009 Melanie Milburne

ISBN: 978-0-263-28077-7

0220

# HIS MISTRESS FOR A MILLION

**TRISH MOREY**

To the Maytoners,
every one of you warm, generous and wise.
This one's for you, with thanks.
xxx

# CHAPTER ONE

REVENGE was sweet.

Andreas Xenides eyed the shabby building that proclaimed itself a hotel, its faded sign swinging violently in the bitter wind that carved its way down the canyon of the narrow London street.

How long had it taken to track down the man he knew to be inside? How many years? He shook his head, oblivious to the cold that had passers-by clutching at their collars or burrowing hands deeper into pockets. It didn't matter how long. Not now that he had found him.

The cell phone in his pocket beeped and he growled in irritation. His lawyer had agreed to call him if there was a problem with his plan proceeding. But one look at the caller ID and Andreas had the phone slipped back in his pocket in a moment. Nothing on Santorini was more important than what was happening here in London today, didn't Petra know that?

The wind grew teeth before he was halfway across the street, another burst of sleet sending pedestrians scampering for cover to escape the gusty onslaught, the street a running watercolour of black and grey.

He mounted the hotel's worn steps and tested the handle. Locked as he'd expected, a buzzer and rudimentary camera mounted at the side to admit only those with keys or reservations, but he was in luck. A couple wearing matching track-suits and money belts emerged, so disgusted with the weather that they barely looked his way. He was past them and following the handmade sign to the downstairs reception before they'd struggled into their waterproof jackets and slammed the door behind them.

Floorboards squeaked under the shoddy carpet and he had to duck his head as the stairs twisted back on themselves under the low ceiling. There was a radio crackling away somewhere in the distance and his nose twitched at a smell of decay no amount of bleach had been able to mask.

This place was barely habitable. Even if the capricious London weather was beyond his control, he had no doubt the clientele would be much happier in the alternative accommodation he'd arranged for them.

A glazed door stood ajar at the end of a short hallway, another crudely handwritten note taped to the window declaring it the office, and for a moment he was so focused on the door and the culmination of a long-held dream that he barely noticed the bedraggled shape stooping down to pick up a vacuum cleaner, an overflowing rubbish bag in the other hand. A cleaner, he realised as she straightened. For a moment he thought she was about to say something, before she pressed her lips together and flattened herself against a door to let him pass. There were dark shadows under her reddened eyes, her fringe was plastered to her face and her uniform was filthy. He flicked his eyes away again as he passed, his nose twitching at the combined scent of ammonia and stale beer. So that was the hired help. Hardly surprising in a dump like this.

Vaguely he registered the sound of her retreat behind him, her hurried steps, the thud of the machine banging against something and a muffled cry. But he didn't turn. He was on the cusp of fulfilling the promise he'd made to his father on his deathbed.

It wasn't a moment to rush.

*It was a moment to savour.*

And so he hesitated. Drank in the moment. Wishing his father could be here. Knowing he would be watching from wherever he was now.

Knowing it was time.

He jabbed at the door with two fingers and watched it swing open, letting the squeak of the hinges announce his arrival.

Then he stepped inside.

The man behind the dimly lit desk hadn't looked up. He was too busy scribbling notes on what looked like the turf guide with one hand, holding the phone to his ear with the other, and it was all Andreas could do to bite back on the urge to cross the room and yank the man bodily from his chair. But much as he desired to tear the man to pieces as he deserved, Andreas had a much more twenty-first-century way of getting justice.

'Take a seat,' the man growled, removing the phone from his ear long enough to gesture to a small sofa, still busy writing down his notes. 'I'll be just a moment.'

One more moment when it had taken so many years to track him down? Of course he could wait. But he'd bet money he didn't have to.

*'Kala ime orthios,'* Andreas replied through his teeth, *I'm fine standing*, 'if it's all the same to you.'

The man's head jerked up, the blood draining from his face leaving his red-lined eyes the only patch of colour. He uttered a single word, more like a croak, before the receiver clattered back down onto the cradle, and all the while his gaze didn't leave his visitor, even as he edged his chair back from the desk. But there was nowhere to go in the cramped office and his chair rolled into the wall with a jolt. He stiffened his back and jerked his chin up as if he hadn't just been trying to escape, but he didn't attempt to stand. Andreas wondered if it was because his knees were shaking too much.

'What are you doing here?'

Andreas sauntered across the room, until he was looming over both the desk and the man cowering behind it, lazily picking up a letter opener in his long-fingered hands and testing its length through his fingers while all the time Darius watched nervously. 'It's been a long time, Darius. Or would you rather I called you Demetrius, or maybe even Dominic? I really can't keep up. You seem to go through names like other people go through toilet paper.'

The older man licked his lips, his eyes darting from side to side, and this close Andreas was almost shocked to see how much his father's one-time friend and partner had aged. Little more than fifty years old, and yet Darius's hair had thinned and greyed and his once wiry physique seemed to have caved in on itself, the lines on his face sucked deeper with it. The tatty cardigan he wore draped low on his bony shoulders did nothing to wipe off the years.

So time hadn't treated him well? Tough. Sympathy soon departed as Darius turned his eyes back to him and Andreas saw that familiar feral gleam, the yellow glow that spoke of the festering soul within. And he might be afraid now, taken by surprise by the sudden appearance of his former partner's son, but Andreas knew that any minute he could come out snarling. Not that it would do him any good.

'How did you find me?'

'That's one thing I always liked about you, Darius. You never did waste your time on small talk. No "how are you?" No "have a nice day".'

'I get the impression you didn't come here for small talk.'

'Touché,' Andreas conceded as he circled the room, absently taking inventory, enjoying the exchange much more than he'd expected. 'I have to admit, you weren't easy to find. You were good at covering your tracks in South America. Very good. The last we heard of you was in Mexico before the trail went cold.' Andreas looked up at the high basement window where the sleet was leaving trails of slush down the grimy glass before he turned back. 'And to think you could still be back there enjoying the sunshine. Nobody expected you'd be fool enough to show your face in Europe again.'

A glimmer of resentment flared in Darius' eyes, and his lip curled into a snarl. The hungry dog was out of its kennel. 'Maybe I got sick of beans.'

'The way I hear it, you ran out of money. Lost most of it on bad business deals and flashy women.' Andreas leaned over and picked up the form guide sitting on the desk. 'Gambled away the rest. All that money, Darius. All those millions. And this—' he waved his hand around him '—is what you're reduced to.'

Darius glowered, his eyes making no apology in their assessment of his visitor's cashmere coat and hand stitched shoes, a tinge of green now colouring his features. 'Looks like you've done all right for yourself though.'

*No thanks to you!*

Andreas' hands clenched and unclenched at his sides while he tried to remember his commitment not to tear the man apart. A deep breath later and he could once again manage a civil tone. 'You've got a problem with that?'

'Is that why you came here, then? To gloat?' He sneered, swinging a hand around the shabby office. 'To see me reduced to this? Okay, you've seen me. Happy now? Isn't that what they say—success is the best revenge?'

'Ah, now that's where they're wrong.' This time Andreas didn't restrain himself, but allowed the smile he'd been headed for ever since he'd set foot in this rat trap. 'Success is nowhere near the best revenge.'

The old man's eyes narrowed warily as he leaned forward in his chair, the fear back once more. 'What's that supposed to mean?'

Andreas pulled the folded sheaf of papers from inside his coat pocket. 'This,' he said, unfolding them so that the other man could see what he was holding. '*This* is the best revenge.'

And Andreas watched the blood drain from the other man's face as he recognised the finance papers he'd signed barely a week ago.

'Did you even read the small print, Darius? Didn't you wonder why someone would offer you money on this dump you call a hotel on such easy terms?'

The older man swallowed, his eyes once more afraid.

'Did you not suspect there would be a catch?'

Darius looked sick, his skin grey.

Andreas smiled again. 'I'm the catch. That finance company is one of mine. I lent you that money, Darius, and I'm calling in the debt. Now.'

'You can't… You can't do that. I don't have that kind of money lying around.'

He flung the pages in Darius' direction. 'I can do it, all right. See for yourself. But if you can't pay me back today, you're in default on the loan. And you know what that means.'

'No! You know there's no way…' But still Darius scrabbled through the pages, his eyes scanning the document for an out, squinting hard when they came across the clause that proved Andreas right, widening as he looked up with the knowledge that he'd been beaten. 'You can't do this to me. It's no better than theft.'

'You'd know all about theft, Darius, but whatever you call it this hotel is now mine. And it's closing. Today.'

The shocked look on Darius' face was his reward. The man looked as if he'd been sucker punched.

Oh, yes, Andreas thought, revenge was sweet, especially when it had been such a long time coming.

# CHAPTER TWO

*ROCK bottom.*

Cleo Taylor was so there.

Her head ached, her bruised shin stung where the vacuum cleaner had banged into it, and three weeks into this job she was exhausted, both mentally and physically. And at barely five o'clock in the afternoon, all she wanted to do was sleep.

She dropped the machine at the foot of her bed and sank down onto the narrow stretcher, the springs that woke her every time she rolled over at night noisily protesting her presence.

*Karma.* It had to be karma.

How many people had tried to warn her? How many had urged her to be careful and not to rush in? And how many of those people had she suspected of being jealous of her because she'd found love in the unlikeliest of places, in an Internet chat room with a man halfway around the world?

Too many.

Oh, yes, if there was a price to pay for naivety, for blindly charging headlong for a fall, she was well and truly paying it.

And no one would say she didn't deserve everything that was happening to her. She'd been so stupid believing Kurt, stupid to believe the stories he'd spun, stupid to believe that he loved her.

*So pathetically naïve to trust him with both her heart and with her nanna's money.*

And all she'd achieved was to spectacularly prove the award she'd been given in high school from the girls whose company she'd craved, but who never were and who would never be her friends.

*Cleo Taylor, girl most likely to fail.*

Wouldn't they just love to see her now?

A barrage of sleet splattered against the tiny louvred window high above the bed and she shivered. So much for spring.

Reluctantly she thought about dragging herself from the rudimentary bed but there was no way she wanted to meet that man in the hallway again. She shuddered, remembering the ice-cold way his eyes—dark pits of eyes set in a slate-hard face—had raked over her and then disregarded her in the same instant without even an acknowledgment, as if she was some kind of low-life, before imperiously passing by. She'd shrunk back instinctively, her own greeting dying on her lips.

It wasn't just that he looked so out of place, so wrong for the surroundings, but the look of such a tall, powerful man sweeping through the low-ceilinged space seemed wrong, as if there wasn't enough space and he needed more. He hadn't just occupied the space, he'd consumed it.

And then he'd swept past, all cashmere coat, the smell of rain and the hint of cologne the likes of which she'd never smelt in this place, and she'd never felt more like the low-life he'd taken her to be.

But she had to get up. She couldn't afford to fall asleep yet, even though she'd been up since five to do the breakfasts and it had taken until four to clean the last room. She reeked of stale beer and her uniform was filthy, courtesy of the group of partying students who'd been in residence in the room next door for the last three nights.

She hated cleaning that room! It was damp and dark, the tiny en suite prone to mould and the drains smelling like a swamp, and if she hadn't already known how low she'd sunk that room announced it in spades. The students had left it filthy, with beds looking as if they'd been torn apart, rubbish spilling from bins over the floor, and an entire stack of empty takeaway boxes and beer bottles artfully arranged in one corner all the way from the floor to the low ceiling. 'Leaning Tower of Pizza,' someone had scrawled on the side of one the boxes, and it had leant, so much so that it was a wonder it hadn't already collapsed with the vibrations from the nearby tube.

It had been waiting for her to do that. Bottles and pizza boxes raining down on her, showering her with their dregs.

*No wonder he'd looked at her as if she were some kind of scum*. After the day she'd had, she felt like it.

She dragged herself from the bed and plucked her towel off a hook and her bag of toiletries, ready to head to the first-floor bathroom. What did she care what some stranger she'd never see again thought? In ten minutes she'd be showered, tucked up in bed and fast asleep. That was all she cared about at the moment.

The bright side, she told herself, giving thanks to her nanna as she ascended the stairs and saw rain lashing against the glazing of the ground-floor door, was that she had a roof over her head and she didn't have to go out in today's weather.

"There's always a silver lining", her nanna used to tell her, rocking her on her lap when she was just a tiny child and had skinned her knees, or when she'd started school and the other girls had picked on her because her mother had made her school uniform by hand and it had shown. Even though her family was dirt poor and sometimes it had been hard to find, there'd always been something she'd been able to cling to, a bright side somewhere, something she'd been able to give thanks for.

*Almost always.*

She sighed as the hot water in the shower finally kicked in and warmed her weary bones. A warm shower, a roof over her head and a bed with her name written on it. Things could always be worse.

And come summer and the longer days, she'd have time to see something of the sights of London she'd promised herself before she went home. Not that there was any hurry. At the rate she was paid, after her board was deducted, it would be ages before she could even think about booking a return airfare to Australia. God, she'd been so stupid to trust Kurt with her money!

A sudden pang of homesickness hit her halfway back down the stairs. Barely six weeks ago she'd left the tiny outback town of Kangaroo Crossing with such confidence, and now look at her. If only she could go home. If only she'd never left! She'd give anything to hug her mum and half-brothers again. She'd even find a smile for her stepfather if it came down to it. But when would that be? And how would she be able to face everyone when she did?

She would be going home humiliated. A failure.

*The bright side*, she urged herself, *look at the bright side*, as she pulled her eye mask down and snuggled under the covers, the cold rain lashing at her tiny window. She was warm and dry and she had at least ten hours' sleep before she had to get up and do it all over again.

'But you can't close the hotel,' Darius protested. 'There are bookings. Guests!'

'Who will be catered for, as will the staff we have on file from your finance application.' Andreas snapped open his phone, made a quick call and slipped the phone back into his pocket. 'I'm sure the guests won't mind being transferred to the four-star hotel we've chosen to accommodate them in and you can be assured the employees will be paid a generous redundancy.'

He cast a disdainful eye around the room. 'I don't foresee any complaints. And now I want you off the premises. I have staff coming in to take over and ensure the changeover is smooth. The hotel will be empty in two hours.'

'And what about me?' Darius demanded. 'What am I supposed to do? You're leaving me with nothing. Nothing!'

Andreas slowly turned back, unable to stop his lips from forming into a sneer. 'What about you? How many millions did you steal from my father? You happily walked away and left my family with nothing. What did you care about anyone else then? So why should I care about what happens to you? Just be grateful you're able to walk out of here with your limbs intact after the way you betrayed my father.'

A buzzer sounded, the security monitor showing a team of people waiting on the front step. 'Let them in, Darius.' The older man's hand hovered over the door-release button.

'I can help you!' he suddenly said instead, pulling his hand away to join the other in supplication. 'You don't need all these people. I know this hotel and I… I'm sorry for what happened all those years ago. It was a mistake… A misunderstanding. Your father and I were once good friends. Partners even. Isn't there any way you might honour that?'

Andreas dragged much-needed air into his lungs. 'I'll honour it in the same way you honoured my father. Get out. You've got ten minutes. And then I never want to see you again.'

Darius knew when he was beaten. Sullenly he gathered his personal possessions, the form guide included, in a cardboard box and slunk away even as the team filed into the office. Andreas took two minutes to go over the arrangements. Someone would email all forward bookings and advise of the change of hotels while the rest of the team would meet guests as they returned to expedite their packing and transfer to the new hotel. New guests would simply be ferried to the alternative premises nearby. There was no reason for the operation not to go like clockwork.

His cell phone beeped again as he dismissed the team to their duties and he reached for it absently, taking just a second to savour what he'd achieved. The look on Darius' face when he'd realised the truth, that he had lost everything and to the son of the man he'd cheated of millions so many years ago, was something he would cherish for ever. Doubly so because his father never could.

He frowned when he looked at the phone. Petra calling again? *Kolisi*, maybe there really was an emergency.

'*Ne?*'

Half a continent away, Petra's voice lit up. 'Andreas!' She sounded so bright he could almost hear the flashbulb.

'What's wrong?'

'Oh, I've been so worried about you. How is it in London? It is all going to plan?'

Andreas felt a stab of irritation. No emergency, then. Merely Petra thinking she had some stake in what was happening here. She was wrong. 'Why are you calling, Petra?'

There was a pause. Then, 'The Bonacelli deal! The papers are here ready to be signed.'

'I expected that. I told you I'll sign them when I get back.'

'And Stavros Markos called,' she continued at rapid pace, as if he hadn't spoken. 'He wants to know if they can book out the entire Caldera Palazzo for their daughter's wedding next June. It's going to be huge. They only want the best and I told them it should be fine, though I have to put off another couple of enquiries—'

'Petra,' he cut in, 'you know they can. You don't have to ring me to confirm. What's bothering you? Is there something else?'

There was silence at the end of the line, and then she laughed, an uncomfortable tinkle. Or at least, it made him feel uncomfortable. 'I'm sorry, Andreas,' she continued. 'It probably sounds silly, but I miss you. When do you think you'll be back?'

Something clenched in his gut, the pattern of her constant phone calls making the kind of sense he didn't want them to make. But there was no other option. She'd been checking up on him, making sure nobody else was occupying his bed or his attentions while he was in London and she was holding the fort back on Santorini.

He murmured something noncommittal before sliding his phone shut. What was wrong with her? He didn't do relationships. Petra, more than anyone, should have understood that. She'd witnessed the parade of women through his life. Hell, she'd been the one to organise the flowers for them when they were on the inner, the trinkets for them when they were on the outer. But he'd made one fatal mistake, broken his own rule never to get involved with the staff.

Drunk on success and the culmination of years of planning, he'd let his guard down when he'd heard the news that Darius had been found and the trap set. He'd been the one to insist Petra go out to dinner with him to celebrate. He'd been the one to order the champagne and he'd been the one to respond when she leaned too close, all but spilling her breasts into his hands. He'd wanted the release and she'd been there.

What a fool! He'd always assumed she was as machine-like and driven as he was. He'd always thought that she'd understood it was always just sex to him. And yet every time Petra called him now, he could almost feel her razor-sharp nails piercing his skin all over again. But why she'd want to be his mistress when she knew which way they invariably went…

Cold fingers crawled down his spine.

Or did she have something else in mind? Something more permanent she thought she was due after working alongside him for so many years?

*Sto thiavolo!*

What had his mother been telling him in her recent phone calls? That maybe it was time for him to settle down and find a wife?

And who did his mother like to talk to first, calling the office line instead of his cell phone, because 'her own son never bothered to tell her anything'?

*Petra.*

Had his mother also confided the news with her good friend's daughter that it was time for her only child to settle down? He'd just bet she had.

Damn. He didn't want to have to find a new marketing director. Petra was a good operator. The best at marketing the package of luxurious properties that Xenides Exclusive Property let to the well-heeled looking for a five-star experience in some of the most beautiful places in the world. She'd single-handedly designed the website that made his unique brand of five-star luxury accommodation accessible to every computer on the planet and made it so tempting that just as many booked through the website alone as booked by personal referral.

He didn't want to lose her; together they made a good team. But neither did he want her thinking she was destined to be anything more to him than a valued employee.

He sighed. What would she do when he found someone else, as he inevitably would? Would she leave of her own accord?

Andreas made up his mind on a sigh. It was a risk he would just have to take. Petra's departure from the business, while inconvenient, was preferable to her making wedding plans. All of which meant one thing.

*He wouldn't be returning to Santorini without a woman on his arm and in his bed.*

She would have to be somebody new, somebody different, someone who could step into the role of his mistress and then step out when he no longer needed her. No strings. No ties.

A contract position. A month should be more than enough.

Now he just had to find her before his flight back to Greece tomorrow.

He looked around the dingy room and sighed, the weight of years of the need for vengeance sloughing from his shoulders. His work here was done, an old score settled and Darius vanquished. There was no need for him to linger; his team knew what to do. He could hear them now knocking on doors and explaining the move, smoothing any objections with the promise of four-star luxury and their bill waived for the inconvenience. They would make the necessary transfers and see to the stripping bare of the furnishings in preparation for the builders and decorators that would turn this place into something worthy of being included in the Xenides luxury hotel portfolio.

Everything was under control.

And that's when he heard the scream.

# CHAPTER THREE

THE earth-shattering sound rang through the basement, followed by a torrent of language Andreas had no hope of discerning. He was down the hallway and at the open door in just a few strides. 'What the hell is going on?'

One of his team was busy backing out of the small room, closely followed by a slipper that flew past his head and smacked into the wall behind. 'I had no idea there was anyone here,' he said defensively. 'It was marked on the plans as a closet. And it's barely six o'clock. What's anyone doing in bed at this time of night, least of all here?'

'Get out!' screeched the voice. 'Or I'll call the manager. I'll call the police!'

So much for everything being under control. Andreas ushered his red-faced assistant out of the way. 'I'll handle this.'

He stepped into the tiny room that smelt and looked more like a broom closet, ducking his head where the stairs cut through the headspace and avoiding the single globe dangling on a wire from the ceiling, under whose yellow light he found the source of the commotion. She was sitting up in bed, or on a camp stretcher more like it, with her back rammed tight against the wall, the bedding pulled up tight around her with one hand despite the fact her fleecy pyjamas covered every last square centimetre below her neck. In her other hand she wielded a second furry slipper.

Her eyes were wide and wild-looking under a pink satin eye mask reading 'Princess' that she'd obviously shoved up to her brow when she'd been disturbed. Some kind of joke, he decided. In her dishevelled state, with her mousy-coloured hair curling haphazardly around her face, she looked anything but princess material.

Then his eyes made sense of the smell. In the yellow light he saw the vacuum cleaner tucked at the end of the bed and the drab uniform draped unceremoniously over the radiator, and one question at least was answered. The cleaner, he surmised, the one he'd spotted earlier in the corridor who'd stunk of beer. No doubt she'd been trying to sleep it off when she'd been disturbed.

He tried to keep the sneer from his lips as he addressed her. 'I must apologise for my people startling you,' he began. 'I assure you, nobody means you any harm. We simply didn't realise you were here.'

'Well, I am *obviously* here and your *people* have a bloody nerve going about bursting into other people's rooms. What the hell are you playing at? Who are you? Where's Demetrius?'

He held up his hands to calm her. She was Australian, he guessed from her accent, or maybe a New Zealander, but her words were spilling out too fast to be sure.

'I think perhaps you should calm down and then we can discuss this rationally.'

Her hand lifted the slipper. 'Calm down? Discuss rationally? You and your henchman have no right barging into my room. Now get out before I scream again.'

*Gamoto*, the way she clung to those bedcovers as if her virtue were at stake! Did she really think he was going to attack her? It would take a braver man than him to tackle those industrial-strength pyjamas she was buried beneath.

'I'll leave,' he conceded, 'but only so you can get dressed. Come out when you're ready to talk. It is impossible to reason with a woman sitting in bed dressed up like a clown.'

Her jaw fell open, snapping shut again on a huff. 'How dare you? You have no right to be here. No right at all.'

'I have every right! I've wasted enough time here as it is. Now get dressed and meet me in the office. I'll speak to you then.'

He spun away, pulling the door closed behind him, but not before the other pink slipper went hurtling over his shoulder like a furry missile.

He'd barely started pacing the office floor, damning Darius for the spitting, snarling legacy he'd left behind, when he heard someone behind him. He turned to find a young woman in jeans and a top standing there, her expression sullen, her feet bare.

He sighed. *What the hell else*, he thought, *has Darius left me to clean up?* 'Can I help you?'

'You tell me. You're the one who demanded my presence.'

His eyes did a double take. This was the cleaner? The banshee ready to scream the house down in the broom closet? He didn't know what to be more impressed by, her speed in complying with his orders—the women he associated with couldn't effect a quick change if their life depended on it—or the radical change in her appearance.

He asked her to shut the door behind her and he leaned back and perched himself on the edge of the desk, watching her as she complied. She'd discarded the fleecy pyjamas and ridiculous eye mask and pulled on faded jeans and a long-sleeved T-shirt, and that brought the second surprise. She wasn't tall, but what she missed out on in height she made up for in curves. He'd never have guessed there was shape under that drab uniform or hidden away under a mound of bed clothes, but her fitted T-shirt and hipster jeans accentuated the swell of breasts and the feminine curve of waist to hip that had been completely disguised before.

Nor would he have guessed she would scrub up so well. Sure, there were still grey shadows under her eyes, but she looked years younger than the haggard wreck he'd seen struggling with the vacuum cleaner in the hallway, and much less frightening than the banshee he'd encountered so recently in the closet-cum-bedroom. With not a hint of make-up and with her damp hair tamed into some kind of loose arrangement behind her head, a few loose tendrils coiled around her face served to soften features that weren't classical in the least.

She would never pass for pretty, he determined, but if she bothered to make an effort she could probably do something with herself.

Although right now it looked as if she'd much prefer to do something with him, preferably involving knives.

He caught the glower as she folded her arms underneath her breasts and wondered if she had any idea that motion just accentuated their fullness. *Or that it drew attention to their peaking nipples.*

So she hadn't bothered to put on a bra? No wonder she'd been so quick to appear. He was surprised to feel his body stir, but then he'd never had a problem with such time-saving measures, or with breasts that looked like an invitation. Despite the inconvenience, he could only be intrigued by the closet-dweller. He was sure he'd seen no mention of her in the reports that had crossed his desk.

Cleo bristled under the relentless gaze. What was his problem? She'd done what he'd demanded—abandoned any hope of sleep to get herself up and dressed and met him in the office and for what? So his eyes could rake over her as if she were some choice cut of meat in a butcher-shop window?

So maybe the look was marginally better than the one he'd given her in the hallway earlier when he'd regarded her as some kind of scum before sweeping imperiously by, but it certainly didn't make her feel any more comfortable.

Quite the reverse. She rubbed her upper arms, not from the chill, but to ward off the prickling sensation his gaze generated under her skin. And if she was lucky the action might just break whatever magnet hold his eyes had on her breasts.

He only had to look at them for her nipples to harden to rocks.

Damn the man! Arrogance shone out of him like a beacon, but the only thing it was lighting up was her temper.

'Are you going to tell me what this is all about or would you prefer to keep ogling me?' She looked around the office. 'Where's Demetrius?'

'The man you know as Demetrius is gone.'

Of course he would speak in riddles. The man was insufferable. 'What are you talking about? Gone where? When will he be back?' She'd never much liked her boss, who'd seemed more concerned with his form guide than with how his hotel was falling down around his ears, but as far as she was concerned, the sooner he was back, the better.

'He won't be back. This hotel now belongs to me.'

His revelation slammed through her like a thunderbolt. Where did that leave her? Her rapidly chilling toes curled into the cracked linoleum while a shudder of apprehension wormed its way into her mind. Whatever had happened must have been sudden. She'd heard Demetrius on the phone to his turf accountant when she'd finished the last room, just before this man had appeared, larger than life. A bloodless coup. And the man in front of her, with his cold eyes and strong jaw, looked just the kind of ruthless man for the job. Ruthless—but also her new boss. She swallowed, horrified at the impression she'd made so far. Hadn't she flung a slipper past his ear? 'What is this, then, some kind of interview? Okay, my name is Cleo Taylor and I've been cleaning here for three weeks, and doing the breakfasts. Demetrius probably told you—'

'Demetrius told me nothing. There was no mention of you in the list of employees we had.'

'Oh? But then, Demetrius paid me in cash. He said it was better for the both of us.'

'He would no doubt think that.' Andreas understood why. So Darius could pay her peanuts and most likely deduct the majority of it in return for the cot she occupied.

She shrugged, looking confused. 'So… You'll still be needing a cleaner, right?'

'Not exactly.'

'Okay, I do more than clean. I get up at five for the breakfasts…'

'I'm not looking for a cleaner. Or a kitchen hand.'

'But the hotel—'

'Is closing.'

The fear that had begun as a shred of concern exploded inside her in a frenzy of panic. It might be the worst job with the worst pay in the world—but it was a job, and it came with a roof over her head. And now she'd have no job. *And, more importantly, nowhere to live.*

Her mouth was drier than a Kangaroo Crossing summer's day. 'You mean I lose my job.'

He gave the briefest of nods. It might as well have been the fall of the guillotine. Once more she'd failed. Once more she'd bombed. She almost wanted to laugh. Almost managed to, except the sound came out all wrong and this was no place or time for such reactions, not with him here, watching her every move like a hawk.

*Oh, Nanna*, she beseeched, closing her eyes with the

enormity of it all, *where's the silver lining to losing the worst job in the world?* Unless that was it. She hated the job. Now she had no choice but to find something else. And hopefully, something better.

But it was so hard to think positive thoughts about losing her job when it also meant she'd be losing the roof over her head with it. She opened her eyes toward the window, the rain still pelting against the glass. A bright side. There had to be a bright side. But right now she was darned if she could see what it was.

'When?' Her voice was the barest of whispers. 'How much time do I have?' She would have to move fast to secure something. The little money she had wouldn't last long and if she had to use it for any kind of rental bond…

'Tonight. You need to pack your things and be gone in two hours. The guests are all being transferred to other premises. The builders and redecorators move in to gut the place tomorrow.'

'Tonight? You're closing the hotel so soon?' And panic turned to outrage. 'No. No way you can just walk in and do that!'

'No? And why is that? Surely not some misplaced loyalty to your former employer? I see he showed you none.'

'No, damn you. But it took me the best part of the day to clean this dump. Every single room from top to bottom and now you tell me you're closing it and I could have knocked off at ten this morning? Thank you very much. You could have saved me the trouble!' She flung out her arms to make the last point and then put a hand to her brow, pushing back the hair from her face. Although it was what the action did to her breasts that had his attention.

He didn't know what he'd been expecting, but it wasn't the impassioned response she'd given him. Or the swaying floor show. No sag. Her breasts were full and round and pointed high. Would they look as good uncovered? Would they fill his hands as generously as he imagined they would? Would he like to find out? He needed a woman…

He dragged in a breath, trying to cool his rapidly heating groin, and forced his eyes away. *Sto kalo*, she was a cleaner. A cleaner with a drinking problem if how she'd appeared earlier was any indication. Petra must really be getting to him if he was getting hot under the collar over a cleaner. 'You're mad at me,' he said, reluctantly dragging his attention back to her face, 'because you've spent all day cleaning? Isn't that your job?'

She choked back a sob. Yes, she probably sounded irrational, hysterical, but what did he expect—that she would turn around and calmly thank him for his bombshell? 'You try being a cleaner in a dump like this. I've just had the worst day of my life. How would you like it if you were a cleaner and someone booby-trapped their rubbish? How would you like it if you ended up smelling like a brewery and wearing someone else's dried pizza crusts and then somebody else told you that you hadn't had to clean it up at all, that you needn't have bothered?'

His ears pricked up. Maybe not a cleaner with a drinking problem after all. Maybe he wasn't quite so crazy… 'You don't drink beer? I thought you were an Australian.'

'So that makes me a drinker? No, for the record, I don't drink beer. I can't abide the taste of it. And,' she continued, without missing a beat, 'then I get hauled from my bed and told that my job is over and that I have to leave. And that you want to throw me out in that!' She pointed to the window, where the rain distorted the light from the streetlamps and turned it into crazy zigzags. 'What kind of man are you?'

He wanted to growl. This was supposed to be the most successful day of his life, a day he'd dreamed about for what seemed like for ever. And here he was, being challenged by the likes of this scrap of a woman, a mere cleaner. He ground out his answer between his teeth. 'A businessman.'

'Well, bully for you. What kind of business is it that throws innocent women out onto the street in the middle of the storm from hell?'

He'd heard enough. He turned and flicked an imaginary piece of lint from his sleeve. 'You must have somewhere else to go.'

'Yes. And it's twelve thousand miles away. Shall I start walking now, do you think?'

'Then why don't you just buy yourself a ticket home?'

'And you think that if I could afford my fare home, I'd be working in a dump like this?'

'Do you need to be so melodramatic?'

'No. I don't need to. I'm just doing it for laughs.' She dragged in a breath and threw her arms out by her sides. 'Look, why can't I stay here? Just for tonight. I'll go tomorrow morning, first thing. I promise. Maybe it will have stopped raining by then.'

'The hotel is closing,' he reiterated. 'It will be locked down tonight in preparation for the builders and redecorators coming in tomorrow. The deal was the hotel would be delivered empty.'

'Nobody made a deal with me!'

'I'm making it now.'

It didn't sound like much of a deal to her. 'So where are the guests going? Why can't I go there?' She held up her hand to stop his objection. 'Not as a guest. Surely they could do with a cleaner, with this sudden influx of additional guests.'

He uttered something in Greek, something that sounded to her dangerously like a curse. 'I'll call and ask. No guarantees. Meanwhile you get your things together. I assume that won't take long.'

She sniffed. 'And if they don't have a job?'

'Then you're on your own.'

'Just like that?'

'Just like that.'

She put her hands on top of her head and sighed, locking her fingers together, and turning her head up high, as if to think about it.

But Andreas couldn't think about it. He was too busy following the perfect shape of her breasts, her nipples pulled up high, their shape so lovingly recreated by the thin cotton layer that was all that separated him from them. Her waist looked even smaller now. Almost tiny in comparison as she pulled her arms high, the flare of her hips mirroring the curve above. His mouth went dry.

Damn it all! He yanked his eyes away, rubbing them with his fingers. Anyone would think he'd never had a woman. She was a cleaner. It wouldn't work. Clearly the day had taken more out of him than he'd realised.

'And what about my wages?' She was looking at him, her eyes wide, her arms unhooking. 'Demetrius owes me for more than a week! And surely I'm entitled to some kind of severance pay, even if he was paying me cash, seeing you're the one to terminate my job!'

Silently he cursed Darius again, along with his own team that had failed to pick up this stray employee. 'How much are you owed?'

Cleo did some rapid sums in her head. Math had never been her strong point, so the calculations were a bit rough, but an entire week and a half, less board, that was a considerable sum. 'Fifty quid,' she said, rounding it off, hoping he wouldn't balk.

He pulled a money clip from his pocket, withdrew a handful of notes and then added a fistful more before handing the bundle to her.

Her eyes opened wide as she took in the high-denomination notes and the number of them. Her math was still lousy, but it was more than clear he'd given her way too much. 'I can't take this! There's heaps more than that here.'

'Then consider it a bonus for doing what I ask and getting out of here. Call it your redundancy package, if you like, with enough for your accommodation tonight and probably for an entire week if you play your cards right. Now, it's time you started packing.'

She looked as if she'd rather stay and keep arguing, her mouth poised open and ready to deliver another salvo, but she must have thought better of it. She jammed her lips shut and wheeled around, marching purposefully towards the door, shoving the wad of notes into her jeans pocket as she went. Not that it was any distraction. He was already looking there, admiring the way her denim jeans lovingly caressed the cheeks of her behind as she went. But she stopped before the door and turned, and he was forced to raise his eyes to meet hers.

'I'll go and pack,' she said, colour in her cheeks and fire spitting from her eyes, 'and I'd like to say it's been a pleasure meeting you, but I'm afraid that isn't possible. I'll leave my key in the door. Not that you need it, apparently.'

And then she swept out with her head held high like the princess on her eye mask rather than a redundant cleaner.

There was no need for him to stay. But he sat there, leaning against the desk, thinking that he'd been wrong. She wasn't pretty by any measure, she wasn't tall and elegant like his usual choice of woman, but there was something about her, a fire in her eyes as she'd protested his closure of the hotel, something that had almost burned bright in the seedy air between them. Would she be as passionate in the bedroom, or would she go back to being the bedraggled mouse he'd seen lurking in the corridor?

Damn! Trust Darius to leave him to clean up his rubbish. But he should have expected it.

He rubbed the bridge of his nose, hating the way his thoughts were going. The woman had a point. He, more than anyone, knew what it was like to be left with nothing and without even a roof over his head. He wouldn't wish that on anyone.

He slid open his cell phone, found the direct number for the manager of the hotel the guests here were being transferred to and hit 'call'. It answered within a moment. 'It's Andreas. Have you a position for another cleaner or kitchen hand? There is one here who requires a position, preferably live-in.'

There was a moment's hesitation, but no argument, no question as to qualifications or referees from the manager. That Andreas himself had enquired was all the assurance the manager required, the moment's hesitation all the time he needed to make the necessary rearrangements. Of course, they could use the help, came the answer. And there would be a bed the person could use in a shared room.

Andreas breathed deep with relief. When he'd thought of getting even with Darius, he'd thought they'd covered all the bases with everyone on the payroll. He'd not thought about any other fallout, the ones Darius had been paying on the sly. But now that fallout was well and truly taken care of. His father had been avenged and nobody had been inadvertently left homeless in the deal. It was the best of all worlds.

He tried to recapture the joy, the exhilaration of the day's events. After what he'd achieved after a lifetime of wanting, he should feel better than this, surely. But something still didn't sit right with him. Maybe it was just the adrenaline let-down now that he'd achieved his goal?

Or maybe it was because he wasn't sure that he wanted someone else taking care of fallout that came complete with sweet curves and lush breasts?

He sighed. He might as well go give her the good news. His car was waiting and he had work to do.

She was already struggling out of her room with an over-sized pack when he emerged and he wondered how she'd walk if ever she got it onto her back. It looked almost as big as her. He leaned down and took it from her, lifting its weight easily. Their fingers brushed and she pulled her hand away, tucking it under her other arm. 'So you pack as quickly as you get changed?'

She looked up at him, her cheeks flaring with colour again as he looked down at her, surprised by the extent of her reaction. Did she not want to touch him that desperately, or was it something else she was feeling? Resentment perhaps, or even hatred that he'd bowled her out into such a night. But she'd dragged on some kind of all-weather jacket and her breasts' reaction was hidden from him. 'Please, you don't have to take that. Not after—all those things I said about you. It was very ungracious after you were so generous. I'm sorry. It's been a long day.'

'I found you a job.'

Her eyes opened wide. 'You did?' They were blue, he realised for the first time, the kind of blue that came with the first rays of light on a misty Santorini morning showing all the promise of a new day. And then she smiled. 'But that's fantastic. Thank you so much. Is it a cleaner's job at the other hotel? Can I stay there?'

He'd never seen her smile. He got the impression she didn't use it a lot around this place, but it was like switching on a light bulb and for a moment it switched off his thought processes. He coughed, his mind busy rewinding, rethinking. 'The job comes with accommodation, yes.'

'Oh, I can't believe it. I'm so sorry for all those things I said back there. I really am.' She reached into her back pocket and hauled out the stash of notes he'd given her, pressing them into his free hand. 'Here. I can't take this now. I won't be needing your money.'

A woman who wouldn't take money when it had been given her? He didn't know many women who wouldn't be hanging around for more, not handing it back. So she worked as a cleaner—maybe she was better qualified than he'd assumed.

A month.

That was all he'd need. She wouldn't be the kind of woman to expect to hang around. She wouldn't want more than he was prepared to give.

*A month would work out just fine.*

# CHAPTER FOUR

'KEEP it,' Andreas said, pushing her hand back, curling his fingers around it. 'You'll probably need some new clothes in your new job.'

Cleo solemnly regarded the notes still curled in her palm, her hand small and warm in his. 'Oh, you mean a new uniform.'

'Something like that,' he said, turning away quickly. 'Come on, my car's waiting outside, I'll give you a lift.'

He hauled her bag up the stairs as if it were a handbag and not stuffed full with all her worldly possessions and from there someone else took one look and relieved him of it, following in their wake, holding an umbrella over their heads as they emerged into the wet night. *Who is this man,* she wondered, *to have his own people to fetch and carry and clean out an entire hotel at his say-so?* A line of minibuses waited at the kerb outside, their exhaust turning to fog in the cold evening air. She recognised some of last night's guests being bundled with their luggage into one of the vans.

She started walking to the one behind. 'No,' he said. 'This one's ours.'

She looked where he indicated and did a double take. He had to be kidding. The black limousine stretched for what looked an entire frontage if not the whole block! She swallowed. She'd never travelled in such a vehicle in her life. She flashed a look down at her outfit. Worn farm boots, denim jeans and an old Driza-Bone coat. She looked longingly at the line of minibuses. She'd feel much more comfortable in something like that.

But the chauffeur had the door open, waiting. 'Are you sure we'll both fit?' she asked, but her companion didn't crack a smile, just gestured for her to precede him, and she had no choice but to enter the car.

It was like being in another world as the vehicle slipped smoothly into the traffic. It was bigger than her bedroom in the hotel and she wouldn't have been surprised to learn it boasted its own en suite. The plush leather seats were more like sofas with not a squeak of springs to be heard and they felt and smelled divine. A cocktail bar sprawled along one side, boasting spirits of every colour imaginable, a row of crystal-cut glasses held delicately in place, and then, just when she thought it couldn't get more amazing, there were stars, or at least tiny coloured lights twinkling all over the ceiling. And even as she watched they changed from blues and greens to oranges and reds and back to blues again.

And then there was him. He sprawled on the seat opposite, his back to the driver, one arm along the back of the seat, and with one leg bent, the other stretched long into the space between them. He'd undone his coat and the sides had fallen apart. Likewise the suit jacket underneath, exposing an expanse of snow-white cotton across his broad chest, all the whiter against the olive skin of his face and hands.

He was watching her, she realised. Watching her watching him. Her skin prickled. How could he do that with just his eyes? But it wasn't just his eyes, it was the slightly upturned mouth, the sculpted jaw and the attitude. Oh, yes, he had attitude to burn.

She pressed herself back into the seat, trying to look less overwhelmed, more relaxed. 'I guess you've never met anyone who hasn't been in a stretch limousine before. My reaction must have been quite entertaining.'

'On the contrary,' he said, without moving his eyes from hers, 'I found it charming.'

*Charming.* Nobody had ever used that word around her before. She wouldn't have believed them if they had. He was no doubt being polite. More likely thinking *gauche*. She felt it. Maybe she should steer the conversation, such as it was, to safer territory.

'Is it far to the hotel?'

'Not far.'

'Do you know what kind of job it is?'

'I think you will perform a variety of tasks. I'm sure you will find them to your liking.'

'Oh.' She wished he could be more specific. 'But it's a live-in position?'

Across the vast interior he nodded, his dark eyes glinting in the light of a passing streetlamp, and for some reason she suddenly felt uncomfortable, as if she'd almost glimpsed something in their otherwise shadowed depths.

'There is just one catch.'

'Oh?' There had to be though, she thought. Why should her life suddenly turn around without there being a catch? 'What is it?'

'The position has a fixed contract. This job will last only one month.'

'I see.' She sank back in her seat. Well, a month was better than nothing. And at least she'd have time to sort something else in between now and then.

'But you will be well compensated.'

She blinked up at him. 'Thank you again for your generosity, Mr…' and she was left floundering, speechless. She was in a car heading who knew where with a man who'd promised her a job somewhere and she didn't even know his name. When would she learn? What the hell kind of mess was she heading for now? 'Oh, My God, I can't believe I'm doing this. I don't even know your name.'

He smiled and dipped his head. 'I assure you, you have nothing to fear. Andreas Xenides at your service.'

Her eyes narrowed. She was sure she'd heard the name, maybe even read something in one of the papers back home before she'd left. But that man had been a billionaire. She didn't tend to meet many of them in her line of business. Maybe this man was related. 'I think there's someone called Xenides with a huge hotel up on the Gold Coast in Queensland.'

He nodded. 'The Xenides Mansions Hotel. One of my best performers.'

She swallowed. 'That's your hotel? You own it?'

'Well, one of my companies. But ultimately, yes, I own it.'

She didn't so much sink back into her seat as collapse against it.

He frowned. 'Does that bother you?'

'Bother me? It terrifies me!' She put a hand to her wayward mouth. Oh, my, the man was a billionaire and she'd thrown a slipper at his head, right before she'd bawled him out in the basement and insisted he pay her wages and find her a replacement job. As a cleaner. And the amazing thing about it was that he had.

Mind you, the way people were running around after him at the hotel ready to do his bidding, he could probably have found her a job as an astronaut if he'd put his mind to it.

What must it be like to wield that much power? She glanced over at him, her eyes once more colliding with his dark driven gaze. So he was a billionaire. That answered a few questions. But it didn't answer all of them.

'There's something I don't understand.'

'Oh.' He tilted his head to one side, as if almost amused. 'What is it?'

'Why would you care about a tiny dump of a hotel three blocks from Victoria Station? Why buy it? There must be plenty of other hotels better suited to a posh outfit like yours.'

And his eyes glistened and seemed to focus somewhere behind her and Cleo got the impression he didn't even see her. 'I had my reasons.'

She shivered at his flat voice as if the temperature had just dropped twenty degrees. Whatever his reasons, Andreas Xenides struck her as a man you wouldn't want to cross.

Cleo looked away, wanting to shake off the chill, and was surprised to see how far they'd come. She'd expected a lift to another small hotel somewhere close by, as he'd intimated, but she could see now that the limousine was making its way towards Mayfair.

His cell phone beeped and she was grateful he had a distraction. She was happy just to watch the busy streetscape, the iconic red double-decker buses, the black taxi cabs all jockeying for the same piece of bitumen and somehow all still moving. 'Petra, I'm glad you called. Yes, I'm finished in London.'

She wasn't trying to listen to his call, but there was no way she couldn't hear every word, especially when he made no attempt to lower his voice, and it was a relief when he dipped into his native language and she could no longer understand his words and she could just let the deep tones of his voice wash over her. When he spoke English his accent gave his words a rich Mediterranean flavour, a hint of the exotic, but when he spoke in Greek his voice took on another quality, on the one hand somehow harsher, more earthy and passionate on the other.

Much like Andreas himself, she imagined, because for all his civilised trappings, the cashmere coat and the chauffeur-driven limousine, she'd seen for herself that he could be harsh and abrupt, that he was used to making the rules and expecting people to play by them. And definitely passionate. Hadn't he set her own body to prickly awareness with just one heated gaze?

It made sense that a man like him would have a Petra or someone else waiting for him. He was bound to have a wife or a girlfriend, maybe even both; didn't the rich and famous have their own rules? She looked around at the car's plush interior, drinking in the buttery leather upholstery with her fingers and wanting to apologise to the pristine carpet for her tired boots. She gazed out of the tinted windows and caught the occupants of passing cars trying to peer in, looks of envy on their faces, and sighed, committing it all to memory. What would it be like to be one of the Petras of this world? To move in such circles and consider this all as normal?

She smiled philosophically. This was not her world. Any minute now he'd drop her at the hotel to take up her new cleaning position and he'd be gone for ever, back to Petra or another, whoever and wherever she was.

'We're flying back tomorrow,' she heard Andreas say, abruptly switching back to English. 'Expect us around five.'

Cleo wondered at the sudden change of language but continued peering out at the scenery outside her limousine's windows, the magnificent park to their left, the lights from buildings and streetlamps making jagged patterns on the wet roads. Even on a dark, wet night the streets of London fascinated her. It was so different from the tiny town of Kangaroo Crossing, where the main street was dusty and almost deserted after six at night. Here it was so vibrant and filled with life at whatever time of the day or night and she would never get sick of craning her neck for a look at the everyday sights here like Buckingham Palace, sights she'd only ever dreamed about one day seeing.

'*Us*, Petra?' Andreas continued. 'Oh, I'm sorry, I should have mentioned. I'm bringing a friend.'

Something about the way he said those last words made Cleo turn her head, some loaded quality that spoke of a message she didn't quite understand. She didn't mean to look right at him, she intended to swing her head around as if merely choosing to look out of the nearside windows, but her eyes jagged on his and held solid. 'That's right,' he said, holding her gaze and her heartbeat, it seemed, in his. 'A friend. Please ensure Maria has my suite prepared.'

He clicked the phone closed and slipped it away, all the while still holding her gaze.

'Is it much further?' she asked with false brightness, wondering what it was she was missing and why she was so suddenly breathless and why he needed to look at her that way, as if she were about to be served up for his next meal.

'No. Not much.'

As if on cue the limousine pulled off Park Lane into a wide driveway and rolled to a gentle stop. She looked up at the hotel towering over the car. 'But this… This is Grosvenor House.'

'So it is.'

The door opened and cold air swept into the warm interior as the concierge pulled open the door. 'But why are we here? I thought… You said…'

'We're here,' he simply said, sliding one long leg out and extending his hand to her. 'If you care to join me.'

'But I can't go in there. Not like this. I look like I've just stepped off the farm.'

'They'll think you're an eccentric Australian.'

'They must have a staff entrance!' But still, she was already moving towards him, inexorably drawn by his assuredness.

'Come,' he said, taking her hand to help her out. 'These people are paid not to take any notice.'

It was no consolation. She felt like someone who should be staying at some backpackers' hotel, not the poshest hotel in Mayfair. She caught sight of her reflection in the glass frontage and grimaced. She looked like a total hick. Why couldn't he have warned her? But Andreas didn't seem to care. The concierge staff swarmed like foot soldiers around him, taking orders, trying to please, while others ferried her backpack onto a trolley as lovingly as if it were the finest Louis Vuitton luggage.

She followed in his wake uncertain, sure someone was about to call Security and send her on her way, but worry soon gave way to wonder.

She stepped from the revolving door into a lobby of white marble and columns the colour of clotted cream and forgot to think. It was amazing. Luxurious. A fantasyland. It took every shred of self-control she possessed not to spin around in a circle to take it all in. Instead she slipped her Driza-Bone from her shoulders and tried to look as if she belonged. Fat chance.

Could it be possible that she'd soon be working here? At Grosvenor House? Andreas left her momentarily while he dealt with Reception, she guessed to inform the housekeeper she was here, and she drank in the luxury and the ambience. Now she would have a reason to call her mother and not feel as if she had nothing but bad news. After the disaster that Kurt had been and her mother worrying about her working long hours in a seedy hotel, she would be thrilled she'd scored a position in one of London's landmark hotels. She wouldn't tell her it was only for a month. If she played her cards right, she'd have a reference from one of London's top hotels and she would be set for another job.

And maybe some time soon she'd be able to save enough money to pay back the money her nanna had given her and she'd lost when she'd entrusted it to Kurt. At least now she had a chance.

Andreas returned and took her arm and steered her past a suite of red velvet chairs on a round signature rug that reeked money.

'Are you taking me to meet the housekeeper? I'm sure I can find her. I've kept you long enough.'

He didn't look at her, simply kept on walking her into a lift. 'I thought you might like to see your room first, see if it's suitable.' He pushed a button and she frowned. 'Did I tell you you'd have to share?'

His question distracted her. 'You think I mind? Just look at this place.' She paused as the elevator smoothly hummed into motion, suddenly making sense of what had niggled at her before. 'Hang on. We're going up. Surely they wouldn't give staff accommodation on a guest floor?'

He held off answering as the lift doors slid open, welcoming them into an elegant elevator lobby decorated in olive and magenta tones, before he directed her to a nearby door and keyed it open. 'It seems you're in luck.'

And the hairs on the back of her neck stood to attention. 'Tell me this is not my room.'

'Strictly speaking, it's not. Like I told you, you'd have to share.'

She swallowed. 'Then tell me whose room it is. Who would even have a room like this in the Grosvenor to start with— Prince Harry?' And even as she asked the question the chilling answer came to her, so unbelievable that she didn't want to give it credence, so insane that she thought she herself must be. 'It's your room, isn't it? There is no cleaning job. And you expect me to share with you?'

His dark eyes simmered with aggravation. 'Come inside and I'll explain.'

'I'm not going in there! I'm not going anywhere except down in that lift unless you tell me right now what's going on. And then I'm probably heading down in that lift anyway.'

'Cleo, I will not discuss this in public.'

She looked around. 'There's nobody else here!'

A bell pinged behind her, followed seconds later by lift doors sliding open. A group emerged, the women chatting and laughing, their arms laden with shopping bags, the men looking as if they could do with a stiff drink.

She looked longingly at the open lift door behind them. Took a step towards it and then realised. She snapped her head around. 'Where is my pack?'

'No doubt still on its way up. Now come in and listen to what I have to say and if you still want to go, you can go. But hear me out first. I do have a job for you.'

'Just not cleaning, right?' Cleo bit her bottom lip. What kind of jobs did Greek billionaires give girls who'd dropped out of high school and made a mess of everything they'd ever attempted? Definitely nothing you needed qualifications for…

But that made less sense than anything else. Her looks were plain, her figure had always erred on the side of full, and she'd never had men lining up for her favours. Cleaning was about all she was suitable for.

'Cleo.'

He made her name sound like a warning, the tone threatening, but maybe he was right. Maybe she should hear him out while she waited for her pack. Besides, if she was going to let fly with a few choice words of her own, maybe privacy was the preferred option.

*And then she'd leave.*

Spider legs skittered down her spine at the thought of going out into the cold wet night with no place to go. But she'd face that later. She wasn't going to let the weather dictate her morals. She strode past him into the room, cursing herself for choosing that particular moment to breathe in, wishing that, for someone so aggravating, he didn't smell so damn good.

Thankfully the room was large enough that she could put some distance between them. A lot of distance. She'd been expecting a bedroom, a typical hotel room. She found anything but.

The room looked more like a drawing room in a palace than any hotel room she'd ever seen, a dining table and chairs taking up one end of the room, a lounge suite facing a marble mantelpiece at the other with the dozen or so windows dressed in complementary tones of creams and crimsons.

But she wasn't here to appreciate the fine furnishings or the skilful use of colour. She didn't want to be distracted by the luxury she could apparently so easily take advantage of. Would it be easy? She wondered.

She dropped her jacket over a chair and turned, dragging in oxygen for some much-needed support. 'Okay, I'm here. What's going on?'

She almost had the impression he hadn't heard her as he headed for a sideboard, opening a crystal decanter and pouring himself a slug of the amber fluid it contained. 'You?' he offered.

She shook her head. 'Well? You told me I had a cleaning job at some hotel.'

Still he took his sweet time, taking a sip from the glass before turning and leaning against the dresser. 'While it's not exactly what I said, it is what I intimated. That much is true.'

'You lied to me!'

'I did not lie. I found you a job cleaning at another hotel. And then I decided better of it.'

'But why? What for?'

He drained the glass of its contents and placed it on the dresser in the same motion as he pushed himself towards her. 'What if I offered you a better job? More pay. Enough to buy your return ticket to Australia and a whole lot more. Enough to set you up for life.'

She licked her lips. If she could pay back her nanna what she'd borrowed... But what would she be expected to do to get it? 'What kind of job are you talking about?'

He laughed, coming closer. 'You see why I knew you would be perfect? Any other woman would ask how much money first.'

She sidestepped around the dining table, until it was between them. 'That was my next question.'

He stopped and started moving the other way, slowly circling, step by step. 'How much would be enough? One hundred thousand pounds? How much would that be in your currency?'

She swallowed, too distracted to concentrate on keeping her distance. Her maths might be lousy but even she had no trouble working that one out. Double at least. Her mouth almost watered at the prospect. But she'd heard plenty of stories about travellers being offered amazing amounts of money to courier a box or a package. And equally she'd heard of them getting caught by the authorities and much, much worse. She might have done some stupid things in her life, but she was so not going there. 'I don't want any part of drug money. I'm not touching it.'

He was closer than she realised, his dark eyes shining hard. 'Cleo, please, you do not realise how much you insult me. This would be nothing to do with drugs. I hate that filthy trade as much as you. I assure you, your work would be legal and perfectly above board.'

Legal. Above board. And it paid in the hundreds of thousands of dollars? Yeah, sure. There were jobs in the paper like that for high-school dropouts every other day. 'What is it, then?' she asked, circling the other way, pretending to be more interested in an arrangement of flowers set upon a side table. The red blooms were beautiful too, she thought, touching her fingers to the delicate petals, just like everything else in this room. Did he really expect her to share it with him? 'So what's the job?'

He didn't move this time, made no attempt to follow her, and because she was ready for it, expecting it, the fact he stayed put was more unnerving than anything. 'It's really quite simple. I just need you to pretend to be my mistress.'

# CHAPTER FIVE

'PRETEND to be your *what*?' Cleo started to laugh. If ever there was a time for hysterical laughter, this moment was tailor-made, but shock won out in the reaction stakes, choking off the sound and rendering her aghast. 'You must be insane!'

'I assure you I'm perfectly serious.'

'But your mistress? Who even uses that word any more?'

'Would you prefer it if I used the word *lover*?

'No!' *Definitely not lover*. And definitely not when it was said in that rich, curling accent. She didn't want to think about being Andreas' lover, pretend or otherwise. 'I don't know where you got the impression that I might say yes to such a crazy proposition, but I'm afraid you have the wrong impression of me, Mr Xenides. I'm sorry, but I'll have to turn down your generous proposal.'

'Call me Andreas, please.'

She looked over her shoulder anxiously, watching the door, before she looked back. 'And why would a man like you even need someone to act as his mistress anyway? It makes no sense.'

He shrugged. 'Maybe I just don't like to be seen as available.'

'Maybe you should just put out a press release.' She looked

longingly at the door again. 'When is my bag supposed to arrive? I want to go.'

'At least think about it, Cleo. It's a lot of money to throw away. Can you afford that?'

'You're crazy. Just look at me.' She held her arms out at her sides, her heart jumping wildly in her chest, her words tumbling over her tongue. 'I'm a cleaner. I muck out bathrooms and rubbish bins and have the split nails and red hands to prove it. I'm short and dumpy and have never once in my life been called so much as pretty, and you're suggesting I could pretend to be your mistress? Who's going to believe that for a start? They'll think you've gone mad and they'd be right.'

He answered her with a raised eyebrow and a half-hearted shrug as he eased closer. 'I think you underestimate your charms.'

Charms? What planet was this man from? 'Why *me*? You could have any woman in the world. You probably already have.'

He turned her implied insult to his advantage. 'Exactly. Which is why I don't want just any woman in the world.' He was close now, so close she could see the individual lashes that framed his dark eyes, close enough to see his pupils flare as he held out his fingers to her cheek. She flinched but he kept coming, tracing the line of her cheek with the backs of his fingers. 'I want you.'

Her heart missed a beat or two. She tried to shake her head but still his fingers remained, his touch feather-light and yet bone-shudderingly deep in effect.

'I don't... I can't...'

And he pulled his hand away, concern muddying his eyes as if something had just occurred to him. 'You're not a virgin?'

The intimacy of the question threw her for a moment. She could feel her cheeks burning up as she fought to find an answer. 'I thought this was about pretending. Why should whether or not I've ever slept with anyone even be an issue?'

He shrugged. 'Because there will be nights we are forced to share a bed to keep up appearances. And it's not beyond the realms of possibility that as a man and a woman, together, we might wish to seek mutual pleasure in each other's bodies.'

*Help!* 'So you expect sex, then, as part of this deal?'

He frowned and drew away, as if the very idea of her asking offended him. 'Not necessarily. Just that it may well be a by-product of our arrangement.'

*Sex as a by-product of our arrangement?*

How formal that sounded. How impersonal. It sounded more like a business deal, which she supposed it was. Not that she'd been involved in too many business deals, especially where they included a sex clause.

'I don't want it,' she ventured, not entirely sure if she meant just the contract or the sex or both. Because there was something about Andreas' touch that sent her senses into overdrive, something about his touch that made a secret part of her ache in ways it shouldn't, especially not for a man she'd only just met, a man she knew nothing about.

'It's a good offer,' he continued, as gently and convincingly as a parent trying to get a child to drink its milk. 'It's a fixed-term contract and in one month you go home. All expenses paid. First-class travel naturally.'

He watched her face, searching for the crack in her resolve. 'And no sex, if that's what you want. Though if it did happen, I can guarantee it wouldn't mean anything.'

His words blurred. *"It wouldn't mean anything."* And all she kept hearing was the echo of the words Kurt had said to her when she'd told him she loved him. And he'd just laughed as he'd yanked up his jeans. *"What's your problem? It didn't mean anything. You really are stupid."*

And all she had felt was the bottom falling out of her world as her newly discovered heart had lain shredded. She'd made a pointless journey, thrown what she'd always believed to be special away on a deadbeat who'd taken everything he could get and left her high and dry.

'You have had sex? Can we be clear on that?' Andreas' uncertain voice came from a long way away and still it brought her hackles up. What did he think now, that she was a complete loser?

'Oh, sure, loads of times.' *Once.* But then why should it matter if he thought her a complete loser? It wasn't as if she hadn't thought the same thing herself.

'Then it's all settled.'

Her head snapped up. 'Hang on, what's settled?' She had a feeling she'd missed something somewhere. Had she said yes and somehow forgotten?

'Tomorrow you will fly with me to my home on Santorini.'

She knew the name. Kurt had wooed her with his promises of travel and sunsets, of short breaks they could take to the Mediterranean, to Corfu and Mykonos and Santorini, of crystal-clear waters and lazy summer days. It had sounded so romantic, but of course, it had all been lies designed to convince her that they had a future together in order to lure her to London. She'd all but given up any hope of seeing anything at all of Europe.

But now she had the chance to go there with Andreas. Was it enough of a reason to say yes?

A buzzer sounded and Andreas moved swiftly to the door, pulling it open to the porter at last with her luggage. 'We will leave at twelve. The morning will be busy with appointments so we will have to start early.

'In the bedroom, thank you,' Andreas directed the porter, pressing a note into his hand.

'No!' she called, surprising them both and causing the porter to wheel around. 'I'll take that.' She grabbed one of the shoulder straps.

'Leave it, Cleo.'

'But there's no point. I was just leaving anyway.'

The porter looked nervously from one to the other, Cleo tugging on the pack, knowing it was her hold on reality and on control, and Andreas glowering until finally the porter decided that discretion was the better part of valour and withdrew, uttering a rushed, 'Call me if you need anything more,' before making himself scarce.

Cleo heaved the backpack onto her shoulder.

'I thought we had a deal.'

'You thought wrong. I never agreed to anything. And I'm leaving.'

'But you have no job, nowhere to go.'

'I'll find something. I'll manage.' She retrieved her Driza-Bone from the back of a chair and bundled it in front of her before being game enough to steal one last glance at him.

*Impossibly good-looking*. That was how she'd remember him. Eyes of midnight-black and hair that waved thick and dark to collar length, an imperious nose and a passionate slash of mouth it was almost a crime for any man to possess. And a face like slate, just like she'd thought in the hotel, until it heated up and the angles took on curves she'd never seen coming.

But so what? She was leaving. It might be a huge amount of money to give up and already she could hear the girls from her high school singing out a familiar chorus of "loser, loser, Cleo's a loser". But she'd been hearing that chorus a long time and she was used to it. She'd been an object of pity ever since her father had walked out on her pregnant mother, never to be seen again.

And besides, she knew she was doing the right thing. For

Andreas' proposal was flawed. She didn't want the chance of 'sex as a by-product' of anything. She'd had sex that didn't mean anything and she'd hated herself in the aftermath. It had made her feel cheap and disposable and had hurt her more than she wanted to admit. She didn't care for the chance of more, no matter how much he might be paying.

'I'll see myself out.'

'I need you,' he said as she turned for the door.

She halted, her fingers around the door handle. 'I get the impression, Mr Xenides, that you don't need anyone.' She twisted and pulled. She didn't belong here. Now she'd made up her mind, she couldn't wait to get away. Had to get away.

The door was open just a few inches when his palm slammed it shut. 'You're wrong!'

She turned to protest but the words sizzled and burned in the heat she saw coming from his eyes. 'How much will it take, then? How much do you want? I thought you didn't care about money, but you're just like the rest, one whiff and you want more. You're just a better actress. Which tells me you're exactly the woman I need.

'So how much, sweet, talented Cleo? How much to secure your services for a month? One hundred thousand clearly isn't enough, so let's say we double it. Two hundred thousand pounds. Four hundred thousand of your dollars. Would that be enough?'

The numbers went whirling around her brain, so big they didn't mean anything, so enormous she couldn't get a grip on them. Four hundred thousand dollars for a month of pretending to be Andreas' companion? Was she nuts to even think about giving that up? She could go home, pay back her nanna, pay for repairs to the farm's leaking roof that her mother always complained about but there was never enough money to repair, and she'd still have enough left over to buy a place of her own.

More than that, she'd be able to go home and hold her head up high. And for once, just once in her life, she didn't have to be a loser.

But could she do it? Could she pretend to be this man's lover and all that entailed and simply walk away in the end?

She shook her head trying to work it all out. She truly didn't know. If she just had some time to think it all out. 'Andreas, I—'

'Five hundred thousand pounds! One million of your dollars. Will that be enough to sway your mind?'

She gasped. 'You have to be kidding. That's an obscene amount of money.'

'Not if it gets me what I want. And I want you, Cleo. Say yes.'

She couldn't think, couldn't breathe, only one note of clarity spearing through the fog of her brain.

*One million dollars.*

How could she walk away from that? It was unthinkable, unimaginable, like winning the lottery or scooping the pools. And she'd even get to live on Santorini for a whole month, the island she'd longed to visit, the island Kurt had only talked about visiting for a day or two. Wasn't that some kind of justice? She licked her lips, once more feeling her hold on the world slipping, swaying. 'Just for a month, you say?'

The corners of his mouth turned up. 'Maybe even less if you play your cards right.'

'But definitely no sex. Just pretending. Is that right?'

A shadow passed across his eyes and was just as quickly gone. 'If that's the way you want it.'

'That's exactly the way I want it. No sex. And in one month I go home.'

'No questions asked. First class. All expenses paid.'

She swallowed against a throat that felt tight and dry and

against a fear that he might soon discover he was making the mistake of his life and she'd be booted out with the week. 'I don't know if I'm the right person for the job.'

He slipped the pack from her shoulder and dropped it on the ground beside them before she'd noticed, relieving her of the weight on her back, but not even touching the fear in her gut. 'You'll be perfect. Any other questions?'

She shook her head. How could she expect him to make sense of anything going on in her mind when she couldn't unscramble it herself? 'No. Um, at least… No, I don't think so.'

He smiled then, as he curved one hand around her neck, his fingers warm and gentle on her skin and yet setting her flesh alight. 'Then what say we seal this deal with a kiss?'

She gasped and looked up at him in shock. That message cleared a way through the fog in her brain as if it had been shot from a cannon. 'We could always just shake hands.'

'We could,' he agreed, both hands weaving their magic behind her head, his thumbs tracing the line of her jaw while he studied her face. 'But given we will no doubt have to get used to at least this, we might as well start now.'

And he angled her upturned face and dipped his own until his lips met hers. Fear held her rigid, that and a heart that had taken on a life of its own and threatened to jump out of her chest. But as his lips moved over hers, gentler than she'd imagined possible, gentle but, oh, so sure, she sighed into the kiss, participating, matching him.

One hand scooped down her back, pressing her to him from chest to thigh, her nipples exquisitely sensitive to the chest that met hers, heat pooling low down between her thighs, making her more aware than she'd ever been of her own physical needs. They called to her now, announcing their presence with logic-numbing desperation until her knees, once stiff with shock, threatened to buckle under her. She trembled, reaching for him, needing something to steady herself as his mouth wove some kind of magic upon her own.

It was just a kiss. Tender almost, more gentle than she would ever expect this man to give, but, oh, so thorough in its impact. Her fingers tangled in his shirt, her fingertips drinking in the feel of the firm flesh beneath and she was sure she felt him shudder. Was this how a man felt, rock-hard and solid, as opposed to a boy? Kurt had claimed to be twenty-six and told her he worked out regularly, but his body had been white-bread soft and just as unsatisfying.

But Andreas felt as if he'd been sculpted from marble, firm flesh over muscle and skin that felt like satin and her fingers itched to feel more. Ached to feel more.

Then just as suddenly the kiss was over, his lips departing, and she was left bereft and breathless blinking up at him. He said nothing, just looked down at her, his dark eyes swirling with questions until a bubble of panic rose up inside her.

Had he spotted her lack of experience? Would he change his mind and toss her out, now that she'd finally agreed to his terms?

'I guess we have a deal,' he surprised her by saying, before letting her go. 'You might want to settle in. I have some work to do with the lawyers and I'll arrange for the necessary papers to be drawn up.'

'The papers?' She'd just been kissed senseless and he expected her to suddenly know what he was talking about. 'What papers?'

'The contract. This is a business arrangement. I think we both need the assurance it will stay that way.'

'Oh, of course.' She nodded as if she understood completely. When what she knew about business law would fit through the eye of a needle. Which was what had got her into her mess with Kurt. *A gentlemen's agreement*, he'd told her, and she'd been fool enough to believe he was gentleman enough to honour the terms. So much for trust.

Andreas clearly wasn't into trust or gentlemen's agreements, for which she should be thankful, even if it rubbed that he might not trust her. But if a contract meant she'd get her money and not get ripped off this time, she could live with it.

A wave of exhaustion suddenly washed over her, the adrenaline rush of the last half-hour, the events of the last twenty-four hours, especially the emotional upheaval of the last four when she'd been wrenched from her bed, catching up with her. She needed sleep and she needed it badly. 'Which way to my room?'

He'd already pulled his cell phone from his pocket and made the connection. He looked up and frowned before turning away, a torrent of Greek pouring into the phone.

Okay, so she'd find it by herself. She hauled her pack over her shoulder and aimed for one of the two doors she knew didn't lead to the hallway outside. One of them would be her room for sure.

She found a bedroom off the living room, a massive king-sized bed covered in almost a dozen pillows taking centre stage. She opened one cupboard and found a line of shirts and trousers hanging inside. Andreas' wardrobe, then. She took another door that led into a massive marble bathroom, complete with bath, shower and bidet, and then took another door out, only to find herself back in the living room where Andreas was still on the phone.

He raised one eyebrow when he saw her emerge and she raised her own. 'My room?' she mouthed quietly and he frowned and pointed to the door she'd first entered and her heart leapt into her mouth. Surely he wasn't expecting them to share? Even though he'd hinted that it might be necessary to maintain the illusion, there was no one else here to pretend for now. And hadn't she made it plain enough that she wouldn't sleep with him? She shook her head and her panicked thoughts must have been laid bare in her eyes. He covered the handset with one hand and pointed to a sofa. 'I'm sleeping there,' he growled. 'The bedroom is all yours.'

She retraced her steps to the bedroom and dug through her bag until she found her pyjamas and toilet bag and ducked into the bathroom, feeling embarrassed and stupid and relieved all at the same time. Of course he didn't want to sleep with her! What the hell had she been thinking? Their deal was for her to *pretend* to be his mistress, not be the real thing. One kiss had scrambled her brain completely. One kiss and she was practically expecting him to make love to her.

She adjusted the water temperature and stepped into the cloudburst of a shower. The pounding of the steamy water was like a salve to her weary muscles and tired body, but still she was out in record time, simultaneously pulling on her pyjamas and cleaning her teeth in case Andreas needed the bathroom. Her stomach rumbled and she realised she hadn't eaten since breakfast. But she was used to that. It was the one reason her jeans fitted her now, rather than stretching at the seams like when she'd first arrived in London. At least her mad job had achieved what ten years of New Year's resolutions had failed to deliver. Anyway, she was too tired to eat now. All she wanted to do was collapse into bed.

She pulled the hair tie from her hair, shaking the damp ends free as she surveyed the object in question. Compared to the camp bed she was used to, the bed seemed to stretch an acre in every direction. And it was all for her. But which side was his? Or did his lordship like to occupy the middle? He might be going to sleep on the sofa outside, but just the knowledge that he'd slept here last night and she could be sharing that same place seemed too intimate, too personal. She hovered at the side a while, before exhaustion got the better of her and she climbed into the closest side, finding herself enveloped in cloud-soft luxury, the scent of Andreas on her pillow, the comforter so soft and warm around her it was like a hug from her nanna.

The bright side, she thought dreamily, was that sooner than she'd expected she'd be home and hugging her nanna again. There was always a bright side.

She pulled her mask over her eyes to shut out the ribbon of light seeping under the door, feeling sleep tugging at her so hard that nothing could keep her awake tonight, not the occasional burst of Greek she could hear coming from the room outside, not regret at making the deal she'd done and not even the fear that, despite his assurances, at any moment Andreas Xenides could walk through that door and climb into this bed.

She yawned. She knew she should care. She wanted to. But not right now. In the morning she'd be able to think straight. In the morning they could set any necessary boundaries.

*In the morning…*

Andreas was still on the phone when Room Service arrived with the meal he'd ordered in between calls to his lawyers and to the concierge to arrange the round of appointments Cleo would need in the morning. He was hungry and he figured she must be too, and until she'd been thoroughly made over there was little point being photographed with her in any of the restaurants or bars. Before and after shots wouldn't help his cause. In any event, there was something to be said for taking a few hours in private to get to know one another. For, as much as he expected she'd be perfect for his purposes, the contracts needn't be signed until he'd made absolutely certain.

He pushed open the door to the bedroom to let her know their meal had arrived and found the room in darkness, lit only with the light spilling in from the room behind. And there she lay, looking tiny in the big wide bed, her flannelette pyjamas buttoned almost all the way up to her neck like a suit of armour with the quilt pulled up almost as high, and that damned Princess mask hiding her eyes.

The blood in his veins heated to boiling point. She was sleeping? He'd just agreed to pay her a million dollars and she was sleeping as if it were no big deal and she could start earning her money tomorrow?

He was just about to rip the damn mask off when she stirred on a sigh and settled back into the mattress, her breathing so slow and regular that he paused, remembering.

She'd been asleep when his staff had woken her hours ago, he recalled, after being awake since the very early hours, the shadows under her eyes underlining her exhaustion. Maybe he should give those shadows a chance to clear and give the makeover experts a fighting chance to turn her into the woman he needed her to be?

Maybe he should just back out of here and let her sleep?

*And maybe he should just climb right in there with her and make the most of his money?* She'd said she didn't want sex but he'd never known a woman to turn him down. That she'd been so adamant grated.

There was a knock at the door outside. Housekeeping, no doubt, come to make up the sofa bed, and he turned and pulled the door closed behind him.

He had no need to take any woman. He had an entire month. She would come to him; he knew it.

# CHAPTER SIX

IT WAS a strange dream, where people faded in and out of focus, the girls from school with their taunts of loser, her half-brothers hugging the father who looked on her as excess baggage, and Kurt laughing at her, his white chest quivering with the vibrations. From somewhere Cleo could hear the sound of her nanna telling her to look for the silver lining. She spun around trying to find the source of her voice, trying to pull her from the shadows and hang onto her message and drown out the chorus behind her, when a different shape emerged from the mist, tall and broad and arrogantly self-assured.

*"I'm scared."* It was her voice, even though she'd not said a word, and she wanted to run, tempted to turn back to the mocking chorus behind her, back to the world she knew and understood so well, back to the familiar, but her legs were like lead and she couldn't move and he kept right on coming until he stood head and shoulders above her. And he smiled, all dark eyes and gleaming white teeth. 'You should be,' and then he'd dipped his head to kiss her and she heard nothing but the buzzing in her ears and the pounding of her heart, and from somewhere in the shadows, the sound of her nanna's voice.

'Rise and shine.' The words made no sense until the blow

to her rump, cushioned with the thick quilt but enough to bring her to consciousness with a jump. 'You've got a busy morning.'

The alarm on the bedside table alongside snapped off and she drank in the scent of bed-warmed flesh. *His bed-warmed flesh*. So the alarm was the buzzing in her ears? But what was causing the fizzing in her blood?

She sat up and pushed her mask above her eyes, and then, remembering his comment about dressing like a clown, swiped it from her head. A moment later she wished she'd kept it on. He was naked. Unashamedly naked as he strode to the wardrobe and pulled out a robe. Too late she averted her eyes and, *oh, my*. She felt the blush rise like a tide as the truth sank in—he was huge! Only to have the blush deepen with the next wayward thought.

*And if he looks that big now?*

She swallowed, pulling her legs up like a shield, wondering why she should be suddenly tingling down *there*. How big he could be had nothing to do with her. It wasn't something she was planning on finding out.

'Hungry?' he asked casually, but her brain had ceased to function on that level. 'You missed dinner,' he explained, slipping into a robe and thankfully tying it at his waist. 'I thought you might be hungry. I've taken the liberty of ordering for both of us. You looked like you could have slept until noon.'

She unplastered her tongue from the roof of her mouth. 'I was tired.'

'Apparently. You slept like the dead. Breakfast will be here in a few minutes and then your first appointment is in under an hour.'

'What appointment?'

'Downstairs in the spa salon. You're booked in for the works by which time the stylist will be here with a selection of outfits. You won't have much time to decide. We're flying out at noon.'

Cleo glanced at the clock; it was only just after seven. 'That's hours away.'

'You'll need every bit of it, so eat up and don't wait for me.' His eyes raked over her and her skin prickled under his gaze. 'You're going to need your strength.'

She shivered as he disappeared into the bathroom. Why did she get the impression he wasn't only talking about her upcoming appointments?

He needn't have worried about her not eating. Room Service arrived with the heavily laden trolley a minute or two later, and the aroma threatened to drive her crazy. The porter had hardly finished serving the breakfast up on the dining table in the next room before she practically fell upon the feast. There was yoghurt and jam, pastries and rolls and toast, along with two massive platters of English breakfast. It was a feast. The coffee was smooth and rich with just the right amount of bitterness to wash it all down. She couldn't remember enjoying a meal more.

Andreas emerged from the bathroom while she was still eating, a towel lashed low around his hips and barefoot, moisture still clinging to his chest and beading in the hair that curled into his neck.

'That's what I like to see,' he said, sitting alongside her at the table. 'A woman with a healthy appetite.'

She managed to swallow her mouthful but it was hard to think about food after that. He was so close she could smell his freshly washed skin, the scent of fine soap and clean flesh challenging her appetite, steering it in another direction completely. He uncovered a platter of croissants, still steaming hot from the oven, and offered it to her.

Turning towards him was one mistake. Looking at him rather than the plate of croissants was a bigger one. His olive skin glistened with moisture under the lights and even as she watched a bead of moisture ran down over his sculpted chest, pausing at the bud of one tight nipple only to sit there, poised on the brink.

She could feel that droplet as if it were on her own skin, feel it rolling down her breast and teetering at her nipple, turning it tight and hard against the soft flannelette of her pyjamas.

She should reach out a fingertip and release it from the tension that kept it hovering. She could at least stretch out one hand and capture the doomed droplet in her palm.

She was too late for either. Gravity won and the droplet fell, swallowed up into his towel. 'Would you care for something?'

She blinked and raised her eyes to find his watching hers, amusement creasing their corners. 'A croissant, or perhaps there's something else you might enjoy more?' Now even his lips had turned up. He was laughing at her and she'd brought it on herself. Nothing unusual in that; she was used to making a fool of herself. It was just she wasn't used to making a fool of herself over a naked chest and a single droplet of water.

'N... No, thank you,' she managed, holding her pyjamas together at the neck as if that would defend her against... Against what? Throwing herself bodily at him? 'I should have my shower. Thank you for breakfast.'

'One thing,' he said, grabbing one hand as she made a desperate bid for freedom, his thumb making lazy circles on her palm as he held her. 'You don't have to thank me for anything. We have a deal. You will act like a mistress and take what is offered you, and I will take what is offered to me. Understood?'

Her hand was dwarfed by his, and so much paler now she'd lost her Aussie year-round tan, and the contrast seemed so much like the contrast between them. Andreas was strong and wealthy and darkly dangerous and she was broke and pale and reduced to making deals to survive. But did he really expect her to offer herself to him? He'd slept out here, the sofa bed still unkempt, sheets and blankets littering the floor, but from the moment he'd awakened her this morning, with his unashamed display of his naked body and his thinly veiled comments, she'd had the sense that sex wasn't far from his mind. *With her?* Surely not.

She swallowed. 'I'll do my job in accordance with the terms of our contract. I can't think what else I could possibly have to offer that would interest you.'

'Exactly what I meant,' he said, his words at odds with the look in his eyes as he let her go.

The rest of the morning passed in a whirlwind. She was ferried down to the salon and secreted away in a private room where it seemed a dozen staff were fully employed in transforming her into someone worthy of being seen on Andreas' arm. Nobody seemed to think it odd, or, at least, nobody made her feel that way and she wondered if Andreas had been right, that the staff were paid far too much to sit in judgement or to care about anything but the service they provided.

Before long, their skilful hands had her relaxing so much that she didn't care. How often did she have a treat like this? Never. She was determined to enjoy it.

In no time it seemed her hair was transformed into a thousand tiny tinfoil packages. A manicure and pedicure followed, along with waxing and a treatment over her new colour before she relaxed into a facial. She felt like a new woman even before the hairdresser studied her, reading her newly coloured hair as a sculptor read the stone, before a make-up artist took her attention, leaving the hairdresser to perform his art.

And finally they were finished. The team gathered around her smiling and waiting for her reaction, but she was too staggered to give one. In the mirror her once-mousy hair gleamed back at her in what looked like a dozen shades of copper to blonde to gold, the skilful cut using her natural wave for fullness while the artful layering somehow seemed to add inches to its length.

And that was just her hair. The make-up artist had turned her eyes into those of a seductress, their blue colouring intensified, the shadows beneath banished, and a woman who had never been pretty felt beautiful for the first time in her life. Tears pricked her eyes and she bit down hard on her lip, trying not to cry, not wanting to ruin all their good work. 'I can't believe what you've all done, thank you so much.' And to the make-up artist, she pointed to her eyes and asked, 'Can you show me how to do this?' and the girl nodded, her smile widening.

'I'd love to. You have such extraordinary eyes to work with. You just have to make more of them. They were just lost in your face before.'

Lost in her face? Or just lost? It could have been the story of her life. But a quick lesson later, Cleo was on her way back to the suite, armed with all the products and cosmetics she would need to reproduce the artists' work.

This time as she walked through the lobby towards the bank of lifts she didn't cringe, didn't expect Security to come running. She was still only clad in jeans and a casual top, but she held her head up high and moved with a confidence she'd never known. One or two heads turned as she passed, and it gave her an unfamiliar buzz. She couldn't keep the smile from her face. Likewise she couldn't wait to show Andreas the transformation.

Except he wasn't in the suite. She shoved aside a stab of disappointment. Of course, he was a busy man; he wasn't going to sit around waiting for her. Besides which, the suite had been turned in her absence into some kind of boutique, with racks of casual, resort and evening wear lining the walls and a stylist named Madame Bernadette who clearly took her job very seriously. No wonder he'd made himself scarce.

Mme Bernadette took one look at Cleo over the top of her glasses, and clucked her tongue. 'Hmm, let's get to work. This may take some time.' She snapped her fingers at an attendant, who meekly bowed and handed Cleo a robe. 'Put that on,' Mme Bernadette instructed. 'We have work to do.'

Two hours later, Cleo was exhausted. She'd lost count of how many times she'd changed, how many times the stylist had poked, prodded and pulled various bits of whatever she had on, analysing the fit, whether it was the sheerest lingerie or the most figure-hugging gown. But she obviously knew her craft, because by the end of it the racks had been depleted. Everything not still hanging was going with them. There wasn't a whole lot left hanging.

For someone who'd survived on the contents of one backpack for six weeks and lately just one pair of jeans and a couple of T-shirts, an entire couture wardrobe for one month seemed like overkill, but Andreas was clearly calling the shots as Mme Bernadette would not be swayed by any talk of moderation.

The dilemma of how it was supposed to fit in her luggage was soon taken care of, as another knock on the door heralded a trolley carrying a suite of designer luggage and two maids who curtsied as they entered—actually curtsied her—before getting on with the business of packing, letting her get on with her own preparations.

It was almost twelve. She had no doubt Andreas would expect her ready on the dot and had no doubt he would also expect to see the new collection put to good use. For that reason she'd chosen a creamy silk blend trouser suit with a silk camisole that skimmed her new shape, no doubt ably assisted with a new bra that was as sexy as it was an engineering masterpiece. It gave her both cleavage and support yet it looked sexy as sin and felt as if it were barely there. With the new sling-backs that added four inches to her height and showed off her newly pedicured toes to perfection, and a blue scarf Mme Bernadette had pressed upon her because it accented her eyes, she felt more feminine than she ever had, as if she'd grown up and made the transition from a child into a woman in the space of just a few hours. She couldn't wait to show Andreas the new her.

Twelve noon came and went. Then twelve-thirty and still there was no sign of Andreas, no calls. She sat in a wing-back chair surrounded by packed luggage, swinging one leg and clicking her newly manicured nails, increasingly nervous about what she was doing.

After a whirlwind morning where there'd been no time to wonder at the recklessness of what she was doing, of agreeing to fly off to somewhere in Greece with a total stranger, she wasn't sure she wanted a chance to think.

Nor did she need the time to wonder if Andreas had suddenly changed his mind, and, having totally sucked her into his plans, he'd left without her. She could imagine he'd worked out that nobody was worth one million dollars for one month of acting. She could equally imagine him laughing at her naivety as he soared thousands of feet above the earth back to his world.

Her stomach clenched. It wouldn't be the first time she'd been cast aside the moment she'd made a commitment. Kurt had chosen his moment with impeccable timing, offering to look after her money and taking everything she'd had to give, first her untested body and then her naïve heart, before cruelly rejecting both. She'd been no more than sport to him, a naïve girl lured overseas and out of reach of family and friends so she could be well and truly fleeced. Once he'd scored both her and her money, he'd discarded her to go in search of fresh prey.

Impatient with the direction of her thoughts, she pushed herself up out of the chair she'd specifically chosen because it was the first thing across the room Andreas would see upon entering, giving up any pretence of appearing cool and calm in favour of striding across the room to the windows, gazing down unseeingly across the busy street to the cool green serenity of Hyde Park beyond.

No, Andreas was no Kurt. He might be arrogant and autocratic, but he would never stoop to such a thing. He'd taken so long to convince her to come with him and he'd gone to such expense. Why do that if he wasn't going to go through with it?

Her hand went to the drapes and she rested her head against it. Although he'd shown no mercy yesterday. He'd invaded the hotel like an army general routing the enemy, the guests evacuated, the sleeping turfed from their beds, and Demetrius summarily vanquished. She shivered. How could a haircut and a suitcase full of new clothes make her blind to what had happened at his behest only yesterday? Was she so fickle?

No, Andreas might resemble a Greek god, but she'd be a fool to assume he would be a merciful one.

The buzzer sounded and she jumped, suddenly all pins and needles as she crossed the room and pulled open the door. The porter nodded. 'I'm here to collect the luggage for the airport. Your car is waiting downstairs, miss.'

She took a deep breath, trying to settle her quivering stomach. So she hadn't been abandoned? That was a good thing, surely? She grabbed her jacket and scarf, threw her bag over her shoulder and marched out, doing her best to play the cool, confident person she was supposed to be when inside even her blood was fizzing. My God, she was actually doing this! She was leaving England for a Greek island with a man she barely knew, a billionaire who needed a pretend mistress.

And yes, he might be arrogant and ruthless and used to

getting his own way, and yes, she'd seen enough of him to know she didn't want to cross him, but it was just for one month. And at the end of that month, she'd walk away a millionaire herself.

How hard could it be?

She smiled as she made her way through the elegant lobby, the waves in her newly styled hair bouncing in time with the tapping of her heels on the marble floor. Finally her luck was changing. Finally Cleo Taylor was going to be a success.

A doorman in a top hat touched a hand to his brow as she emerged. 'Miss Taylor,' he said, as if she were some honoured guest he'd been waiting for and not the hick girl who'd walked in wearing cowboy boots less than a day before, and he pulled open the door to a waiting limousine.

She dipped her head and climbed inside, sliding onto the seat behind the driver, opposite where Andreas was sitting totally engrossed in some kind of report perched on his knees.

'I thought you could probably use the extra time,' he said by way of explanation, flipping over a page without looking up.

'You mean you're blaming me for you being late.'

He looked up at that, looked ready to take issue with her words, but whatever he'd been about to say died before it ever got to his lips. He didn't have to say a word, though, not with the way his eyes spoke volumes as they drank her in, slowly and thoroughly, from the tip of her coloured hair to the winking toenails peeking out at him from her sandals, a slow gaze that ignited a slow burn under her skin, the flames licking at her nipples, turning them hard, before changing direction and licking their way south.

'Cleo?'

'You were expecting someone else?'

The report on his lap slid sideways, forgotten. She smiled. 'Well? Do you think you got your money's worth?'

They'd done something with her eyes, he realised. They'd done something with her hair too, so it was no longer mousy and shone in what looked like a hundred different colours, and her clothes were a world apart from her jeans and cowboy boots, but it was her eyes that looked most different. Before they'd been the misty blue of a Santorini morning, but now suddenly it seemed the mists had cleared and they were the perfect blue of a still summer's day.

'Have I had my money's worth?' he mused, finally getting to her question. She was happy with the results, that much was clear, but not half as happy as he was. His hunch had been right. She would be perfect. 'Maybe not yet. But I fully intend to.' She gasped, colour flooding her cheeks almost instantly, and it was his turn to smile. Her reactions were so instantaneous, so honest. He hoped she'd never lose that. At least, not for the next few weeks.

He picked up the abandoned report and returned to his reading. He didn't want to have to work late.

Not tonight.

Tonight he hoped to have better things to do.

The Jet Centre at London City Airport ushered them through with a minimum of fuss, expediting immigration and customs requirements so that they were ready to board less than forty minutes after leaving the hotel.

She recognised the logo she saw on the side of the small jet they were approaching, the same stylised X she'd seen adorning Andreas' luggage. 'Isn't that your logo?'

Andreas nodded. 'You recognised it?'

She shook her head. He was missing the point. 'You own a plane? Your own jet?'

'Not entirely,' he responded, stepping back to let her precede him up the short flight of steps. 'The company leases it. Along with the helicopter we have for short-haul flights within Greece itself. It is a tax-effective arrangement.'

She shook her head. He imagined she was interested in his financing arrangements? For someone who'd only recently made her first ever flight in a commercial airline, and then cramped in cattle class with three hundred other tortured souls, the concept of having one's own plane at one's beck and call was mind-boggling. She'd thought the limousine was the height of luxury and here he was with his own private jet. *And* a helicopter.

'But there must be two dozen airlines flying between London and Greece every day.'

He shrugged. 'I expect so. But not when I want to.'

That was at the heart of it, she guessed, and what Andreas wanted, Andreas got. After all, wasn't that what she was doing here? And if he could afford to throw away a million dollars plus expenses on her, clearly a million dollars didn't mean very much to him. He had money to burn.

A smiling stewardess greeted her, directing her to a seat, showing her where to store her bag and taking her jacket before disappearing again. Cleo settled herself in, looking around the cabin in wonder and doing a rapid rethink.

The interior oozed comfort, a centre aisle flanked by no more than half a dozen ultra-wide armchairs in dove-grey leather that looked more suited to a fireside setting than to any plane travel she'd ever heard of. She thought about the cramped conditions on her flight to London, the lack of space to store her own things let alone the pillows, blankets and toiletry packs they weighed you down with so that you couldn't even sit down when you boarded, of the man in the seat in front who'd jerked his seat back the first chance he'd had and left it there the entire flight and the child two rows back with the spluttering cough. Who wouldn't choose flying like this over queues and delays and airline food if they could afford it? If you had money to burn, there were no doubt worse ways to spend it.

Andreas dropped his briefcase down on a timber table-cum-desk that extended from the other wall, slipping into the seat alongside her as the attendant reappeared, this time bearing a tray with two filled champagne flutes. 'Enjoy your flight,' she said. 'We'll be taking off shortly and I'll be serving lunch as soon as we're level.'

Andreas took both glasses, thanking her and passing one to Cleo as the plane started taxiing from the apron. 'This toast is to you,' he said, raising his glass, 'and to our month together. May it be mutually—satisfying.'

The glass paused on the way to her lips. How did he make just one innocent word sound so sinful? And what was it about him that provoked her thighs to suddenly squeeze down further into the seat? He watched her over the rim of his glass as he took a sip of the sparkling wine, his lips curled, his eyes charged with a heat that was soon washing through her, closely followed by a crashing wave of fear that sucked the air from her lungs.

He could be a panther sitting there, rather than a man, a big dark cat watching its next meal, waiting. She could even imagine the lazy flick of his tail as he pretended there was no rush...

Oh, God, what was she even doing here? She was an imposter, a charlatan. She'd had sex once in her life and it had been lousy. And here she was, contracted to play the role of this man's mistress for an entire month. Never had she been so unqualified for a position. Never so unprepared.

'You don't like the wine?'

Condensation misted the glass between her fingers. 'I'm not very thirsty. Maybe with lunch. How long is the flight?' She grasped onto anything that might steer the conversation, and her thoughts, into safer territory.

'Four hours, give or take. Unfortunately after our late departure we will have missed the sunset, said to be the most beautiful in all of Greece. You haven't been to Greece before?'

There was that sunset thing again. Maybe that was one thing Kurt hadn't lied about, and now she'd have the chance to experience Santorini's sunset for herself. The bright side, she thought as she shook her head in answer to Andreas' question, definitely a bright side.

'Ah. Then you are in for a treat. I promise you will love Santorini.'

His enthusiasm was infectious and she found an answering smile with no hesitation. 'I look forward to it.'

The jet came to a brief halt at the end of the runway before the engines powered up and the plane moved off. Again Cleo was struck by how different this felt from the hulking jumbo jet that had seemed to take for ever to get going, panels vibrating and overhead lockers rattling as it lumbered along the runway before somehow managing to haul itself up into the air. This jet was small and powerful and accelerated as if it had been fired from a gun.

She held onto her stomach but there was none of the lurching motion that had made her feel queasy in the seven four seven. Instead the ground fell sharply away as the plane pierced the air like an arrow, and Cleo watched the rain-washed view in fascination until cloud cover swallowed both it and the plane. A few moments later they had punched their way through and bright sunshine poured through the large portholes, filling the cabin with light.

'I have some work I must attend to,' Andreas told her, retrieving his briefcase. 'But I have a copy of our contract for you to look over and sign. Will you be comfortable?'

*Much more comfortable than if you didn't have work to do.* The traitorous thought was as sudden as it was true. When he looked at her in that heated way that he did, it was impossible to think straight. And after the intensive morning she'd had, she could do with a few hours of quiet time curled up in a good book, or a good contract for that matter. 'I'll be fine,' she said a little uncertainly, taking the papers he offered.

He watched her a while, trying to search behind her eyes for what she was really thinking, but he found no hint of machination. Instead her clear blue eyes held without shifting or looking away. He nodded then, turning back to his report, before she might read too much into his gaze.

A woman who didn't need constant pandering, who didn't sulk and was content to let him work when he needed to? She was definitely a rarity. A pity about her 'no sex' demands. *If she were any good in bed, she'd be just about perfect.*

# CHAPTER SEVEN

THE cloud cover cleared after lunch when they were somewhere over the south of France, revealing a coastline that was
staggeringly beautiful even from this height, the world below
like a rich tapestry of colour and texture of sea and land and
mountains complete with their frosting of snow. Cleo watched
the colours change below as they sped towards the night, the
shadow moving over the earth as night claimed more and more
for its own.

The contract had taken no time at all to deal with, the terms
reasonably straightforward, even to her unbusinesslike brain.
One month of partnering Andreas in exchange for one million
Australian dollars and an all-expenses first-class fare home.
Simple really, if she didn't let herself think about whom she
was contracting with. No sex seemed such a crystal clear
notion until she looked at him and felt that increasingly familiar
tingle in her flesh, a tingle that felt too much like longing.

So she wouldn't look at him. Instead she pushed back in the
wide armchair that felt more like a bed, shucking off her shoes
and tucking her legs beneath her. Once in Greece she'd be four
hours closer to home, a four-hour head start when she left in
a month to return to Kangaroo Crossing. She smiled when she
thought about seeing her mum and her nanna again, and her

rough-and-tumble half-brothers who were happiest in their own company and probably hadn't even realised she'd gone yet. She'd send them a postcard the first chance she got, let them all know she was a few hours closer to coming home...

The next thing she knew, she was waking up with a start, struggling to sit up with her chair reclining to near horizontal, a weightless but snug mohair rug covering her.

'You're back with us, then,' Andreas said, putting away his laptop. 'We'll be landing soon.'

She put a hand to her hair, and then to her eyes, worried she'd just undone all the good work of the morning. 'I must have drifted off.' She looked outside her window but it was inky blackness outside, clusters of lights visible way down below, but, more importantly, no reflection to assure her she wasn't wearing panda eyes. Or, worse still, just the one.

'You look good.'

She blinked and turned slowly, not sure she'd heard right or that he was even talking to her.

He was stashing his briefcase away in the compartment alongside his knees, and for a moment she thought she must have misheard or been mistaken. Until... 'If that's what you were worried about.' Now he did turn, and once again she was staggered by the intensity of his gaze and the power he had to skewer her with just one glance. 'Stunning, in fact. I don't suppose I told you that before.'

*Nobody* had ever told her that before. Let alone a man whose five o'clock shadow only served to increase his eye appeal. Along with his white shirtsleeves rolled up and the dark V of skin at his unbuttoned neck, he looked more like a pirate now than a property magnate. She licked her lips. Boy, she could do with a drink. 'Um. Thank you.' She wanted to believe the butterflies in her stomach were all to do with the fact the pilot had chosen that second to commence his descent, but she'd be lying to herself. For the hungry look she'd seen in his eyes when she'd got his attention in the car was back again, and that had been enough to start the fluttering sensation, enough to switch on the slow burn inside her.

Nobody had ever called her anything approximating stunning before. Nobody. Even her own mother had never got beyond cute. Hearing Andreas say it made it all the more real.

*And made him all the more dangerous.*

She injected a lightness into her voice that was at odds with the pounding of her heart. Why let him know how much he affected her? That was never part of the deal. 'Well, it's good to know all this morning's work didn't go to waste.'

She unclipped her seat belt and stood, heading for the bathroom, and she was halfway to escape when the ground went from under Cleo's feet, her stomach suddenly in her mouth. With Cleo thrown offbalance, it took only a jerk of Andreas' hand to steer her towards him. She landed in his lap a moment later, appalled that he'd borne the brunt of her weight as she'd collided against him.

'This is no joking matter,' he warned, showing no discomfiture for her sudden landing, indeed, giving every impression that he welcomed it as he nestled her deeper into his lap. 'This is serious.'

She could see it was. She could feel it was. She looked up at his shadowed face, so supremely confident while she lay there breathless and terrified, her heart thudding like a drum as she battled to get her wayward stomach under control. She was no good in turbulence, she knew from experience, the unexpected motion flipping her stomach end to end.

And right now, sitting on Andreas' lap, was no ordinary turbulence. Flames under her skin licked and curled in all the places their bodies met—where his hands touched her and where her legs lay across his before they spilled over the arm rest, where her breast rested heavy and full against his chest and, most of all, where her bottom pressed tight into his lap. Where something growing and rock-hard pressed back.

She squirmed, embarrassed at the intimacy of the contact. He felt huge, so much bigger than he had looked this morning before his shower, so much bigger than Kurt, and she didn't want to know. Didn't need to know. 'Andreas,' she pleaded, not even sure what she was pleading for as she squirmed some more, the urge to escape such intimate contact warring with an inexplicable need to get even closer.

But his eyes were closed, a frown pinching the skin between his brows, the skin drawn tight across his cheekbones. 'You really should stop wriggling...' he said cryptically, and then he opened his eyes and she read desire in their swirling depths and it only served to confuse her more. 'Unless you're planning on rescinding that no sex condition.'

She launched herself from his lap, scrabbling to get herself upright and away from him. 'Don't flatter yourself! It was you who yanked me into your lap, remember?'

He smiled as she headed, chin up, for the bathroom. 'How could I forget? But it wasn't me who was wriggling.'

Clusters of lights clung to the hilltops off to one side, but it was the air Cleo noticed first as they stepped from the plane, so clear and fresh after London's heavy atmosphere, it seemed to have been washed with the very ocean itself. She inhaled deeply and tried to relax. It wasn't working. The plane might have landed but the flock of butterflies in her stomach hadn't come down with it.

'Welcome to Santorini,' Andreas said, drawing her into the circle of his arm and pressing his lips to her hair as they headed towards a waiting car, its headlights lighting their path. She shivered, as much from the cool night air as from his sudden and unexpected touch, and he squeezed her closer so she had to tuck her arm around him. Clearly the pretence had already begun.

It was no hardship to hold him, there was a firmness about his body that made him a pleasure to touch, and the closer she was to him, the more of his delicious masculine scent she could consume, but it was impossible to relax. Her legs felt stiff, her steps forced, her features tense. It was all for show, all to give the appearance they were lovers. And all of it was fake.

'Smile!' he ordered. 'Anyone would think you were about to meet a firing squad.'

Maybe not, but Andreas was paying her a million dollars to pretend to be his mistress and it was a role she had no concept of. A million-dollar mistress who couldn't sell what she knew about being someone's mistress for one dollar.

She should have told him, should have confessed that her experience with the opposite sex was limited to one lousy time instead of claiming to have had sex 'loads of times'. He'd expect her to know what was expected of her and how to act and he'd have every right to be furious when she didn't. She glanced up at him but his profile was set hard, his jaw line rigid as he scowled at the waiting car, and she thought better of it. Whatever he seemed so upset about, now was hardly the time to confess her inexperience.

Whatever was bothering him didn't stop him hauling her closer to him so that they were joined from shoulder to hip, their legs brushing every time they took a step, limb against limb, flesh against fabric until his heat radiated through her. She looked down at her feet and took a deep gulp of the clear night air. Did he feel it too, this delicious friction? Or was he so used to the feel of women that he didn't even notice? She was sure there was no way she would ever get used to the touch of him.

'Cleo?'

She turned her head up towards his. 'Yes?'

And suddenly he was kissing her. No tender kiss, this one; instead his mouth plundered hers with both savagery and skill that left her once-stiff knees jellied and her senses reeling.

She found her fingers in his thick hair, his breath in hers, and all she knew was that she wanted more. How could he do this to her with just one kiss? She could have been back on the plane, feeling the press of his erection hard against her thigh, the same desperate need building inside like a furnace suddenly given oxygen until she was thinking insane, irrational thoughts. Such as she needed to be closer. Horizontal. *Naked.*

He let her go just as abruptly and it was all she could do to stand. 'Wha…? What are you doing?' She clung to him, breathless, her lips swollen and aching as he scowled again even as he smoothed her hair where his fingers had tangled in it.

'Come on,' he said impatiently. 'There's someone I want you to meet.'

It was a contest which one was the most sleek. The Alpha Romeo had smooth fast lines and sexy red duco. The blonde leaning against the door with the amused look on her face was even sleeker. Skinny blue jeans, a white top and a gold belt all atop a pair of killer sandals had never looked less casual. Despite the new clothes, Cleo immediately felt lumpy and inferior and completely ill at ease.

'Cleo,' Andreas said, 'I'd like you to meet Petra Demitriou, my right-hand man, or, as it turns out, my right-hand woman.'

Petra laughed and shook her golden head, showing off her effortlessly sophisticated up-do and, courtesy of the same movement, the long smooth sweep of her neck. 'Oh, Andreas, and I thought you'd never noticed.' She elegantly unwrapped her long arms from over her ample chest and extended a hand to the visitor, while her razor-sharp eyes gave her the once-over. Cleo got the feeling she missed nothing. The way Petra blinked as her smile widened told Cleo she'd been found wanting.

It was hardly her fault. She was still battling to regain her land legs after that kiss. It hadn't been an air pocket she'd hit this time, it had been an Andreas pocket that had sucked the oxygen from the air and knocked her off her feet.

'Hello, Cleo, it's always nice to welcome another of Andreas' guests.'

The woman had an accent that sounded as smooth as honey and yet came with a chilli bite. So Petra wasn't impressed with Andreas' passing parade of women? But then, who could blame her? No doubt she'd be equally unimpressed if their roles were reversed. So instead of reading anything into the critical once-over and the clearly unwelcoming welcome, she thanked her and took the woman's hand.

Petra's fingers were long and slender and cool to touch and clearly weren't aiming to linger. In the next movement they'd been withdrawn and the other hand was holding out a car key to Andreas. 'I thought you might like to drive the new Alfa Romeo. It just came in today. Cleo and I can sit in the back.' Cleo caught something distinctly unfriendly in her expression the moment before her mouth turned into a smile. 'We could get to know one another while Andreas test-drives his new toy.'

Cleo did a rapid reassessment. Maybe she'd only imagined that sneer? She shrugged, confused by it all, confused by what was expected of her and not wanting to offend anyone. 'Lovely. Thanks.' Anything right now to escape the confusion the man alongside her could wreak with a single kiss.

'I wondered why you decided to meet us, rather than send Nick.' Andreas sounded annoyed, his words clipped.

Petra laughed his comment off as she offered the keys up at eye level like a temptation, her lips pouting seductively behind them. He remembered the pose. It was the same one she'd given when they'd been at that restaurant in Oia and she'd said she'd had too much to drink and asked if he could drive them both home, her hand on his thigh the entire way…

'I know how much you were looking forward to a ride. I thought you might appreciate the key.'

Breath hissed through his teeth. He hadn't had too much to drink tonight and the only ride Andreas was looking forward to right now was apparently off limits. But that Petra could be so obvious when it was clear he had found someone else to spend his nights with only served to confirm he had been right to bring someone home with him.

Thank God he hadn't turned up tonight alone. *Sto thiavolo*, he should have chosen someone who could be a bit more convincing! Cleo was as rigid and stiff in his arms as a store dummy. Even his kiss, designed to show Petra that they were completely and sexually into each other, had backfired. Your mistress wasn't supposed to ask what you were doing when you kissed her, as if you'd taken some liberty. No, it would take some doing to make Cleo more comfortable, and more convincing in her role, but if sex was off the agenda he didn't know what would do it.

He hadn't needed Petra turning up at the airport. Had she imagined that one look at her and his desire would be rekindled, the new lover forgotten? Or had she hoped he'd been bluffing, and that there was no woman? Why else would she dress so provocatively, in clothes that clung to her body like a second skin? He was suddenly beginning to get a new appreciation of his right-hand woman. She'd always been a good operator but he'd never realised just how cunning she was.

'Would you mind if I asked you to drive, Petra? Cleo and I have had such a long day. Haven't we, sweetheart?' The implication hung on his words that he'd had a long night and was expecting another to follow. The endearment was meant to convince Petra. Meanwhile a wide-eyed Cleo looked up at him like a rabbit caught in the headlights. He pulled open a rear door and ushered her in, wishing that just once she might act like the mistress he was paying her to pretend to be.

Petra, left with no other choice but to comply, smiled meekly and slid into the driver's seat.

'Have you eaten?' she asked a moment later as the car's powerful engine turned over. 'I've made you a booking at Poseidon.'

Andreas couldn't fault her logic. It was what he normally did if he arrived with a woman in the late afternoon or evening. Sometimes they'd be in time to catch the sunset, sometimes they'd miss it, but a platter of fresh seafood and a Greek salad filled with olives, feta and fresh tomatoes bursting with Greek sunshine ensured that they would be fuelled for the night ahead.

But not tonight. Not when his so-called mistress was as jumpy as a kitten. Maybe she might relax at the house.

'No, take us straight to the house. We had a late lunch. We will eat later.'

There was silence from the driver and yet Andreas could almost hear her mind ticking over, wondering just what was so important that they would rush back to the house and pouncing on the answer in the very next thought. He wondered how far Petra could be pushed. Would she leave if she could see her position was hopeless? He hadn't wanted to lose her expertise but maybe that would be for the best. No one was indispensable. And he couldn't have her thinking she had claims on him.

Likewise he couldn't have the woman alongside him thinking that she could just sit there, as far away from him as she could get and gaping out of her window like some tourist on a coach tour. Damn it, she was supposed to be interested in him!

He leaned across and wrapped an arm around her, cursing when her startled response earned raised eyebrows from their driver in the rear-vision mirror.

'It's not far to Fira,' he told Cleo as the car powered up the road from the airport.

It was as he said. Within a few minutes the car had climbed its way past small picturesque villages and scattered white-washed hotels to a road along the very edge of the island where it became more built up. On one side the land sloped down gently to where they'd just come, the lights of the airstrip bright in the dark night. On the other side, the land fell away steeply, to a dark flat sea. A scattering of lights shone across the waters while in front there seemed a sweeping curve of lights into the distance that curved in tiers down a hillside before being swallowed up by the darkness.

'It is hard to appreciate in the dark,' Andreas told her, the stroke of his thumb on her upper arm doing all kinds of crazy things to her breathing, 'but Santorini is actually a collection of small islands, the remnants of an ancient eruption. Fira, the capital, is built on the lip of the crater. The lights you see further on belong to the town of Oia. Like Fira, it is a very beautiful town, full of narrow cobbled streets and beautifully restored buildings, centuries of years old. Some say the sunset in Oia is the best in the world. I will take you there if you like.'

She suspected he was merely acting his part, she knew she should be, but still the very picture of sharing a sunset with this man worked its way into her soul so much that she almost wanted it to be real. Her voice, when she found it, was breathless and short, and it was no trouble for her to inject into it the necessary enthusiasm. 'I would like that, very much.'

There was a strangled sound from the front seat, followed

by a cough and a murmured apology. 'Andreas is right, Cleo,' Petra said, steering the car through a succession of narrower and narrower streets, past ornate iron gateways and walls of polished white set off with colourful bougainvilleas that caught Cleo's eye. 'It is only a small island, but there is much to see on Santorini. Will you be staying long?'

Cleo shot a look at Andreas, who was scowling again, and she wondered if it was because she'd made such a hash of things that he was already regretting their deal and the time he'd said they'd have together. 'Maybe a few weeks,' she offered nervously, 'maybe less…'

In the rear-view mirror she saw their driver's eyebrows shoot up as she pulled up before a private garage alongside a red-brick building that wouldn't have looked out of place in Venice and waited for the automatic door to roll up. 'That long? How lovely for you. It will be like a wonderful holiday.'

'Of course,' Andreas added with a growl as Petra steered the car into the garage and pulled to a stop. 'There's every chance she may stay longer.'

'Why did you say that?' Petra had bid them goodnight and left them in the lobby, retiring to her own suite, and meanwhile Cleo had been playing and replaying the words over in her head, so much so that she'd barely taken in the details of the house, other than just a handful of impressions. Grand proportions, furnishings that were both elegant and exquisite, it was more a palace than any humble home she'd ever seen.

'Say what?' Andreas sounded almost bored as he instructed the hired help to take care of the luggage and led the way to his suite of rooms, and yet there was too much coiled tension in his every step, his every movement, for her to believe that. Even his words were brimming with tension. The sound of her heels clicking on the terrazzo floor only served to ratchet it up.

'Why did you say I might stay longer?'

'Because you made it sound like you weren't planning on staying at all.'

'I wasn't sure you'd want me to.'

'And I thought we had a deal.'

Maybe so, but she knew he wasn't happy with her, knew she'd failed to impress him with her acting skills. But what did he expect when she'd never been a mistress, didn't know how a mistress was supposed to act? It wasn't as if she'd blown it in front of his business partners. It had only been his driver—his right-hand woman. *An exceptionally beautiful right-hand woman.*

Could the act all be for her benefit?

'Petra is very beautiful.'

He shrugged, but gave every impression of knowing who he was talking about. 'Is she? She's good at what she does.'

'And she lives here with you, in this—' she looked around her, at the exquisite wall hangings and period furniture '—this *house*?'

'The offices of Xenides Properties are here. I'm often away and Petra works long hours. It's an arrangement that works well for both of us.'

There was no hint of any attachment in his words or the tone of his voice. In fact he could have been talking about any employee. Maybe her hunch had been wrong. Maybe he was just aware of Petra's obvious resentment for his lifestyle and his constant change of companions? Or maybe he was just angry with her own hopeless acting skills. She could hardly blame him if he was.

'Here we are.' A pair of carved timber doors stood at the end of a passageway. He pushed them both open and her eyes opened wide. 'The sitting room,' he said, still moving.

She stayed where she was and let herself gape. By now she

should have been used to the luxury—luxury suites in London hotels, a personal private jet with wrap-around leather and champagne on tap—but still the sheer opulence of his everyday lifestyle made her jaw drop. For this was no rented accommodation or flying office, this was his home. And this one room was large enough to house her entire family back home.

'How much money do you have?'

And he turned and looked at her, a cold expression charging his eyes. 'Does it matter?'

'Well, no. It's just…'

'Do not fear, I have more than enough to pay for you.'

His words shouldn't have stung but somehow they did. The notion he was paying to have her here, to stroke her hand with his thumb and kiss her when he needed to look as if he had someone to kiss.

It wasn't as if he were paying her for sex. She was merely acting. Pretending. And yet there was no pretence about the impact his touch and his kisses had on her. It made no sense. She'd been the one to insist on no sex, so why was it that his touch made her think of nothing else? Why did his kisses make her hunger for that which she had refused to entertain? Did he really not feel it too, this ribbon of desire that seemed to tug her ever closer to his side?

No! Andreas was right. This was a commercial arrangement, not some fairy-tale Cinderella story. In a month's time, or however long it took, she'd leave Santorini and go back to her home in Kangaroo Crossing, albeit a million dollars richer than when she'd arrived. For a girl with her background and her chances in life, surely that was fairy tale enough. And yes, clearly there was no question he couldn't afford it.

'Come on, then,' he said gruffly as he tugged off his tie, pointing towards a door on the far side of the room at the same time. 'Let's get this over with.'

## CHAPTER EIGHT

'WHA...? What do you mean?'

Andreas sighed. What the hell had he been thinking to contract this woman to act as his mistress? As an actress Cleo was as stiff and unyielding as a block of cement. As a mistress, she'd been a total failure. And she would continue to be, until she got over this problem she had with being with him. He tossed the car keys Petra had given him onto a dresser where they slid straight off and fell with a clatter to the tiled floor. Behind him she did the startled thing again, jumping as if he'd just thrown the keys at her. And the quicker she got over it, the better. 'What do you think I mean?' He tugged off his already loosened tie and shrugged off his jacket.

Pointless!

She stood there in the doorway to the bedroom, knowing only that he was furious. Meanwhile Andreas had kicked off his shoes and peeled off his socks, tossing them into a corner. The shirt was next, exposing once again that muscled chest to her gaze. She wanted to look away, but she couldn't. She was transfixed.

'Couldn't you have even pretended to be my lover? Why do you have to jump like a startled rabbit every time I touch you?'

'Because you do startle me. I can't help it!'

He swore under his breath. 'We should have slept together last night. Instead we wasted a perfect opportunity to get comfortable with one another.'

His trousers hit the ground and he kicked them carelessly aside. She wanted to resent him for his arrogance, for his knowing that the hired help would pick them up, for his wealth that allowed him to be that way, and most of all for assuming that she would abandon the one condition she'd set on this arrangement. But he made it so hard, too hard, when, instead of mustering a defence, she was busy admiring his lean powerful legs and the way his muscles played under his olive skin with the action.

Her mouth was dry, her blood thick and thumping slow. 'I don't understand. I told you I wasn't prepared to sleep with you.'

He looked up at her then. 'No, you didn't. You said no sex. I told you there would be times where we would have to share a bed and you made no protest.' He looked up at her, her feet still stuck to the floor in the doorway. 'Go on, then, get undressed.'

Her mouth went dry. *Get undressed.* She could be in a doctor's surgery, awaiting an examination, but then the order would be a request and it would be gently and considerately done, with a curtain provided for her modesty and discretion. Here, she was somehow expected to take off her clothes and climb into bed with Andreas glowering at her, dissatisfied and unrepentant. 'Andreas, I…'

But he was already leaving the room, striding barefoot through a door to a room she could see brimming with marble and gilt. Seconds later he returned, stopping dead when he saw her still there, rooted to the spot. 'You're planning on going to bed fully clothed? At least I won't have to put up with that flannelette armour.' The black silk pouch that was his final barrier hit the floor next, leaving him gloriously naked before her. He was beautiful clothed, carrying himself with an authority and presence that turned heads, but naked he was magnificent, broad shoulders that tapered down to a tightly packed waist and lean hips. He was so beautiful, just the sight of him caused her blood to sizzle. She closed her eyes and swallowed hard against a throat filled with cotton wool as he flipped down the covers and slid into the bed.

'Last night,' she began. 'Last night I had my own bed. Why can't I now?'

'Last night we were in London. I told you we might have to sleep together, to keep up appearances. Given there is only one bedroom in this suite and the fact my offices are here, it wouldn't look good if word got out that my latest mistress was sleeping on the sofa, because I certainly don't intend to. Don't worry, I'm sure I can resist you.'

She didn't doubt it. But sharing the same bed as him, lying alongside his naked body when she already knew how his touch turned her flesh alight, she only wished she could be so sure she could resist him.

He pushed himself up on one hand. 'I'm losing patience, Cleo. Are you going to take your clothes off,' he growled, with more than a hint of menace in his voice, 'or am I going to have to come over there and do it for you?'

She shook her head, fear congealing like a ball in her gut. God no, the last thing she wanted was Andreas undressing her. She'd claimed she was experienced. She could do this. But she wasn't about to do it in front of him. She bolted for the bathroom, taking several minutes to calm herself, cooling her burning cheeks with water from the tap. Her luggage had not yet been delivered or if it had, Andreas wasn't telling, so she stripped herself down to the camisole, bra and knickers and wrapped herself in a voluminous robe she found hanging on the back of the door. It would have to do. This wasn't about sex, or so he'd claimed. So what she wore to bed shouldn't matter.

She emerged from the bathroom a good ten minutes or more after she'd entered to find the lights dimmed and Andreas facing away, his eyes closed as if asleep.

Please God he was!

She padded silently to the bed, stood there a second watching him breathe and decided this was it. She'd practically told him she was a woman of the world, claiming she'd had sex loads of times, so just sleeping with a man in the same bed should hardly throw her. She unlaced the tie at her waist and let the robe slip from her shoulders. Andreas didn't stir and she gained confidence. He wouldn't even know she was here. She turned off the light and slipped between the covers, hovering so close to the edge there could be no way he would feel her presence, and he gave no sign that he did, his breathing slow and regular, a pattern that calmed her own frantically beating heart.

On tenterhooks she lay there listening to his breathing, feeling foolish and naïve, even as the curtains of sleep descended one by one, closing around her and pulling her into their embrace, until she was surrounded by them, warm and comforting and reassuring.

And if those curtains felt as if they'd grown arms and legs and were fashioned of silken flesh rather than velvet, and breathed as if the mild night air moved through them, the brush of them on her shoulder like the warm brush of a lover's lips, she could feel no less comforted.

Cleo woke alone in the wide bed to the spill of sunshine through tall narrow windows and a feeling of disbelief suffusing her veins. She was here. She was really here, lying in bed in a centuries-old mansion on a Greek island and last night—last night she'd slept with a real Greek billionaire, a Greek billionaire who'd honoured her condition that sex was no part of this deal!

A shiver ran down her spine. Four weeks, the contract had stipulated. Four weeks she could be here, sharing Andreas' bed. After last night the prospect was suddenly more thrilling than threatening. Scattered remnants came to her then, of a warm hand and a silken touch, of the press of thigh and a puff of breath at her neck, and the press of lips…

She must have been dreaming again.

She pulled on the robe she'd left lying on the end of the bed just as the chimes of a clock on a mantelpiece rang out, drawing her eye. Ten in the morning! Even allowing for the two-hour time difference with London, she hadn't slept in so late for months. No wonder Andreas wasn't here. He'd probably gone to work hours ago. And no wonder she was so hungry, it was hours since they'd eaten on the plane. She was halfway to the bathroom when it caught her eye, a patch of blue through the whisper-thin gauzy curtains billowing in the soft breeze, so blue that she was compelled to draw the curtain and investigate.

What she saw took her breath away. There was a terrace outside the window, whitewashed and dazzling in the morning sun, and then the earth must have fallen away beneath them, for a long way below shimmered a sea of the brightest blue she'd ever seen, a sea that stretched before another island that rose, tall and long and dusted with white buildings. And to the left sat another islet, low and wide and dark.

So this was Santorini? No wonder Kurt had raved about it to her. Even if he had never visited, even if he'd never intended bringing her here, maybe for once he hadn't been lying. It was breathtakingly beautiful.

And now she had four weeks to enjoy it, to share it with Andreas...

'You're up, then.'

She turned with a start to see him standing in the doorway. He looked as fresh as the morning, his hair damp at the ends where it curled over his collar, a white shirt and fitted trousers making the most of his lean shape.

And suddenly she wasn't sure what to be the more embarrassed about, finding herself staring hungrily at the delicious V of olive skin where his shirt was unbuttoned, or the knowledge that without intimacy they'd slept together and would do again, tonight. Damn it if her nipples hadn't already tightened under the robe in anticipation, her pulse sending blood to all the places that shouldn't even know he existed, but seemed to anyway. It was only sleep with him they had to look forward to, but that seemed to make no difference; she tingled all over.

'I thought you'd gone to work.'

'There were some things I had to attend to.' He stopped in front of her and curled a hand under her hair, skimming her neck with his fingertips and drawing her closer, his eyes on her mouth. She sensed he was going to kiss her and she made no move to shift away, her eyelids fluttering closed on a sigh. Why should she when his touch felt so good, and when he'd agreed to her terms? Sex might be out but a kiss was definitely within the bounds of conditions she'd set. She could deal with that. Surely this was the best of all worlds?

'Good. You didn't jump,' he said, abruptly letting her go before their lips had even connected.

She blinked, swaying momentarily until she regained her bearings. 'I what?'

'We seem to be curing you of your habit of jumping every time I touch you. This is a good start. Perhaps now you will be more convincing.'

'Oh, of course.' She studied her toes, while she pushed her hair back behind her ears, feeling a total fool for thinking he wanted to kiss her, a total fool for being so eager. 'That is good.'

He was already turning to go when he turned back. 'Breakfast is being served on the terrace if you're hungry.'

She nodded, looking to his eyes for a hint, hoping to find a trace of the warmth and comfort she'd felt last night in her sleep, but there was nothing there and she knew what she'd felt had been a dream.

'I'll be along as soon as I'm dressed.'

There was nothing to feel disappointed about, she told herself as she took a shower in the luxurious marble bathroom, the spray from the shower more like a downpour, raining down sense on an otherwise wayward brain. What was her problem? She had a job to do for four weeks and then she would return home, a millionaire. Tenderness didn't come into it.

She stepped out onto the sun-washed terrace and any remaining sense of disappointment evaporated in the wonder of the place he'd brought her to. What she'd glimpsed through the bedroom window had been magical. But outside on the terrace the view was simply breathtaking.

She could see from one end of this island to the other, the sweeping curve of dark cliffs topped with whitewashed villages that clung to the very edge of the cliff like icing spilling over the sides of a cake.

Andreas sat at the table already but, despite her growling stomach, she was too excited right now to sit and eat. How could she even think about eating when there was so much to devour with her eyes?

A breeze toyed with the ends of her hair as she stood at the balustrade, the air pure and clean as she gazed out across the sapphire-blue waters. The light was wonderful, more like the bright sunlight of home rather than the grey misty blanket that so often shrouded London, defining everything with sharp detail, so that even islands far beyond this ring of cliffs could be clearly seen.

Either side of her, the town of Fira spread across the clifftop, a jumble of closely packed buildings, some adorned with splashes of colourful bougainvillea and punctuated by stairways and narrow paths that somehow combined harmoniously to create a picture of charm, while far below two sleek cruise ships sat anchored. For a second memories of Kurt once more invaded her thoughts, but only for a moment. She was no day visitor here; she was living here for a month.

'What do you think?'

Andreas appeared at her side, his arm looping casually around her shoulders. *Appearances*, she told herself, willing away the jag in her heart rate, *he's merely keeping up appearances for the maid busy filling up coffee cups.* But it didn't matter so much any more, not when she was being treated to a place of such amazing beauty that the man-made seemed not to detract from but to complement the natural.

'It's the most beautiful place I've ever seen. I don't know how you can bear to leave it.'

He smiled as if pleased with her reaction. 'It is always good to come home. Come.' He drew her further around the terrace, pointing out the various islands. 'This is the main island, known as Thera. The island across the water is called Therassia, and the tiny one between is known as Aspronisi.'

'What about that one?' She pointed to the low dark isle she'd noticed earlier.

'That is Nea Kameni, the volcano.'

Her head swung around. 'Volcano!'

He laughed, a rich deep sound that in normal circumstances would allay her fears. But these were hardly normal circumstances. He expected her to live on the edge of a volcano? 'Like I was telling you last night, this ring of islands and these cliffs are the remains of the caldera after an eruption thousands of years ago. The empty chamber filled with sea water causing a massive explosion into which the volcano collapsed. This ring of islands is all that's left.'

Despite the warming rays of the sun, Cleo shivered. The island cliffs formed a crater that was enormous. That something so beautiful could be created from something so devastating beggared belief. 'But it's safe now, isn't it?'

'Oh, yes, the volcano hasn't erupted for some decades.'

Cleo wrapped her arms around her midriff. 'You mean it's still active?'

Andreas shrugged, a wry smile on his face. 'The volcano is rebuilding itself. Sometimes the island rumbles with the reconstruction, and sometimes she makes herself known in more obvious ways and lets off a little steam, but for the most part the earth is quiet. You are no doubt much safer here than on the streets of London.'

She breathed out. 'Maybe you're right, but Kangaroo Crossing is looking better by the minute. We lack the views of course, there's nothing but red dust and Spinifex bushes as far as the eye can see, but at least it comes with no nasty surprises.'

'You mean you don't have poisonous spiders or snakes? What part of Australia is this?' And she had the grace to blush.

'Come,' Andreas said, 'let's eat, and then I must return to work. There is a pool on the lower terrace where you can swim or you can explore the town on foot. Do you think you will be able to amuse yourself during the day?'

'I'm sure I will,' said Cleo, surprised by his apparent interest in her, but her attention snagged as she sat before the breakfast table laden with what looked more like a feast. There were bowls of creamy yoghurt drizzled with honey and platters of pastries and rolls along with a selection of cheeses and fruit from which to choose.

'Good,' he said, 'and then tonight I will show you the sunset and you will see it's not so bad to live on a cliff top overlooking a volcano.'

'I'll take your word for that,' she said, ridiculously pleased with herself when she caught his answering smile.

Refreshing was the word, he decided as he headed towards the suite of offices housed within the mansion. There was an innocence about her, a lack of sophistication that was charming.

Did she really fear for her safety here on Santorini when she came from a country with a reputation for its dangerous wildlife? It was laughable.

'Andreas, you're back at last.' Petra perched herself on the edge of his desk, crossed her legs and smiled, flashing two rows of perfect white teeth between blood-red lips. 'Your mother called.'

He didn't miss the show of leg revealed by the split in the skirt, a skirt he'd never seen before. Was it his imagination or was Petra putting up a fight for his attention, first with her skin-tight clothes display last night, and now a skirt that was split to her thigh? 'Did she leave a message?'

'She said she'd like you to visit, said she hasn't seen you for ages. I said you'd call her back later.'

Andreas wondered what else she might have said. 'Was there anything else?'

Petra looked miffed, the coffee she'd brought them both forgotten. Coffee together in his office around this time of day had been almost a daily ritual, where they would discuss whatever business had arisen or opportunities that might be in the offing. To him, there'd been nothing more in it than one colleague talking to another. Clearly Petra had read things differently.

'No, nothing.' She eased herself off his desk, straightening her skirt with her hands, the motion accentuating her cleavage. So different from Cleo's ingenuous innocence that he almost felt sorry for her. Cleo didn't have to play games to draw attention to herself. He'd noticed her attributes even before the makeover experts had woven their magic. Hers was a natural beauty, fragile, buried under a lifetime of feeling not good enough.

Cleo was more than good enough. Having her in his bed last night and trying not to touch her had been sheer torture. Only when he had been sure she'd drifted off, he'd allowed himself to gather her against him and breathe in the subtle scent of her skin and hair. Without even realising, she'd spooned her body next to his and it had taken every shred of self-control he owned to leave her sleeping when every part of him had been screamingly awake.

'Although,' Petra continued so abruptly that he looked up, surprised to see her still there, 'I guess I should remind you about the Kalistos ball tonight. You'll be taking Cleo, I imagine. Otherwise you and I could travel together...'

'Of course, I'm taking Cleo,' he barked as he sent her on her way. He suppressed a groan as he leaned back in his chair. What was wrong with him? It was clearly marked on his diary, but at breakfast he'd forgotten all about the ball and was thinking in terms of sunsets with Cleo instead. He knew what he'd rather do. But with Kalistos still to give his decision on Andreas' latest proposal to tie their businesses together, a proposal that could benefit both companies to the tune of millions of Euros, there was no way he couldn't show up. As for taking Cleo, she was starting to relax with him, but ideally he'd like another day or two before he could be sure she'd be completely convincing on his arm.

Another day or two he didn't have.

Cleo had never been more nervous in her life. She'd wondered why Mme Bernadette had insisted on her taking the numerous gowns and had half suspected she'd been merely feathering her own nest—a Greek island sojourn surely wouldn't require ball gowns?—and yet here she was, dressed in the pale gold halter-neck gown, her hair piled high on her head with coils trailing around her face courtesy of the hairdresser Andreas had sent to their suite, curtailing her sightseeing plans for today.

Andreas hadn't helped relax her when he'd taken one look at her and whistled low through his teeth, sending her pulse and her senses skittering. And he certainly wasn't helping relax her now as they drove down the windy switchback road to the port.

'Constantine Kalistos is not only one of the major business and political leaders on the island, but also owns the largest charter boat operation in Greece,' he told her, in a tone that suggested she should be taking notes. 'He's considering a business proposal I put to him and he's the main reason we're here tonight. He's the perfect host but, at the same time, he's a man you don't want to offend.'

Cleo battled to absorb the information, growing more nervous by the second as the car pulled closer to a wharf lit with coloured lanterns, music spilling from the massive yacht moored alongside, couples dripping with jewellery and designer fashions emerging from the limousines and sports cars lined up before them.

*Help.* She'd never been on a boat bigger than a canoe and she'd never been to any function more glamorous than the Kangaroo Crossing Bachelor and Spinster Ball, where Akubras were just as likely sighted as bow ties. She swallowed. There were no Akubras here.

Andreas followed her from the car, his hand collecting hers, and she'd never been more grateful to have him alongside. She was so nervous she was sure she was going to wobble straight off her gold kidskin spike-heeled sandals, especially as she stumbled with the gentle movement of the gangplank under her feet.

'Relax,' Andreas whispered, setting her coiling hair dancing around her ear. 'And smile. You'll be fine.' And then he was tugging her forward, onto the brightly lit boat with the even more brightly lit people, and they were greeting Andreas and giving her openly curious glances and she wondered how a girl from Kangaroo Crossing got to be here, in a softly swaying yacht filled with Santorini's who's who with clearly the most handsome man on the island. One look around at the glittering attendees was enough to confirm that.

'Are you okay?' Andreas asked softly, breaking off a greeting to someone, and she looked up into his dark eyes, confused. 'I thought you wanted something,' he added. 'You squeezed my arm.' And she smiled and nodded, not even having realised she'd done it. 'I'm fine,' she told him, wishing for nothing more than for the butterflies in her stomach to settle down.

Something passed between them then, some spark of approval or warmth, she didn't know what to call it, but she felt it in his glance all the way down to her lacquered toenails, and she knew from his answering smile that he'd felt it too. So what if the only thing that bound them was a business contract? Would it be so wrong to like the man into the deal?

Someone slipped a glass of champagne into her hand as the boat slipped from port and Cleo felt the first uneasy twinge as the vessel rocked sideways before pulling away. Slowly it built up speed in preparation for its circuit of the islands and Cleo prayed that they'd soon find calm water as the butterflies turned to moths. Somersaulting moths. She forced a smile to her lips as Andreas introduced her to more and more people, all of whom seemed oblivious to the motion, and all the while shuffling on her stiletto heels in search of the ever-elusive balance as the boat sliced through the gentle swell.

She abandoned the barely touched glass of champagne, exchanging it for water, which still failed to settle her stomach. The fresh air on deck didn't help, not when all she could notice was the line of lights atop the cliffs moving up and down and the passenger catamaran skipping away from them on the seas. When perspiration started beading at her forehead, she knew she was in trouble.

'Andreas,' she said, one hand on her stomach as they moved between groups on the deck. 'I don't feel—'

'Andreas! There you are.'

Cleo stepped back, wondering if she could just slip away as Andreas was swept into a man's embrace, his back slapped by one beefy hand. It was no mean feat given the man barely came up to Andreas' shoulders, his black jacket widest around his ample stomach, and his features creased and heavy with age and excess.

'Constantine,' Andreas said, 'it is always a great pleasure. Allow me to introduce Cleo Taylor, all the way from Australia.'

'Ah,' said the beaming Greek, his eyes sizing her up and taking her hand gallantly. 'Then it is in fact my pleasure.' He held out a hand and gestured around him. 'Tell me, what do you think of my little runaround?'

It was hitting the ferry's wake that did it. Her stomach felt as if it had speared into the sky only to be slammed down again and she knew it was too late. If she opened her mouth, she was lost. She pushed her glass into Andreas' free hand, shoved a path between the two men and bolted for the bathroom.

# CHAPTER NINE

WHAT had he been thinking? Cleo was hopeless. A blow-up doll would have made a more convincing mistress. And the look Constantine had given him when they'd been offloaded back on shore had spoken volumes. Andreas wasn't holding out for good news in that department any time soon. The 'I told you so' look Petra had thrown his way as they'd disembarked hadn't helped.

The car slowly wound its way up the cliff-face road, the lights of Con's yacht heading once more for the sea, the music and laughter drifting upwards on the breeze, rubbing salt into his wounds, while alongside him Cleo sat hunched and looking despondently out of her window.

Damn it, was it too much to ask to get *something* for his million dollars?

Carrying her shoes in one hand, Cleo made straight for the bathroom where she spent at least five times the recommended daily time with her toothbrush and at least that again holding a cold towel to her red and swollen eyes. Andreas had thankfully kept silent all the way home, although she'd known that simmering silence would erupt at some stage, especially after the pleasure boat had had to make a special trip back to the wharf to drop them off.

So be it. She knew she was already a disappointment to him. And now she'd probably blown a million-Euro business deal. But she'd warned him she wasn't the right woman for the job. Maybe now he might listen. Maybe now he would let her go. If he didn't throw her out first.

She sniffed, close to tears again. Did it matter? Either way, she was going.

He was sitting on the bed, flinging off first one shoe and then the other when she emerged. Following them with his silk socks. Without following her progress across the room, he spoke. 'Why didn't you tell me you get seasick?'

She stopped, just short of pulling open the wardrobe door. So the volcano was about to erupt? She was surprised he'd kept quiet this long. 'Maybe I didn't know.'

This time he did look up, disbelief plain on his features. 'How could anyone not know?'

'I've never been on a boat before. There's not a big call for boats where I come from.'

He answered with nothing more than a grunt. 'It could have been worse,' she offered, trying to sound light but having to bite down on her lip to counter the prick of tears.

'Do you think? Do you really think it could have been worse?'

'Sure. I could have thrown up all over the both of you.'

'You might just as well have, for all the good taking you tonight is going to do me.'

She closed her eyes and swayed against the door, liquid spilling from her eyes, and the sound of his clothes hitting the floor piece by piece like a series of exclamation marks. 'I know. I'm sorry.' She took a deep breath and reached in, hauling out her pack from the depths of the wardrobe. 'It won't happen again. There's no way it will happen again.'

Andreas seemed to come from nowhere, his arms forcing

her around even as she clung onto the pack. 'What the hell are you doing?'

She couldn't bring herself to look at his face. But it was no compensation that her eyes were met by the wall of his naked chest, a naked chest she'd never see the likes of again after tonight. 'I can't do this, Andreas,' she said as her mind set about imprinting every square centimetre of his perfect skinscape on her memory while he slipped the pack from her hands. 'I'm going home.'

'You can't go. We have a contract!'

'I can't do this. I'm sorry, I'm hopeless in this role, and you know it.'

'No! That's not true.' He didn't know where the words came from. Hadn't he thought the very same thing himself tonight? But he had no answer for that mystery. All he knew was that he couldn't let her go, couldn't let her walk out of his life. Not like this. Not when he knew the sunshine of her smile. Not when he knew he was the one who had taken it away from her.

She tried to shrug away, even as his thumbs stroked her collarbone. 'You don't have to try to be nice to me. I know you're angry and you have a right to be. I told you I wasn't the right person for this job. I'm a cleaner. A cleaner who jumps every time you touch her. A cleaner who's just discovered she gets seasick. Not exactly an asset to you.'

'Not every time.'

She blinked up at him, frowning. 'What?'

'You don't jump every time. You're not jumping now. And I'm touching you. And I'd like to go on touching you.'

Her blue eyes widened. 'Andreas?'

And he answered her question the only way he knew how. With a kiss that he hoped would tell her he wanted her to stay. That he didn't want her to leave. He drew her closer against him, until the silk of her golden gown pressed warm and slippery and seductive against his skin. He managed to prise his lips away from hers long enough to say the words. 'I want to make love to you, Cleo.'

She was gasping for breath, and no doubt searching for reason. 'The contract…' she uttered.

'This is nothing to do with the contract. This is between you and me. Make love with me, Cleo.'

Did he mean that? Her thought processes were blurred, her senses packed to overload. What he could do to her skin with the touch of one thumbnail. What he could do to her breasts with just the brush of one fingertip. What he could do with one whispered request…

*'Make love with me.'*

He wasn't playing fair. Sex as a by-product of their arrangement—it should be clinical and dispassionate, surely. And then she could be rational and sensible in her rebuttal. But this assault was like a drug, winding logic into sensual knots, feeding into those parts of her that longed for more of what Andreas could provide.

His hands slid down her arms, captured her breasts and forced the air from her lungs. *'Make love with me.'* And the only answer she could find was to lift her hands behind her neck and unclip her halter top, so that the fabric slid down over the hands that now supported her breasts.

He growled then, and swept her into his arms, carrying her like a prize and laying her down on the bed, peeling down the silk until her breasts lay exposed to his gaze. She watched him watching her, her hands around his neck, his dark eyes heavy with longing, and never had she wanted anything more.

And then she felt nothing beyond the ecstasy of his hot mouth on her breast, his tongue hungrily circling her nipple.

'Andreas,' she implored, not knowing why or what she wanted. He growled a laughing response and she almost cried out in despair when he withdrew and cold air replaced where he'd been, only for his mouth to claim the other. His hands scooped her sides, moulding to her flesh, drinking it in as his lips drew her breast deeper into the furnace of his mouth.

Somewhere in some vague recess of her mind, she was aware of his hand at her back, and the downward buzz of a zipper, but it was the sensation of the silken gown sliding down her body that took precedence and the feel of his hot mouth at her belly.

Some time, she couldn't remember when, she'd wrapped her arms around his neck and tangled her fingers in his hair. It was thick and silky, the waves curling around her fingers possessively.

And then there was nothing between them but underwear, nothing that could disguise his need or hide her want.

*Oh, God!*

The panic welled up even as his hand scooped down her body, from shoulder, over breast, to stomach, to *there*, where she forgot about panic and ached instead with something that felt like desperation. His fingers slipped under the lace, scooping low, driving her crazy with his feather-light touch.

And then so gently, so tenderly he parted her and her back arched from the bed. She could feel what he could, her slickness, the moistness that let his fingertips glide against her tender flesh like satin over silk, while his thumb circled a tight bud of nerves that combined agony with ecstasy, the pressure building and building until they screamed for release.

His lips found her nipple and it was Cleo who screamed, Cleo whose world fractured and split apart in a blinding explosion of colour and sensation that left her shattered and gasping in his hands.

She was more responsive than he'd imagined and now he wanted her more than ever! He dispensed with his underwear and reached for protection in almost the same movement. The scrap of lace hit the floor in the next as he kissed his way up her still-shuddering body, positioning himself over her. He'd known he would enjoy her body. She was lush and curvy and her breasts filled his hands better than he could have hoped.

His erection bucked, eager now, and more than ready. Still, he took a moment to lap at one rose-coloured nipple, to nuzzle at her neck before brushing the hair from her turned-away face and pressing his lips to her cheek, only to taste salt.

He took her chin in his hand and pulled it around to face him. Tracks stained her cheeks, moisture clung to the lashes of her closed eyelids and her lips were firmly pressed together. 'You're crying? Did I hurt you?'

Reluctantly her blue eyes opened to him. Awash with tears, they looked the colour of the sea as she slowly shook her head, swiping at her eyes with one hand. 'I'm sorry,' she sniffed, 'but that's never happened to me before. I didn't know…'

*Never happened?* Confusion clouded his mind for a moment, clearing just as quickly as a wave of fury rolled over him. He sat up. 'You are a virgin!' *Vlaka!* He was such a fool. He left the bed and strode across to a wardrobe, plucking out a robe that he lashed around himself, giving the tie a savage tug. No wonder she had been so coy, so sensitive to his touch. No wonder she had been so bad an actress! She had been touched by nobody!

He rounded on the bed, to where the girl now sat huddled over her knees, scrabbling for her golden gown in an effort to cover her nakedness. A virgin! That was the last thing he needed. 'You told me you had slept with men before! You told me you were not a virgin. What the hell are you doing here?'

She dropped her head onto her knees as a fresh flood of tears spilled from his eyes, only magnifying his fury.

'What kind of woman are you? Were you so hungry for money that you would risk that which is most precious to you?'

'No,' she cried, raising her tear-stained face up at him, 'because I'd already thrown that away for nothing!'

She sniffed again and swiped the back of one hand across her cheeks, swinging her legs over the side of the bed and standing, the gown bunched ineffectually around her. 'I'm not a virgin, if that makes you feel any better. So you don't have to worry about deflowering me. Somebody else got there first.'

He supposed he should have been relieved. He watched her flight for the bathroom while he stood there wondering why all of a sudden that thought was somehow so very unappealing.

'You made out like you'd had sex plenty of times.'

She didn't even turn around. 'So sue me.'

'But you've never even had an orgasm.'

This time she did, glaring over her shoulder at him. 'I don't recall seeing that condition in the fine print.'

He consumed the distance between them in a handful of purposeful strides, catching her by the arm just short of the bathroom door and swinging her around to face him.

'So why not? How many times have you had sex? How many men?'

She looked down at his hand on her arm, before turning her face slowly up to his. The tracks of her tears had messed up whatever had been left of her make-up. There were dark smudges under her blue eyes and her hair was still tangled and messy from thrashing her head around when she'd climaxed. *When she'd climaxed for the very first time.*

*He'd given her that.* Despite the tears and smudges and tangled hair he saw only that. He felt the thrum of blood return, the heaviness building once again in his groin.

'How many?'

'One.'

And he felt himself frown. 'One man?'

Her eyes looked sad and pained at the same time, before she blinked and turned her head away and he knew.

'Why didn't you tell me?'

She flinched and tried to pull away and he couldn't blame her. He'd growled out the words so harshly that even to his own ears his question had sounded more like an accusation. But damn it, she was supposed to be pretending to be his mistress. 'You should have told me, instead of making out you'd had sex plenty of times.'

Her head snapped around, her blue eyes blazing. 'You think it's easy to admit to someone you barely know that you've had sex only once and it was so lousy anyway you really wish you hadn't bothered? Especially when sex isn't part of the deal.' She gave an exaggerated shrug to accompany a wide-eyed look of innocence. 'And you so understanding. Heck, why didn't I tell you?'

He wanted to shake her. He wanted to tell her she'd been wrong ever thinking she could pull this off, that she should have admitted the truth when he'd first put his proposition to her, and maybe he would do both of those things, but first of all there was a raw pain in her liquid eyes that made him want to tear somebody else limb from limb first.

'Who was he?'

'It doesn't matter. He was just some guy. It was just for a laugh.'

But her eyes told him differently.

He cupped her neck in one hand and drew her head to his shoulder. For a moment she stayed stiff but the strumming of his fingers on her skin soon soothed away her resistance. 'But it was no good. At least, not for you.'

She gave what he suspected was meant to be a laugh, but came out more like a hiccup. 'It was awful. It hurt and it was over in no time but I thought…'

He drew her closer into a hug. What kind of man was so uncaring of an innocent? 'You thought what?'

She shrugged and tried to lift her head. 'It doesn't matter.' Her voice was flat and lifeless but her body was warm and pliant against his, as if she'd forgotten to be afraid. His fingers stroked her neck, tracing the bones of her spine up into her hair and then down again.

Her scent surrounded him, the smell of her hair, the remnants of her fragrance and the warm scent of her earlier arousal. She had come apart in his arms. His and nobody else's and the knowledge made him hard. She was almost a virgin and she needed to know it could be better. He kissed her hair and breathed deep.

'He was a fool. He did not deserve the gift he'd been given.'

She raised her face and blinked up at him. 'I thought you would be mad with me. *Were* mad with me. And you'd have every right. I'm sorry. I know I should never have agreed to do this.'

He listened to her words and nodded on a sigh. 'You're right. You clearly do not have the experience necessary for the job.' And he felt her stiffen in his arms and try to pull away.

'But perhaps that is something we could remedy together.'

It felt as if her heart had skipped a beat. Or maybe it had just stopped altogether. But no, she was still standing and there was her heartbeat, pounding louder than ever in her ears.

She looked up at him, afraid she'd misconstrued what he meant, afraid in case she hadn't.

*Afraid.*

And he took her face in his hands and pressed his lips to hers.

'I promise you your second time will be better.'

She was in his arms in the next moment, bundled still with the golden dress tangled around her and feeling strangely disjointed and other-worldly.

'Andreas,' she whispered as he placed her like a treasured prize in the centre of the bed. 'What if I can't? I mean—' She felt the heat flood to her face. 'You're so…big.'

And he smiled as he unwrapped her from the coverlet, uncovering her bit by bit until she lay naked on the bed before him. 'I will not hurt you,' he said, and his dark eyes held a promise as intense as their desire so that even when he untied his own robe and revealed the full extent of his arousal she believed him.

Time became irrelevant in the minutes following. Colours blurred and merged with her feelings into a sensual overload. And nothing mattered but the sensations Andreas conjured up inside her as he worked his brand of slow magic upon her body.

No part of her escaped his attention. Nowhere was ignored by his clever fingers or his heated mouth or the hot flick of his tongue.

Until she was burning with a need that she'd never known.

Burning for completion.

'Did he do this to you?' Andreas asked as he parted her thighs and dipped his head lower. And she tossed her head from side to side, the sensations inside her robbing her of the power of speech.

'Did he make you feel this way?' He wanted to know as he pressed his hot mouth to her very core, almost tipping her over the edge.

'Did he make you call his name?' he demanded.

Her cry was torn from her, his name on her tongue as he sent her once again over the edge. 'Did he?' he demanded, raining hot kisses on her eyes and on her mouth. Hot kisses that tasted of him and of her.

'No' she breathed when finally she could talk once more, her head still spinning, her body humming. 'No.'

'Then he was not a man. He gave you nothing and so what he took from you was nothing.'

She shuddered under him, though whether from the intensity of his message or from the obsidian gaze meeting hers, she couldn't tell. Nor could she think as she felt the nudge of him against her.

She gasped and felt a moment of panic but his eyes stayed her.

'You are ready,' he told her. 'Trust me.'

Strangely she did. And this time there was no stab of pain, no discomfort. This time she felt her muscles slowly stretching as he eased his way inside, until he filled her completely, all the time his dark eyes not leaving hers.

He kissed her then, a slow, deep kiss that spoke of possession as he started to move inside her. She gasped into his mouth as he slowly withdrew. She gasped again when he returned, awakening nerve endings she'd never known she possessed, inviting their participation in this sensual dance.

Every part of her felt alive. Every part of her awake to his slow seduction, welcoming him as he increased the pace and the rhythm. And still his eyes didn't leave her face.

She clung to him, inside and out, feeling it building again, that relentless ever-increasing tension as he took her higher and still higher with each deep thrust until there was nowhere left to climb, nowhere left to go.

And then her world exploded, shattering into tiny fragments as he pushed her over the edge. And this time she wasn't alone. This time he came with her.

* * *

Clearly the man had been a fool. Andreas lay there listening to the sound of her deep even breathing as the moonlight spilled through the long window and over her creamy skin, giving it a pearl-like sheen. He'd always made a point of not bedding virgins. He didn't want to build false hopes. He didn't want attachments based on first times. He didn't want attachments full stop.

So whoever had clumsily relieved Cleo of her virginity had handed him a gift. She was unbelievably responsive, her delight in an unfamiliar act refreshing and light years away from that of the women he normally associated with, who tended to go mechanically through the motions with a brisk, businesslike efficiency. Not that there was anything wrong with that; it was no different from the way he himself operated. But now that he had been handed this prize, it would be refreshing to spend a few weeks having sex with someone who wasn't quite so practised, someone for whom the art of love-making would be more of a novelty.

Far from being the disaster he'd been contemplating earlier tonight, his four-week plan had been inspired, now that she'd clearly dispensed with that no-sex clause. A few weeks with Cleo in his bed would suit him perfectly and then she'd depart back to wherever she'd come from and meanwhile Petra would have well and truly got the message.

He sighed, congratulating himself as he relaxed back into the bed, the scent of a woman's hair on his pillow, the scent of their love-making in his bed.

A few easy-to-take weeks with Cleo, and life would be back to normal.

# CHAPTER TEN

ANDREAS started work early the next day, hoping to work out a way of getting Constantine back on side, but he wasn't returning calls and with growing frustration Andreas picked up a file from his desk, flipped it open and found documents he'd been waiting on since before his trip to London. Good. He glanced over them once and frowned when he couldn't remember a thing he'd just read. Took a second look and still nothing stuck. He closed the file, pushing it away as he leaned back in his chair, spinning it around to face the view of the caldera from his office.

What was Cleo doing today? He'd left her snug in bed, the scent of their recent love-making perfuming the air. Had she decided on a late breakfast and a swim? Or had she decided to explore the streets of Fira on her own after he'd curtailed her exploration yesterday? She didn't speak Greek. Santorini's tourist venues catered for tourists of course, but still…

'Where are you going?'

'I'll be back,' he told Petra as he strode past. 'Later.'

An hour later he *was* back, his mood foul because he'd missed her, still no call back from Con and still the damned papers made no sense. He opened another file. Signed some papers awaiting his signature, relegated some more marked for his attention to the out-tray, read and reread another batch of files before he decided his heart wasn't in it and he pushed his chair back with a rush.

Where was she? He'd told the staff to let him know the moment she returned, and he'd heard nothing. Surely they couldn't have forgotten his instructions.

Maybe they had. By four o'clock he'd had enough of waiting and guessing. How much time did one woman need for shopping? Fira wasn't *that* big a town.

He found her in the suite preparing to take a shower, already in her robe, and he knew he'd been right to suspect she was up to something because not one shopping bag littered the room. 'Where the hell have you been?'

She turned, startled, her cheeks reddening. 'You told me I could go out.'

And he had. He exhaled, trying to rid himself of hours of frustration in one single breath. 'You were gone a long time. You clearly weren't shopping. What were you doing?'

Her face brightened again, warily at first, gaining enthusiasm as she spoke. 'Fira is amazing! The paths and the houses and even the gates. Did you realise how wonderful the doorways are here? They beckon you with a glimpse of paradise, a snatch of view, like some wicked temptation, and opening to stairs you don't even know are there and that lead to terraces hidden below. It's incredible. I've never seen anything like it.'

She was like a powerhouse, so lit up with the joy of her discoveries that her joy fed into him. He should be used to the everyday sights that surrounded him but she made them all fresh and new and now he wished he'd been there to see it through her eyes and feel the joy of her discovery with her.

'And there are donkeys with ribbons and beaded headbands that carry people all the way up and down to the port…'

For a moment her blue eyes misted and lost a little of their joy. She shook her head. 'I walked. I felt a bit sorry for them. But then,' she said breathlessly, her eyes lighting up again as if she'd discovered the meaning of life itself, 'then I found the Archaeological Museum.'

'You what?' He smothered a snort of disbelief, but it was only just. Nobody he'd ever brought to Santorini had bothered to look it up. Not one of his former women had ever been interested, preferring to shop for the gold jewellery the island was renowned for or designer trinkets to take home. 'Why did you go there?'

'I was curious about Santorini, and it was amazing! I couldn't believe the history of this place. There was an entire city buried under ash. A whole city buried, just like Pompeii, but thousands of years earlier and they'd found pots and urns and the most incredible artworks.' She held out her hands and sighed, her blue eyes bright with discovery, her cheeks alive with colour and all he knew was that he wanted that enthusiasm and joy wrapped around him. He wanted her. *Now.*

He saw the change in her eyes as she realised, saw the movement in her chest as she hauled down air and felt the air crackle between them as if it were alive. 'Andreas?' And then she was in his arms as they tumbled together onto the bed.

Last night's tenderness was history. They came together in a heated rush, Cleo grappling with his shirt buttons and his belt while he plundered her mouth with his kisses and drove her to the edge with the hot sweep of his hands before plunging into her depths. It was brutal and savage and fast but they both wanted it that way, needed it to be that way, the all-consuming fire of their need driving them on. Her cries melded with his as he drove into her one final time, sending them both spinning and weightless and once more into the crater.

Panting and slick with sweat, he cursed himself for his lack of control. That was no way to take a woman with so little experience. 'Are you all right?'

She blinked her blue eyes up at him, eyes that were still dizzy and lacking focus. 'Wow.'

'Was I too fast? Did I hurt you?'

'Oh, no. Just, wow.'

Strangely, in a place he didn't even know he had, he felt a surge of pride. Still inside her, not caring that he was still half dressed because he didn't want to be apart, he cradled her face in his hands and kissed her softly. 'What was that for?' she breathed.

'Just because.' He traced a hand down her throat and up the incline to one perfect breast. 'Did you see the women, how they were portrayed in the wall paintings?' She gasped as his fingers circled her nipples, her flesh firming, responding to his touch. He growled in appreciation. So responsive and yet she'd just come. And in turn, so was he. He felt the change in direction in his blood. Felt the heat return. 'Did you see how they were dressed?'

She blushed the delightful way she did. 'Did the women really go bare-breasted? I wasn't sure.'

He arched over her and flicked her nipple with his tongue. 'They did. The Minoans celebrated life and nature and all things beautiful. And these…' he dipped his head to her other breast '…are beautiful. You would have been a goddess in those times,' he said, feeling himself swell once again, feeling the need to take her once more. 'A fair-headed goddess from across the seas.'

This time the rhythm was slower, more languid and controlled and he watched the storm once more build inside her, her arms woven around his neck, her legs anchored at his back. He watched her face as she neared the summit, he watched her azure eyes widen as the waves of pleasure lifted her higher and ever higher and then he watched her features freeze into that mask of ecstasy as her muscles clamped down around him and took him with her.

It seemed like for ever until he could breathe normally again. Slowly, gently, he withdrew and found reason to curse himself all over again.

*Vlaka!* Like some hot-under-the-collar schoolboy he'd forgotten to use protection. What the hell had he been thinking? But he hadn't been thinking, not beyond being inside her and sharing that glorious enthusiasm that had streamed out of her like sunshine.

'Cleo, are you safe?'

The words made no sense in the context of their love-making. She was safe. She felt safe being with Andreas. Until a cold wave of realisation washed over her. They hadn't used protection!

'Oh. I…' When was her last period? Was it three weeks, or only two? 'I don't know. I can work it out, though.'

'So work it out,' he said gruffly as he tore off what was left of his clothes and headed for the shower.

She curled up behind him on the bed. 'You make out like it's my fault.'

He took a deep breath. In a way it was. He'd never lost control like that before. Never been so obsessed with being inside a woman that he'd forgotten something as basic—as necessary—as protection. Who else's fault was it?

*His.*

He looked over his shoulder to where she now sat, huddled on the bed, her robe drawn back tightly around her like a shield. 'You're right.' He forced the words through his teeth. 'I'm sorry. But sorry isn't much good if you become pregnant.'

*Pregnant?* Oh, God. She'd been so blown away by Andreas' love-making that she hadn't stopped to think of the consequences. Pregnant. No wonder he was so angry. It couldn't happen, could it? Surely life wouldn't be that unfair when she was going home in just a few weeks.

Although knowing her luck…

She swallowed. She'd be going home pregnant and unmarried. A loser. Again.

Or would she?

The bright side, she thought, knowing she was probably being irresponsible to even think this way. The bright side was she'd be going home with Andreas' baby. Would it matter that she was pregnant if she had something of Andreas to keep for ever? Was it wrong to think that way? At least the money she was going home with would ensure that their baby would want for nothing.

And the chances were, nothing would happen, and she would go home alone.

She jacked up her chin. 'We'll deal with that *if* it happens. But I don't have stars in my eyes, Andreas. I know I have a use-by date. I'm not looking for more.'

He nodded and told her she was welcome to join him before stepping into the bathroom. He didn't expect she would now, he thought as he turned on the powerful jet of spray and adjusted the temperature, the familiar smell of salt from the mineral-rich water thick in the steamy atmosphere. Which was a shame. He would enjoy her body slick with soap and water.

Another time.

He could see he'd hurt her and that bothered him. Not that he'd hurt her, but that he even cared. Especially when her words should have given him comfort. She didn't want any more from him. That was good, wasn't it?

He lifted his face up into the stream of water and soaped his body. He'd make it up to her. Petra could hold the fort for a few days. He'd show Cleo his Santorini, the world that he loved, seeing as she was interested in more than just the usual souvenir shops.

After all, if they only had a month, they might as well enjoy it.

The next few days passed in a blur for Cleo. Andreas surprised her by wanting to tour the island with her and he was a consummate tour guide. He took her to the town of Oia at the very tip of the island and let her explore the narrow laneways and discover the blue-domed churches and the elegant remnants of Venetian occupation and the windmills that clung to the sides of the cliff.

And then he delighted her by taking her to the mountain of Mesa Vouno where hand in hand they climbed the path to the ruins of Ancient Thera, the remnants of an ancient Greek and later Roman city. With the wind whipping in her hair she discovered more of that fascination for the ancient that she'd found while touring the museum. People had lived here, thousands of years ago. They had left their mark on the earth in the walls and the columns still standing and in the engravings on the rocks, of eagles and dolphins and strong-featured men.

Andreas could be one of them, she thought, chiselled and strong-jawed and handsome beyond belief. He caught her watching him, the wind in his hair so that it looked alive. 'What are you thinking?'

And she smiled and celebrated a brand-new discovery: that a girl with no education and no career wasn't necessarily doomed to clean rooms all her life, that she'd found something she could be passionate about. 'I'm going to go home,' she announced, on the top of a mountain overlooking the entire island, 'and study. I'm going to find a course where I can learn about the people who lived here and left these marks on the rocks. I want to know more.' And she spun around laughing.

And he laughed too, because her mood was infectious, even though he suspected she'd go home and the memories would fade and she'd forget all about a bunch of old rocks on the top of a mountain somewhere halfway across the world.

They stopped for lunch at a *kafenio* in a nearby village on the way back and enjoyed simple fare of the freshest vegetables and seafood cooked superbly and that tasted better than anything she'd ever eaten before, and they walked it off again along a black sandy beach.

And wherever they went, it was to a backdrop of azure seas and sky, black volcanic rock and whitewashed buildings that all melded with incredible beauty.

'You are so lucky,' she sighed later that night as together they watched another fiery sun sink into the ocean, the sky a painter's dream of scorching red and gold. They hadn't missed a sunset since that aborted ball and she knew that she would never get sick of the sight.

She turned to see if he'd heard and caught him watching her, the intensity of his eyes sending vibrations down her spine that converged on her heart and made it lurch. 'The sunset. You're not watching.'

And he smiled. 'I'm watching it reflected in your expression. I never knew how beautiful our sunset was until this moment.' He curved a hand around her neck, drawing her closer into a kiss. 'How long do we have left?' he murmured, his lips in her hair, his breath tickling her ear.

She trembled against him. She knew exactly what he was asking. She'd been counting off the days and nights since she'd arrived, at first with enthusiasm, and lately with a sense of dread. 'Um, two weeks and four days.'

And he pulled her closer until their bodies were aligned, length to length. 'Then let's not waste a minute of it.'

\* \* \*

Half an hour in the mornings was all he needed these days to clear his desk of anything needing his attention. He was sick of looking at files that meant nothing, sick of worrying about unreturned calls and he'd discovered the joy of delegation and the freedom it brought. Half an hour was enough to clear his desk and his day for Cleo. So it was lucky she chose then to call.

'Sofia.' He grimaced, remembering he was supposed to call his mother back days ago. 'I was just about to call you.'

'We need to talk,' she said. 'It's been too long.'

It had been. And he had things he needed to tell her, things he'd meant to tell her when he'd returned from London. 'Aren't we talking now?'

'Come to Athens,' she said. 'I need to see my son. I have news I can't tell you over the phone.'

Ice slid down his spine. 'What's wrong?'

There was a moment's hesitation and he sensed her wavering, almost able to see his mother holding onto the edge of the table for support. 'Come to Athens.'

There would no doubt be a breeze later, she'd learned enough about the weather since she'd been here to know that it would whip up over the clifftops around midday, but for now the waters of the caldera showed barely a ripple under the perfect spring sun, and the waters of the infinity pool stretching out before Cleo showed even less. In the distance she could hear the odd group of tourists passing by, exclaiming over the perfect photo opportunity—there seemed to be one around every corner on Santorini—but the pool deck was private and tucked away from the main tourist trails and their voices and snatched words drifted away and all was quiet again. She was breathless from the slow laps she'd done but that was good. She had a pile of books on Santorini, its history and archaeological treasures to read, and that was good too. She needed to keep busy, given Andreas wouldn't be back until at least tomorrow.

She clamped down on the stab of disappointment that accompanied that thought. Soon enough she wouldn't see him at all. Surely she could live with his absence for a couple of days?

But after the bliss of their last few days and nights together, the news that Andreas had taken the helicopter to Athens and would be away overnight had been a major disappointment. She liked being with him. She liked his company and his conversation and she'd surprised herself by loving being in his bed. Then she'd received the message he would be another night at least.

Two days to fill. Two nights alone in his bed, with the smell of him on his pillow and the empty space alongside her where he should be.

How quickly she'd become accustomed to his touch. And how quickly she'd abandoned the concept of pretending to be his mistress.

Every night they made love. As far as she was concerned, she didn't have to pretend. To all intents and purposes, she was his mistress, in every sense of the word.

She put down the book she couldn't concentrate on and dived back into the pool. She needed to do more laps. The more tired she was, the less she would notice the empty space beside her in bed and the better she would sleep. And the better she slept, the less she would miss his magic touch.

Strange, how she could think his touch so magic after just a few nights. But for the first time in her life, she had felt like a woman. Andreas had done that, unleashing sensations within her that she'd never imagined were there, sensations that yearned to be released again.

Lap after lap she drove herself until, weak limbed and

gasping, she staggered from the pool and collapsed into a lounger. She closed her eyes and tried to blank her mind, but it was still pictures of Andreas she saw, pictures of what they might do together on his return. She'd already decided it was time to be more proactive, to take matters into her own hands.

She could hardly wait to surprise him.

'*Kalimera*. I hope I'm not disturbing you.'

Cleo came to with a start. With Andreas away she'd assumed Petra would be busy in charge of the office. She hadn't expected her to turn up poolside wearing the black-scrap-of-nothing bikini with tie-around skirt that, given its brevity, did nothing to protect her modesty and everything to accentuate her endless legs.

'*Kalimera*,' Cleo replied with almost the extent of her Greek, instantly on edge. Her own bikini was a Moontide original that Mme Bernadette had insisted she take, swirls of blue and green that accentuated her eyes and complemented her skin now that it was starting to take on the tan she'd lost while in England. She knew she looked good in it, but compared to the tall, slender Petra she felt awkward and lumpy. And definitely too exposed. 'I didn't expect to see you,' she said, reaching for a towel to cover her on the pretext of drying her knotted hair. Anything to protect her from the other woman's laser-sharp scrutiny. 'I thought you'd be flat out in the office with Andreas away.'

Petra unhitched the tiny skirt and let it flutter to the lounger alongside, an action clearly designed to draw attention to her legs. It worked. Cleo instantly felt short and squat. 'It is very busy, of course, but I was feeling a little queasy this morning and thought a swim would refresh me before the afternoon's appointments.' She put an impeccably manicured hand to her waist.

Cleo followed the movement and wished she hadn't. Did the woman not have a bulge anywhere? 'You're not well?'

The woman gave a shrug and checked her hair. 'We had a reception with lunch yesterday. Most likely just something that disagreed with me.' She walked lithely to the water's edge, descending the stairs into the pool's liquid depths as regally as a Miss Universe contestant, where she breast-stroked two lengths of the pool without a splash, emerging from the water with her hair as sleek and perfect as when she'd gone in.

'Ah, that's wonderfully refreshing,' she said as she lowered herself to the lounger. 'And finding you here is even better. We haven't had much of a chance to get to know one another, have we? Andreas selfishly keeps you all to himself.'

'I guess not.'

'I love your swimsuit,' Petra said, patting herself dry with a towel. 'Those colours are wonderful on you.'

Cleo blinked. The words sounded sincere enough, and she wondered if she'd misjudged the woman. All she'd had to go by was one car trip from the airport and she'd been tired. Maybe she'd imagined the snippiness. 'Thank you. Yours looks gorgeous too.'

Petra smiled and nodded her thanks. 'You're Australian, aren't you?'

Cleo relaxed a little. At least here was a safe topic. 'That's right. From a little outback town called Kangaroo Crossing. It's dry and dusty and nothing at all like here.'

'I've always wanted to go to Australia. Tell me about it.'

Cleo obliged. It was good to talk of home, of a place that was so much a different world from this one that it could have been on another planet, of a place of endless drought and strug-gling families and mobs of kangaroos jumping across paddocks of red dust. And the more she spoke of home, and the more the other woman smiled and laughed, the more she relaxed. It was good to talk to another woman. She'd missed that in London.

'Now I simply must go and visit your homeland. But Andreas said you met in London. What were you doing so far from home?'

Cleo shook her head. 'You really don't want to know. You'd think me a total fool if I told you.'

'Oh, no, never.' She reached one long-nailed hand over to Cleo's and patted it. 'It's all right. You can tell me. I'll understand, I promise.'

And then, because it had been so long since Cleo had been able to pour her heart out to anyone, it all came out in a rush, how she'd found Kurt through an Internet chat room and how he'd seduced her with his promises of romance and travel and how she'd fallen for it, hook, line and sinker. She didn't tell her about his making love to her, of relieving her of her virginity and then casting her aside. She'd had no choice but to tell Andreas, but that part was nobody else's business.

'So you were stuck in London? You poor thing. But surely you had a return ticket?'

She shook her head. 'I'd only enough money for one way. I never thought I'd need to head home so soon. Except my nanna had lent me the return fare just before I boarded the bus to the city, just in case the worst happened. Only I didn't have a bank account so Kurt said he'd look after it for me…'

'And he took your money? What kind of man was he?' She patted her arm again. 'You are much better off without him and here in Santorini.'

'I know.' She took a deep breath. It felt surprisingly good to get that all off her chest. All the emotions and guilt and self-flagellation that had plagued her every day since he'd dumped her felt as if they were sloughing away, as if she'd confessed her sins and all would be right with the world.

'And how fortunate for you to meet Andreas after all that had happened to you. You must feel very lucky.'

'I do,' Cleo agreed, sure Petra hadn't meant that to sound as it had.

'So how are you enjoying Santorini, then?' she asked, changing tack. 'This is your first time here?'

Cleo relaxed again, certain she'd been reading too much into the other woman's tone. Santorini was another topic she could easily and honestly enthuse about. 'It's so beautiful! You're so lucky living here, being surrounded by all this—' her arm swept around in an arc '—every day. The sights and atmosphere, even the history is amazing.'

'I'm so glad you're enjoying it. We're very proud of our island home. We want visitors to be happy here.'

'I'm very happy. The sunsets are amazing.'

'Honeymooners come here just to experience Santorini's sunset. It's supposed to be very romantic. What do you think?'

Cleo suddenly felt too tied in knots to answer. It was romantic, or it would be, if you were here with the right person. But Andreas wasn't the right person, was he? They'd just been forced together by circumstances and soon she would leave. Although the way he'd looked at her the other night on the terrace… 'I guess it could be, if you were here with the right person.'

'Oh, I'm so sorry. I'm making you uncomfortable.'

'It's okay. It's not like I'm here for the romance exactly.'

The other woman's eyebrows arched approvingly. 'No? Well, I guess in your place that's the best way to think about it. Andreas has quite a reputation for moving on. And now I must get back to work. Thank you so much for talking with me. I feel like we're going to be good friends while you're here.'

'Are you feeling any better?' she asked as Petra retied the tiny skirt around her hips.

'Oh, I'm feeling *much* better, thank you.'

Cleo watched her slip on her gold sandals and wander away, wondering why it should be that she was suddenly feeling so much worse.

'It's just a lump, Andreas. There's no need to go on about it.' Sofia Xenides stiffened her spine and sat her slim body higher on the chaise longue, her ankles crossed demurely beneath her, her coffee balanced on her knees. Andreas knew the posture, recognised it as his mother closing the subject down again.

To hell with that.

'You should have told me.'

'You were busy. In London apparently. And then with who knows what?'

He bristled. 'You could have called me on my cell phone.'

'And told you what? That I had a lump? And what could you have done besides worry?'

'I would have made you see a doctor.'

'Which is exactly what I did do. And tomorrow I will get the results of the biopsy and we will know. There was no point worrying you unnecessarily before, but I am glad you will be with me tomorrow. And now we have more important things to discuss. When were you planning on telling me what exactly you were doing in London?'

Andreas sighed. 'You know, then?'

'Petra tells me you found Darius. Is that true?'

'I found him. He'd gambled the last of the money away, all he had left was a seedy hotel filled with mould and rising damp. He was ripe for a low-interest loan in order to fund his gambling habit.'

'So you found him, and you exacted the revenge you have been looking for all these years. I imagine you ruined him in the process.'

'It is no more than he did to us!'

'Andreas,' she sighed, 'it is so long ago. Perhaps now you can put the past behind you?'

'How can you say that? I will never put the past behind me. Don't you remember what he did to us, what it was like back then? He destroyed Father and he walked away and left us with nothing. *Nothing!*'

She shut her eyes, as if the mention of her late husband was still painful, but a breath later she was still firm. 'And it has driven you all these years, my son. Now that you have achieved the goal you have aimed for all your life, what are you going to do with the rest of your life?'

Andreas stared blankly out of the window and shrugged, the question unnerving him. Hadn't he been feeling an unfamiliar lack of motivation lately, avoiding the office because suddenly it was all too uninspiring? Below the terrace lay the rolling expanse of Athens city, apartment blocks jostling with antiquities in the sprawling city. No, he was just temporarily distracted with Cleo, that was all. Soon she would be gone and he would refocus on his work again. 'I will go on with my business,' he said, resolutely. 'Already the Xenides name is synonymous with the most prestigious accommodation on offer across all of Europe. I will make it even bigger, even better.'

She gave another sigh, except this one sounded less indulgent, more impatient. 'Maybe there is another goal you might pursue now.'

'What do you mean?'

'Perhaps it is time you thought about family.'

'I have never neglected you!' Even though he felt a stab of guilt that he'd never returned her call as he'd intended.

'Did I say you had? But the time for looking backwards is past. It is time to look to the future, and to a family of your own.'

He sighed. If this was about getting married again... And then something he'd never seen coming hit him like a brick. 'You want grandchildren.'

'I am a Greek mother.' She shrugged. 'Of course, I want grandchildren. Maybe now you have satisfied this lifelong quest for vengeance, you might find the time to provide me with some, while I can still appreciate them.'

'Mother—'

She held up one hand to silence him. 'I am not being melo-dramatic. It is not just that I have had this scare and I must face the prospect of the results not going the way I would prefer, but you are not getting any younger, Andreas, and neither am I. I do not want to be too old or too sick to appreciate my grand-children when they eventually come.'

'Stop talking this way! I'm not about to let you die.'

'I have no intention of dying! At least not before you bestow upon me the grandchildren I crave. I am not blind. You have quite a reputation with the women, I believe. After all this experience, do you not know what kind of woman would suit you for a wife?'

It was ridiculous to feel like blushing at something his mother said, and he wouldn't, but still her veiled reference to his many lovers made him so uncomfortable he couldn't bring himself to answer. Besides, could he in all honesty answer? The women he had through his bed had one resounding attribute, but it hardly made them wife material.

'Petra said you have a woman staying with you.'

He almost growled. Petra had always been like family,

they'd practically grown up together, but there were times he resented the closeness and the fact Petra knew his mother so well. This was one of those times.

'It's none of Petra's business. Or yours, for that matter.'

'Tsh, tsh. Who else can ask if I can't? Petra said she's an Australian woman. Quite pretty, in her own way.'

She was more than pretty, he wanted to argue, until another thought blew all thoughts of argument out of the water.

*And she could be pregnant.*

They'd had unprotected sex. Twice. Right now she could be carrying his seed.

A baby. His mother could have the grandchild she yearned for. And as for him? *He would have Cleo.*

Strange, how that thought didn't send his blood into a tailspin.

But marriage? Was that what he wanted? He took a deep breath. But his mother would expect it, and, besides, there was no way he could not marry the mother of his child. Especially not now.

Granted, they'd shared but a few short days, less than two weeks, but those days had been good. The nights even better. Surely there could be worse outcomes?

'Petra said—'

He snapped away from possibilities and turned back to the present. 'Petra talks too much!'

'Andreas, she only wants the best for you, just as I do. In fact, I once wondered if—'

It was like a bad soap opera. Or a train wreck where you couldn't look away. He had to keep going till the bitter end. 'Go on.'

'Well, you and Petra have lived together for a long time now.'

'We share a building, not a bed!' And the mood his mother was in, he wasn't about to confess that they had. *Once.*

'And,' she continued, without missing a beat, 'you have so much in common.'

'She works for me. Of course, we have a lot in common.'

'Anyway,' Sofia said with a resigned shrug of her shoulders before she turned her attention to pick at an invisible speck of nothingness alongside her on the sofa, 'sometimes we don't realise what's right there in front of us, right under our noses. Not until it's gone.'

His teeth ground together. 'I'm not marrying Petra.'

She smiled up at him, blinking innocently as if his outburst had come from nowhere. 'Whoever said you would? I just wondered, that's all. And there's nothing wrong with a mother wondering, is there, Andreas? Much better to consider the options than to let the grass grow beneath your feet.'

The grass was feeling comfortable enough where he was standing right now. Or it had been, until his mother had laced its green depths with barbs that tore at the soles of his feet and pricked at his conscience.

'About this appointment tomorrow to see your doctor…'

'I get the point, Andreas. But enough about doctors too. Would you like some more coffee?'

# CHAPTER ELEVEN

CLEO was in the pool resting her elbows on the edge, one of her glossy history books perched in front of her. Hungrily Andreas' eyes devoured her, from the streaked hair bundled up in a clip behind her head, her bare shoulders and back, and her legs making lazy movements in the water. She looked browner than he remembered, her skin more golden. Clearly the weather here suited her better than that dingy hotel in London where her skin was never so much as kissed by the sun.

And an idea, vague and fuzzy inside him, found dimension and merit. She could be pregnant with his child, even now. And even though the news for his mother had been good, the tests had come back negative, that still didn't change the fact that his mother yearned for grandchildren.

Sofia was right. She wasn't getting any younger, although he'd never thought of his mother as a number with a finite span. And he'd never thought of his own age and the possibilities of family. Because he'd thought of nothing beyond the one thing that had driven his life for more than a decade.

*Retribution.*

And now he'd achieved it all, he'd built himself up from nothing until he could exact the revenge he'd been planning for twelve long years, and yet somehow he didn't get the same buzz from the achievement any more. He didn't even care any more if Constantine turned his proposal down flat, and that had never happened before. But the prospect that the grandchild his mother hungered for could already be in the making caused a new and unfamiliar buzz.

Fate? He shook his head. You made your own opportunities in this life, he knew. He'd lived by that mantra for years. He believed in it. It had been what had kept him focused, until he'd found Darius and pulled what was left of him down.

He'd made this opportunity. And like any other, he'd make the most of it.

He padded noiselessly to the side of the pool. He doubted she would hear him anyway, even if he had made a noise. The books she'd bought on Santorini and its ancient civilisations seemed to have her completely in their thrall. Maybe it wasn't just talk, maybe she really was interested in more than a superficial picture of the island. Or maybe she was just killing time until his return.

Option B, he much preferred.

She turned a page, the angle of her head shifting, still totally oblivious to his presence.

*She wouldn't be for long.*

He dived into the water and crossed the pool, taking her by the waist as he erupted like a sea god from the water.

'Hey!' She turned, her fright turning to delight when she saw who her assailant was. 'Oh, you're back.'

Her legs were cool where they tangled with his, her shoulders deliciously warm from the sun and her lips so slick with gloss he wanted to find out if they were as slippery as they looked. 'Did you miss me?' he asked, his hands caressing curves they had sorely missed.

'Not really,' she lied, unable to keep the smile from her face or the tingling from her skin. 'I was kind of busy here, catching up on my reading. You know how it is.'

'Liar!' he said. 'Believe me, I know how it is—' before pulling her into a deep kiss that had them both spinning together into the depths. They came up gasping but Andreas wasn't finished with her yet. Already he'd untied her bikini top, one hand at her breasts while the other pushed at her bikini bottoms.

'Andreas…'

'Do you realise how long I've dreamed about having you in water?'

'Andreas…' She clung to him. She had no option but to cling as he brought her flesh alive and made her blood sing. His hands pushed inside her bikini, rounded her buttocks and delved deeper.

'I've missed you,' he growled, burying his face at her throat, his words so heavy with want it made her head spin. 'And I want you, so badly.'

'I… I got my period.'

He lifted his head slowly and gazed at her, his vision blurred by a rush of blood. Bad blood. 'I see.'

'But that's good news, isn't it? I thought you'd be pleased. Now there are no complications. That's what you wanted.'

He let her go and turned towards the edge of the pool, powering himself up with his hands to step from the pool like an athlete. He pulled a towel from a nearby stack and buried his face in it. 'Yes, it's good news. Of course.' Only it didn't feel like good news. It felt as though all the shifts he'd made, all the changes he'd made in his thinking were for nothing, and he was left stranded. He didn't like the feeling.

He could have done with the odd complication. It would have suited his purposes well.

*So much for making opportunity happen.*

Petra brought them both coffee as he checked his files the next day. Or she brought him one. Her nose twitched as she deposited the cup on his desk. 'You're not having one?' he queried, surprised she wasn't joining in with this long-time ritual.

Her nose twitched again. 'I seem to be off coffee. Don't know what it is. Probably just that time of the month.'

Andreas blanked out. He was over that time of the month, big time, and he certainly didn't want to hear about Petra's. He was irritable, he was short-tempered, and the sooner he got Cleo back where he wanted her, the better for all concerned. And maybe he'd even forget to use protection all over again. Only she'd probably be gone before she was fertile…

Damn.

Mind you, he could always change the contract terms… His mood brightened considerably. That was definitely one option worth pursuing.

'Poor Cleo,' Petra said, sifting through mail as she perched herself on the edge of his desk in her usual way, 'what a dreadful thing to happen, being cheated of her money like that.' She slapped a couple of papers down in front of him. 'Though I guess she brought it on herself to a large extent.'

His ears twitched at the mention of Cleo's name. He'd almost forgotten Petra was there again, already working out how best to tackle the subject of an extension to their terms. 'Brought what on herself?'

She shrugged. 'She must have told you. She went to London to meet this guy she'd hooked up with on the Internet and he ripped off the money for her return fare and left her with nothing. Awful. Mind you, you'd have to be pretty stupid to fall for something like that.'

Andreas sat back in his chair, letting the silence fall between them like an anvil. He knew for a moment that his scowl would say everything he needed to while he untangled the threads of his anger in his mind.

'Are you saying Cleo's stupid?'

'No! I mean… Well—' she shrugged and screwed up her nose, like she was making some kind of concession '—maybe just a bit naïve.'

'Or are you saying that my father was stupid?'

'Andreas! It's hardly the same thing.'

'Isn't it? My father trusted someone and lost everything to him. Cleo trusted someone and suffered the same fate. Tell me how it's different.'

He stood up and peeled his jacket from the back of his chair, shoving first one arm and then the other into it. 'You deal with the mail, Petra. I've got more important things to do.'

'Andreas, I didn't mean anything, honest.'

No? He was sick of the niggling, sick of Petra's snippy put-downs of Cleo with just a look or a snide remark. He'd been wrong to think she would take a not-so-subtle hint. Maybe it was time for a more direct approach. 'It's not going to happen, Petra, so don't think it is.'

She looked innocent enough, but he knew there was a computer inside that was as sophisticated as it was devious. 'You and me. That night was a mistake. It won't happen again.'

He found Cleo sitting out on the terrace overlooking the caldera and reading another of her books. In spite of the still-smouldering anger that simmered inside him, he smiled. In a lemon-coloured sundress that made the most of her newly acquired tan, she looked both innocent and intent at the same time.

She looked around, almost as if she'd been able to feel his eyes on her, and she smiled that heart-warming smile as her azure eyes lit up with enthusiasm. 'Back already? You'll never guess what I just read.'

Her enthusiasm was infectious. So infectious he didn't want her to leave in however many days they had left. It was to his advantage she was in a good mood. It would be easier to convince her to stay. 'Tell me,' he said, pulling up a chair alongside.

'Well, when the volcano erupted going back three thousand years or so ago, it wiped out not just the cities on the island itself, but some think it brought down the entire prehistoric Minoan civilisation with it.'

'It's possible,' he acknowledged with a nod. 'Nobody knows for certain, but it could explain why the Minoans were such prosperous sea traders one minute and wiped from the face of the earth the next.'

Her azure eyes sparkled like the waters of the caldera itself. 'But this is the really exciting bit. Some say that the eruption and the fallout are the origins of the legend of Atlantis. A world that sank beneath the sea—and this is where it all happened! Do you believe it? Do you think Santorini is actually what's left of Atlantis?'

His cell phone interrupted them and he pulled it out, took one look at the caller ID and switched it off. Petra could wait.

'I think it's highly possible,' he conceded, repocketing his phone.

She sighed, hugging the book to her chest, and looked over to where the volcano, now silent, spread dark and low in the midst of the waters. 'I believe it. I did a Google search and found a Classics course in Sydney.'

'Cleo…'

'I'm going to enrol in it as soon as I get home. I'll be able to afford to live there now, thanks to you.'

'About going home.'

She turned her head, the spark gone from her eyes. 'Do you want me to leave earlier? I… I don't mind, if that's what you want.'

And he almost laughed at the idea. He shook his head. 'No. I don't want you to go earlier.'

'Then, what is it?'

He took a second to frame his thoughts. 'What's waiting for you at home? I mean, you've never talked about your family. Are they close?'

She gave a curious smile, her eyes perplexed. 'Well, not really. My mum's great, but the twins, my two half-brothers, keep her pretty busy and she's got a baby coming apparently.' She screwed up her nose. 'And then there's my step-dad, of course.'

'What's he like?'

She shrugged. 'He's okay, a bit rough around the edges maybe, but a lot of blokes are like that out there, but Mum loves him and he's good to her.'

'And to you?'

*Excess baggage.* The words were indelibly inscribed on her psyche. She sucked in a breath. 'We moved out there when Mum got the job as his housekeeper. I think he always saw me as a bit of an add-on, always hoping I'd make something of myself and move out. He'll be relieved I'll finally be off his hands.'

'Is that why you took off for the UK?'

She put the book she'd been holding up on the table and rubbed her arms. 'What's going on?'

'What do you mean?'

'Why all the questions? You've never bothered about all this personal stuff before.'

'Maybe we had something else to keep us busy then.' And even under her tan she managed to blush the way she did that made him warm all over. 'And maybe I'm just interested.'

She looked up at him warily through lowered lashes, as if she still didn't quite believe him. 'Okay. I guess wanting to prove myself was part of the reason I left. The job opportunities at home were non-existent and I kind of fell into cleaning, like

Mum had.' Her hands knotted in her lap, her grip so tight it sent the ends of her fingers alternately red then white. 'I thought meeting Kurt was the opportunity of a lifetime and the chance to escape. I was so desperate to make a success of myself, I made every mistake in the book. I was such a fool.' She fell silent on a sigh, moisture sheening her eyes.

He reached over and untangled the damp knot of her hands, taking one of them between his own, lifting it, and pressing his lips to its back. 'It's no crime to trust someone.'

She blinked up at him, trying to clear her vision. Why did he have to be so kind? It had been easier when she'd thought him completely ruthless, easier when she remembered the way he'd taken over the hotel, issuing orders like a general in battle.

But lately he'd been beyond kind. The way he'd abandoned his work to escort her around the island, the way he'd watched sunset after sunset with her because she didn't want to miss a single one because she wanted to store them all up and remember when she went home, and the way he'd woken her softly just this morning with a kiss and brought her to climax with his clever fingers and his hot mouth.

And now he was listening to her as if what she said mattered. As if he cared for her as much as she was beginning to care for him.

She gulped down a breath.

*Oh, no, don't go there! Don't imagine it for a minute.* Because once before she'd thought someone cared for her. Once before she'd fallen for him because of it. Look where that had got her.

No, she'd made a deal. Under the terms of their contract, she would leave here in little more than two weeks and they'd never see each other again.

She turned her eyes away from the thumb now stroking her hand, his long, tapered fingers and neat nails, up, and up to his face, knowing he was waiting for some kind of response, something to show that she'd put what had happened in the past behind her. But it wasn't what had happened in the past that was bothering her. It was what lay ahead that scared her most of all.

Two weeks of sharing Andreas' bed and pretending to be his mistress, *being his mistress*.

Two weeks of guarding her fragile heart.

And two weeks to work on not falling in love with Andreas Xenides.

She dragged in oxygen to steel her resolve. She'd learned from her mistake with Kurt. It wouldn't happen to her again. She wouldn't let it. She couldn't afford to let it.

'Thank you,' she managed at last, trying to keep things as impersonal as possible. 'I appreciate it.'

'How much?'

It had taken her ages to form a response. She wasn't ready for his. 'Pardon?'

'How much do you appreciate it?'

She shook her head, still uncertain. 'What do you mean?'

'Would you consider an extension to our contract?'

'No.' This time it was her rapid-fire response that took him by surprise. He jerked back, as if she'd fired a shot from a gun. 'I mean, I'm not sure that's possible, with this course, and everything I've got planned.' She plucked at a crease in her dress, her mind in turmoil. Leaving after another two weeks would likely be hell. How would she calmly walk away if she stayed longer?

'I'll double what I'm paying you. Two million Australian dollars.'

'It's not about the money!' And it wasn't. Just lately the thought of being paid for what she was experiencing here on Santorini sat uneasily on her. If he'd been a bully and as ruthless as he'd first seemed, she might have felt as if she deserved it for putting up with him, but he wasn't like that. He was kind and generous and he seemed as if he cared.

'But you like it here. You like being with me.'

She pushed herself out of her chair, striding to the balustrade, her hands grasping at its reassuring solidity. The season was warming up. Three cruise ships lay at anchor today, lighters zipping through the spring mist between them and the port with their cargo of today's photo-hungry tourists.

*It's no crime to trust someone.*

His words came back to her. Andreas was right. It was no crime to trust someone. Once. But it was a fool who let themselves be burned a second time.

How could she tell him she was scared? He was a businessman. He dealt in contracts and clauses and certainties. Those he understood. Those he lived by. And that would have to be her angle.

She sensed when he joined her at the terrace edge, on the very lip of the ancient crater where the fresh salty wind met the sky. Her skin prickled, her blood fizzed and her flesh became alive with want.

'You *do* enjoy my company, don't you?'

There was no point answering his question. The truth would get her nowhere. 'We have two weeks left, Andreas. Maybe we should just make the most of them.'

A noise alerted him, something other than the cry of seabirds or the distant buzz of conversation and exclamation as tourists wended their way through the narrow paths and came upon another magnificent photo opportunity. He swung his head around and saw her standing there, in the doorway leading to the terrace. *Gamoto*. How much had she heard?

'Petra, what can I do for you?'

'*Kalimera*, Cleo,' she started. 'I'm sorry to interrupt, but, Andreas, your phone was switched off and I had to talk to you.'

'Can't it wait?' He didn't care if he sounded rude. The last thing he needed was Petra spying on them. Already she'd somehow wormed more information out of Cleo than he had wanted her to, and if she'd been here while he'd been talking about the contract…

'I am sorry. But you must excuse me. I'm not feeling very well, Andreas. I wanted to let you know I really think I'm not much good in the office today. I'm hoping it's all right with you to go to my apartment and lie down.'

Damned time of the month again, he supposed, though why all of a sudden she had to fall victim to the curse, he didn't know.

'Are you still feeling unwell?' Cleo asked, moving away from him to take Petra by the arm. 'Can I get you anything?'

'I really don't want to interrupt you,' Petra protested, and then with a smile, 'but that would be so sweet. I am feeling a little dizzy.'

And Andreas watched in bemusement and not a little frustration as the woman he had brought here to deflect the attentions of another was now giving that woman all of hers.

'Come straight back,' he called out to her. 'I want to take you shopping.' And she waved her hand to him, acknowledging she'd heard, even as she shepherded Petra into the building. It wasn't really a lie, he thought as he paced the length of the terrace waiting for her, watching the last of the morning mist burn off the deep blue waters of the flooded crater. She wasn't big on shopping, preferring to explore the churches and villages than the flash boutiques and jewellery stores, but there was something he wanted to buy her, something special he knew would remind her of the intense blue of the sun and sea of Santorini and would at the same time be the perfect complement to her eyes.

And something that might even help persuade her to stay.

Why she was so vehement about leaving, he didn't understand. She loved it here, she loved all of it, even coming to terms with the fact the islands were part of a volcanic system that had been changing over thousands of years and would keep on changing.

But he was determined to make her change her mind and he was confident he could do it. Everyone had their price. A million dollars had got her here.

He didn't care how much it took to keep her.

An hour later, Andreas excused himself to make a phone call and Cleo happily agreed to wait, a rack of blue-beaded key rings catching her attention. It was probably time she thought about buying a few souvenirs to take home. The last two weeks had gone in a flash. The next couple of weeks would probably fly past even quicker.

She dodged out of the way of a group of tourists taking up the width of the street. The streets of Fira were busy today, the day tourists growing in number by the minute, making the narrow lanes and streets even more crowded. If she'd known, she might have stayed at home.

*Home.*

Now there was a notion. Since when had the mansion she was temporarily occupying ever been her home?

A silver donkey key ring caught her eye, strung on blue cotton with blue beads that looked like eyes. She selected two. Her half-brothers would both love one. She found another, with spinning letter beads that spelt out SANTORINI with more of the eye beads and a beautiful blue stone at the base. Her mother, she decided instantly, slipping it from the rack.

Now she just needed something for her step father. She looked over the racks and decided that with the blue beads there was nothing 'blokey' enough, so her gaze widened, her eyes scanning the contents of the store for that perfect easy-to-pack memento.

And that was when she saw him.

# CHAPTER TWELVE

HE WAS checking out the postcards, his face and chest puffier than Cleo remembered, or maybe that was just because they were both pink from the sun, and his arm looped around the shoulders of a girl who looked as stringy as her hair.

*He was here.*

The key rings slipped from her fingers, clattering to the floor.

'I'm sorry to leave you so long.' She registered Andreas' voice, clung onto the sound like a lifeline even as he bent down to pick up the items she'd dropped. 'Cleo, what's wrong? You look ill.'

'That's him,' she croaked through a throat clamped as tight as every muscle and organ in her body. 'That's Kurt.'

Kurt chose that moment to widen his own search, scanning the shop for opportunities. He looked around, the skin between his eyes creasing into a frown when he saw Andreas scowling at him, a frown that became confused when he looked at the woman alongside the stranger, until the moment he recognised her and his expression became one of abject terror. He tugged, already half outside the shop himself, at the girl next to him who was busy trying on sunglasses. Kurt didn't care, the need to escape clearly paramount, as he dragged his protesting girlfriend out with him, the unpurchased sunglasses still covering her eyes.

'Stay here,' Andreas said, barking out orders to the proprietor in Greek in the same breath before he took off after Kurt. A moment later a woman brought Cleo a chair, insisting she sit down, clucking over her like a mother hen as she pressed a bottle of spring water into her hands. Cleo didn't argue. She was still punch-drunk from seeing Kurt.

So he'd come to Santorini. All that talk of the Greek Islands hadn't been for nothing. But who was the girl? Someone he'd picked up on the Internet who did make the grade? She didn't want to feel hard done by, she had had a complete wardrobe and cosmetic makeover, but surely even before all that she'd been a cut above her?

God, was she that much of a loser that she couldn't even hang onto a man like Kurt?

The woman returned to her side, pressing a small plastic Santorini shopping bag into her hands. The key rings of course, she thought as she felt the beads inside. Andreas must have passed them on to her. She reached for her purse but the woman waved her away. 'No charge,' she said, smiling, bowling Cleo over with more of the warmth and hospitality she'd found everywhere on the island, so that her eyes threatened to spill over with it.

It seemed to take for ever but it was probably only fifteen minutes and Andreas was back. She stood to greet him. 'How are you feeling now?' he asked, collecting her inside his arm.

'Better, thanks. What happened to Kurt?'

'I'll tell you once we're alone.' And she understood why. There was a crowd gathered around the store now, sensing the excitement, wanting to find out what was happening and be part of the action, a crowd that seemed suddenly fascinated in blue-beaded key rings and postcards and bookmarks featuring church domes and cats.

She turned to the beaming proprietor, who was busy exchanging Euros for trinkets, but not too busy to be able to do two things at once. *'Efharisto poli,'* she said, in her slowly improving Greek, repeating it in English in case she'd made a complete hash of the words. 'Thank you, so much,' and the woman beamed and nodded and replied with a torrent of words Cleo was at a loss to understand. 'What did she say?' she asked as soon as they'd re-entered the busy street and he'd steered her towards the mansion.

Andreas didn't look at her, his gaze fixed somewhere ahead, his jaw tight. 'She said we would have beautiful children.'

'Oh. How…quaint.'

Andreas didn't answer. He was too busy wanting to believe it.

'I believe this is yours.' Staff had brought coffee and pastries to a table on the mansion terrace overlooking the caldera that Cleo knew should be listed as one of the wonders of the world, when Andreas handed her the envelope.

She eyed it suspiciously. 'What is it?'

He pressed the envelope into her hands. 'Take a look.'

She opened the flap and peered inside. A stack of notes sat plump and fat inside. She frowned. 'What is this?'

'I had a chat to your former friend.'

'You mean Kurt? You're kidding! You got Nanna's money back. I don't believe it!'

'It seemed he was only too happy to refund you the money he'd borrowed from you in order to escape a charge of shop lifting, plus a bonus for the inconvenience he caused you along the way.'

'Shoplifting?'

'The sunglasses. His girlfriend didn't have time to put them back on the rack. It ended up being a handy levering device.

It seems he didn't want to hang around on Santorini and explain it to the police when his cruise ship was sailing tonight.'

It really didn't matter how or why, it didn't matter that soon Cleo would have more than enough money to repay her many times over, the simple fact was it was her grandmother's money she was getting back, the money she had entrusted to Kurt and haplessly thrown away in the same instant. And getting it back was as if she hadn't lost it at all. 'Thank you,' she said, throwing her arms around his neck. 'I love you so much.'

It wasn't so much hearing her own words. It was feeling his hands still at her sides that alerted her. She slid down his body, appalled at the gaffe she'd just made. 'That's just a figure of speech in Australia. A kind of thank you. Because I really appreciate what you've done.'

'I understand,' he said, but still putting her away from him as he was suddenly craving distance. 'I need to drop by the office, check everything is all right, given Petra is sick. Will you be okay?'

She nodded stoically, thinking that if Andreas had wanted her to stay longer before, he'd no doubt now want her gone tomorrow. 'Of course. I'll see you later.'

And then Andreas was gone and Cleo was left alone, in the sun and breeze and clear blue sky. There were clouds gathering in the distance, she noted absently, thinking that maybe they were in for a storm, while at the same time wishing that one day she would learn not to be so impetuous and admit things she didn't really feel.

Because she hadn't really loved Kurt. She could see that now. She was in love with the idea of being in love and being loved and she'd wanted it to work. So desperately that she'd thought that once they'd had sex, she should tell him that she loved him.

And she didn't really love Andreas either. Not really. He was just kind and she was just grateful and it was crazy to think, that just because he had behaved better to her than Kurt, this gratefulness she felt for him was somehow love.

*Liar.*

An inner voice brought her to task. She didn't want to stay because she knew what would happen. Not that she was at risk of falling in love with him, but because she would be at risk of loving him more.

Because she already loved him.

The wind whipped stronger around her, the cruise ships below straining at their chains. Kurt was down there, she realised, on board one of those ships and soon to sail once more out of her life.

But Kurt was nothing to her now. As Andreas had said, that first night they'd made love—*had sex*—Kurt had given her nothing.

It was Andreas who had given her everything. It was Andreas who had opened her heart.

*It was Andreas she loved.*

Andreas reread the fax with increasing frustration. There was a problem with the paperwork on the takeover of Darius' hotel. The bank needed more signatures. His. Or the papers could not be processed and the transaction could not proceed and Darius would retain ownership by default.

He would have to go to London.

It would take no time. A day. Two at the most. Cleo could come with him.

*'I love you so much.'*

Her words came back to him in stark relief. Sure, she'd tried to explain it away, to get him to accept it was some kind of Australian equivalent for thank you. But he wasn't buying that.

There was no way he could take her. As much as he wanted her and hungered for her, as much as he'd wished she'd been already incubating his child—maybe it was better that she didn't come with him.

Maybe, he thought with a tinge of reluctance, maybe it was even better that he sent her home early. He'd never wanted to get involved with virgins and with good reason.

Cleo had been the closest he'd got to having a virgin and maybe this experience had proven him right. Virgins and almost virgins. They were looking for someone to love, looking for someone special to make this huge physical leap they were taking into something emotional. Even if there was nothing there.

*Except that his mother wanted a grandchild.*

Cleo would be beautiful pregnant, her body rounded and blooming, her belly swelling with his seed, but she didn't want to stay and now he wasn't sure she should.

Maybe his trip away would do them both good, and put things into perspective, a perspective he was admittedly having trouble with himself. And then it would all make sense when he came back.

The idea appealed. Logic appealed.

Although, strangely, leaving her again didn't.

She'd blown it. Whatever sense of camaraderie had been building between them, she'd blown it with a few thoughtless and ill-timed words. He'd told her he was leaving in one breath and he was gone in the next, with barely a backward glance and even less warmth. She hadn't even rated a peck on the cheek.

It hurt, his physical withdrawal from her. It hurt more than the fact he would be gone for a day or two, because eventually he would return to Santorini, but things would be different between them.

At least it would be easier for her now to leave. Now there was no way he would want her to stay.

Restless and unable to settle into her books, she wandered into the town, to a small travel agent she'd seen tucked away alongside a heaving souvlaki shop. There was no reason why she shouldn't make enquiries about flights to Australia, the two weeks she had left would soon pass, but still she felt guilty, as if she were going behind Andreas' back. Which was ridiculous, she told herself as she forced herself to enter the narrow shop-front. It was not as if he didn't know she was going to leave. Not as if he didn't know when. What harm would it do to ask?

Then she saw it on the cover of one of the faded and tatty brochures that lined the walls, a picture of Ayers Rock amid a sea of red dust, and a wave of homesickness crashed over her. That was her world, a dusty, hot land where it never seemed to rain. That was where she belonged, not this island paradise, with its to-die-for-views and romantic sunsets and a man who would never really be hers.

A little over two weeks and she could be home.

Maybe it would be wise to make a booking now.

She found Petra in their suite, rifling through the drawers on Andreas' side of the bed. 'What are you doing here?'

'Ha!' the woman said, clearly not feeling guilty in the least as she turned, holding up a fistful of papers. 'There was nothing in the office but I knew I'd find it here.'

'What is it?' she asked, while fear uncurled in her stomach like a viper, hungry and hissing. 'What have you got?' But Cleo knew what it was. Andreas' copy of the contract. Their contract. And she remembered being out on the terrace and discussing an extension and them turning to see Petra watching them. Listening. She swallowed as the woman's greedy eyes drank in the details. 'That's none of your business.' She marched across the room and tried to snatch it from Petra's hands, but Petra whipped it away, staring at Cleo with such a look of triumph that Cleo was momentarily afraid.

'One million dollars! He's paying you one million dollars to sleep with him?'

'No, he's not! Give that back!'

'What does that make you? Some kind of high-priced whore?' Her eyes raked her as effectively as a blast of burning-hot Kangaroo Crossing dust. 'More like an overpriced one.'

'It's not like that. I didn't have to sleep with him.'

'No? But you are, aren't you? I've seen the way you look at him. I know what you're doing. How is that not selling yourself? How is that not whoring?'

'Get out! It's nothing to do with you.'

'Isn't it? I wondered where Andreas had dredged you up from, acting more like some frightened schoolgirl than one of his women. I knew something was up the minute you stepped from the plane. It was all a charade, all for my benefit.'

'What are you talking about? Why should it be for your benefit?'

'Because Andreas was my lover, until you showed up!'

Cleo reeled, feeling blind-sided. 'What?'

'And he didn't know how to tell me it was over. So he employed you—' she gave a theatrical toss of her head '—to be his whore.'

'Andreas wouldn't do that.' But even as she put voice to the words, the doubts she'd had from the start doubled and redoubled in her mind. Why had he needed someone to act as his mistress? To deflect gold-diggers generally, or one woman in particular? She couldn't believe it. Didn't want to believe it.

'But why couldn't he just tell you? Why go to so much trouble?'

'To totally humiliate me, why else?'

The other woman glared at her, as if she belonged here in this place and Cleo didn't, and a wave of revulsion rolled over her. Had Petra occupied this bed in this room before her arrival? Had Petra spent the nights lacing her long legs around Andreas' back as he drove himself deep into her? She closed her eyes, trying to block the pictures out.

No wonder the woman didn't like her. She'd been right from the start: Petra's edgy friendship had been laced with hidden meaning and snide digs.

But whatever his tactics and however repugnant they might be, Andreas had clearly made up his mind. It gave Cleo a much-needed foothold in the argument. 'So Andreas didn't want you, then.' It was her turn to smile. 'And you just can't take no for an answer.'

'You bitch! Do you really think he wants you, a woman who is so stupid she falls for someone over the Internet and loses everything? Do you really think he would prefer your type than someone who can talk business with him and understands his needs?'

Even while Cleo berated herself for revealing so much to this woman—too much—she was so grateful she hadn't revealed absolutely everything. And at least she had the advantage of knowing Andreas wanted her, at least for now. 'Clearly,' she countered, 'you ceased being one of his needs some time ago! Did you overhear while you were eavesdropping on the terrace that he'd asked me to stay longer? Tell me then, who is it he needs—you, who are so loyal to your boss that you skulk around in his bedroom looking for dirt, or me, who he would happily part with another million dollars to have stay?'

And Petra pulled out her trump card. She collapsed on the bed and burst into tears, the contract slipping from her fingers onto the coverlet. Cleo reached down and snatched it up, although the damage had already been done, the cat well and truly let out of the bag. But as for what to do next? Comfort the hysterical woman after the things she'd said and the names she'd called her? Not likely.

'Do you want me to call a doctor?'

Petra sniffed and shook her head, for once her perfect hair unravelling at her nape like the woman herself. 'There's no point. I know what's wrong with me.' She snatched a tissue from the holder on the bedside table and blew her nose.

Maybe she really was heartbroken, thought Cleo. Maybe she'd really loved Andreas and thought he'd loved her back and she couldn't bear the thought of someone else having him.

'I guess it wasn't easy seeing me here.' She wasn't hoping for conciliation. She still hadn't sorted out how she felt about being used by Andreas to ward off his previous lover.

Petra responded with a snort. 'You could say that.'

'It's always hard when the person we want doesn't want us.' Hell, she'd been there herself. 'But sometimes it's for the best. Sometimes they're not the right choice for us after all.'

The woman looked sideways at her, her eyes red-rimmed and swollen. 'So now you're giving me advice. How sweet. Perhaps you might give me advice on another matter?'

Okay, so she probably wasn't the best person to be comforting this particular woman. But at least she was trying. 'I'll do my best.'

'Do you think I should have an abortion?'

# CHAPTER THIRTEEN

LIGHTS swam behind her eyes, blood crashed in her ears and Cleo felt the urge to run. Run as fast and as far as she could. Run till her lungs burst and her legs collapsed under her. Run till she hurt so much she couldn't feel any more pain.

'You're pregnant, then.' It all made sense, Petra's morning queasiness by the pool, her dizziness this morning and her mood swings and tears.

'How clever you are. And have you similarly worked out whose child it would be?'

And Cleo's fantasy world crashed down around her. Andreas' child. His baby.

*'It's not a crime to trust someone.'*

Maybe not. But it should have been a crime to make the same mistake, over and over and over, like a broken record. *The bright side, Nanna, where's the bright side?*

*You have a booking to go home in two weeks,* a voice in her head told her. *Change it.*

And Cleo knew that was what she had to do. She had to leave, and now, while Andreas was away. Staying was pointless. She didn't want anything to do with him any more, a man who could treat women as he had, pitting one against the other like queens battling it out on some chessboard.

Besides, there was Petra to consider, and a baby. Andreas' baby.

She put a hand to her own stomach. For a few days there, the possibility had existed that it could have been hers. That she too could have been pregnant.

Thank God it had never happened! What a mess that would have been.

'He doesn't know, then?'

'Not yet. I only just found out myself.'

'I think you should tell him as soon as he comes back. I'm sure… I'm sure he'll do the right thing.'

Petra nodded, still looking at the floor. 'I know he will. His mother desperately wants grandchildren. At least she will be delighted.'

Oh, God. More words she didn't need to hear. More words that rocked the foundations of her soul. Andreas had forgotten to use protection with her that time. Surely not intentionally? And yet he'd seemed almost annoyed when he'd learned she wasn't pregnant. He'd offered her more money to stay—to give him more time to get her pregnant? It didn't bear thinking about. She didn't want to know the answer.

'I'm leaving,' Cleo told the woman still hunched and bowed on the bed. 'I'll pack my things and be gone this afternoon.' It was still early in the day. She was sure she could get some kind of link to Athens, be it by plane or ferry. She'd get out now, before Andreas returned and threw her out because there was no point continuing with their charade. She'd get out now while she still held some shred of pride intact.

Petra sighed and sent her a watery smile. 'That's probably for the best.'

Halfway to London, Andreas was growing restless, still searching for the answer to a question that had been plaguing him for hours. Why had she told him she'd loved him? Why would she do that?

She'd turned down a million-dollar offer to stay. Turned him down flat, talking about returning home as if she couldn't wait to be out of there.

And then he'd given her an envelope full of Kurt's money and she'd told him that she loved him. It made no sense, no sense at all.

He toyed with the plate of dips and antipasto, took a sip of his cold *Mythos* beer and watched the landscape beneath his window slowly roll by. What did she want by saying such a thing?

He sighed and pushed back into his seat, smiling about how excited she'd been when she'd told him what she'd learned about the legend of Atlantis. Why did she want to go home so badly to study when all she wanted was all around her here? She couldn't study in a more perfect place. No, she had to stay, there was no question.

But she wouldn't take his money. What else could he offer? *Family.*

The idea was so simple! If she were part of his family she would stay. And she could bear him the children his mother so desperately wanted. He wasn't interested in looking for a wife. He couldn't even think about it with Cleo occupying his bed and his thoughts. And she had said that she loved him. It was perfect.

He took a celebratory swig of his beer and sighed. He'd marry her. Hadn't he come to terms with that very idea when he'd thought she could be pregnant? So what was to stop him marrying her when she was not? She would be pregnant soon enough then.

It was all settled.

He picked up the phone that connected him with the pilot. 'Change of plans. We're going back to Santorini.'

There was no argument, no question from the flight deck. They were turning around. So he wouldn't make it to London to sign those papers, but did he really care about Darius anyway? He'd put the fear of God into him. Wasn't that enough? He could do what he damned well liked with the hotel; one more wasn't going to make any difference to the Xenides portfolio. And the kicker would be that Darius would still have to pay him back the loan.

He put his hands behind his head and leaned back into the soft upholstery. It was perfect.

'Three weeks, Mother, that's right. Are you busy that weekend?'

'Too busy for my son's wedding? Tsh. Of course not.' Even here, standing at the window to his office overlooking the caldera, he could hear the tremor of excitement running through her voice, could imagine that five minutes after this conversation the entire who's who of Athens would know about the upcoming nuptials. 'Although I have to admit to being a little surprised.'

'Really?' Not half as surprised, he'd bet, as he had been when he'd returned home to find Cleo gone and a teary Petra apologising, not making any sense. Petra and tears. He'd never expected to see the day.

He'd been about to head straight back to the plane and follow Cleo when Petra had dropped the bombshell that she was pregnant. He wouldn't wish the news she'd given him on his worst enemy. It wasn't the world he'd imagined so perfect, with Cleo sitting on the terrace, her belly swelling, ripe with their child. But it was a child. *His child.* And there was no way he could walk away. 'Why's that?'

'Well, you seemed so sure when you were last here that you weren't planning on marrying Petra.'

'It was something you said,' he said, clutching at the excuse.

'Something about not realising what was right there under your nose.'

'Oh.' There was a short silence and for a moment he thought the line had dropped out. 'I guess I did say that.'

Strange, Andreas thought, as one of his staff slipped a note to him. He'd imagined his mother would be delighted with that little snippet. He could see her even now telling all her friends at bridge that she'd played matchmaker.

'Anyway, I'll send over the helicopter for you a few days in advance.'

'That would be lovely. I'll enjoy coming over to help with everything. And, Andreas?'

'Yes?'

'It all seems such a rush. I know I put some pressure on you and, while that's a mother's prerogative, I'd hate to think you were rushing into something you might regret later. Are you sure you're making the right decision?'

His head collapsed back, his hand going to his brow. It was the right decision, wasn't it? Morally. Ethically. For the sake of his child. He was doing the right thing. The note in his hand fluttered against his brow. He looked at it, trying to focus, trying to make sense of the words it contained in the context of the query he'd sent to the clinic.

We are unable to provide information on our patients but can advise that we have no patient by the name of Petra Demitriou.

And it was signed by the very doctor Petra had claimed had confirmed her pregnancy.

No wonder she hadn't wanted him to accompany her!

'Andreas? Are you still there? I asked if there was any chance you were making a mistake.'

He was, but his teeth were grinding together and it took a force of will to prise them apart. *Thank God he hadn't told his mother why it was all such a rush!* 'Very possibly, Mother. I'll have to call you back.'

'Possibly? What do you mean?'

'I'll call you back.'

Right now he had something more important on his mind.

He found her in his suite, supervising the removal and packing of Cleo's clothes. 'What the hell are you doing?'

'Andreas! I didn't hear you coming.'

'Who asked you to take Cleo's clothes away?' He gestured to the staff, clearing the room with a click of his fingers.

'Andreas, Cleo's gone. I thought I should make room for my things, seeing as I'll be moving in soon.'

He swallowed back on a surge of revulsion. He hadn't been able to stomach the thought of Petra back in his bed when he could still smell Cleo's scent on his sheets, the smell of her hair on his pillow. Although Petra had made it clear she'd like to resume sexual relations ten minutes after she'd dropped the double-barrelled blast that Cleo had gone and that she was carrying his child.

And now she was planning on moving in. It was all he could do to keep a tenuous hold on the contents of his stomach.

'When's your next appointment with the clinic?' he asked disingenuously. 'I'd like to come too.'

She smiled and closed the wardrobe doors, he guessed so he couldn't see how empty they now were. Empty of Cleo. As empty as he now felt. 'There's no need for that. It's just routine. Tests. You know.'

'No, I don't know. And neither, it seems, does Dr Varvounis.'

'Wha…? What do you mean?'

'You're not registered at the clinic. He's never heard of you. You haven't been, have you?'

'You probably have the wrong clinic—'

'I think I have the wrong fiancée.'

'What's that supposed to mean? I'm the one who's having your baby!'

'Are you? Or is it as fabricated as your affection for me? You made it up, didn't you? Made the whole story up in one final desperate attempt to get rid of Cleo and get your talons into me. And it nearly worked. Well, no more. The wedding is off. And you are no longer in my employ. I want you out of here.' He turned on his heel and strode out of the room and suddenly she was there, tugging at his arm.

'But I love you, Andreas! We can make a baby just like your mother yearns for, I know we can.'

Fury flared inside him. 'What did you say? Did she tell you that? Is that how you came up with this plan to trap me? I'm sorry, Petra. Maybe I wasn't clear enough before. I don't want you. I never really did. I want Cleo.'

'She wasn't good enough for you. She was young and naïve and stupid.'

'I love her!'

And her eyes went wide. 'You couldn't. You can't. Andreas, please, listen to me—'

'Get out, Petra. I never want to see you again.'

And then she was gone and he was alone. Alone to the re-alisation that had shocked him as much as it had Petra.

He loved Cleo.

*And he was going to get her back.*

# CHAPTER FOURTEEN

So MUCH for autumn. Cleo wiped the sweat from her brow as she lugged the vacuum cleaner along the balcony of the Kangaroo Crossing Hotel, the last pub, the sign boasted, this side of the Black Stump.

It might be April but a last hoorah from summer had the sun shining down like a blowtorch, turning the already parched earth to yet more red dust. As if they needed more. A convoy of four-wheel drives roared down the main street, turning the air red and rich with diesel fumes.

Welcome to the outback, she thought as she tackled the sticky doors of yet another balcony room.

Inside was thankfully cooler, the thick stone walls protecting the rooms from the worst of the heat, but still she managed to work up a sweat as she cleaned the last of the rooms.

She'd been lucky to score this job. Her mum had had to give up work as her pregnancy was now quite advanced and she was happily awaiting the arrival of her baby. Cleo couldn't help but be excited for her, not only because she'd been able to take over the cleaning job from her. She could even supplement her income by pulling beers in the bar at night.

And the best thing was the job came with its own accommodation. True, it was in the basement, but it was nothing like the poky closet she'd endured in London. This was a real room with a real bed, and so much the cooler for being underground.

She'd save up now she was home and when she had enough she'd enrol in that Classics course in Sydney. She'd discovered she could do it by correspondence and hopefully she'd be able to start next semester. She could hardly wait. The books from Santorini she'd brought home were so well read they were dog eared and slipping from their covers.

She looked around and gave a small sigh of satisfaction as she straightened the last kink out of the queen bed's coverlet and stopped to smell the roses she'd salvaged from the twisted climbers covering the beer garden. A VIP had booked for tonight, the manager had proudly advised, the room had to be perfect. And it was. Dubbed the honeymoon suite because it boasted its own bath and loo, it was the grandest room the hotel had to offer. She smiled. Some honeymoon suite. Nothing at all like the suites she'd shared with Andreas in London and Santorini. But then, this was Kangaroo Crossing, and if she was ever going to have a honeymoon herself this was the best she could hope for.

Not that that was likely. Since coming home, she'd sworn off men for good. Clearly she had no idea how to fall in love with the right one. She hauled the vacuum cleaner and her gear back out into the hot still air, allowing herself just a second to remember what it had been like in those first few giddy days and nights she'd shared with Andreas on Santorini, when there'd been times she'd actually believed he'd cared about her, those perfect days before she'd discovered she was being used as some sort of shield between him and Petra, the woman who was carrying his child, the woman he was probably already married to.

The vacuum cleaner thumping almost reassuringly against her shin brought her back to reality. Her time with Andreas had been nothing more than a fantasy. This was her life now. This was her world, a world that had shrunk in the last two weeks to one big wide dusty stretch of highway lined with low timber-board buildings.

Another car was making its way through the town, a trail of red dust behind it, a car impossibly shiny and as low slung and inappropriate for the outback roads as you could imagine. She stopped to watch for a moment, expecting it to keep right on going, only to see it slow to a halt, pulling up alongside the hotel in the shade of an ancient gum tree. Could this be their VIP, then? Kangaroo Creek didn't get many of those. She put down the machine and rested her arms on the timber balustrade to watch. And then the driver stepped out and the air was punched from her lungs.

*Andreas.*

Dressed in light-coloured chinos, a white shirt unbuttoned halfway down his chest and a gold watch glinting against his olive-skinned wrist, he looked cool and urbane. And then she thought of what he'd done to her, of his hot mouth and his clever tongue, and the very concept of cool and urbane tripped into overload.

Dry-mouthed, she clung to the railing now, knowing that if she didn't her legs would never hold her up. Why was he here? What could he possibly want?

Unless it was to show off his new wife…

The honeymoon suite. A VIP. It all made sense. But why bring her here? Surely Andreas wouldn't stoop that low?

But he was alone, and as she watched he tugged a single leather holdall from the boot. She should go before he saw her. She should disappear back to the basement and hide.

And then he looked up, and their eyes jagged, and her heart flipped over. *Please*, she thought, *please, I want to hate you for what you did. I want to be angry about how you used me. I want to forget. Please don't make me remember…*

But just one look at him was enough to know that she still hungered for him, and then he pulled the sunglasses from his face and she knew that he wanted her too.

Oh, God, why was he here? What could it mean? And why did she have to look such a bloody mess? She pushed back from the railing, preparing to flee, when he raised a hand and spoke.

*'Kalimera, Cleo,'* he said, in that gorgeous accent that always made her insides quiver. It was probably the first time the greeting had ever been uttered in Kangaroo Crossing. And probably the last, if she had anything to do with it.

'What the hell are you doing here?'

'I love Australian women,' he shouted from below. 'They always speak what's on their mind.'

There was a murmur of agreement from below, no doubt from the blokes lining the verandah watching the occasional car go by, but she was already intent on her reply. 'Have you known that many to know?' And instantly she wished she'd fled when she'd had the chance because it seemed as if half the pub's contents had suddenly spilled out onto the verandah below to watch the proceedings.

'Only one,' he admitted. 'But that was more than enough.'

A ripple of laughter drifted up from the crowd. They'd all seen the car, they'd all seen the man that had stepped from it like some Greek god dripping with money and influence. She didn't have to see their glances to know what they were all thinking. That anyone would be mad to turn this man away. But they didn't know what he'd done. They didn't know he had a woman back home pregnant with his child.

'Go to hell, Andreas!' Damn him. She battled the vacuum cleaner down the outside stairs, thankfully in the opposite direction from where he was standing, and headed inside for the basement stairs, her mind too confused to deal with whatever was going on, her heart too filled with hurt to assist.

She was too slow. He met her in the lobby, where the entrance hall met the stairs going down to the basement. 'Cleo.'

'How ironic,' she said, her feet riveted to the ground, 'that we should meet like this again. Have you plans for taking over the Kangaroo Crossing Hotel, then? Should I start looking for another job?'

'I didn't come for the hotel.'

'No?' She clutched the rounded stairway newel like a safe haven. If she hung onto that, surely her legs would keep working. Although maybe she should be more worried about her heart. Right now it felt so big it was a wonder it didn't spill right out of her mouth. 'Then what are you doing here?'

'I came here to see you.'

There was no way her legs were going to get her down those stairs, not with the way he was looking at her now.

'And what if I don't want to see you?'

The noise from the bar next door was almost overwhelming as the customers spilt back into the cool interior, one topic of conversation and conjecture clearly discernible amongst the shouts and laughter.

'We need to talk. Not here. Somewhere private. Have dinner with me tonight and I'll explain.'

'Mr Xenides, I presume?'

Daphne Cooper, the manager's wife, primped her hair and giggled like a schoolgirl as she spun the register around to face him. 'If you'd just sign here, please. And if you need somewhere private,' she continued with a wink in Cleo's direction, 'I can serve dinner for two in the honeymoon suite?'

'I would appreciate that very much,' she heard him say before Daphne's answering giggle, and Cleo took advantage of the interruption to flee.

She slammed her door, grabbed her bathroom gear and escaped to there before he would have a chance to follow her.

Why was Andreas here? Why now, when he hadn't bothered to contact her in all the days since she'd fled Santorini and she'd made a start at a new life and forgetting…?

Who was she trying to kid? she asked herself, when she stepped under the shower. She would never forget those perfect few days and nights in paradise.

There was a card under her door when she returned.

*Join me for dinner*, it simply said, with a time and a room number. The honeymoon suite. What a joke. For a moment she was tempted to send a note back, telling him what he could well and truly do with his kind invitation, before sense got the better of her.

Why shouldn't she listen to what he had to say, the excuses he had to offer? Why shouldn't she hear him out? And then she could tell him exactly what she thought of him and tell him to get the hell out of her life once and for all.

She refused to hang around the hotel wondering what he was doing all afternoon, so instead she hitched a ride out to the homestead to see her mum, thinking that helping her with the washing or just sorting out the twins would distract her for a few hours. Nanna was there too, full of baby stories that made her laugh and made her almost forget the queasy feeling inside. She didn't tell them about Andreas. She didn't want to hear Nanna's take on the bright side. Because there wasn't one. Not this time. There couldn't be, except that soon he would be gone.

Her stepfather, Jack, wandered in for afternoon tea around four, his khaki work clothes dusty, his hair plastered to his scalp where his hat had been stuck all day. 'G'day all,' he said as he plonked his big frame down on a chair, and as Cleo's mum fussed with getting more tea and cutting slabs of cake. 'Bit of a commotion down at the pub. This mate of yours, Cleo, what's he doin' here?'

Her mother and nanna swivelled their heads simultaneously, their voices in chorus. 'What mate?'

'This rich bloke, from Greece, they reckon. Come to see our Cleo.'

Her head swung around to look at Jack. *'Our Cleo'?* Where had that come from?

But everyone else was apparently more interested in the rich bloke. Questions fired at her from all sides. They'd known it had all gone wrong with Kurt, but this job she'd had in Santorini she'd said precious little about. What was her former boss suddenly doing here? And why?

She fended them off the best she could. After all, she didn't know the answers herself. But she promised she'd let them know. First thing tomorrow when she came out on her day off. By then he'd be no doubt long gone and might cease to be a topic of conversation.

Her stepfather offered to run her back into town, another surprise. But the biggest surprise was when he pulled up outside the hotel. She was halfway out the door when a big beefy hand landed on her arm. She jumped and swung her head around. Her stepfather's face looked pained, preferring to study the steering wheel than look at her. 'Cleo, one thing. Close the door, love.' He suddenly nodded towards the line of men sitting outside on the verandah, sipping their beers. 'There's a pack of vultures out there waiting for any hint of gossip to brighten up their sad lives.'

She pulled her leg back in and closed the door and he resumed his scrutiny of the steering wheel, crossing both his wrists at the top.

'I know we've never been close. I know I've never made you feel welcome. And I should have. Because you're family. I was glad when you came back. Your mum was beside herself with worry and...' He sighed. 'Well, it was just good to know you were home, safe and sound. And I just want you to know that if this bloke tries to take advantage of you, or tries to hurt you, I'll wipe the bloody floor with him myself.' He swung his head around. 'Understood?'

She'd never known Jack to make such a long speech. She'd never known him to more than grunt in acknowledgement, and here he was, letting her know he'd defend her. As part of his family.

She flung her arms around his beefy neck and hugged him. 'Thank you.' And then, because she was as embarrassed as he was, and close to tears, she flung open the door and was gone before either of them could say goodbye.

She dressed carefully, or as carefully as she could given her now limited wardrobe. A wraparound skirt and vest top with mid-height sandals were the best she could do, although she could still use the make-up she'd been given in London to make the most of her eyes. She wasn't interested in seducing him, she told herself as she applied mascara. She just wanted him to see that she was surviving, and surviving well.

And then she was ready. She took one last look at herself, took a gulp of air and headed upstairs.

He was waiting for her knock, opening the door and standing there, all Greek god and potent male, so potent that the words almost dried in her throat and would have, but that there were questions she needed answers to. 'What are you doing here, Andreas? What is it that you want?'

He looked at her hungrily, as if she were the meal. 'Dinner is served,' he said, fuelling the feeling, and despite the desperate logical waves from her brain that told her to cling to her anger, to hold onto her hatred of what he'd done, her body hummed with his proximity as she let him usher her inside.

The door closed with a snick behind her, the table laden with dishes awaiting. The steaming dishes could have smelt good, the cooking here was renowned as the best country cooking could offer, but right now her senses were full of the scent of him, and nothing incited her appetite more. Oh, no. She had to get out of here. She couldn't do this!

She turned suddenly, 'Andreas, I—', and was surprised to find him so close behind her that they almost collided. He reached out and steadied her with his hands at her shoulders, warm and strong, and the feeling was so intoxicating, so real after the memories she'd been hanging onto, that she forgot what it was she wanted to say. She felt the tremor move within him then as he exhaled, as if she wasn't the only one fighting their demons. But that was crazy. What demons could possibly plague Andreas?

*Unless he felt guilty about seeing a woman while his child grew within another.*

'Come,' he said at last. 'Sit.' And so she did, watching him pour them both wine, knowing she dared not touch it for fear of losing her resolve. 'How are you?'

'Andreas. Can we please cut to the chase? What are you doing here?'

He took a deep breath, and placed an envelope before her plate. 'You left without this.'

With trembling hands she picked up the envelope and pulled the paper from inside. A cheque. For five hundred thousand pounds. 'You left without your money.'

She stared at the cheque feeling sick. So that was what this was about. Mr Businessman handling the money aspect, ensuring all the i's were dotted, all the t's crossed. Of course. Strange, though, when he could have just posted it. Although then she would never have had the opportunity to do this…

She slipped it back in the envelope and pressed the flap down with her thumb, her eyes not leaving his. His mouth was halfway to a smile, as if he was expecting her to pocket it, which in turn made her smile. And then, over a snowy china plate, she ripped the envelope in half, and tore those two pieces into half again, over and over, until the tiny fragments fluttered to her plate. And then she stood. 'I don't want your money. So if that's all?'

He was on his feet, blocking her exit, 'What the hell is wrong with you? We had a deal. The money's yours. You earned it.'

'No. I didn't. I left before the contract term expired. Besides which, even if I had stayed, I wouldn't want your money anyway. I don't want anything of yours, don't you understand that?'

His features looked strained, the flesh across his cheek-bones drawn tight. Clearly a man unused to not getting his own way. 'I pay my debts, Cleo. We had a contract and I—'

She wanted to scream, suddenly grateful for the foresight Daphne had had to organise dinner for them here in a private room as opposed the dining room, where this discussion would have provided gossip for the next decade at least. 'I will not take your money! You will not reduce those days I spent with you, making me feel like some overpriced whore!'

It was Andreas' turn to stand. 'I never thought of you like that!'

'No? But Petra did. She found the contract in your suite and made it clear that's what I was. Remember Petra,' she charged, 'the mother of your child?'

'You don't have to remind me about Petra,' he said, his teeth clenched. 'Petra was the woman who took you away from me.'

How could he be so blind? How could he avoid the truth that had sent her away? The truth that meant he shouldn't be here with her now or ever, whatever the reason. 'She never took me away from you. You did that all by yourself, when you got her pregnant and used me as some kind of human shield. How do you think that made me feel? Knowing that all the time I was in your bed, your previous lover was already carrying your child!'

'She was never my lover and she was never carrying my child!'

Cleo felt the wind knocked out of her sails. 'She what? But she was pregnant. She told me… And she said you were paying me to humiliate her…'

His hand raked through his hair; the other rubbed his neck. 'We had sex. Once. It was a mistake and I told her. But she knew my mother wanted grandchildren, and that she'd had a cancer scare and was worried I'd never get around to it. She admitted as much to Petra, who decided she'd have to bring out the big guns if she was going to get rid of you and clear the way for her. She faked the pregnancy to trap me.'

'But she was sick, dizzy…'

'All of it put on. All of it designed to make everyone believe it was true.'

It was too much to take in. Too much to accept. And there was still so much that didn't make sense.

And yet hadn't Petra said the very same thing—that Andreas' mother wanted grandchildren? And hadn't Cleo remembered his unexpected response when she'd informed him her period had arrived?

She swallowed. 'Is that why you're back here? Because you need a child and you think I'll provide it for you?'

'What? Cleo, what are you saying?'

'You wanted me to be pregnant, didn't you? You seemed strangely disappointed that I wasn't. That was right after visiting your mother, wasn't it? She told you then that she wanted grandchildren.'

He took a step closer, knowing the bridge between them was much longer and way more fragile than he'd realised. 'Cleo—'

'And then you asked me to stay longer, offered to pay me more. Why do that if you weren't going to try and get me pregnant?'

'It wasn't like that.' Except he knew that it was. Hadn't that been his exact plan? Keep her longer, get her with child. *Make his mother happy.*

'And then you discover Petra was faking it and you turn up on my doorstep.'

'No! I'll admit—' He spun away, troubling his hair again with his fingers, raking his scalp with his nails until he flung himself back, his arms slashing through the air. 'Yes, I'll admit I was hoping, that it seemed like an easy option. I'll admit that I wanted you to stay because I thought you might fall pregnant. But that's not why I'm here now. I didn't come for a child, Cleo, I came for you.'

Her chin kicked up, her blue eyes liquid and shimmering in the rays from the sun setting outside the window. 'And you expect me to believe that?'

'Cleo, I know I don't deserve your trust. I know I'm the last person to deserve that. But on that flight to London when I'd left you behind, I learned something. That I wanted you. That I wanted to marry you. And so I turned the plane around and came home.'

Her face was paler now, her fingers clawed around the back of her chair. 'Isn't it the same thing? Why decide to marry me, unless it was to keep me around longer and increase your chances of having a child?'

His features were tight, his jaw line growing even tighter before he conceded in a nod. 'Okay, that's what crossed my mind—initially—and no, I'm not proud of it. And then I got home and learned you'd already left and was about to follow you and bring you back, except there was Petra saying she was pregnant and I knew I had no choice but to let you go.'

He held out his long-fingered hands in supplication. 'Do you have any idea how that feels? To bow to responsibility when it feels wrong and when your heart wants something different, even if it doesn't understand why?'

She swallowed again and he followed the movement in her throat and down to where she crossed her arms under the breasts he'd missed so much, but not just because of their perfection, he'd learned, but because of the woman he missed more.

'So tell me, Mr Businessman, what is it that your heart wants?'

He took a deep breath. 'You once said you loved me.'

'A figure of speech—'

'So you said. I promise you, at the risk of thoroughly humiliating myself here, my declaration won't be.' He watched her perfect blue eyes, saw the questions, the suspicion and maybe, maybe, just a flicker of hope to mirror his own. 'I love you,' he told her. 'I don't know when it happened, or how, or why it took me so long to realise that that was the reason I couldn't let you go, that you had to stay. And you will probably never forgive me for the way I treated you and for being so blind for so long, but I pray you will, because I love you, Cleo, and I had to come and ask you, beg you if necessary, if you would do me the honour of becoming my wife.'

Time stood still. There was the odd shout from the verandah downstairs, the odd drift of laughter through the French doors and outwardly her world hadn't changed. But inside it was as if someone had taken the pieces of her world and rearranged them and everything was suddenly new and unfamiliar.

'Cleo, for God's sake, say something.'

And she blinked to find Andreas still there, not a dream, not some wild imaginings of a woman who'd been too long in the sun.

'Me? You love me?' Cleo, the high-school dropout. Cleo, the cleaner, who would never amount to anything. A bubble of hope burst from her heart. 'You want to marry me?'

And she must have looked so shaky that he snatched her in his arms and held her so close that she could feel his heart thudding powerfully in his chest, but still she couldn't quite trust him. 'And babies, then. I guess you want babies.'

And he stilled for a moment and held her away from him with his big broad hands until he could see her face. 'Right now, all I want is you. I love you, Cleo. And if a child never happens, so be it, my mother will have to deal with it. Because it's you that I want, nothing more. '

Her eyes swam with tears, happy tears, as she looked up into his perfect face. 'I guess you've got me, then, Andreas.'

His dark eyes still looked uncertain. 'Is that a yes?'

And she flung her arms around his neck and held him tight. 'Yes!' she cried. 'Because I love you, Andreas, I love you so much!'

And he kissed her and swung her into his arms and carried her, the meal laid out for them forgotten, to the soft embrace of the queen-sized bed.

Later, much later, when the passion of their reunion had temporarily abated, they stirred. 'There's something else I brought you,' he whispered, nuzzling her cheek, before disappearing for a moment to withdraw a small package from his jacket. He didn't hand the box to her; instead he snapped on her bedside light before holding the pendant up before her. She loved it immediately, the geometric Greek pattern in gold surrounding a circle of amazing blue gemstone that looked as if it were on fire.

'I bought this in Fira,' he said as he clipped the chain around her neck, 'but I never had a chance to give it to you. But I think it signifies everything about us. For this,' he said, tracing one finger around the gold border where it lay on her chest, 'is the Greek, while the core, the inner beauty is an Australian opal, that shows, like your eyes, every colour of the sea and sky.'

'It's so beautiful,' she said, lifting and cradling the pendant in her hands so she could study its colour and depth.

'It's you and me,' he said. 'The Greek and the Australian, together.'

And they kissed and held each other tight.

'There's one thing I still don't understand,' she murmured a little while later as she nestled against him.

'What is it?'

'You said you turned the plane around. Didn't you go to London? I thought you had to go or you could lose the hotel deal.'

His fingers stilled momentarily in her hair, and she nestled closer, allowing her own hand to explore the perfection of his chest, the feel of his satin skin, the wiry dusting of dark hair that coiled around her fingers, the nub of a masculine nipple. 'It was important, as you say. But suddenly the hotel didn't seem to matter any more. And neither did getting even with Darius—or Demetrius, as you knew him.'

'What happened to the deal, then?'

He shrugged. 'Last I heard, he was back in charge. Probably still losing money hand over fist to his turf accountant.'

It was her fingers' turn to still. 'You let the deal fall through? I thought you hated him so much.'

He sighed. 'I did. Once.'

Troubled now, she let her fingers resume their exploration,

down his chest and circling his navel with her fingertips. 'But why? What did he do to deserve that?'

'Does it matter?'

'I need to know the kind of man I'm marrying. I need to understand. You seemed so ruthless then, so driven.' She shivered and he tucked her in closer, his thumb stroking the nipple of one goose-bumped breast and flicking her thermostat to simmer.

'A long time ago he was my father's partner. They'd built a strong business together and everything seemed to be going well. But he'd asked my mother to marry him once, a long time before my father had married her. It seems he'd never forgiven him for that. Or her. So he bided his time watching the business grow and waiting for the perfect opportunity, when the business was cashed up and ready to make a major investment. He took the lot and left us with nothing. My father died barely a year later, a broken man, and I swore on his grave that I would one day get even.'

'Oh.' He'd tensed with his words, and her fingers worked to massage the pain away, stroking his flat belly and following the trail of hairs that arrowed downwards where she encountered him, thick and pulsing once more into life. 'I understand now,' she said, and she did. 'I can see why you needed to get even.'

He flipped over her then, so suddenly that she didn't see it coming. 'It's history,' he said as he buried his face in her neck and settled between her legs. 'And it doesn't matter any more. My mother tried to make me see that, but it was you who made me understand.'

She shook her head as his hot tongue circled her nipples, first one and then the other, his breath like a heated caress where his tongue didn't touch. 'How?'

But she did see the foil packet he had ready in his hand. She shook her head. 'I want you, this time,' she whispered. 'It's you I want to feel inside me, your flesh against mine.' And he cast it aside and kissed her, hot and desperate and soul deep.

She gasped into his mouth as he entered her in one tight, fluid stroke, gasped again when he started to move inside her, the delicious friction of his increasing rhythm sending tremors through every part of her. 'For too long,' he muttered through teeth clenched tight, 'I was looking to the past. But in you…' He stilled for a moment, poised at the brink as he looked down at her, caressing her face with the pads of his thumbs. 'In you, I found something different. In you I found my future. I love you, Cleo.'

And he lunged into her again, his cry rent from him like a cry of freedom, as together they spilled into their future.

# EPILOGUE

HER mother was hanging out sheets on the line, her nanna sitting in the shade of the ancient peppercorn tree, when Andreas' car pulled up alongside the homestead late the next morning. Cleo had warned them they were coming but still her mother turned and stared, while the twins bowled around a corner of the house, shooting each other up with guns they'd improvised from sticks and rubber bands and skidding to a halt when they saw the red sports car Andreas was unfolding himself from. 'Wow,' they said in unison. 'Is that your car?'

Andreas turned on his million-wattage smile as he pulled off his sunglasses and shook his head. 'Sadly no, it is a hire car,' and the boys' faces dropped. 'But I have one much better than this back on Santorini,' and they wowed again and positively drooled as they circled the car like a couple of sharks.

'I'll give you a ride a little later,' he said. 'That is, if you like.' Their eyes lit up on their combined, 'Awesome!' Cleo laughed and wondered how he could read children so well when he'd had so little to do with them. Maybe he'd make a pretty good father, she figured, if his reaction to her half-brothers was any indication. Maybe having his babies wouldn't be such a hardship.

*Making them, she already knew, would be nothing but sheer pleasure.*

Her cheeks colouring into a blush she suspected she shouldn't be brandishing when she was about to introduce the man she loved to her family, she slipped her hand in his and led him to where her mother stood, her eyes as wide as her expanding stomach, while Nanna's watched on keen and interested. 'Mum, Nanna, I'd like you to meet Andreas Xenides, the man I love, and the man I intend to marry.'

'That is,' Andreas added, turning on his dazzling smile again and bowing as he took first her mother's and then her nanna's hand in greeting, 'if you permit me your daughter's hand in marriage.'

'Oh, my,' her mother said, the concerned look she'd had on her face when they'd driven up transforming into her own wide smile. 'Jack!' she called as the screen door slammed and her husband emerged from the house. 'Jack, come and meet Andreas. Cleo's getting married!'

Jack didn't rush. He took his own sweet time, Cleo thought, as he let his laid-back stride carry him closer, his beefy arms swinging loosely by his sides and his eyes narrowed by the sun and still drinking in the scene, missing nothing. He pulled up a metre shy and the two men faced each other off, the Greek billionaire in the white shirt, with money clearly at his fingertips, and Jack in his moleskins, his sandy hair for once not flattened by his hat, and who clearly felt that out here, even being the dirt-poor farmer he was, he was king.

He nodded, extending a wary hand. 'Mr Xenides, Jack Carter.'

'Call me Andreas, Mr Carter.'

He nodded. 'Andreas, it is. And just plain Jack is fine with me. I hear you made quite a ruckus in town with your fancy car. And now, I hear, you want to marry Cleo.'

Beside her Andreas smiled. 'That's about the size of it, if you'll allow me to, that is.'

And Jack turned to Cleo. 'And is this what you want, lovey?'

Cleo beamed at the endearment. 'It's everything I want, but only on one condition.'

Her stepfather's face turned dark and he looked ready to take Andreas on, in case he took issue. 'And what's that?'

'That you walk me down the aisle and give me away.'

And she could have sworn her sun-hardened stepfather melted right there before her eyes.

'Well,' said her mum with a tear in her eyes, wiping her hands on her apron and looking for something to fill in the stunned-mullet silence from her husband, 'you will both be staying for lunch? I've got a lamb roast on.'

And they did stay, and afterwards Andreas rang his mother while his new family were busy with dessert, knowing it was morning now in Athens. 'I have a surprise for you,' he told her.

'You're marrying the Australian woman after all?'

And he did a double take. 'You knew?'

She laughed. 'Didn't I tell you? Sometimes you don't know what's right there under your nose until it's gone.'

Andreas laughed then too. 'You did,' he told her, wondering if somehow she hadn't known all along but still not understanding how.

Then after dessert he took the twins for a spin in the car, after which they put their own two and two together.

'You're leaving again?' they asked Cleo, almost simultaneously, sounding disappointed that with Andreas gone they might be deprived of an occasional ride in a sports car.

And their nanna nodded wisely, as always. 'But look at the bright side, boys, you'll be able to visit Cleo and Andreas on Santorini and have a ride in his sports car there. Isn't that right, Andreas?' And Andreas nodded and Cleo laughed and knew right then and there she could stop looking for her own bright side, because she'd found it.

*Love.*

There was no brighter side.

# PROUD GREEK, RUTHLESS REVENGE

**CHANTELLE SHAW**

In memory of my darling dad, Bob Gibbs, who encouraged me to write and was so proud of me.

# CHAPTER ONE

'TAHLIA, you look divine.' Crispin Blythe, owner of the contemporary art gallery Blythe of Bayswater, greeted Tahlia Reynolds effusively. 'Those baubles you're wearing must be worth a small fortune.'

'A large fortune, actually,' Tahlia replied dryly, moving her hand to the ornate sapphire and diamond necklace at her throat. 'These "baubles" are top-grade Kashmiri sapphires.'

'Let me guess. A present from Daddy? Reynolds Gems' profits must be booming.' Crispin's smile faded slightly. 'It's good to know that some businesses are unaffected by this wretched recession.'

Tahlia frowned at the faintly bitter note in Crispin's voice. She had heard rumours that the gallery was suffering from the downturn in the economy, and for a moment she was tempted to reveal that things were far from rosy with her father's jewellery company, but she kept quiet. Reynolds Gems' financial problems would be public knowledge if the company went into liquidation, but they were not at that point yet. Perhaps she was being unrealistic, but she refused to give up hope that the company her father had built up over the past thirty years could be saved. It would not be for want of trying, she thought grimly. Her parents had used all their savings trying to keep

Reynolds afloat, while she had worked for no salary for the past three months, and had traded in the sports car her father had given her three years ago, for her twenty-first birthday, for a battered old Mini.

In desperation she had even sold her few items of jewellery, as well as many of the designer clothes that she had once been able to afford. The dress she was wearing tonight was on loan from a friend who owned a boutique, and the sapphire and diamond necklace was not her own—though it was one of Reynolds Gems' most valued pieces, stunningly beautiful and instantly eye-catching. Her father had asked her to wear it tonight in the hope of drumming up new business for Reynolds, but she was terrified of losing it, and knew she was going to spend the evening constantly checking that it was still around her neck.

She followed Crispin into the gallery, accepted a glass of champagne from a waiter, and glanced around at her fellow guests who were congregated in groups, admiring the paintings by the artist Rufus Hartman. Tahlia nodded to one or two acquaintances and allowed her eyes to drift. They came to an abrupt halt on the man who was standing on the other side of the room.

'Who is that?' she murmured curiously, feeling her heart jolt violently beneath her ribs. In a room packed with good-looking, successful men, the simmering virility of this particular man set him apart from the crowd.

'I assume you're referring to the Greek hunk in the Armani?' Crispin said archly, following the direction of her gaze. 'Thanos Savakis, billionaire head of Savakis Enterprises. He bought out the Blue-Sky holiday chain a couple of years ago, and owns several five-star hotels around the world. Careful, darling, you're drooling,' Crispin murmured wickedly as Tahlia continued to stare. 'A word of warning: Savakis has a reputation as a womaniser. His affairs are discreet, but numerous—and short-lived. Commitment is not a word associated with Thanos Savakis—unless it's his commitment to making even more money to add to his enviable fortune,' Crispin finished with a theatrical sigh.

'Workaholic womanisers are definitely not my type,' Tahlia murmured faintly, dragging her gaze from the man and taking a sip of champagne. But her eyes were drawn inexorably towards him, and she was glad that he was looking down at the dainty blonde who was hanging onto his arm because it gave her a chance to study him.

Tall and lean, with broad shoulders sheathed in an expertly tailored jacket, he was mesmerising, and Tahlia quickly realised that she was not the only woman in the room to be fascinated by him. With his classically sculpted features, bronzed skin and gleaming black hair, which was cropped short to emphasise the proud tilt of his head, he was stunningly handsome. But teamed with his blatant sex appeal Thanos Savakis possessed some indefinable quality—a magnetism and self-assurance that set him apart from other men. He would command any situation, Tahlia decided. She sensed his innate arrogance, and although he appeared to be giving his full attention to the pretty blonde at his side, she detected the giveaway signs that he was growing impatient of his companion's chatter.

The woman was a little too eager, Tahlia mused. Instinct told her that a man as self-possessed as Thanos Savakis would be irritated by any hint of neediness, and as she watched he carefully but firmly extricated himself from the blonde's grip and strolled into the adjoining gallery.

Gorgeous, but definitely out of her league, Tahlia decided, giving herself a mental shake as she slowly became aware once more of the babble of voices around her, and the clink of champagne flutes on a silver tray as a waiter walked past.

She was shocked by the effect the sexy Greek had had on her—especially as the width of the room had separated them and he hadn't even glanced in her direction. She could not remember ever being so aware of a man. Not even James.

Her mouth tightened. Six months ago her relationship with James Hamilton had come to a shocking and explosive end, and since then she had struggled to piece her shattered heart back together. But the bitterness she felt towards him still burned as corrosively as on the night she had discovered his treachery.

'Tahlia, darling, that's vintage Krug you're gulping down, not fizzy water.' Crispin's laconic drawl dragged Tahlia back to the present. 'Can I get you another?'

She grimaced as she glanced down and saw that she had drained her glass without realising it. 'No, thanks. I'd better not.'

Crispin gave her an impatient look. 'Oh, live daringly for once. A few glasses of bubbly will help you relax.'

'Correction, a few glasses will have me giggling inanely,' Tahlia said dismally. 'And, after the recent press stories about me, I really could do without being snapped by the paparazzi clearly the worse for drink.'

Crispin gave her an amused glance. 'Yes, the tabloids do seem to have excelled themselves,' he agreed. 'The headline "Gems girl Tahlia Reynolds blamed for marriage break-up of TV soapstar Damian Casson" was particularly attention-grabbing.'

Tahlia flushed. 'It isn't true,' she said tensely. 'I was set up. I've only ever met Damian once, when we were guests at a book launch party held at a hotel. He was knocking back champagne all night and kept pestering me. I told him to get lost. The next morning he came over to my table at breakfast to apologise. We got chatting, and he told me he'd got drunk the previous night after he'd rowed with his wife and she had refused to go to the party with him. When I left, he offered to carry my bag to the car—hence the picture of the two of us emerging from the hotel together. Neither of us had expected the media to be hanging around at nine o'clock on a Sunday morning—or at least,' she said slowly, 'I hadn't expected them to be there.'

Anger formed a tight knot in Tahlia's chest at the realisation that Damian had undoubtedly been aware of the presence of the media.

'I was shocked when a journalist asked about our relationship, but Damian told me to leave it to him and he would explain that we were simply friends.'

Instead, the handsome young actor had told the press a pack of lies about their 'amazing night of sizzling sex', Tahlia thought bitterly. If Damian's intention had been to make his wife jealous, it had obviously worked. Beverly Casson had been quoted saying she was 'distraught' that 'party girl' Tahlia had stolen her man. The story had been a scoop for the journalists—the sort of thing that would boost sales of the tabloid, and no one seemed to care that it was untrue, or that Tahlia's reputation was now in tatters.

'This sort of adverse publicity is one of the drawbacks of allowing myself to be in the public eye,' she said dully. 'For months the press have made me out to be a vacuous bimbo who turns up to every event—even the opening of an envelope. It's the price I've had to pay for promoting Reynolds Gems.'

Tahlia bit her lip. When she had graduated from university three years ago her father had made her a partner of his company and given her the role of PR executive. But the global recession had hit Reynolds hard, and in an attempt to raise the company's profile she had reluctantly agreed to feature in an advertising campaign. She had then appeared in glossy magazines, attended numerous social events, modelling fabulous diamonds and precious gems from the Reynolds Gems collection.

Before she had left for the gallery tonight she had learned that all her hard work had been for nothing.

Peter Reynolds had looked grave as he'd explained that, despite the campaign, profits at all three of Reynolds Gems' jewellery shops were down. 'To be frank, Tahlia, Reynolds is facing bankruptcy,' he'd told her. 'I've approached every major bank and financial institution for help, but they've all refused to lend us any more money.' Tahlia's heart had ached when her father had dropped his head into his hands in a gesture of utter despair. 'I'm at rock bottom,' he'd admitted hoarsely. 'I've no more money left to stave off our creditors. The only glimmer of hope on the horizon is an equity firm, Vantage Investments, who have expressed an interest in buying out the company. I've arranged to meet their CEO next week.'

Tahlia could not forget the lines of strain of her father's face, but she forced her mind back to the present and glanced around the gallery, aware that fretting about Reynolds' financial situation was not going to help. She had dreaded the prospect of attending the exhibition tonight, when her supposed love-life was headline news, but Rufus Hartman was a close friend from her university days and she could not have missed his first major exhibition.

As she strolled around the gallery with Crispin she was conscious of the curious stares from some of the other guests. 'I wonder how many people here tonight think I'm a heartless marriage-breaker,' she muttered bitterly.

'No one believes a word that's written in the gutter press,' Crispin assured her breezily.

Tahlia wished she shared his confidence, but for a moment she was tempted to slink into a quiet corner and remain there for the rest of the night. But that was ridiculous; she had done nothing to be ashamed of. Her hand strayed to her necklace. She had come to the art gallery tonight not simply to support Rufus. She had a job to do, she reminded herself.

Crispin had mentioned that a wealthy Arab prince would

be attending the exhibition. Apparently Sheikh Mussada enjoyed buying gifts for his new wife, and Tahlia hoped that if she could catch his attention he might be impressed by the sapphire necklace and request to see more Reynolds Gems jewellery. If Reynolds could earn the patronage of an Arab prince they might not need to sell to Vantage Investments after all, she mused, so lost in her thoughts that she did not realise that Crispin had led her into the second gallery until he addressed a man who was studying one of the paintings.

'Thanos—I hope you're enjoying the exhibition. May I introduce you to a fellow art-lover?' Crispin drew Tahlia forward. 'This is Tahlia Reynolds. Her company, Reynolds Gems, have sponsored Rufus throughout his career, and she has an expert knowledge of his work.'

Shock ripped through Thanos as he stared at the woman at Crispin Blythe's side. She had dominated his thoughts for so long that for a few seconds his brain struggled to comprehend that she was standing in front of him, and it took all his formidable will-power to school his expression into one of polite interest rather than murderous rage.

He had arrived in London three days ago, and at a dinner party with friends had been introduced to Crispin, who had invited him to this exhibition at his art gallery. Thanos had no particular interest in art, but these events were always useful for social networking. You never knew who you might meet, he thought derisively, as his eyes raked over Tahlia Reynolds's slender form.

He recognised her instantly. Hardly surprising when her face was plastered over the front of all the red-top tabloids, he thought sardonically. But the photos of her in the newspapers, even the artfully posed pictures in the glossy magazines, showing her in couture gowns and stunning jewellery, did not do justice to her luminescent beauty. His eyes swept over her close-fitting blue silk cocktail dress, which matched the sapphires at her throat and was cut low to reveal a tantalising glimpse of the upper curve of her breasts.

She was exquisite, he acknowledged grimly. He welcomed the wave of black hatred that surged through him, but to his disgust another, unbidden emotion stirred within him. Nothing had prepared him for the impact of seeing Tahlia in the flesh, and to his fury he felt an unmistakable tug of sexual interest.

An awkward silence hovered in the air after Crispin's introduction, and as the gallery-owner cleared his throat Thanos acknowledged that he could not give in to his inclination to fasten his hands around Tahlia's slender neck and squeeze the life from her body.

'Miss Reynolds,' he murmured smoothly, extending his hand to her. He noted that she hesitated before she responded, and her hand shook very slightly when she placed it in his. Her fingers were slim, and as pale as milk. It would take a fraction of his strength to crush them in his grasp. He tightened his grip rather more than was necessary, and when her eyes flew to his face he stared at her impassively.

The brief pressure on her fragile bones could not compare with the pain his sister endured every day, he thought savagely. Melina had been in hospital for six long months, and would have to undergo many more weeks of physiotherapy before she would walk unaided again. Thanos did not blame the driver of the car which had ploughed into Melina. The police had assured him that the man behind the wheel had stood no chance of avoiding the young woman who had run into the road without looking.

No, he held two other people responsible for the accident which had almost ended Melina's life—and those same two people had callously broken her heart. Tahlia Reynolds was a predatory bitch who had been having an affair with Melina's husband, James Hamilton. Melina had been distraught when she had discovered them together in a hotel bedroom, and she had fled outside onto an unlit country road, straight into the path of an oncoming car.

Thanos released Tahlia's hand but continued to scrutinise her intently. According to the recent press reports she had been up to her old tricks with another married actor. Did this woman have *any* scruples? he wondered savagely. How dared she stand there staring at him with her startling bright blue eyes, her mouth curved into a hesitant smile?

Soon she would have little to smile about, he brooded. He had already dealt with his ex-brother-in-law. Immediately after Melina's accident James had fled to L.A., but the actor had quickly discovered that no Hollywood director would work with him after Thanos had threatened to withdraw his financial backing of various film projects if James Hamilton was given so much as a walk-on part. James's acting career was dead and buried, and Thanos was determined that it would never be resurrected. Now he wanted revenge on James's mistress.

Tahlia's hand was still tingling as if she had received an electric shock. Some indescribable force had certainly shot from her fingertips all the way up her arm when she had shaken Thanos Savakis's hand, and now she felt strangely light-headed. The champagne must have gone to her head, she thought ruefully. The peculiar feeling that had swept over her when Thanos's skin had briefly come into contact with hers was *not* an intense reaction to the sexiest man she had ever laid eyes on, she told herself firmly. And yet she could not deny that he unsettled her.

'It's a pleasure to meet you, Mr Savakis,' she said politely.

'Are you here in London on business, or…?' She tailed away uncertainly, entranced by the sudden smile that lifted his features from handsome to breathtakingly gorgeous, and revealed a flash of white teeth which for some inexplicable reason made her think of the story of Red Riding Hood and the cunning wolf.

'Business…and pleasure,' Thanos drawled, relieved that he was once more in control of his hormones. He trailed his eyes over Tahlia. She was exquisitely packaged: designer dress, shoes and handbag, not to mention an eye-watering collection of sapphires and diamonds that sparkled enticingly against her creamy skin. Her outfit must have cost a fortune, he thought cynically. Tahlia was clearly used to the finer things in life, and he was going to take enormous pleasure in putting an end to her pampered, self-indulgent lifestyle.

He had expected her to show some sort of reaction when he introduced himself, but there had been no flicker of response in Tahlia's eyes at the name Savakis. Presumably she had been unaware of James Hamilton's wife's maiden name— no doubt she and James had not spared a thought for Melina during their secret assignations. Molten fury seared his insides. He wanted to vent his anger and denounce her as the heartless whore who had wrecked his sister's life—let the members of London's high society who were gathered in the gallery hear what a cheap little tart she was. But with a huge effort of will he resisted the urge. There would be time enough to tell her what he thought of her after he had brought her to her knees.

'I see that Earl Fullerton has just arrived,' Crispin Blythe murmured. 'I'll leave you two to have fun. I suggest you ask Tahlia to give you a tour of the gallery, Thanos. She has a special relationship with the artist, and is the best person— apart from Rufus himself, of course—to talk about his work.'

'Oh, but…' Tahlia stared after Crispin, unbearably embarrassed by the obvious way he had manoeuvred her and the sexy Greek together. Thanos's mouth was still curved into a smile, but the faintly derisive gleam in his eyes unnerved her, and she could not shake off the idea that for some reason he had taken an instant dislike to her. 'I mustn't monopolise your company, Mr Savakis,' she murmured, glancing rather desperately around the gallery, in the hope that she would spot someone she knew.

'What exactly is the nature of your "special relationship" with Rufus Hartman?' Thanos queried coolly. 'Is he one of your lovers?'

For a moment Tahlia was too taken aback to reply. With a sinking feeling she realised that Thanos had probably seen the newspaper reports of her supposed affair with Damian Casson. Her temper flared. So much for Crispin's assertion that no one believed the rubbish that was written in the downmarket tabloids. 'I really don't see that it's any of your business,' she said coldly, 'but as a matter of fact Rufus isn't attracted to women,' she added. She was not sure why she had lowered her voice, because Rufus was quite open about the fact that he was gay. 'He is a good friend with an incredible talent.'

Thanos's dark eyes roamed lazily over her, as if he were mentally undressing her, and Tahlia felt horribly exposed in her low-cut gown. Her eyes seemed to be drawn to his face of their own volition, and she could not help but focus on the sensual curve of his mouth. His kiss would not be gentle. The thought crashed into her head and her face burned as she imagined him lowering his head and covering her lips with his. Heat coursed through her veins, and when she tore her eyes from him and glanced down she was mortified to see the outline of her nipples clearly visible beneath her dress.

Tahlia had turned her head again, and seemed to be scanning the room for someone. 'Are you searching for anyone in particular?' Thanos queried, his eyes narrowing when she shrugged her slim shoulders. Her skin was so pale it was almost translucent. He noticed a dusting of gold freckles along her collarbone and the slopes of her breasts and felt a tightening sensation in his groin. His fierce awareness of her was both unexpected and infuriating, but it was satisfying to see the evidence that she was equally aware of him.

If she had been any other woman he would have wasted no time in seducing her. With her track record he doubted she would need much persuading into his bed. Disgust swept through him and he ruthlessly banished the image of peeling the straps of her blue silk gown down her shoulders and exposing her slender naked body. She was his brother-in-law's whore, he reminded himself grimly, and it was inconceivable that he could desire her when he had sworn revenge on her for the pain she had caused his sister.

Thanos's accented voice was deep and sensual, and it sent a little shiver of awareness down Tahlia's spine, but she was determined to ignore the effect he had on her. 'I'm looking for an Arab prince—Sheikh Mussada,' she said coolly. 'Do you know him?'

'I know of him—as, I imagine, does everyone else here tonight, seeing that he has recently taken over a major high street bank.'

'Yes, I believe he is the fifth richest man in the world,' Tahlia muttered distractedly, supremely conscious of the exotic scent of Thanos's aftershave. She wondered if it would appear impolite if she walked away from him, and then—recalling his dig about Rufus being 'one of her lovers'—wondered why she should give a damn what he thought of her. The Prince must have arrived by now, she thought, as she craned her neck to peer into the larger gallery.

Thanos frowned, wondering what had caused the hectic

flush on Tahlia's cheeks. 'Didn't Sheikh Mussada marry recently?' he queried tersely, a sudden suspicion forming in his brain.

'Yes, but apparently his wife hates flying, and never travels abroad with him.'

Tahlia thought of the business cards in her purse. As she had driven to the gallery she'd indulged in a daydream in which Sheikh Mussada admired her sapphire necklace and asked her where he could buy something similar. That would be Tahlia's cue to invite him to visit one of the Reynolds Gems shops—she would arrange to open the store out of hours if the Sheikh preferred, and expert assistants would be on hand to help him purchase a gift for his wife. In the daydream, Sheikh Mussada was so impressed by Reynolds' stock of jewellery that he requested their catalogue to take back to Dubai. Soon afterwards they would be flooded with orders from the Prince and his numerous wealthy relatives.

'Oh, that must be him.' Tahlia felt a spurt of excitement as the throng of guests parted and she glimpsed a man wearing traditional Arab robes. This was her chance to save her family's business. The sapphire collection she was wearing tonight was truly spectacular, and Sheikh Mussada was reputed to be an enthusiastic collector of top-quality jewellery. All she had to do was somehow gain his attention.

'Hey, don't run away.'

Warm breath feathered Tahlia's neck, whispering across the stray tendrils of hair at her nape, and she jerked her head around, startled to discover that Thanos had moved and was now standing much too close for comfort.

'Sorry?' For a few seconds she had been so caught up in her daydream about the Sheikh that she had almost forgotten about Thanos. Almost, but not entirely, she conceded ruefully. He was not an easy man to forget, and as she stared at his beautifully sculpted face and glimpsed the flare of sensual heat in his eyes her breath snagged in her throat.

'Our host has assured me you are an expert on Rufus Hartman's work, and I wholeheartedly approve of his suggestion that you should give me a guided tour of the exhibition,' he murmured.

'I assure you I'm no expert,' she replied quickly, feeling as though she were drowning in Thanos's dark eyes. His lashes were ridiculously long for a man, she mused, and his skin gleamed like polished bronze, stretched taut over his magnificent cheekbones. He swamped her senses, and her heart slammed painfully beneath her ribs when he reached out and trailed one finger very lightly down her face.

'Your skin is as soft as satin,' he said, his gravelly accent sending a frisson of awareness down her spine. 'I have to admit that I am captivated by your beauty, Tahlia.'

He had to be kidding, Tahlia decided as she struggled to drag oxygen into her lungs. Surely the sexual hunger blazing in his eyes could not be real, when a few moments ago he had been sending out distinct vibes of barely leashed hostility? She was puzzled by his sudden change of attitude, and even more confused that he was staring at her as if she were his every fantasy rolled into one.

'I…' She seemed to have lost the ability to think. She moistened her parched lips with the tip of her tongue, saw him focus intently on the betraying gesture, and felt liquid heat surge through her veins.

'Why don't we start with the landscape in the corner?' Thanos suggested briskly, and he slid his hand beneath her elbow and steered her firmly across the room—out of Sheikh Mussada's view.

Did she get a kick out of seducing other women's husbands? he wondered furiously. He had noted the determined gleam in her eyes when she'd spotted the Sheikh—the way she had stroked her fingers over the sapphire necklace, drawing attention to her slender throat and the provocative swell of her breasts. Beneath her beautiful shell Tahlia Reynolds possessed a cold and calculating heart. James Hamilton was not blameless, but Thanos was convinced that Tahlia had deliberately seduced his sister's husband—and now she was planning to turn her sorcery on the happily married Sheikh Mussada.

Not if he could help it, he vowed grimly. He was not going to let Tahlia out of his sight for the rest of the evening—even if it meant having to pretend that he had fallen under her spell.

# CHAPTER TWO

TAHLIA glanced surreptitiously at the clock on the gallery wall
and was shocked to see that almost an hour had passed since
Thanos had asked her to act as his guide around the exhibition. She could hardly believe she had spent so long in the exclusive company of the sexiest man in the room, and she could
not help but find his attention flattering. His hand was resting
lightly in the small of her back, and she was agonisingly aware
of his lean, hard body, so close to her that she could feel the
warmth that emanated from him and smell the subtle scent of
his cologne. He seemed in no hurry for them to part company—but she was supposed to be networking, offering business cards to anyone who admired her necklace. So far she
hadn't done a very good job of drumming up new business.

'I'm sure Rufus will be able to discuss his work in far more
depth than I can,' she murmured, as Thanos halted in front of
a painting that looked as though the artist had flung splodges
of vivid colour onto the canvas, and which to Tahlia's eyes did
not resemble anything vaguely recognisable.

Thanos followed her gaze across the room to where the
long-haired and bearded Rufus Hartman was chatting with a
group of guests.

'But he is not nearly such an attractive guide,' he

drawled, a gleam of undisguised sexual interest in his eyes as he turned back to Tahlia, stealing her breath. Thanos Savakis was an outrageous flirt, and her common sense told her she should walk away from him and keep on walking. But her usual caution seemed to have deserted her; she was blown away by his charismatic charm, and when his mouth curved into that devastatingly sexy smile her heart began to race.

Thanos glanced back at the picture. 'Mr Hartman's abstract paintings are the sort of thing I'd like to have in my new hotel. They're contemporary and eye-catching and would suit the modern design of the building.'

'I understand you own a chain of hotels? Crispin mentioned it,' Tahlia admitted, flushing at Thanos's quizzical expression.

What else had Crispin told her? he wondered sardonically. That he was a billionaire with a penchant for blondes? Had Tahlia asked the gallery-owner to introduce them, confident that he would find her red-gold hair and milky-pale skin intriguingly different from the dozens of bleached blonde, sunbed-tanned women who were milling around the gallery, eyeing him rather than the artwork on display?

'I own hotels in many parts of the world, including the Caribbean and the Maldives, and I'm currently in negotiations to buy the Ambassador Hotel, where I am staying on this trip to London.'

Tahlia's eyes widened. The Ambassador was one of the most exclusive hotels in the capital. She had taken little notice when Crispin had said that Thanos was a billionaire, but now it struck her that he could probably buy Reynolds Gems out of his petty cash.

'My latest development is in one of the Greek Islands,' Thanos continued. 'The Artemis is a five-star hotel, offering the ultimate pampering experience—superbly equipped gyms, spas and beauty parlours, together with shops selling designer clothes and jewellery.'

'It sounds wonderful,' Tahlia murmured, her mind focusing on Thanos's mention of jewellery shops within his hotel. Unconsciously her hand strayed to the row of sapphires and diamonds around her neck. The ornate necklace was not the sort of thing she usually wore, but it was undoubtedly impressive, and tonight she needed to impress.

Thanos's gaze followed the movement of her hand. 'Your necklace is almost as exquisite as the woman wearing it,' he remarked.

She blushed. 'It's just one of a wide range of pieces made by the expert goldsmiths and designers at Reynolds Gems. Our gemologists source the finest precious stones and diamonds to ensure that every piece of jewellery is of top quality.' Tahlia hesitated. Was it fair to subject Thanos to the hard sell when they were at a party, not in a boardroom? Their business needed all the help it could get, she reminded herself, and she had to seize every available opportunity to promote the company.

'Perhaps you might like to consider selling a selection of Reynolds Gems jewellery at the Artemis?' she said carefully. She opened her purse and extracted a business card. 'I believe it could be a mutually beneficial arrangement. Reynolds has an excellent reputation for superb craftsmanship, which would be in keeping with the high quality of your hotel. And we are an expanding company,' she added, as Thanos studied the card she had handed him.

'Really…?' He gave her a razor-sharp glance, and Tahlia felt the colour rise in her cheeks.

'Oh, yes. We have a dynamic management team which is always on the look out for exciting new ventures.' That, at least, wasn't a downright lie. She knew her father would jump at the chance to improve Reynolds' profits.

Thanos's slow smile once more sent heat surging through Tahlia's veins, yet at the same time she was again reminded of a wolf stalking its prey.

'That's certainly a very interesting proposition, Tahlia. I'll give your suggestion serious consideration,' he murmured.

'You will?' She forgot that she was supposed to be a hard-headed businesswoman and grinned at him. She felt as though Christmas had come early—and maybe it had, she thought excitedly. Thanos owned up-market hotels around the world, and if he allowed Reynolds Gems to promote their jewellery to his wealthy clientele it could completely turn around the company's fortunes.

Thanos's eyes narrowed on Tahlia's face. Gone was the exquisite and rather haughty-looking socialite. In her place was a young woman with an impish smile and sparkling blue eyes which were more beautiful than the most priceless of sapphires. How could she lie so blatantly and yet look so innocent? And how could he hate her and want her with equal intensity? He despised her, but at this moment he despised himself more—because he could not deny his longing to pull her into his arms and claim her soft, smiling mouth with his lips.

Suddenly he was tired of the game he had been foolish enough to start. He should have revealed from the beginning that he was her lover James Hamilton's ex-brother-in-law. He was tempted to tell Tahlia there was not a chance in hell he would enter into any 'mutually beneficial arrangement' with her or her company, but he swallowed the words. He had laid his plans carefully, and now he was poised to destroy Reynolds Gems. His moment of revenge would be sweet, and he wanted to savour the expression on her beautiful face when she realised that she had lost everything.

There was no reason to remain with her any longer. Sheikh Mussada had left the gallery some fifteen minutes ago, he reminded himself, infuriated by the knowledge that he had prolonged his time with her because he had found her intelligent and witty conversation utterly captivating. He glanced around the gallery and saw that the blonde who had attached herself to him like a limpet when he had first arrived was giving him baleful looks. To his annoyance he could not help but compare Lisette's fluffy platinum blonde curls and her sequined dress with its plunging neckline and thigh high skirt to Tahlia's graceful elegance.

His jaw tightened and he gave Tahlia a cool smile. 'I must ask you to excuse me, Tahlia. I'm expecting a business call and need to return to my hotel.'

'Oh, but…' Tahlia stared at Thanos's retreating form, startled by his abrupt departure. He was striding away across the gallery. She felt embarrassed at the thought of calling him back, but she might never have this opportunity again. 'Can I look forward to hearing from you when you've had time to consider my idea about selling Reynolds Gems jewellery in your new hotel?' she called desperately.

Thanos paused and glanced back at her, his expression unfathomable. 'Oh, you'll certainly be hearing from me, Tahlia,' he promised softly. But for some reason his words sent a frisson of unease down her spine.

Tahlia woke early on Monday morning, with a heavy sense of dread in the pit of her stomach. Today her mother was due to see a specialist, to hear whether a mastectomy followed by a course of chemotherapy had destroyed her breast cancer. In the past few weeks Vivienne had regained some of her strength, and her hair had grown back enough that she no longer needed to wear the brightly coloured silk scarves mother and daughter had chosen together before the start of her treatment.

Her mother had been so brave, Tahlia thought, swallowing the lump in her throat. The past two years since Vivienne had been diagnosed had been a nightmare for both her parents, and she hoped with all her heart that today they would be given the news that she was completely cured.

The future of Reynolds Gems was another worry, she acknowledged grimly as she stepped into the shower. She was not hopeful that Thanos Savakis would agree to promote their jewellery at his new hotel, and if Vantage Investments decided against a buy-out, she did not know what would happen to the company her father had devoted his life to.

She would try and find out more about the situation today, she decided as she applied minimal make-up and swept her hair into a loose knot on top of her head.

The May sunshine streaming through the window was warm enough for her to choose a lightweight outfit. Her pale grey pencil skirt and matching jacket were years old, but the precarious state of her finances meant that new clothes were out of the question. She was grateful that her mother had taught her to choose classics rather than high fashion items, because the suit still looked good, and she teamed it with a lilac blouse, slipped her feet into kitten heels and checked her handbag for lipstick, keys and various other essentials, before hurrying out of her flat, praying that her ancient Mini would start this morning.

Tahlia was puzzled to see her father's car in the car park when she arrived at the Reynolds Gems shop just off Bond Street, and she raced upstairs to the office. 'I wasn't expecting to see you,' she greeted him, her smile fading when she saw the tense expression on Peter Reynolds's face. 'What's wrong?' She paled. 'You can't have heard from the hospital this early?'

'No.' Her father sought to reassure her. 'Your mother's appointment is still scheduled for eleven-thirty. I'm here because I received a call from Vantage Investments at eight o'clock this morning, informing me that they've changed the date of our meeting from Wednesday to midday today.'

'But today is impossible. Ask if we can reschedule for tomorrow.'

'I tried,' her father said wearily. 'But they say we can meet today or not at all.'

'You have to go to the hospital with Mum,' Tahlia said urgently. 'Nothing is more important than her appointment with Mr Rivers. What about asking the hospital if they can rearrange your meeting with him?'

'I've tried that too, but he's flying off to a conference later today.' Peter sighed heavily. 'I hate to put this on you, Tahlia, but I've told Steven Holt from Vantage that we'll go ahead with the meeting, although only one of the directors will be present. This will just be a preliminary meeting, but it sounds as though they are seriously interested in making a deal. Obviously if it all goes to plan I'll be involved in the negotiations, but today it's all down to you. Do you think you can handle it?'

'Of course I can,' Tahlia assured him firmly, her heart contracting when she noted the deep lines furrowing his brow. Her father looked as though he had aged ten years since her mother's illness had been diagnosed, and she was willing to do anything to alleviate his stress. 'Leave the figures for me to read through, and I'll do my best to convince Vantage to buy Reynolds Gems. You need to go home and keep Mum calm before her appointment.' She bit her lip and added huskily, 'Ring me as soon as you have any news, won't you?'

'I will,' her father assured her gravely. 'All the paperwork is on my desk,' he added distractedly, and Tahlia knew that the only thing on his mind right now was her mother.

'Go,' she said gently, giving him a little push towards the door. And with a ghost of a smile he walked out of the office.

Two hours later, Tahlia put down the documents which outlined the company's financial situation and picked up her cup, grimacing when she took a sip of cold coffee. Only a miracle could save them, she acknowledged dully. It was clear that Reynolds Gems' profit margins had been low for the past couple of years, but despite that her father had gone ahead with a costly refit of all three shops, and had had to borrow a huge amount from the bank to do so.

Now, because of the global recession that had affected so many businesses, the bank was demanding that the loan be repaid—and, as was obvious from the figures, Reynolds did not have enough money to clear its debts. Tahlia could see from various letters that her father had pleaded with other banks for help, but in the present financial climate no one was interested in rescuing a failing company.

If she failed to persuade Vantage to buy Reynolds Gems the company would go bankrupt—it was as simple as that, she acknowledged sickly. The responsibility was terrifying, and as she gathered up her briefcase and handbag she felt a churning sensation in her stomach that grew worse as she walked briskly out of the office.

Vantage Investment's offices were in the heart of the city. Tahlia knew that parking would be a nightmare, so instead of driving she took the tube to Cannon Street, arrived much too early for her meeting and had twenty agonising minutes to kill before she finally pushed open the glass doors and walked through the plush reception area, her heels echoing loudly on the marble floor. The receptionist directed her to the lift, and on the journey up to the seventh floor she peered at her reflection in the stainless steel walls. She quickly applied another coat of lipgloss, dismayed to see that her hand was shaking.

'Miss Reynolds? I'm Steven Holt,' a sandy haired man greeted her when she emerged from the lift.

'It's a pleasure to meet you, Mr Holt,' Tahlia returned the greeting with a nervous smile, hiding her surprise that the CEO had met her, rather than his secretary or a junior manager.

He made no further conversation as she followed him along the corridor, and her confusion increased when he ushered her into a room and quietly closed the door after her. She stared blankly at the solid wood. Was she supposed to sit here and wait for him to return? Tension knotted her stomach as she turned into the room, and her heart almost leapt from her chest when she caught sight of the man sitting behind the desk, his broad shoulders and the proud tilt of his head silhouetted against the bright sunshine pouring through the window.

*'Mr Savakis?'* She halted abruptly and stared at him, her pulse-rate accelerating as her eyes swept over his thick black hair and hard-boned handsome face, then lowered to his impeccably tailored jacket, blinding white shirt and navy silk tie. He was even more gorgeous than the man who had tormented her dreams: a suave, sophisticated billionaire businessman—but what business did he have here at Vantage Investments, with her?

Thanos was watching her impassively, his dark eyes cold and—the word filtered into Tahlia's mind—pitiless. He made no response to her uncertain smile, simply dipped his head to indicate that she should sit down.

His silence unnerved her, and her voice was unnaturally high-pitched when she burst out, 'I don't understand. I'm here for private discussions with Mr Holt.'

'Steven Holt is the chief executive of Vantage Investments, and in ordinary circumstances your discussions would have been with him,' he told her coolly. 'But these are not ordinary circumstances, Tahlia.' For a split second emotion flared in his eyes, and Tahlia caught her breath at the look of simmering fury he directed at her before his lashes fell, masking his expression. 'Vantage is a subsidiary company of Savakis Enterprises.'

'I see,' Tahlia said carefully, shaken by the look he had given her, and utterly bemused by it. 'Then…you must know why I'm here?'

'Oh, yes, Tahlia. I know exactly why you're here,' Thanos leaned back in his seat and brought the tips of his fingers together. He was a remote and forbidding figure, and he made no attempt to disguise the contempt in his eyes as he raked them over Tahlia's designer suit. No wonder Reynolds Gems was in trouble if Tahlia paid herself a salary well above average to finance the luxurious lifestyle she obviously took for granted, he mused cynically.

'You are hoping to persuade me to buy out your company and save it from bankruptcy. The same company that you assured me is an expanding operation with a dynamic management team,' he said mockingly.

Tahlia felt her cheeks burn as she recalled her suggestion that he might consider allowing Reynolds Gems to sell their jewellery at his new hotel. Clearly he had never had any intention of taking the idea seriously. For some reason he had just been playing her along, and the knowledge sparked her temper.

'Why didn't you tell me of your connection with Vantage Investments, instead of letting me believe there might be a way to save Reynolds?' she demanded angrily. 'Did you enjoy making a fool of me?'

'I admit I found the situation mildly amusing.'

The expression in his eyes chilled her to the bone. 'But why?' she choked. 'What have I ever done to—?' She broke off and stared at the photograph of a young woman that he had pushed across the desk—for a second her heart stopped beating.

'I believe you have met my sister?' Thanos asked, in a dangerously soft tone.

'I…' Tahlia groped for words, her brain in freefall.

'I imagine it was not a long meeting. And there would have been a certain awkwardness to the situation, seeing that you were in bed with Melina's husband at the time. Of course my sister no longer looks as she does in that photo,' Thanos went on, in the same chilling tone of barely suppressed aggression. 'And it is unlikely she will ever dance again—which is a pity because, as you can see from the picture, she loved to dance.'

Tahlia could not formulate a reply as she stared at the photograph of the beautiful young woman whose face was so shockingly familiar. In the picture her dark hair was swept up into a chignon, rather than falling in a mass of curls around her shoulders as it had been on the night Tahlia had seen her, but there was no mistaking that this was James's wife.

'Melina was distraught after she caught you and Hamilton together. She fled from the hotel, and as she dashed across the road she was hit by a car,' Thanos said harshly. 'Eyewitnesses said she was thrown at least twenty feet into the air before she hit the ground. She was in a coma for three weeks, both her legs were broken, and she suffered spinal damage.' He ignored Tahlia's horrified gasp and went on remorselessly, 'For a while the doctors believed she would be in a wheelchair for the rest of her life. Thankfully her last round of surgery was successful, and she is having intensive physiotherapy to help her to walk, but she will never dance again,' he finished grimly, a nerve flickering in his cheek as he picked up the photo of his sister and stared at it.

The silence in the room screamed with tension, until at last Tahlia forced herself to speak. 'I…I didn't know,' she whispered.

Thanos gave a savage laugh. 'You mean you didn't hear the ambulance sirens? Or you did hear them but you were not sufficiently interested to go and find out who had been injured? Presumably you and Hamilton continued with your sexual gymnastics after Melina left?' he snarled contemptuously. 'Neither of you had the decency to follow her, even though it must have been obvious—even to a heartless bitch like you—that she was devastated at finding the man she loved in bed with his whore.'

Tahlia bowed her head while Thanos's savage fury crashed over her. His anger was no less than she deserved, she acknowledged sickly, and her mind relived that terrible night six months ago, which had started off so wonderfully.

She had felt excited and a little nervous when James had checked them in to the hotel he had booked for a romantic weekend.

'Just one key?' she'd queried tremulously, her heart thumping.

'One key, one room—one bed,' he'd replied, with that disarming grin that melted her heart. 'You know I love you, Tahlia,' he had murmured when they'd reached their suite, and he had pulled her into his arms and kissed her. 'And you love me—don't you, baby? Making love is the next step in showing our love for each other.'

She had been unable to resist him: good-looking, easygoing James, who had swept her off her feet. She had been ready for them to become lovers, and when James had started to undress her she had not hidden her eagerness. But as they had tumbled onto the bed the door had burst open, and a woman had stumbled into the room.

She would never forget the look of shock on the woman's face, the tears streaming down her cheeks and her voice crying brokenly, 'How could you, James? How could you? I am your *wife*...'

'I didn't know about your sister's accident,' she insisted shakily, dragging her mind back to the present. 'I left James almost immediately.' After his sulky confirmation that, yes, he *was* married—'but that's no reason to get hysterical, Tahlia.' 'I ran down to my car, parked at the rear of the hotel. Melina must have run out of the front of the hotel, and I drove home along a different road. I don't remember hearing sirens or anything—but I was in shock,' Tahlia said falteringly, remembering how she had driven away, desperately trying to hold back her tears until she reached her parents' home. 'I had no idea that James was married.'

'*Liar.*'

The solitary word cracked through the air like a whip, and Tahlia jumped. 'I swear I didn't know—' she began, but Thanos silenced her with a savage glare.

'Of course you knew. Just as you knew that the actor you've been having an affair with recently was married. Far from attempting to hide your relationship with him, you brazenly flaunted it, allowing yourself to be snapped by the press leaving a hotel with him.' Thanos's lip curled. 'Tell me, do you enjoy a feeling of power when you have sex with other women's husbands? Women like you disgust me.'

Women like his father's mistress, Thanos brooded grimly. Wendy Jones had known that his father had a wife and children, but that had not stopped her flirting with Kosta Savakis and pursuing him with single-minded determination, uncaring of the pain and destruction their affair caused. Wendy and Tahlia were two of a kind—predatory, heartless bitches who lacked any moral decency. His hatred of the woman who had become his stepmother had burned inside him for years, and as he stared across his desk at Tahlia's pale face his fury threatened to choke him.

The icy anger in Thanos's eyes sent a shiver down Tahlia's

spine, and she said frantically, 'I promise you I did *not* know James was married. If I had I would never have dated him, let alone agreed to spend a weekend with him.' She jumped to her feet and gripped the edge of the desk, breathing hard so that her breasts rose and fell jerkily. 'When your sister burst into the hotel room and announced that she was James's wife I felt *terrible*. I felt as though I were the lowest life form on the planet.'

'An apt description,' Thanos snapped, his jaw hardening. 'And I have no doubt that you felt terrible—you'd just been caught out, and you knew James was likely to end his affair with you so that he could try and persuade his wealthy wife to forgive him. I don't understand what you saw in my brother-in-law,' he added scathingly. 'James Hamilton is a penniless, talentless waste of space. But, according to the press reports, you seem to get a kick out of sleeping with other women's husbands.'

The colour leached from Tahlia's face, and for a second she was tempted to flee from the room, but she forced herself to meet Thanos's cold stare. 'The reports in the tabloids about my supposed affair with Damian Casson are a complete fabrication,' she said stiltedly. 'And I have instructed my solicitor to proceed with legal action against the papers involved.' Her eyes dropped to the photograph of Thanos's sister and she swallowed. 'I am so sorry,' she whispered. 'I wish I could apologise to Melina, and explain to her that James deceived both of us.'

'Do you think I would allow you anywhere near my sister?' Thanos demanded harshly. 'Melina has suffered enough, without having to hear your lies.'

He had also risen to his feet, and was surveying her with visible contempt. She could understand why he was angry, Tahlia conceded, but his refusal to listen to her and his determination to believe the worst of her sparked her temper.

'I am not lying,' she told him with quiet dignity. 'And I am not the woman portrayed by the tabloids. I had no idea that James had a wife.' Tears stung her eyes, and she lowered her head so that Thanos would not see them. She had felt a fool that night in the hotel, when James's treachery had been revealed, but her emotions were of little significance compared to the pain—both mental and physical—that Thanos's sister must be suffering.

'I'm so sorry,' she repeated shakily. She had been an innocent pawn in James's game, but she still felt responsible for his wife's terrible accident.

'It's too damned late to be sorry,' Thanos grated. 'It's a pity you did not feel this touching remorse *before* you slept with my sister's husband.'

'I never slept with him,' Tahlia said quickly. 'Although I realise that will be small comfort to Melina. I admit that I had intended to become James's lover. The night that Melina found us at the hotel would have been our first night together.' She swallowed, but forced herself to go on, aware that Thanos and his sister deserved her honesty. 'I had fallen in love with James—although I realise now that I never really knew him at all,' she added bitterly.

She was good, Thanos conceded grimly. She almost had him convinced that she was as innocent as she protested—and the shimmer of tears in those beautiful blue eyes was a nice touch. If it wasn't for the story in the tabloids about her affair with another married actor he might have been tempted to believe her.

But perhaps he *wanted* to believe that Tahlia had been hoodwinked by James Hamilton because of his own inconvenient physical attraction to her? he brooded irritably. Today she was the epitome of understated elegance: her slim-fitting skirt skimmed the gentle flare of her hips, and the cut of her jacket emphasised her tiny waist, while her soft lilac-coloured blouse complemented her creamy complexion. The scattering of freckles across her nose and cheeks matched her red-gold hair, while the long lashes fringing those startlingly blue eyes were a slightly darker shade of gold.

She might be lovely on the outside, but inside she was rotten to the core, and all the evidence proved that she had known just what she was doing when she began her affair with James, Thanos reminded himself. He was not going to be duped by her lies simply because his hormones were raging out of control. His mouth tightened and he forced himself to move away from her, strolling across the room to stare out of the window at the view of the city.

Tahlia watched him, her eyes roaming over his broad shoulders and the arrogant tilt of his head. Despair settled like a lead weight in her stomach.

'You never had any intention of buying out Reynolds Gems, did you?' she said dully.

'None whatsoever,' he replied coolly. 'It seemed entirely fair that you should suffer a fraction of the misery my sister has suffered, and so I decided to destroy your company. But, to be honest, bringing about Reynolds Gems' downfall has not been difficult. Some of the decisions taken by the company during the last two years have been downright reckless, and they are directly responsible for Reynolds' current financial situation. I simply tricked you into thinking that Vantage Investments would offer a rescue package, and you were gullible enough— or more likely greedy enough—to be fooled into believing you could hang on to your self-indulgent lifestyle.'

It was no coincidence that Reynolds Gems' problems had begun at the same time as her mother's illness had been diagnosed, Tahlia acknowledged. During that terrible time business had come a long way down her father's list of priorities, and she felt guilty that she had not become more involved with running the company.

'Reynolds Gems is my father's company, not mine,' she said quietly. 'If you destroy it you will be hurting him.'

'You became a partner three years ago. My investigations were very thorough,' Thanos said coldly, turning away from the window to give her a sardonic look. 'It's too bad your father will lose the company he built from scratch, but he shouldn't have brought his daughter up to be an immoral slut.'

Anger, swift and white-hot, churned inside Tahlia. Her eyes flew to the clock above the desk and she felt a pang of dread. Had her mother been told that her battle with breast cancer had been successful? Or, as the specialist had warned might happen, had the cancer spread? Even if the news was bad, her father would hide his fears and support Vivienne, just as he had done every day for the past two years. Only Tahlia knew that sometimes he sat alone in his study and wept. Peter Reynolds, of all people, did not deserve Thanos's disdain.

Shaking with fury, she marched across the office and stood directly in front of Thanos. 'Think what you like about me, but don't you *dare* say a word against my father. He is a better man than you will ever be.'

'Not in business,' Thanos drawled sarcastically.

Tahlia flushed. 'I accept he had made some unwise decisions, but there were reasons…' She glanced at Thanos's mocking expression and halted abruptly. She refused to discuss her mother's health problems with him when she was sure he would accuse her of lying to gain his sympathy. Her anger dissipated as quickly as it had arrived, leaving her feeling drained and despairing as the realisation hit her that there was no hope of saving Reynolds Gems from the administrators.

'I wish more than anything that I'd never met James

Hamilton,' she said huskily. 'And I hope with all my heart that your sister makes a full recovery.'

She swung away from him, choking back the tears she was determined would not fall until she was outside his office. Her knee collided painfully with the coffee table.

'Damn it!' She stumbled, dropped her briefcase, and bit back an oath as it burst open and spilled its contents over the floor.

No doubt Thanos was enjoying seeing her on her knees, she thought furiously, as she knelt and began to scoop up the pages of figures that spelled the demise of Reynolds Gems. She dashed her hand over her eyes and froze when she realised that he had crouched beside her and was helping to gather up her paperwork.

'Thank you.' She took the papers he handed her and slowly lifted her head, startled to find him so close. The tang of his cologne drifted around her, teasing her senses, and she could feel the dry heat emanating from his body. How could she be so agonisingly aware of him when he had made it clear that he despised her? she wondered despairingly.

It was suddenly imperative that she stood up and moved away from him, before he realised the effect he had on her, but her muscles had seized up. Her eyes were drawn to his—and shock ricocheted through her when she glimpsed the unmistakable feral desire blazing in their depths.

# CHAPTER THREE

How could he feel this overwhelming sexual attraction to Tahlia when he loathed her? Thanos wondered furiously. His brain acknowledged that she was an immoral slut, but his body was responding with humiliating eagerness to the delicate fragrance of her perfume. He could not tear his eyes from the soft curve of her mouth, and the tantalising fullness of her lips was proving an irresistible temptation. His desire for her was an unexpected complication that filled him with self-disgust, but no amount of reminding himself of Melina's injuries could banish the fierce urge to crush Tahlia's lips beneath his.

Thanos was going to kiss her. Tahlia saw the smouldering intent in his eyes seconds before he lowered his head, and she was stunned by the realisation that she wanted him to. He believed she had slept with his sister's husband, and he had made his opinion of her quite clear, but for reasons she could not understand she made no attempt to deny him and simply waited, heart thumping, for his mouth to claim hers.

The first brush of his mouth sent a quiver of reaction through her. His lips were firm, sliding demandingly over hers, but Tahlia's pride belatedly came to her aid and she clamped her mouth shut, fighting the overwhelming temptation to respond to him. He hated her, she reminded herself. And he thought he had good reason to destroy Reynolds Gems in a bid to hurt her. He adamantly refused to believe that she had not set out to deliberately steal his sister's husband, and if she gave in to the urgent clamouring of her body and kissed him back it would surely confirm his belief that she was the immoral slut he had accused her of being.

But she had recognised the sizzling sexual chemistry between them at the art gallery, and now it was raging out of control, consuming them both. When he caught hold of her hand and drew her to her feet she went unresistingly—now they were standing so close, yet not quite touching, and her senses were inflamed by the subtle scent of male pheromones, the intoxicating heat emanating from his hard body that made her long to close the gap between them and have him crush her against his muscular chest.

His lips hardened, became more urgent, and her will-power crumbled beneath the onslaught. With a little gasp she opened her mouth, and he immediately thrust his tongue deep into its moist warmth, exploring her with shocking eroticism as he snaked his arm around her waist and jerked her close, hip to hip, her soft breasts pressed against his rock-solid body.

His hungry passion was like nothing she had ever experienced before, and it drove every thought from her head other than her frantic need for him to continue kissing her. She forgot that they were standing in his office, forgot that he owned Vantage Investments and had refused to save Reynolds Gems from collapse. She was only aware of him, of the demanding pressure of his lips and the faint abrasion of his jaw against the softer skin of her cheek as he angled her head and deepened the kiss to another level that was flagrantly erotic.

She was aware of the melting warmth between her thighs, and the rigid proof of his arousal pressing into her belly. With a low moan of capitulation she moved her hands to his shoulders. She would have wound her arms around his neck, but he abruptly snatched his mouth from hers and jerked his head back, his eyes glittering with contempt as he stared down at her.

'What's the matter Tahlia—has Damian Casson come to his senses and dumped you in favour of his wife? Surely you won't find *me* a good substitute to relieve your sexual frustrations when you're only attracted to married men?' he taunted, his voice dripping with sarcasm that made her skin crawl.

Tahlia gasped, and acting purely on impulse she raised her arm and cracked her hand across his cheek. 'You arrogant bastard,' she choked, shaking with anger and humiliation. '*You* kissed *me*. What were you trying to do—prove how irresistible you are?'

'I certainly proved something,' Thanos drawled as he strolled back across the room and leaned his hip against his desk, folding his arms across his chest in an indolent stance that disguised the fact that his heart was slamming beneath his ribs. 'The sexual alchemy between us is as potent as it is inexplicable, and I admit I kissed you because I was curious to see how you would react.' His eyes narrowed on her white face. 'Hit me again and I promise you will regret it.'

Tahlia stared at the livid red mark on his cheek and felt sick. She had never struck another human being in her life, and she was shocked and ashamed by her violent display of temper. It was no good reminding herself that Thanos had deserved it. He had kissed her, but she had wanted him to, she owned miserably. Despite knowing his low opinion of her, she had been unable to resist him. What did that say about her morals? she wondered despairingly.

Thanos kept his expression deliberately blank, giving no clue to the internal battle raging inside him as he sought to bring his hormones back under control. Kissing her had been a mistake, he acknowledged grimly. He was furious with himself for succumbing to the temptation of her lush mouth, and his temper was not improved by the knowledge that he wanted to kiss her again, to slide his lips down her throat to the pulse beating frenetically at its base, then tug the pins from her hair and run his fingers through the pale red silk.

He studied her dispassionately, wondering if the tears clinging like tiny sparkling diamonds to her lashes were meant to make him feel remorse or pity. He felt neither. She deserved to lose her company, and she would still not suffer a fraction of the trauma his sister had suffered.

He had planned Tahlia's downfall during the endless days and nights he had sat at Melina's bedside, waiting for her to regain consciousness. He had felt so helpless and so afraid, he remembered grimly. He who had never feared anything, who had fought his way out of poverty to the pinnacle of success, had been scared that he was going to lose the one person in the world he truly loved. Now Melina was out of danger, and slowly recovering from her injuries, but he would never forget the accident that had so nearly claimed her life— and he would never forgive the two people he deemed responsible for it.

In the current financial climate Tahlia would never find another buyer for Reynolds Gems. Everything was going just as he had planned. But that was not entirely true, he acknowledged irritably. He could not remember the last time he had wanted a woman as badly as he wanted Tahlia and his hunger for her angered him. He had first-hand proof that she was a woman like his father's mistress, yet still he was consumed with this damnable longing to possess her.

Maybe he should seize what he wanted and be damned, he mused grimly. He had planned to take revenge for his sister by fooling Tahlia into believing that his company would buy

Reynolds Gems and then withdrawing his offer of financial support at the last minute. He had no interest in saving Reynolds' three failing jewellery shops, but those shops *were* in prime London locations. The current recession meant that the property market had all but collapsed; he knew Peter Reynolds had tried and failed to sell the shops, and that now his creditors had run out of patience, but eventually the financial climate would improve and the shops would be lucrative investments.

Thanos's business brain told him he would be a fool to turn down the opportunity to increase his property portfolio—and wouldn't his revenge be all the sweeter if he made it personal? Buying out Reynolds Gems would save Tahlia from financial ruin, but he would demand repayment in full—in his bed!

The tense silence stretched Tahlia's nerves, and her skin prickled beneath Thanos's intent gaze. He appeared relaxed, but he reminded her of a panther: sleek, dark and dangerous as it eyed its prey. She had to get out of his office, she thought wildly. Gather what little dignity she had left and leave.

She retrieved her briefcase from the floor, where she had dropped it, and turned towards the door.

'There might be a way I could be persuaded to buy Reynolds Gems…'

His soft drawl stopped her in her tracks, and she swung back to face him, her heart thumping. It was probably a trick, she told herself, or a joke at her expense, but she was desperate for a lifeline—however tenuous.

'How?' she demanded baldly.

'The time-honoured tradition of bartering—each of us has something the other wants,' he elucidated, when she stared at him blankly. 'It's possible we could negotiate a deal.'

Tahlia frowned. 'What do I have that you want? I have nothing.'

Dark eyes burned into her, and she felt a fierce tugging sensation deep in her pelvis. 'Don't be naïve, Tahlia,' he said, in a faintly bored tone. 'You know perfectly well what I want.' He crossed the room in two strides and slid his hand beneath her chin, holding her prisoner and forcing her to meet his gaze. *'You,'* he said bluntly. 'I want to take you to bed and enjoy the delectable body that you share so willingly with your numerous lovers.' He ignored her gasp of outrage and continued coolly. 'In return for your sexual favours I am prepared to buy Reynolds Gems for the full asking price.'

A bubble of hysteria rose in Tahlia's throat. She had been right; it *was* a cruel joke. But there had been no hint of amusement in Thanos's voice, and the feral heat in his eyes scorched her skin. 'But…you don't like me,' she faltered, picking from the random threads of thought that whirled in her head.

That did seem to amuse him, and he laughed derisively. 'It is not necessary for me to *like* you. I want to have sex with you; I'm not suggesting that we become best friends.'

Tahlia flushed at his mockery. 'I have always thought that lovers should also be friends.' Thanos could not have made it clearer that he was only interested in using her body for his sexual satisfaction. 'I am not a piece of meat,' she told him scathingly, 'and I am not for sale.'

Thanos's eyes narrowed. How dared Tahlia speak to him in that contemptuous tone when, according to the press reports, she dropped her knickers for any Z-list celebrity who gave her the time of day?

'Everything and everyone is for sale for the right price,' he told her mockingly. 'You should be grateful of my offer. Who else do you think will be prepared to shell out a six-figure sum for a failing company? That's a damn good rate for even the most inventive hooker. And besides,' he drawled, tightening his grip on her chin when she tried to jerk out of his grasp, 'we both know you would not find it such an ordeal to share my bed. You might want to deny the sexual chemistry that burns between us, but your body is more honest.'

At that moment Tahlia would have given her life to deny his sardonic taunt, but from the moment he had moved close to her the exotic tang of his aftershave, mixed with another subtle masculine scent, had pervaded her senses and lit a flame inside her. Her breasts felt heavy, and she caught her breath when he trailed his free hand down her front and discovered the hard peaks of her nipples jutting beneath her silk blouse.

Anger was her only weapon against the insidious warmth that licked through her veins. He thought she was no better than a prostitute. She would not, *could* not give in to the voice in her head which urged her to agree to his outrageous proposal. It would be devastating to lose Reynolds Gems, but far worse to sacrifice her pride and her self-respect.

'Hell will freeze over before I agree to your disgusting suggestion,' she snapped.

He shrugged. 'Are you prepared to stand by and allow your father to lose the company he has devoted his life to for the past thirty years?'

Tahlia swallowed the lump that had formed in her throat. 'Emotional blackmail is despicable. My father would never expect me to sell my body, even if it means losing everything he owns. You seem to think that your wealth gives you special privileges. Obviously you were born with a silver spoon in your mouth,' she flung at him, remembering that Crispin Blythe had said that Thanos was a billionaire. 'You believe your money can buy you anything. But it can't buy me.'

'In that case I may as well take what you give away freely to so many other men,' he bit out savagely, seizing her shoulders and slamming her against his chest. He lowered his head and captured her mouth with bruising force. Tahlia gave a shocked cry, and he took advantage of her parted lips to thrust his tongue between them, exploring her with a bold eroticism that made her tremble. Anger came to her rescue and she pushed against his chest, but he merely tightened his arms around her until she felt as though she were trapped in a vice. She was determined not to respond to him, but he seemed to sense her resolve and eased the pressure of his mouth a fraction, changing the kiss from one of domination to a sensual tasting that she found utterly irresistible.

She felt as though her bones were dissolving. Her legs no longer seemed capable of bearing her weight, and she sagged against him, relaxing her balled fists and splaying her hands over his chest, feeling the heat of his body through his shirt. She felt his fingers slide up her nape and with a deft movement he released the pins from her chignon so that her hair uncoiled and fell in a scented silky curtain around her shoulders. He made a muffled noise in his throat and buried his hands in her hair, angling her head while he deepened the kiss. She responded helplessly, closing her eyes as she sank deeper into the velvet softness of his caress.

Lost in a world of sensory pleasure, she was unprepared when he suddenly lifted his head and stared down at her. The cold contempt in his dark eyes doused her in a wave of humiliation as she realised that she was clinging to him.

'My offer still stands,' he said coolly.

She jerked away from him, tears of shame burning her eyes. There was no evidence in his mocking expression that he had been stirred by the kiss, while *she* was a seething mass of emotions and could not disguise the effect he had on her.

'My answer is still the same,' she said curtly. 'I am not for sale.'

She was sure he would taunt her with the fact that she had offered no resistance when he had kissed her again, but he shrugged uninterestedly and flicked back his cuff to glance at his watch.

'In that case I believe we have covered everything,' he said coolly. 'Perhaps you'll have better luck securing a rescue plan for Reynolds Gems elsewhere?'

He must know that her father had approached a number of banks for help and had been refused. But pleading with him would be utterly pointless, and would decimate what little dignity she had left. Somehow she forced her limbs to move, snatched up her briefcase, and even managed to bid him a cool goodbye before she swept out of his office with her head held high, determined to deny him the pleasure of witnessing her utter devastation.

Tahlia caught the tube back to Bond Street on auto-pilot, stunned by the events that had taken place in Thanos's office. She could not believe he had made the foul suggestion that she should sleep with him in return for him buying Reynolds Gems. When she had first met him at the art gallery her instincts had warned her that he was ruthless, but now she knew just what kind of a man he was: a man who would pay for sex with a woman who he had admitted he despised. Unquestionably she had made the right decision when she had turned him down. There was no way on earth she would ever agree to be Thanos Savakis's whore. She was furious with herself for allowing him to kiss her—and worse by far was the fact that while she had been in his arms she had forgotten everything—even her mother.

Her phone rang as she walked into her office, and her heart lurched when she saw that the caller was her father. 'Is it good news?' she asked him tensely, hardly daring to breathe as she waited for his reply.

'The best,' he assured her gently. 'The consultant gave your mother the all-clear.'

Tahlia could hear the relief in Peter Reynolds's voice, and tears stung her eyes. 'Thank God,' she whispered shakily. 'Mum must be overjoyed.'

'We both are,' Peter said in a choked voice. 'We're going out to dinner tonight to celebrate—my credit card can just about take it. Will you come?' He hesitated, and then added, 'There's something I need to discuss with you.'

'Of course I'll come,' Tahlia agreed, puzzled by her father's tone. Her mother had beaten cancer and the world was suddenly a wonderful place, so why did he sound so tense? 'Dad, what's the matter?'

There was another long pause before Peter spoke. 'I've had a letter from the bank, threatening to repossess Carlton House.'

'What?' Tahlia's legs gave way and she dropped onto a chair. 'What do you mean? I don't understand. How can the bank repossess Carlton when you and Mum jointly own it?'

'I had to remortgage the house as well as take the loan when we refurbished the shops,' Peter explained flatly. 'Your mother agreed to it because I assured her it was just a temporary solution to a cashflow problem with the company, and she thinks I've already repaid it. I was hoping the bank would give me some leeway, but I'm behind with the repayments and they are demanding I pay the arrears immediately. 'There's no money left, Tahlia. I've used every penny of my personal savings trying to keep Reynolds afloat. I hope to God Vantage Investments are serious about buying Reynolds Gems,' he said thickly, 'because if not I will be solely responsible for losing Carlton and breaking your mother's heart. How did the meeting go?' he asked; a note of desperation audible in his voice. 'Steven Holt sounded pretty keen when I spoke to him a few days ago.'

Tahlia's brain seemed to have stopped functioning. Her parents could not lose Carlton House. It was inconceivable.

In her mind she pictured the graceful old manor house that had been built during the reign of Elizabeth I and which had been passed down through her mother's family for generations. The house was a listed building and had been a serious drain on her parents' finances for years, but they had swiftly dismissed any idea that they might be better to sell Carlton and move to a smaller house which required less upkeep.

Her mother would be utterly heartbroken if she was forced to move from the home she loved now, and after the past two gruelling years of fear and chemotherapy she did not deserve to suffer further misery.

'Yes.' She uttered the word instinctively, because she could not bring herself to say no—to reveal that the meeting had not gone as she or her father had expected, and that the CEO of Vantage Investments had been instructed to sound enthusiastic about buying out Reynolds by Thanos Savakis, head of Vantage's parent company Savakis Enterprises, a man whose only agenda was revenge.

'As you said, it was only a preliminary meeting. There are still a few points to discuss before a buy-out is absolutely certain. Leave things with me while you concentrate on Mum,' she added hurriedly. 'Why don't you take her to Cornwall and stay with Aunt Jess for a few days? You could both do with a break, and Jess would love to see you both.'

She gripped the phone, willing herself to remain calm. 'Dad…you're not serious about the possibility of losing Carlton, are you? I mean, there has to be a way…'

'The only way I can settle the debt on the house is by selling the company,' Peter said flatly. 'A while back there were a couple of other firms who were interested in buying Reynolds, but I turned them down because Vantage Investments offered the best deal. If Vantage should change their mind I'm sunk. The bank is putting pressure on me, and there's no time to find a new buyer. You say that a few things need to be ironed out? I think I should call Steven Holt.'

'*No.*' Tahlia fought to keep the panic from her voice. If her father phoned Vantage he would learn from Thanos that there was no deal and never had been, that the offer to buy Reynolds had just been part of a cruel trick designed to punish *her.* This was her fault, she thought despairingly. If Vantage had not approached her father he would have sold Reynolds to one of the other firms who had been interested, and Carlton House would be safe.

'*Are you prepared to stand by and allow your father to lose the company...?*' Thanos's voice mocked her. The thought had torn her apart, but she had rejected his solution, vowing to find another way to save Reynolds. The defeated note in her father's voice now made it clear there was no other way. It was not simply the company that was in danger but Carlton House, and her parents' happiness and peace of mind.

'*Each of us has something the other wants.*' Thanos was a billionaire who had the means to buy Reynolds, and in return he wanted...

A tremor ran through her. He wanted to have sex with her. She couldn't do it, she thought wildly. But hard on the heels of that thought came the acknowledgement that she had no choice. Her father had admitted he was at rock bottom, and she was at the limit on her own overdraft and credit cards. She could not raise enough money to cover one mortgage repayment on Carlton, let alone clear the arrears.

'There are just a couple of minor points that need clarification before Vantage agrees to the deal,' she told her father, forcing herself to sound calm. 'I'll get back to them and sort it out. Can I speak to Mum?' she asked quickly, before her father could argue.

'Oh, yes—of course…' There was a moment's silence, and then Vivienne's voice sounded down the line.

'Tahlia! Isn't it wonderful?' she said tremulously. 'I feel as though I've been given a second chance at life.'

The raw emotion in her mother's voice tore at Tahlia's heart, and she swallowed the tears that clogged her throat. 'I hope you enjoy every minute of it, Mum,' she whispered. 'You and Dad deserve to be happy.'

And she would do everything in her power to help them, she vowed fiercely as she put down the phone. Even the unthinkable.

Thanos emerged from the *en suite* bathroom and padded across the bedroom to answer the phone, his brows lowering in a frown as he listened to the message relayed by the receptionist. He hesitated for a few moments, wondering why Tahlia Reynolds was standing in the lobby of his hotel at eleven o'clock at night, and silently acknowledged that he was intrigued.

'Inform Miss Reynolds that I will see her in my suite in fifteen minutes,' he murmured, before he replaced the receiver. It wouldn't hurt Tahlia to cool her heels, and if the reason for her unexpected visit was sufficiently important she would wait until he was ready to see her. He also needed to get dressed—unless he intended to greet her wearing nothing but a towel around his hips. When he recalled his body's involuntary reaction to her at their last meeting it was clear that clothes were a necessity, he conceded, his mouth curving into a self-derisive grimace.

To his annoyance his curiosity grew over the following quarter of an hour, and after pouring himself a liberal malt Scotch he paced restlessly around his suite. What did Tahlia want? Had she, after all, decided to offer her body in return for him saving her father from financial ruin? His mouth twisted as he recalled her scathing refusal to sell herself to him earlier in the day. Her reaction had surprised him, he acknowledged. He had first-hand evidence that she had the morals of an alley cat, and the recent story of her affair with another married actor was not the first time her love-life had been reported in the press.

He had been certain that she would agree to sleep with him in return for his agreement to buy Reynolds Gems, but instead she had looked as scandalised as if she were a vestal virgin—which was a laughable notion, he thought sardonically.

*'Hell will freeze over before I agree to your disgusting suggestion,'* she'd flung at him with icy scorn. So why was she here now? Undoubtedly she wanted something. In his experience women always did, he thought cynically. He stared out of the window at the night-time view of London: the myriad lights of buildings and cars glowing like bright jewels against the black velvet sky, the illuminated London Eye sparkling like an enormous static Catherine wheel. His mind flew back six months to another hotel—this time in Athens—and another woman whose visit had been unexpected.

He had been shocked when Yalena had phoned him out of the blue and suggested they meet up. Fifteen years had passed since the woman he had loved had broken off their engagement and married his best friend, and he admitted he had been curious to gauge his reaction when he met Yalena and Takis again. But Yalena had come to his hotel alone, dressed like a tart and clearly confident that Thanos would not turn down her offer to leave her husband for him. She had made a mistake all those years ago, she had told him tearfully. She realised now that she loved him, not Takis—although Thanos noted that she had only arrived at that conclusion since his name had been included on the list of the world's top one hundred richest men.

Yalena had been dismissive of the fact that her husband

adored her, and worked hard to give her a good lifestyle, and Thanos had felt a mixture of disgust and disappointment that he had been so wrong about her. For years he had put her on a pedestal—the discovery that she was an avaricious gold-digger, just like every other woman he had ever met, had filled him with contempt and the bitter realisation that he had been a fool to waste his emotions on her.

The knock on the door dragged him from his memories. Tahlia was here. He finished the whisky, savouring its warmth as it slid down his throat. What would he do if she *had* come to offer herself to him? He felt a tightening sensation in his groin, and his nostrils flared as sexual heat flooded through him. He wanted her badly, and he could afford her. Why not indulge himself? he brooded. He hadn't had sex for months. Combining visiting Melina in hospital with running a billion-pound company had meant that he'd had neither the time nor the inclination for his usual meaningless sexual liaisons with lovers who knew better than to expect commitment from him. Celibacy did not suit him, he owned as he strode across the suite. His body felt taut, hungry for satisfaction, and antici-pation licked in his veins.

The door of Thanos's suite swung open and Tahlia wondered if he could hear her heart beating frantically against her ribs.

'Tahlia,' he greeted her coolly.

His heavily accented voice caused a delicious little shiver to run down her spine, and at the same time exacerbated the tension that had shredded her nerves during the fifteen minutes she had been forced to wait downstairs in the bar. He stood back for her to enter, and for a few seconds her resolve wobbled, and she was tempted to turn tail and flee. But somehow her legs continued to propel her forward—like a lamb into the wolf's lair, the voice in her head whispered as she moved into the centre of the room. Another tremor ran through her when she heard the click of the door closing behind her.

'You are the mistress of surprise,' Thanos drawled as he strolled towards her.

'What do you mean?' she queried sharply, colour storming into her cheeks. The word *mistress* touched a raw nerve. Thanos believed she had been James Hamilton's mistress. He assumed that she was sexually experienced. The fact that she was not made what she was about to do even harder.

'I did not expect to see you at the art gallery, and I did not anticipate you turning up here tonight.' Nor had he anticipated his reaction to her when he had opened the door—the way his heart had slammed in his chest at the sight of her, looking utterly exquisite in the same blue silk gown she had been wearing the other evening. His desire for her weakened him, and he resented the effect she had on him. 'What do you want, Tahlia?' he demanded tersely, moving away from her to avoid the subtle drift of her perfume that teased his senses.

Tahlia shot him a quick glance that encompassed his black silk shirt, open at the throat to reveal a few inches of bronzed skin covered with crisp, dark hairs, and his superbly tailored black trousers which drew her attention to his lean hips and muscular thighs. The table lamps placed strategically around the room emitted a soft apricot glow that threw his sculpted cheekbones into sharp relief and danced across his gleaming jet-black hair.

He was unfairly gorgeous, and her stomach muscles clenched as she relived those moments in his office when he had crushed her against his body and his lips had claimed hers with untamed passion. No woman would ever tame Thanos, she brooded. Beneath his veneer of urbane sophistication she sensed power and ruthless ambition, a magnetism that com- manded the respect of other men and drew beautiful women to him in droves—yet none would own him or control him, and only the most foolish would try.

The expression on his coldly handsome face was not encouraging, but she had spent the evening listening to her mother's excited chatter about her plans for the garden at Carlton House while her father had looked increasingly strained and haunted. She had finally accepted that she would do whatever it took to prevent her parents from losing their home.

Her mouth felt dry. She licked her lips nervously and prayed that when she spoke her voice would not waver. She did not want him to know how much this was costing her. 'I've come to tell you that I accept your offer,' she said baldly, lifting her head and meeting his midnight gaze steadily. 'I'll sleep with you in return for you buying Reynolds Gems, for the price my father stipulated to Vantage Investments.'

# CHAPTER FOUR

FOR several long, agonising seconds Thanos said nothing, but then his brows rose and he drawled mockingly, 'I will expect you to do rather more than *sleep* in return for paying a fortune for your family's failing company.'

His body had reacted predictably to the knowledge that Tahlia was his for the taking; his arousal had been instant and uncomfortably hard. But inexplicably he'd also felt a surge of savage disappointment. When she had rejected his offer earlier that day he'd felt a grudging sense of admiration for her, but now he felt nothing but contempt. She was prepared to sell her body to protect her financial security. She was a gold-digger. He would have no compunction about taking her to bed and sating his inconvenient desire for her.

He dropped his gaze to the low-cut neckline of her dress and the provocative thrust of her breasts. *Theos,* she was beautiful. Heat surged through him and he ruthlessly ignored the faint whisper of regret that it had to be like this, that making love to her would be nothing more than a business transaction. What else could it be? he brooded. He wanted her; she wanted him to bail out her father. It was as simple and clinical as that.

Tahlia caught her breath when Thanos reached out and removed the diamanté clip that secured her chignon. Her hair fell down around her shoulders as soft as silk against her skin, and she watched his eyes darken as he wound a few pale red-gold strands around his fingers. He stayed like that for timeless seconds, his dark eyes scorching her, and then she gasped when his strong arms suddenly closed around her and he jerked her hard against his chest, his dark head swooping and his mouth claiming hers in a kiss of pure possession.

His dominance was absolute as he forced her head back on her slender neck and kissed her fiercely, demanding her complete compliance and proving beyond doubt his mastery. Instinct warned her that Thanos would be a skilled and highly experienced lover, but he had no idea that she was a novice— a virgin who had no real idea of how to please a man.

The hard ridge of his arousal nudging insistently against her thigh was proof that he wanted her, and his low growl of satisfaction when he slid his tongue deep into her mouth filled her with a mixture of apprehension and feminine triumph that she could have such an affect on him. Her senses were swamped by the subtle scent of his aftershave, and fire licked through her veins when she placed her hands on his chest and traced the bunched muscles beneath his shirt. He was so intensely, intoxicatingly male, and he aroused feelings inside her that no other man had ever made her feel.

But the voice of caution in her head, which she had ignored during the taxi ride to his hotel, was demanding to be heard.

This had gone way too far. She should never have started it in the first place, she thought frantically when he finally broke the kiss and drew back a fraction to stare down at her, his eyes glittering with sexual hunger. She ran her tongue over her lips; swollen and sensitive from the unsparing pressure of his mouth, and felt a lightning flare of reaction at her mental image of him making love to her. Her decision to offer herself to him had been born of a desperate desire to help her father.

But to sell herself to a man who despised her, who made no effort to disguise his contempt of her? That was beyond desperation—it was insane.

She opened her mouth to tell him she had made a horrendous mistake. But as she was about to utter the words a picture flashed into her mind of her mother as she had been a few months ago, painfully thin and fragile, with a silk scarf wrapped around her head to disguise the fact that she had lost her hair after numerous bouts of chemotherapy. Tonight, Vivienne had still looked fragile, but her head was now covered in baby-fine curls and her smile had been that of a woman who had cheated death and was looking forward to the rest of her life. Her parents had suffered enough, Tahlia thought fiercely. She could not sit back and allow them to lose their home.

'You don't come cheap, Tahlia,' Thanos murmured, with a deliberate inflexion on the word *cheap* that brought a flush of colour to her cheeks. 'Before I agree to pay such a substantial sum for Reynolds Gems, I think it only fair that I should see what I'm getting for my money.'

'I don't understand,' she faltered, snatching a sharp breath when he hooked his finger beneath the shoulder strap of her dress and drew it down her arm.

'I think you do,' he said softly. 'Your dress is charming, but I want to see what is beneath the pretty packaging. Take it off,' he ordered, when she remained rigidly unmoving.

*End this now,* the sensible voice in Tahlia's head urged frantically. *Tell him you've changed your mind, and get out of here fast.*

And then what? demanded the reckless voice inside her that she had not known existed until tonight. Go back to her parents and watch her father's emotional devastation as he broke the news to her mother that they would have to leave Carlton House?

She stared wildly at the door while her mind engaged in a fierce debate. Go—or stay, and sell her soul to the devil?

'How can I be certain that you will buy Reynolds Gems?' she asked Thanos shakily. 'I need some sort of assurance.'

'My word is the only assurance I'm prepared to give.' Thanos's eyes narrowed when she opened her mouth to argue. 'Take it—or leave it,' he shrugged uninterestedly. 'We can call the deal off.'

Tahlia's brain was racing. She had no option but to take him at his word. He was calling the shots. One night in his bed would mean that her parents' retirement would be free from financial worries. They need not know what she had done to secure their future. No one would know apart from her. And faced with the choice of sacrificing her self-respect or ensuring her parents' happiness there was no contest.

Without giving herself time to reconsider, she reached behind her and slowly slid the zip of her dress down her spine. She shot him a lightning glance, and her stomach dipped when she found him watching her intently, the expression in his dark eyes unfathomable. Don't think. Just get it over with, she told herself. And, taking a deep breath, she drew the straps of her dress down, revealing inch by inch the silver-grey strapless bra she was wearing beneath. She prayed he could not see that her hands were shaking. For this one night she must play the part of seductive temptress.

Her silk dress whispered against her skin as she drew it down over her stomach and hips and allowed the material to slither down her thighs and pool around her ankles. Her French knickers matched her bra, and her stockings were gossamer fine, topped with a wide band of lace which secured them around her slender thighs. She stepped carefully over her dress, terrified that she would stumble on her four-inch stiletto heels. She could not bring herself to look at him, but he slid his hand beneath her chin and tilted her face to his. The sultry gleam in his eyes filled her with trepidation, and at the same time a fierce jolt of shameful excitement.

She was exquisite, Thanos acknowledged, his heart kicking in his chest. He hated himself for his reaction to her, for the urgent tide of desire that swept through his body that weakened and unmanned him. He knew Tahlia possessed the morals of a whore, and he knew the pain she had caused his sister, but his awareness of her consumed him and overrode every other consideration but his need to make love to her.

He inhaled sharply, re-imposing control over his hormones, and trailed his eyes over her in a cool assessment.

'Very nice,' he drawled, watching in fascination as twin spots of colour flared on her pale cheeks. Her ability to blush at will was a useful trick in her armoury, as was her air of innocence, he reminded himself impatiently. But he could not prevent himself from reaching out and tracing the fragile line of her collarbone. Her skin felt like satin beneath his fingertips, and her long pale amber hair fell in a curtain of silk around her shoulders. He brushed it aside to reveal the slender column of her throat, then lowered his mouth to the pulse beating frenetically at its base. She smelled divine, her light floral perfume tantalising his senses and driving every thought from his head other than his burning need to possess her.

Tahlia held her breath when Thanos trailed his lips along her jaw in a feather-light caress that sent a tremor through her. Was he going to make love to her right now? Remove her bra and knickers and stroke his strong hands over her naked body before tugging her down onto the sofa? His mouth was tantalisingly close, and the gleam in his eyes filled her with apprehension—and at the same time a wild and uncontrollable excitement. There was no point in kidding herself; she wanted him to kiss her. She snatched a frantic little breath as he slowly lowered his head.

He claimed her mouth in a kiss of determined intent, forcing her lips apart and thrusting his tongue between them to explore her with erotic thoroughness. To her shame, Tahlia was lost from the first touch; he was so big and powerful, and she knew that if she fought him she would lose. Besides, she did not *want* to fight him, she acknowledged with searing honesty. Heat was coursing through her veins, and she felt boneless and supremely conscious of the melting warmth pooling between her thighs.

He increased the pressure of his mouth and slid one hand into her hair, while the other roamed up and down her body, skimmed her hips and slender waist, then curled around one breast. The brush of his thumb pad over her nipple caused it to harden beneath her sheer lace bra.

She had not expected the firestorm of emotions that raged through her. Her whole body seemed to be burning up, and the throbbing hardness of Thanos's arousal thrusting into her pelvis turned the fire into a raging inferno. She slid her hands over his chest, feeling the heat of his body through his silk shirt, and suddenly it was not enough. She wanted to feel his bare flesh beneath her fingertips. Fingers shaking slightly, she began to unfasten his buttons, revealing olive-gold skin covered with fine dark hairs, but before she had reached halfway down his abdomen he lifted his head, and his hands closed over hers in a vice like grip.

'Your eagerness to share my bed is flattering,' he drawled, watching dispassionately as colour surged into Tahlia's cheeks. 'But we have an early start in the morning, and I prefer to wait and enjoy you at my leisure.'

He had known from the moment he had taken her in his arms that one night would not be enough to pacify the ravenous beast that had taken charge of his body, Thanos acknowledged. His desire for her was beyond anything he had experienced with any other woman, and he would not be satisfied with a hurried sex session—a few snatched hours of pleasure before he left for an urgent business meeting tomorrow. For reasons he could not fathom Tahlia was a drug in his veins, and he intended to make her his mistress for as long as it took to slake his hunger for her.

'*We* have an early start?' Tahlia mumbled, so excruciatingly embarrassed by her ardent response to him and his cool rejection of her that she wanted to crawl away and die. 'I don't understand.' Had he changed his mind about wanting her? Sick fear surged through her. Had he ordered her to take off her dress because it had amused him to tease her before he revealed that he would not buy Reynolds Gems?

'It's quite simple,' he told her, picking up her dress and handing it to her. His harsh, 'Cover yourself,' brought another flare of scorching colour to her cheeks. 'I'm flying to the Greek island of Mykonos to visit my new hotel first thing in the morning—and you're coming with me. I shall require your services for one month,' he continued smoothly, ignoring Tahlia's gasp of shock. 'That should satisfy my more basic urges. I've no doubt I'll have grown bored of you after you've shared my bed for a few weeks.'

'I'm not going anywhere with you and—and certainly not for a month,' Tahlia stammered when she finally found her voice. She wobbled precariously on her high heels as she stepped into her dress and tugged it up over her hips, with scant regard for the fragile material. She thrust her arms through the straps, gasping when Thanos spun her round and slid the zip up the length of her spine.

He swung her back to face him and cupped her chin in his hand, forcing her to meet his sardonic gaze. 'You are exceptionally lovely, Tahlia, but even *you* must admit that a six-figure sum for one night of sex with you would be an extravagance—even for a billionaire.'

She blanched at the flare of contempt in his eyes, and accepted that she had taken leave of her sanity when she had agreed to sell herself to him. 'I have responsibilities here—commitments, a job…' Although she would not have one for much longer if Thanos bought out Reynolds Gems, she acknowledged dismally. The future was frighteningly uncertain. 'I can't spend a month in Greece with you,' she said dully. 'It's impossible.'

Thanos shrugged and withdrew his mobile phone from his trouser pocket. 'That's a pity, because I was just about to call Steven Holt and instruct him to proceed with buying Reynolds Gems. But if you've changed your mind I'll tell him not to go ahead.'

She was halfway across the room, heading for the door. But his words stopped her in her tracks. She turned slowly back to face him, her brain whirling. 'You can't phone him now—it's almost midnight,' she pointed out.

'I can do whatever I like,' he informed her, with a supreme arrogance that took her breath away. 'I did not make my fortune by working nine till five. My employees know that I expect them to be available whenever I need them.'

Presumably he would have the same expectation of her if she went to Greece with him? A tremor ran down Tahlia's spine at the thought. She could carry on walking out of the door and out of Thanos's life—and all her instincts were screaming at her that she *should* walk away—but he was offering her the chance to save Carlton House from repossession, the voice in her head argued. The price was high. Could she survive a month as Thanos's mistress? What was one month compared to the rest of her parents' lives?

She snatched a breath and squared her shoulders as she met his hooded gaze. 'I want written assurance that you will honour our deal. I'm afraid I don't trust your word.'

Anger surged through Thanos at her disdainful tone, but he refrained from pointing out that she was not in a position to demand anything. 'My legal team will take care of it,' he told her dismissively. 'Would you like your duties to be listed—how many times a night I will expect you to pleasure me, perhaps a description of positions…?'

'That won't be necessary,' Tahlia said sharply, conscious that her face was burning hotter than a furnace. 'I just want to be sure my father's financial worries will be over.'

'How very altruistic of you,' he murmured sardonically.

She frowned. 'What's that supposed to mean?'

He crossed to the door and held it open. 'Don't waste your breath trying to convince me that your desire to save Reynolds Gems from bankruptcy is to help your father. You have expensive tastes,' he drawled, sliding his finger over the diamanté strap of her dress and then trailing an insolent path down to her cleavage. 'Your sole interest is in ensuring your own financial security—isn't it, Tahlia?' He paused, his eyes narrowing as he glimpsed the sudden shimmer of her tears, and for a second something tugged at his insides at the knowledge that he had hurt her. He dismissed the thought ruthlessly. She deserved to be hurt—just as she had hurt Melina. 'I'll drive you home,' he said brusquely, standing aside for her to precede him out of his suite. 'You need to pack.'

There was simply no point in arguing with him, Tahlia accepted miserably as she followed him into the lift. Thanos had judged her, and he was so pig-headed that nothing she did or said would change his opinion of her. But she had glimpsed the flare of feral hunger in his eyes before his lashes swept down and hid his expression. He desired her, and he had agreed to buy Reynolds Gems in order to have her in his bed for one month. She could only pray that she would not spend the rest of her life regretting her decision to become his mistress.

After giving Thanos stilted directions to her flat Tahlia lapsed into silence, and he seemed to be lost in his own thoughts.

'I'll pick you up at eight o'clock tomorrow morning,' he told her as he parked outside her flat. 'Don't keep me waiting. And Tahlia?' he called, when she flung open the car door and hurried up her front path. 'Remember the reason why you're accompanying me on this trip and pack accordingly, won't you? I'm already fantasising about seeing you in sexy underwear like the tantalising wisps of lace you're wearing tonight.'

Face flaming, she bit back a retort which would have singed his ears and stepped into her flat, slamming the front door behind her and sagging against it. What *had* she done? she thought despairingly, burying her face in her hands as the enormity of the deal she had struck with Thanos sunk in. She had saved her parents from the devastation of losing their home, she reminded herself grimly. And with that thought in mind she dug out a suitcase from the cupboard under the stairs, pulled open her wardrobe and began to sort through its meagre contents for outfits suitable to take to Greece.

'Are you ready?' Thanos demanded curtly, when she opened the door to him at one minute past eight the following morning.

'Almost,' she muttered, annoyed that her heart immediately began to race at the sight of him, in a lightweight stone-coloured jacket and trousers, teamed with a cream shirt which was open at the throat so that she could see a tantalising V of bronzed skin. His black hair gleamed like jet in the early morning sunshine, and his beautifully sculpted features and sensual mouth caused a peculiar dragging sensation in the pit of Tahlia's stomach. 'Unfortunately Charlie is proving rather stubborn to persuade out of my bedroom.'

Black eyebrows winged skywards. 'Spare me the details of your tangled love-life,' he drawled, in the sardonic tone she detested.

'Charlie is my cat,' Tahlia informed him tightly. 'He's actually the laziest cat on the planet, and spends most of his time sleeping on my bed.' She noted Thanos's impatient frown and chewed on her bottom lip. 'You'll have to help me get him into the cat-carrier.'

She disappeared through a door and Thanos followed, glancing curiously around her bedroom. He had expected something more…seductive, he mused. The soft lemon walls, pale carpet and floral curtains and bedspread were fresh and pretty, but he could not imagine her entertaining a stream of lovers here.

A hissing sound like a kettle coming to the boil came from under the dresser, and he stared in surprise at the fat ginger cat whose yellow eyes were fixed menacingly on him. Tahlia was on her knees, dangling a rubber toy in front of the cat to tempt it into the carrier.

'Come on, Charlie,' she crooned. 'Come and play.' The hissing grew louder, and the cat suddenly sprang, hooking its claws in Tahlia's hand. 'Quick—grab him!' she yelled.

'You must be joking.' Instead Thanos manoeuvred the carrier over the cat, and after a brief tussle Tahlia managed to deposit the ball of orange fur inside and hastily secured the door. Blood was running down her hand and the cat was still spitting furiously. *'Theos,'* he muttered. 'What breed is it—a wild cat?'

'He's just a bit sensitive,' Tahlia told him seriously. 'I got him from the cat rescue centre, and I think he was badly treated by his previous owners. He's a sweetie, really.'

'I'll take your word for it. You'd better put some antiseptic on that scratch.' Thanos frowned. Giving a home to a stray cat with homicidal tendencies did not fit in with his image of Tahlia, he brooded irritably. He picked up her suitcase and cast another look around her room, pausing at the photograph on the bedside table. 'Is this your brother?' he asked curiously, as he studied the picture of Tahlia and a tall man with bright red hair.

'No, I don't have any siblings.' She slipped on her jacket and flicked her hair back from her face. 'That's Michael. We met on my first day at university, when he told me that redheads should always stick together.' She smiled softly at the memory. 'Michael was studying to be a vet, but he died of meningitis a few months before he graduated.'

Thanos heard the sudden huskiness in her voice. 'Was he your boyfriend?' he queried abruptly, irritated with himself for his curiosity. Tahlia's personal life had nothing to do with him.

She shrugged. 'We'd been dating for a few months.' Over the years she had come to terms with losing Michael, but only her closest friends knew how devastated she had been by his death. She had no intention of confiding in Thanos. She picked up the cat-carrier and glanced at him. 'I'm ready to leave now.'

Tahlia's tone warned Thanos that she did not want to continue the conversation, and he was suddenly impatient to leave. He did not want to hear that she had suffered a tragedy in her past. For the past six months he had envisaged her as a cold-hearted bitch, and he refused to contemplate any possibility that he might have been wrong.

'I hope you're not planning to try and smuggle that cat through Customs?' he said tersely as they walked out to the car.

'Of course not. Hobson is going to look after him. He used to be my parents' butler, but he's semi-retired now, and lives in an annexe of Carlton House,' Tahlia explained. 'We'll have to take Charlie over to him.'

'Is the house on the way to Gatwick?'

'The opposite direction, I'm afraid. But I can't leave Charlie to fend for himself. I guess it's a case of love me, love my cat,' she quipped, as Thanos deposited the cat carrier on the back seat and opened the front passenger door for her.

'Hell will freeze over before I do either,' Thanos said violently.

He fired the ignition and pulled away from the kerb, but his scathing comment hung in the air between them, and Tahlia quickly turned her head and stared out of the window, wondering why her eyes were stinging with stupid tears. Thanos could not make it plainer that he hated her, but she was shocked at how much his contempt hurt.

She said nothing more, apart from giving him directions to Carlton House, and only glanced at him when he drove through the gates and gave a low whistle.

'I see why your parents are so keen to hang on to the house,' he said dryly, as he stared up at the ivy-covered walls and the three storeys of mullioned windows glinting in the sunlight. 'It's spectacular.'

'For many generations it was passed down to the oldest son of the family, but my mother was an only child so she inherited it,' Tahlia explained. 'It's a Grade I listed building, and to be honest the cost of its upkeep is a nightmare. My parents do their best to maintain it, even though it's a drain on their resources, and Mum is very proud of her heritage. She loves Carlton House. It would break her heart to leave it—'

She broke off, blushing at the knowledge that she had agreed to become Thanos's mistress to keep Carlton House safe. The front door of the house suddenly swung open, and an elderly, impeccably dressed man walked slowly down the front steps.

'Who is that?'

'That's Hobson.'

Thanos frowned. 'He can't still work for your parents, surely? He must be ninety.'

'We think he's in his late seventies, although he won't actually admit his true age,' Tahlia explained as she climbed out of the car and took the cat-carrier from the back seat. 'He started working here as a butler for my grandparents; my parents feel that Carlton is as much his house as it is theirs. My father has promised Hobson that he will always have a home here.' Her smile faded as the implication of her words struck her. If Carlton was repossessed, where would Hobson go? He had no family, and he would be as distraught as her parents if he had to leave the house that had been his home for fifty years.

It wasn't going to happen, she reassured herself as she walked up the drive to greet the butler. Thanos had promised to buy Reynolds Gems, Carlton would be safe, and she would take the secret that she had sold herself to him to her grave.

'I was wondering how you had booked me onto a flight at such short notice,' Tahlia murmured an hour later, as she followed Thanos across the tarmac at Gatwick airport. 'I suppose I should have guessed you own a plane.'

'I travel extensively for my business, and the Lear jet is more convenient than relying on scheduled flights,' he replied, his eyes narrowing on her faintly stunned expression as she followed him onto the plane. His lip curled into a sardonic grimace as he watched her glance around at the plush leather seats. Women were always impressed by the jet, and several of his ex-lovers had been eager to join the mile-high club. He could spend the flight to Greece enjoying Tahlia's gorgeous body in the luxurious bedroom at the far end of the plane— she was hardly likely to object, he mused cynically. She had made it clear she would do whatever pleased him in return for him shelling out a lot of money for Reynolds Gems.

He could not deny he was tempted, he thought irritably, and he skimmed his eyes over her, from her silky red-gold hair—worn loose today, and falling in a smooth sheet down her back—to her elegant cream skirt and jacket teamed with a sapphire-coloured blouse which matched the startling blue of her eyes, finally to her shapely legs sheathed in fine hose, their slender length emphasised by her three-inch stiletto heels. She looked cool and classy, and he felt a violent urge to lower his head and kiss her until her lips were no longer coated in a pale gloss but were red and swollen, as she parted them invitingly beneath his, as she had done in his hotel suite the previous night. Beneath her haughty façade this aristocratic English rose was hot, and she had already shown her willingness to explore the sexual chemistry that simmered between them. But he wanted to enjoy her at his leisure. He would have to curb his impatience until they reached Greece.

Four hours later, Tahlia stared out of the window as the plane swooped low over a cobalt-blue sea sparkling beneath a cloudless sky, dotted with several emerald islands. 'I hadn't expected the land to be so green,' she murmured, her spirits lifting as she absorbed the spectacular view of the Cyclades Islands.

'That's Mykonos just ahead of us.' Thanos's deep voice sounded close to her ear, and she jerked her head around to find that he had closed his laptop, which he had been working on for the entire flight. 'The smaller island closest to it is Delos. It is uninhabited, but it's one of the most important archaeological sites in Greece, and is believed in Greek mythology to be the birthplace of the goddess Artemis—hence the name of my new hotel,' he added with a faint smile.

Tahlia's eyes were drawn to the sensual curve of his mouth and her heart flipped. She had been agonisingly conscious of him during the flight, but as soon as the jet had taken off he had become absorbed in his work and not spared her a word or glance. He had not brought her to Greece for her conversational skills, she reminded herself heavily. Her sole duty for the next month was to please him in bed—but considering her lack of experience in that department she feared he was going to be disappointed.

The Artemis Hotel was situated a few kilometres from Mykonos Town, at the charming beach resort of Agios Ioannis. The vast white-walled, flat-roofed building was impressive, and the reception area no less so, with its pale marble floors and pillars teamed with beautiful leather sofas and chairs in muted shades of blue and grey.

'The whole place is stunning,' Tahlia commented when Thanos had given her a lightning tour of the four dining rooms, six bars and the spa and leisure complex.

'I'm pleased with it,' he replied as he led the way along a velvet-carpeted corridor. The walls were hung with numerous works of art, many of them contemporary pieces, and Tahlia wondered if Thanos had bought any of Rufus Hartman's paintings from the art exhibition where they had first met. She grimaced. Was it really only a few days ago? It felt like a lifetime.

'This is my private suite,' he explained as he halted at the end of the corridor and flung open a door.

Tahlia followed him into an airy sitting room, her heart suddenly beating too fast as she glanced through a door to her right and glimpsed a king-sized bed. She wondered if Thanos expected her to begin her duties as his mistress immediately, but he had walked over to the long wall of windows and opened the French doors leading to the terrace. She followed him, and caught her breath at the uninterrupted view of the crystalline sea and an aquamarine swimming pool below them.

'The suite has its own pool,' he explained, indicating the rectangular pool to one side of the terrace. 'The main pool you can see below us is actually a salt-water pool, separated from the sea by a terraced area where guests can sunbathe and enjoy the view of the bay.'

'It's beautiful,' Tahlia murmured as she stared down at the hotel's pool, which had been cleverly designed so that it appeared to spill into the sea beyond. She lifted her face to the sun, her hair rippling in the warm Aegean breeze.

Thanos resisted the urge to wind the silky strands around his hand, pull her in and capture her mouth in a hungry kiss that he knew instinctively could only end when he swept her into his arms and carried her through to the bedroom. She unsettled him more than he cared to admit, and he found his reaction to her intensely irritating. Even forcing himself to think of Melina—now staying at a rehabilitation clinic in the US, where she was slowly learning to walk again—did not diminish his awareness of the woman at his side.

Had his father struggled to control his attraction to the English tart Wendy Jones, who had become his mistress? he brooded. For the first time in his life he understood the guilt associated with wanting a woman when it was morally wrong to desire her.

He swung round abruptly and walked back across the terrace. 'You have the rest of the day to enjoy the view. I have a meeting scheduled with my management team, which I imagine will last for several hours.'

Tahlia frowned, unsure of exactly what her role in his life was to be. 'What do you expect me to do while you're gone?' she asked as she followed him back inside.

He shrugged dismissively. 'Whatever you like. You can swim, or read—all the rooms at the Artemis have a selection of current magazines. And of course you will need to prepare for tonight.'

Tahlia's mouth suddenly felt dry at the prospect of the

night ahead. In what way did he expect her to prepare? Did the Artemis also leave copies of the *Kama Sutra* in the rooms, for guests to flick through? she wondered, panic churning in the pit of her stomach.

Thanos's eyes narrowed on the hectic flush staining her cheeks. 'Tonight we're dining with the mayor of Mykonos and other council dignitaries. You'll need to dress up.' He gave her a mocking smile. 'Wear something sexy, hmm…? After all, the sole reason you are here is to please me.' He gathered up his briefcase, but instead of heading for the door he walked towards her, his mouth curving into an amused smile that was not reflected in his cold eyes. 'You can start by pleasing me now,' he said coolly, and he cupped her chin in his hand and bent his head, bringing his mouth down on hers before she had a chance to pull away.

The kiss was hard, almost brutal, a statement of possession and a warning of intent that tonight he would demand so much more. Tahlia wanted to deny him, wanted to firm her lips against his probing tongue, but to her shame the moment he touched her she was lost, swept up in the fire that consumed them both. She had been acutely aware of him ever since he had picked her up from her flat that morning, and now her senses were set alight by the scent of his cologne and another, totally masculine scent that belonged to this man alone.

He caught her despairing sigh and ruthlessly took advantage of her parted lips to thrust his tongue between them, exploring the moist warmth of her mouth until she was boneless and clung to him, sliding her hands to his shoulders and running her fingers through the thick dark hair that curled at his nape.

He was breathing hard when he finally released her, and Tahlia took a tiny shard of comfort in the fact that he could not hide the evidence that he was affected by the wild passion they shared.

'I'll see you later,' he said tersely, stepping away from her, but she had the impression that his control was balanced on a knife-edge, and that if she gave any indication that she wanted him to stay he would seize her in his arms once more and kiss her until kissing was not enough for either of them.

She remained silent, shocked and ashamed by her reaction to him, and with a curt nod he strode from the room. Only then did she release her breath. It was crazy and utterly inexplicable, she thought shakily as she held her fingers against her swollen mouth. Thanos believed he had good reason to despise her, and she was well aware that his one aim was to punish her. Yet neither of them, it seemed, could control the wildfire sexual attraction which blazed between them.

# CHAPTER FIVE

THERE was no sign of Tahlia when Thanos walked into his private suite that evening, but it was late, and he assumed that she was getting changed for dinner. His meeting had overrun by several long and frustrating hours, and the discovery that preparations for the party to celebrate the official opening of the Artemis were way behind schedule had put him in a foul mood. He needed to have been in Greece these past few months, to oversee the completion of the new hotel, but thanks to Tahlia and his sleazeball ex-brother-in-law he had been at Melina's hospital bedside in the States instead of running his company.

He crossed to the bar and poured himself a large Scotch, added ice to the glass and took a long sip as he strolled onto the terrace. Dusk had fallen, painting the sky in hues of purple and indigo, and the first stars glimmered as brightly as the lights of the tavernas and hotels that delineated the coast. But the peaceful scene did nothing to lift his mood, and when a faint noise from behind him alerted him to Tahlia's presence he swung round, his brows lowering in a slashing frown as he studied her.

'What made you think that dressing like a nun would please me?' he queried, in a dangerously soft tone. He noted her mutinous expression and his mouth curled into a hard smile. 'Or did you deliberately choose your most unattractive outfit to flout me?'

His guess was not too far from the truth, and Tahlia blushed. At the same time she felt a spurt of annoyance at his description of her as unattractive. It was true her faithful black skirt was years old and unfashionably long, and her cream silk-organza blouse with its high neck and a row of tiny pearl buttons running down the front could in no way be called sexy. But she had swept her hair up into an elegant chignon and taken care with her make-up. She didn't think she looked a complete frump. Thanos, however, clearly held a different opinion.

'I'm not taking you to dinner when you look like my maiden aunt,' he said tersely. 'Go and get changed while I shower, and be ready to leave in fifteen minutes.' His brows rose when she did not move. 'Of course I could always strip you myself—but if that happens I can guarantee we will miss dinner altogether.'

Tahlia flushed at the hungry gleam in his eyes. 'You can't tell me what to do. You don't own me,' she said angrily, frantically trying to banish the image of Thanos removing her clothes and then his, and the even more shocking idea of them showering together.

His mocking smile told her he had read her mind, and her insides squirmed in embarrassment. 'For the next month I can do exactly what I like with you,' he warned her, in a voice laced with such blatant sexual intent that a shiver ran the length of her spine. His patience suddenly evaporated, and he caught hold of her hand and marched her across the lounge to the bedroom. 'I'll find you something suitable to wear,' he growled, but his frown deepened when he flung open the wardrobe and flicked through the few outfits she had brought with her.

'Why did you bring so little with you when you knew you

were coming to Greece for a month?' His eyes narrowed. 'Or did you hope I would grow bored of you sooner?' He reached out and tugged the clip from her carefully arranged chignon, so that her hair tumbled around her shoulders. The sultry gleam in his dark gaze sent a tremor through Tahlia's body as stark awareness uncoiled in the pit of her stomach. 'If so, then I fear you will be disappointed,' he murmured, lowering his head so that his breath fanned her lips. 'The sexual chemistry between us is at combustion point, my beautiful English rose, and I am seriously beginning to doubt that one month will satisfy my desire for you.'

His mouth was so close to hers that Tahlia shut her eyes, certain that he was about to kiss her. The exotic scent of his cologne swamped her senses, and there was no thought in her head to resist him. But to her shock he suddenly moved away from her. Startled, she let her lashes fly open, and she found that she was standing with her mouth still parted in readiness for his kiss. The sound of his soft, mocking laughter filled her with mortification at the shameful sense of longing that he would snatch her into his arms and ravage her mouth with primitive passion.

Thanos closed the wardrobe with a decisive snap. 'There is nothing in there that excites me,' he said bluntly. 'You will have to stay as you are tonight, but tomorrow you will go shopping. We'll be attending many social events while we are here and you'll need several evening dresses, as well as daywear.'

Tahlia thought of her latest credit card bill, which she had no means of paying off, and shook her head. 'I can't afford to buy new clothes,' she admitted wearily, her temper flaring at Thanos's sardonic expression. He believed she led the life of a pampered princess, but nothing could be further from the truth. 'The clothes I've brought with me are all that I own. My father hasn't been able to pay my salary for the last three months. Every penny went into keeping Reynolds Gems solvent. I worked for nothing in the desperate hope that we could save the company,' she explained when he looked disbelieving. 'I sold most of my clothes, and my jewellery, but I didn't make enough to cover my bills and living expenses. I'm struggling to cover even the minimum payment on my credit cards, and a shopping spree is out of the question. You'll just have to take me as I am,' she finished defiantly, and then blushed scarlet as she realised what she had said.

'I am very much looking forward to taking you, Tahlia,' Thanos assured her gravely, the glinting amusement in his eyes masking his shock at her assertion that her life in London had *not* been one of luxury and over-indulgence, as he had assumed.

Of course she could be lying, he mused. Experience had taught him that most women were accomplished liars—none more so than Yalena, when she had been sleeping with one of his closest friends at the same time as swearing her love for him. But his gut instinct told him that Tahlia was telling the truth about her financial situation. No wonder she had agreed to be his mistress in return for him buying her father's company, he thought cynically. He knew from the numerous photos of her in the press that she liked to dress in haute couture. No doubt she would spend her share of the proceeds of the sale of Reynolds Gems on restocking her wardrobe.

He glanced at his watch, and then strolled towards the *en suite* bathroom. 'We're running seriously late, so I'll have to wait until tonight for the pleasure of taking you to bed,' he drawled. 'As for shopping—I will be paying for your clothes. Think of it as one of the perks of being my mistress,' he said in a harder tone, when she opened her mouth to argue. 'I want to see you in sexy clothes that flatter your gorgeous body. Not in an outfit that makes you look as though you are auditioning for a role in *The Sound of Music.*'

Dinner was the ordeal Tahlia had expected. In ordinary circumstances she would have enjoyed the stunning décor and the ambience of the Artemis's gold-star restaurant, where a celebrated French chef had prepared four superb courses. But from the moment Thanos led her over to the table where his guests were already seated and introduced her as his 'companion' she felt so painfully self-conscious—everyone must have guessed she was his mistress—that she could do no more than toy with her food.

As well as the dignitaries from Mykonos, three of Thanos's top executives were also present, and although everyone spoke in English rather than Greek, her attempts at conversation with them were stilted. They clearly thought she was a bimbo, and one of the executives, a man Thanos had introduced as Antonis Lykaios, watched her avidly throughout the meal, trailing his eyes over her as if he were mentally undressing her.

Tahlia was torn between longing for the evening to be over and praying that it would last for ever—because what was to come next was certain to be a hundred times worse, she brooded. Her eyes were drawn to Thanos. He looked breathtaking tonight, in a black dinner suit and a white silk shirt, his dark hair swept back from his brow and the flickering light from the table's centrepiece of candles highlighting the sharp edges of his cheekbones. He was urbane, sophisticated, and no doubt a skilful lover, she thought, feeling a rush of shaming heat flood through her when he looked across the table and their glances locked.

The voices around her faded, and she was reminded of the first time she had seen him at the art gallery, when she had felt as though they were the only two people in the universe.

She watched his eyes darken with a sensual promise that made her mouth run dry, and butterflies leapt in her stomach. It was not Thanos she was afraid of, she acknowledged bleakly; it was herself and her pathetic inability to resist him. It was utterly ridiculous to feel so drawn to a man who openly admitted that he despised her, but when she had first seen him at Rufus Hartman's exhibition—before she had learned that he blamed her for his sister's accident—she had felt an emotional bond with him which defied logic or common sense. A voice in her head had whispered that he was the 'the one' she had been waiting all her life to meet.

'Would you like more wine, Tahlia?' Antonis Lykaios leaned towards her, proffering a bottle of Chardonnay, and Tahlia was so grateful for the excuse to drag her eyes from Thanos that she forgot how her skin had crawled when Antonis had leered at her and smiled at him.

Across the table Thanos fought the urge to rearrange his junior executive's handsome face with his fist—before continuing the caveman tactics by throwing Tahlia over his shoulder and carrying her off to his bed. How *dared* she flirt with Lykaios in front of him? he thought furiously. But what had he expected? In recent months the British tabloids had regularly reported on her energetic love-life with Z-list celebrities. Clearly she would flirt with any man under seventy.

He gave a brief nod to his chief executive, indicating that it was time to bring the evening to an end, before his gaze strayed back to Tahlia. His initial opinion that her outfit was unflattering had been wrong, he thought irritably. At first glance she looked chaste and demure in the high-necked blouse, but look closer and it was possible to see the outline of her breasts beneath the sheer material. His fingers itched to unfasten every one of those tiny buttons and slowly reveal her delectable body. With her pale red-gold hair falling in a silky curtain around her shoulders and a subtle pink gloss on her lips she looked incredibly sexy, and he was infuriated by the knowledge that he was not the only man at the dinner table who could not keep his eyes off her.

The dinner party eventually came to an end, and Tahlia stifled a sigh of relief when the guests stood up from the table. Antonis Lykaios seemed to have taken her smile as a sign that she was interested in him; twice she had had to forcibly remove his hand from her thigh beneath the table-cloth, and she forced herself not to flinch now, when he lifted her fingers to his mouth and kissed them in a theatrical farewell gesture. She saw Thanos's brows lower in a slashing frown, and her sense of foreboding escalated when they crossed the marble vestibule to the lift and he surveyed her in a brooding silence as they travelled to the top floor.

'I realise that you automatically flirt with anyone in trousers,' he drawled as followed her into his suite, discarding his jacket and tie and flinging them carelessly over the back of a chair. 'But Antonis Lykaios is engaged, and I will not allow you to sink your predatory claws into him.'

'I pity his fiancée,' she snapped, her temper flaring at the undisguised contempt in his voice. 'Your executive was flirting with *me*, and I'd be grateful if you would tell him to keep his sweaty hands to himself in future.' She closed her eyes against the pain stabbing at her skull, aware that her headache was due as much to the two glasses of wine she had drunk although she had eaten very little dinner, as to her rising nervous tension. Thanos was heart-stoppingly sexy, with his dark hair falling onto his brow, but he also looked grim and forbidding, and the prospect of giving her virginity to him when he had made it plain that he despised her was suddenly unendurable.

She lifted a hand to massage her temples, and pleaded shakily, 'Thanos, can we talk?'

His dark brows lifted in an expression of arrogant amusement. 'Talking is the last thing I have in mind for tonight.' He strolled towards her and drew her hand away from her face. 'We made a deal, Tahlia,' he reminded her, his voice suddenly harsh and his eyes glittering with cold indifference. 'And now the time has come for you to honour your side of it.'

Her heart was thudding so hard that it hurt to breathe. 'Please…' she cried urgently. 'I swear I had no idea that James was married to your sister…'

She was prevented from saying any more when Thanos placed his finger across her lips. 'Save your lies—and your tears.' He surveyed her over-bright eyes dispassionately, and brushed away the single tear that slipped down her cheek with his thumb. 'I'm not taken in by either,' he said savagely, and lowered his head, capturing her mouth in a punishing kiss that sought to dominate as he forced her lips apart with a bold flick of his tongue.

Once again he had moved with the speed of a panther, pouncing for the kill, and once again Tahlia was unprepared for the molten heat that swept through her the instant he touched her. What was wrong with her? she wondered despairingly. Pride dictated that she should remain stiff and unresponsive in Thanos's arms, but he intoxicated her senses so that she could not think logically, and she was conscious only of the slight abrasion of his cheek against hers, the tingling sensation in her breasts as he crushed her against his chest.

Thanos finally lifted his head and stared down at her, his eyes gleaming when she unconsciously traced her tongue over her swollen lips. 'This madness is not mine alone. You feel it too,' he grated, his fury and frustration palpable—and yet Tahlia sensed that his anger was directed as much at himself as her, and she knew that, like her, he was startled by the intensity of the sexual chemistry which blazed between them. 'You are like a fever in my blood,' he said hoarsely. 'I wanted you from the moment I saw you, and now I cannot wait any longer.'

'Thanos…no!' She gave a shocked cry when he moved his hands to the neck of her blouse and wrenched the fragile material apart, so that little pearl buttons pinged in all directions. Before she had time to react he reached around and un-snapped her bra, casting the delicate scrap of lace to the floor so that her small pale breasts were exposed to his heated gaze.

He was breathing hard, and Tahlia watched in fascination as dull colour flared along his magnificent cheekbones. The feral hunger in his eyes made her tremble with a mixture of apprehension and an unbidden shivery excitement. No man had ever looked at her the way Thanos was doing now, and she instinctively tried to cover her breasts with her hands.

He caught her wrists and tugged them down to her sides. 'Don't hide yourself from me,' he said harshly. 'I want to feast my eyes on every inch of your delectable body.'

His words made Tahlia tremble—not with fear, she ac-knowledged, but with a feverish excitement she could not deny. Her heart slammed in her chest when he pushed her hair over her shoulders, then slid his hand down her body and curled his fingers possessively over her breast. She tensed, ex-pecting him to be rough, but his palm was warm on her bare flesh, and when he stroked his thumb-pad across her nipple in a feather-light caress she gasped as exquisite sensation arced through her.

'Not just beautiful, but delightfully responsive,' Thanos drawled.

She blushed scarlet at the undisguised satisfaction in his voice, but her body seemed to have a will of its own, and she could do nothing to prevent the dusky nipples from swelling into taut peaks. He moved his hand to her other breast and rolled the swollen nipple between his thumb and forefinger, sending another lightning bolt of sensation spiralling down to the pit of her stomach. She caught her breath when he tugged her backwards and lowered his head to the slender arch of her body.

He flicked his tongue back and forth over her nipple, building her pleasure to a level that was almost unbearable, and she gave a choked cry when he finally desisted in teasing her and clamped his mouth around the provocative peak. The sensation of him suckling her was so breathtaking that her lashes drifted down and she gave herself up to the storm he was creating, gasping with pleasure when he moved to her other breast and laved the throbbing peak with firm, wet strokes of his tongue.

She was dimly aware of Thanos dragging her skirt over her hips, and he muttered something in Greek in a hoarse tone when he eased away from her and trailed his eyes down from her pouting breasts to her flat stomach, then lower to her black lace knickers and gossamer-fine black stockings. Tahlia held her breath when he placed his hand on the strip of creamy flesh above her stocking-top, and she felt liquid heat flood between her thighs. Was he going to take her here and now? Drag her to the floor and spread her beneath him on the carpet?

Tension gripped her. Until now she had always believed that she would only ever make love when she was in a loving relationship. She had loved Michael, but their gentle romance had still been in its early stages when he had been snatched from her; she had thought she loved James, but he had lied to her, and she was glad she had discovered his treachery before they had become lovers. Maybe it was time she gave up on love, she thought bleakly. There was no love between her and Thanos. Just mistrust and dislike and a searing passion that obliterated every logical thought and demanded to be appeased. She had agreed to have sex with him in return for her parents' financial security and she would not back out now. But it was only fair that she tell him she was not the experienced seductress he believed.

Thanos stared down at Tahlia's semi-naked body and drew a ragged breath, his nostrils flaring as he fought to bring his raging hormones under control. The delicate skin of her inner thigh felt like satin beneath his fingers, and the urge to move his hand higher and slip it beneath her lacy knickers was so strong that it took every ounce of his formidable will-power to deny himself the pleasure of touching her intimately. His brain acknowledged what she had done—how she had hurt Melina—but his body did not seem to care that she that she was an immoral slut, and it was on fire for her.

'Thanos… I have to tell you…' Her voice shook, but he ruthlessly hardened his heart against her.

'But I don't have to listen—and certainly not to more of your lies and excuses,' he said harshly, disregarding her startled cry as he swept her up into his arms and strode towards the bedroom.

Tahlia was shaking so badly she was sure Thanos must feel the tremors running through her body. Perhaps he thought she was trembling with excitement? She could not bear to meet his gaze and see his familiar mocking expression, so instead she curled her arms around his neck, pressing her face against his shoulder while he carried her. It was not too late to stop this, a voice whispered in her head. She could tell Thanos she would rather sell her soul to the devil than trade her body for hard cash. But what about her parents? another voice screamed inside her. How could she allow them to lose their home and the worry-free retirement they deserved?

Thanos shouldered open the door of the master bedroom, strode over to the bed, and laid Tahlia down on the peacock-blue satin bedspread. Her glorious hair fanned across the pillows in a halo of shimmering gold. He could not resist winding a long silky strand around his fingers, and heat surged through him as he lowered his eyes to her breasts and feasted on their milky-pale beauty.

Why Tahlia? he asked himself angrily. He had never wanted any woman the way he wanted her. His desire was mindless, desperate, an irresistible force clamouring to be assuaged, and his body shook with need as he stretched out beside her and pressed his mouth to the fragile line of her collarbone. She tasted of ambrosia, her skin as soft as rose petals beneath his lips, and he could not resist tracing them down her body, pausing at each breast to anoint its blush-pink tip, relishing the feel of her nipples swelling inside his mouth before he moved lower still.

Her sweetly puckered navel invited him to explore it with his tongue. He felt the tremor that ran through her, but she made no effort to touch him, and lay passive while he caressed her, as if she were somehow detached from her surroundings— from him. Anger coiled inside him. Did she think she could simply lie there, as unresponsive as a marble figurine while he took his pleasure? When he had finished with her would she wash herself clean of his touch? Believing that the price she had paid for her parents' house had been worth soiling herself for? He did not want a sacrificial offering, he thought grimly. He wanted her warm and willing in his bed, and he was determined that soon she would be begging for his possession.

Tahlia stiffened when she felt Thanos's hand slip between her thighs. Until the moment he had laid her on his bed she had been cocooned in a curious sense of unreality. It seemed impossible to believe that she had actually agreed to have sex with him, that he really would make love to her. But the feel of his hands and mouth on her skin, moving ever lower down her body, had catapulted her back to reality, and now fear churned in her stomach at the prospect of giving her virginity to him.

Hysteria formed a bubble in her throat as she imagined his reaction if she asked him to be gentle. He was convinced that she had been his brother-in-law's mistress, and she could hear his scathing laughter if she told him that this was her first time. He would not believe her. And if he did—if he realised that she was innocent—he might well reject her and call off their deal. She could not risk that happening. She was going to have to put on the act of a lifetime, she thought numbly, and pretend that she was as experienced as he assumed.

His palm felt warm and faintly abrasive on the sensitive skin of her inner thigh, and she forced herself to relax as he hooked his fingers in the waistband of her knickers and slowly drew them over her hips.

'Beautiful,' he murmured, his voice thick with sexual tension. She felt his hand brush gently through the triangle of gold curls, and her heart slammed in her chest when he ran his finger lightly up and down the lips of her vagina, so that they swelled and opened like the petals of a flower, moist and sweetly scented with her arousal, ready for him to explore her. He leaned over her to claim her mouth in a slow, drugging kiss that lit a flame deep inside her and banished her fears. His lips no longer sought to dominate but were gently persuasive, decimating her resistance so that she opened her mouth beneath his and kissed him back with hungry fervour.

Her breath hitched in her throat when she felt him gently part her, and she heard his low growl of satisfaction when he discovered the slick wetness of her arousal. She felt boneless, mindless, and she allowed him to spread her legs wider, excitement cascading through her when she felt his finger probe her velvet folds and slip between them. How could it be wrong when it felt so utterly and exquisitely right? she wondered dazedly. Instinctively she arched her hips so that he could slide his finger deeper into her, and she could not hold back a moan of pleasure when he stretched her wider and inserted another finger, moving his hand with delicate skill so that she writhed with the pleasure he was creating.

'Undress me.'

The starkness of his command sent a jolt of trepidation through Tahlia, but her apprehension was mixed with irresistible sexual curiosity. His wickedly inventive fingers had aroused her to a fever pitch of desire, and she wanted... She did not know what she wanted, she acknowledged as she shifted her hips restlessly. This was all new to her. Her body felt tense and strung out, and only Thanos could soothe the dragging ache deep inside her.

She fumbled with his shirt buttons, her movements jerky and uncoordinated, but finally she spread the material aside and skimmed her hands over satin skin overlaid with crisp dark hairs. She could feel the heat emanating from him, and her senses flared as she inhaled the sensual musk of his cologne mingled with the subtle perfume of male pheromones. He dominated her mind and captivated her soul so that the world faded and nothing existed but Thanos, and the erotic glide of his hands and mouth over her trembling body.

Her lashes had drifted down, as if she could blot out the reality of what she was doing, but she was aware of him easing away from her as her skin quickly cooled, bereft of the warmth of his powerful body. She opened her eyes to discover that he had stripped down to his underwear. His black silk boxers could not disguise the jutting strength of his arousal, and when her gaze flicked upwards to his face the feral gleam in his eyes caused her heart to miss a beat. There was no going back; the message thudded in her brain, and she licked her suddenly dry lips with the tip of her tongue as he stepped out of his boxers and stood before her, his bronzed, muscle-bound body as beautiful as a work of art, his powerful erection jutting proudly forward as he strode purposefully over to the bed.

'I want you so badly I'm in danger of exploding,' Thanos said hoarsely, his Greek accent sounding very pronounced. His capacity for logical thought had deserted him and his self-control was non-existent, while his body throbbed with a level of need that he had never experienced before. Tahlia's slender, pale beauty summoned him, and the drumbeat of desire pounding in his veins overwhelmed him. 'I apologise for the lack of leisurely seduction, but I have to have you *now*. And you are ready for me, Tahlia,' he said thickly, his voice deepening with satisfaction as he slipped his hand between her thighs and discovered the drenching sweetness of her arousal.

He could not wait, and swiftly donned protection before joining her on the bed. The mattress dipped as he positioned himself over her and pushed her legs wider apart. He surged forward, rubbing the sensitive tip of his manhood against her until she opened for him. She was tighter than he had expected, and as she tensed he hesitated, confused by the sudden flare of panic in her eyes. He frowned and drew back a little, but already her muscles were stretching to accommodate him, drawing him into a velvet embrace so that he could think of nothing but thrusting into her again, deeper this time, so that he filled her with his swollen shaft.

Tahlia's muscles had clenched at the realisation that Thanos was about to join his body with hers. She had always dreamed that this moment would be special, that she would give her virginity to the man she loved. A wave of intense sadness surged up inside her, but there was no time to think or refuse him, and her eyes widened in shock as she felt the hard length of his arousal push insistently against her femininity. She had no choice but to accept him into her.

To her surprise there was no pain, just an unfamiliar feeling of fullness, and she released her breath on a shaky sigh as he drew back a little and then eased forward once more, until their bodies were locked together in the most intimate embrace of all. Thanos was part of her. She had given herself to him. In some deep and elemental way she was now his for all time, she thought wonderingly as he moved inside her, setting a rhythm that she knew instinctively would take her to somewhere wonderful but as yet remained frustratingly out of reach.

Thanos slid his hands beneath her bottom and lifted her hips, driving into her with faster, deeper strokes. There was no tenderness in his actions. This was sex at its most basic, Tahlia acknowledged, urgent and hungry, driving them both towards the edge. She was dimly aware that her breath was coming in shallow gasps, and when she opened her eyes she saw that Thanos's face was a rigid mask, the cords on his neck standing out as he drove relentlessly into her.

'Don't stop…don't stop…' She was unaware of her urgent cries, her whole being concentrated on the insistent throbbing deep in her pelvis.

Thanos snatched a harsh breath, fighting for control, but the battle had been lost from the moment he had penetrated Tahlia's body and found her tight and hot and utterly irresistible. To his utter shock he realised that he could not hold back. It had never happened to him before, this complete loss of self-control, but he could not help it. His mind and body were focused on reaching that magical place where he would experience the release he craved, and with one final savage thrust his control shattered. A primal groan of male satisfaction was wrenched from his throat as his whole body convulsed with pleasure.

For a few moments he remained slumped on top of her, his chest heaving as he dragged oxygen into his lungs. He was still stunned by what had happened, by the tidal wave that had swept through him and demolished his restraint so that he had selfishly snatched his own pleasure.

Shame seared him, and he lifted his head to stare down at her.

'I'm sorry,' he grated harshly.

'For what?' she whispered.

'Don't you know?' He frowned, puzzled by the look of genuine confusion in her eyes. It could not possibly have been her first time, he reminded himself forcefully. He had evidence that she had been James Hamilton's mistress. Her air of innocence was an illusion. Yet he could not forget her expression when he had first thrust into her, the fleeting fear in her eyes that had been replaced by a look of wonderment. Could it be that she had never experienced an orgasm with any of her previous lovers and so did not know what she had missed?

His male pride was hurt by the knowledge that he had been no better than the other men she had slept with. Driven by his overpowering need for satisfaction he had been impatient, had come before she had climaxed. He rolled off her, propped himself up on one elbow, and skimmed his hand lightly over her stomach, down to the cluster of gold curls between her legs. His mouth curved into a small smile when he felt the tremor that ran through her. His hunger for her had overwhelmed him, but now he was sated—temporarily, at least, he acknowledged wryly as his body stirred—and he knew that with patience he could bring her to the peak of ecstasy.

He lowered his head to her breast and flicked his tongue lazily across her swollen nipple, heard her sharply indrawn breath when he drew the reddened crest fully into his mouth and suckled her. She twisted her hips restlessly, and he smiled again against her skin as he moved to her other breast and meted out the same exquisite torture before trailing his lips down over her flat stomach.

'Thanos…? Tahlia murmured uncertainly when he pushed

her legs apart. The knowledge that he was looking intently at the most intimate part of her body was shockingly arousing, and the dragging sensation in her pelvis, which had eased when he had withdrawn from her, uncoiled in a sharp tug of desire. 'No!'

Too late she realised his intention, and gripped his hair, but his tongue was already probing between her silken folds the sensations he was arousing so utterly incredible that her cry of denial faltered.

'Relax, and I will show you what you've clearly been denied by your previous lovers,' he promised thickly.

Mortified, she tried to bring her legs together. But he held them apart and dipped his head once more, the skilled flick of his tongue making her whimper with pleasure. 'You can't,' she pleaded. But he could, and did, and when his lips closed around the tiny, ultra-sensitive nub of her clitoris she sobbed his name and dug her nails into his shoulders, clinging to him as ripples of delight began deep inside her.

He moved swiftly to position himself over her, lifted her hips and drove his powerful erection deep into her, thrusting fast and hard and driving her ever upwards. And now she was almost there, at the place she had sensed the first time he had made love to her. He withdrew almost completely, and then sank into her so deeply that their bodies imploded simultaneously. She gave a startled cry as she experienced wave after wave of ecstasy crashing through her, causing her entire body to tremble with the power of a storm, before slowly ebbing away to leave her spent and utterly replete in his arms.

Dear heaven, she had never known it would be so…so awesome, so astounding. She could not find the words. She curved her hands around Thanos's back, loving the feel of his satiny sweat-slicked skin beneath her palms. He was lying on top of her, his body lax and heavy, but she did not want him to move. The erratic beat of his heart thundering in unison with hers was strangely comforting. Was it possible that in the shattering moments of his climax he had experienced the same feeling that had swamped her—a feeling that their souls had united and soared to a place that was uniquely theirs?

It was just sex, she told herself—awesome, amazing sex. Although admittedly she did not have any other experience to compare it with. But surely it was nothing more than the pairing of two people who were held in the thrall of a powerful sexual chemistry? It would be stupid to allow her emotions to become involved, yet she felt a bond with him that went far beyond the physical intimacy they had shared.

Thanos finally rolled onto his back and stared blindly up at the ceiling, more stunned than he cared to admit by the power of the passion they had just shared, the feeling of oneness that he had never experienced with any other woman. It made no sense. He despised Tahlia, and his contempt for her had intensified when she had agreed to sell herself to him. But instead of telling her what he thought of her he had succumbed to the temptation of her fragile beauty and taken her to bed. Lust had made a fool of him, and now his hatred of himself threatened to choke him. He was no better than his father, he acknowledged bitterly. Kosta Savakis had fallen for the charms of an immoral woman and had abandoned his family for his mistress. And now he, Thanos, had sacrificed his self-respect and had sex with the woman who had broken his sister's heart.

He had bought her, he reminded himself grimly as he swung his legs over the side of the bed, not sparing her a glance as he strode into the *en suite* bathroom. Tahlia was a whore, and he was paying a fortune for her. It would have been damnably disappointing if the sex *hadn't* been good. He stood beneath the shower, but the powerful spray did nothing to ease his tension. Sex with Tahlia hadn't just been good, it had been the best he'd ever had, he conceded. He was already hardening again, anticipation licking through his veins as he snatched a towel and roughly dried his body.

But when he returned to the bedroom he discovered her curled up beneath the sheet, one hand beneath her cheek, her long gold lashes making crescents against her flushed skin. Once again he was struck by her air of innocence, and something indefinable tugged in his gut when he saw a single tear slip silently down her face. The sight of her vulnerability shook him to the core, and in moment of absolute clarity his brain finally accepted what his soul had instinctively known when he had joined his body with hers. He was aware of a curious drumming in his ears, and realised that it was the sound of his blood pounding through his veins. His logical mind grasped at straws, recalling all the tabloid stories he had read about her torrid love-life, but when she lifted her lashes and he saw the hurt in her eyes his heart accepted the truth.

'You were a virgin, weren't you?' he said quietly.

She did not reply, but the sudden flare of colour on her pale cheeks filled him with guilt and remorse, and a whole host of other emotions he could not define.

Anger at his crass stupidity swept through him, and his throat felt as though he had swallowed glass as he rasped, 'Why the hell didn't you tell me?'

# CHAPTER SIX

THE look of fury on Thanos's face inflamed Tahlia's temper and she sat up, glaring at him as she dragged the sheet across her breasts and pushed her hair over her shoulders. 'What would have been the point?' she demanded bitterly. 'You thought I was an immoral slut who had seduced your sister's husband as well as half the male population of London. Would you have believed me if I'd admitted that I was completely inexperienced?'

Somehow her defiant tone, and the way she hastily dashed her tears away with the back of her hand, emphasised her innocence—an innocence he had taken with all the finesse of a boor, Thanos thought grimly, regret searing him as he recalled his impatience when he had made love to her.

'Probably not,' he conceded honestly. 'But *Theos mou…*' He raked his hand through his hair, his frustration palpable. 'Melina found you in bed with James Hamilton.'

'I told you I didn't sleep with him.'

But he hadn't believed her. He had assumed, as Melina had, that Tahlia and James were lovers, Thanos acknowledged. And during the long hours he had sat at Melina's hospital bedside his hatred of Tahlia had made him determined to seek revenge for the pain he had thought she had caused his sister.

'How do you explain all the stories written about you in the tabloids?' he demanded. 'For the past few months rarely a day has gone by without a picture in the British newspapers of you and one of your seemingly inexhaustible supply of boyfriends at yet another social event.'

'I only went to the parties to promote Reynolds Gems,' Tahlia defended herself. 'My father persuaded me to front an advertising campaign, and then he thought it would give a personal touch if people saw me wearing the company's products. Those men weren't my boyfriends. They were male models hired from an agency. It was all part of the image,' she explained, when Thanos looked sceptical. 'I was photographed by the press wearing couture gowns that were loaned to me by design houses and fabulous jewellery from the Reynolds Gems collection, escorted by a handsome partner. But there was never any romance. Most of the models were too in love with themselves,' she added with a grimace.

'So your party princess image was just a PR stunt?' Thanos gave a harsh laugh. He had certainly been convinced that Tahlia was a good-time girl, and he was still struggling to accept that he had unwittingly stolen her virginity. 'What about the other married actor, Damian Casson? Do you expect me to believe that the photos of the two of you leaving a hotel together were also to promote Reynolds Gems?'

'I don't give a damn what you believe,' Tahlia snapped. 'Damian set me up to make his wife jealous, and as I already told you my solicitor has threatened the papers involved with legal action unless they retract their story of our supposed affair. I hate being in the public eye,' she admitted. 'But I would have done anything to help my father. I just wish all those hours I spent on the PR campaign had done some good.'

'It would have taken a miracle to turn around Reynolds' fortunes,' Thanos told her bluntly. 'Your father had made a catalogue of terrible decisions in recent years, and with the current economic crisis bankruptcy was almost inevitable.

'It wasn't his fault.' Tahlia sprang to her father's defence. 'My mother has been seriously ill, and Dad was so busy caring for her that he couldn't concentrate on running the company. He was terrified he was going to lose her…we both were,' she said huskily, emotion clogging her throat as she acknowledged how afraid she had been that her mother would die.

That fear had haunted her every day of the past two years, and it was only now her mother was well again that she realised how much of a strain it had been to keep smiling and encouraging her parents to think positively when inside she had been racked with worry. Tears stung her eyes and she blinked furiously to dispel them. She had cried on the day her mother had been diagnosed, but since then she had suppressed her emotions and focused on helping her mother through her treatment. Now it felt as though a dam inside her had burst, and two years' worth of tears were flooding out.

She desperately did not want to cry in front of Thanos, and she stared down at the sheets while she tried to regain her composure. But the weeks and months of worry about her mother's health, and her fears that her father could lose his company, combined with the emotional trauma of giving her virginity to a man who despised her, had shattered her tenuous hold on her self-control, and she buried her face in her hands in a frantic attempt to muffle the sound of her weeping.

Once the storm had begun, it raged out of control. She did not know how long she cried, and was only vaguely aware of the mattress dipping as Thanos dropped down onto the bed beside her. She stiffened when she felt his hand on her shoulder, unbearably embarrassed by her breakdown but unable to check the sobs that still tore through her body. Her chest hurt, and her head felt as though it were about to explode, but the hand on her shoulder slid up her neck to massage her nape in a soothing motion that gradually calmed her.

'I'm sorry,' she choked at last, scrubbing her eyes with the back of her hand and staring fixedly into her lap, so mortified by her outburst that she could not bring herself to meet his gaze. 'I'm not usually so pathetic.'

The hand on her neck continued its gentle stroking, and when she dared to glance up she discovered that Thanos had donned a black bathrobe and was sitting so close to her that she could see the tiny lines that fanned around his eyes. He was watching her impassively, but she was startled to glimpse the faintest hint of compassion in their depths.

'What was wrong with your mother?' he asked quietly

'She had breast cancer. It was a particularly aggressive form of the disease, and her initial prognosis was not good.' Tahlia took a shaky breath, shocked by the ferocity of the storm that had ripped through her. 'She had surgery immediately to remove the tumour, followed by intensive chemotherapy which left her desperately weak.' She swallowed, wondering why she was confiding in Thanos, but the words kept tumbling out.

'At one point it seemed that she would not survive the treatment, but somehow she found the strength to keep fighting. My father did everything he could to help her; he went to every chemo session with her, and we took it in turns to sleep in a chair by her bed every time she went into hospital. It's strange how those few hours before dawn seem to last for ever,' she said in a low tone. 'You can't sleep, but you dare not move away from the bed, and as the first light glimmers between the blinds you pray that this is the day there will be some improvement, a turning point.'

'Yes.' Thanos's voice was harsh, and she jerked her head up, catching her breath at the agony etched on his face. 'And every evening, when all hope has gone from that day, you pray that tomorrow will bring the sign you have been waiting for. And so it goes on, day after day. In Melina's case, week after week.'

Tahlia's hand flew to her mouth. How could she have been so crass as to bring up the subject of hospitals when Thanos's sister had been in a coma for weeks? She tensed, expecting him to be angry with her again, and accepted that in all honesty she could not blame him. Since she had learned about the accident she had been tormented by guilt that she should have run after Melina—although it was difficult to imagine what she could have said to the young Greek woman. Even if she had managed to convince Melina she had not known James was married, nothing would have changed the fact that he was a liar and a cheat.

'I can only imagine how awful it must have been,' she said softly, her heart clenching as she pictured Thanos's vigil at his sister's bedside. 'Did other members of your family come to the hospital to wait with you?'

He shrugged. 'I have no other family. My parents died when Melina was five years old, leaving me to bring her up. At first my aunt helped to look after her, but she was elderly and passed away a few months later. Then it was just the two of us.' A nerve flickered in his cheek and he looked away from Tahlia, battling to bring his emotions under control. 'There were times when Melina showed no sign of coming out of her coma and I feared I would be the only surviving member of the Savakis family.'

He must have felt so alone, Tahlia thought gently. As powerless as she had felt as she had watched her mother struggle with the illness that could so easily have ended her life. Instinctively she placed her hand over his, but when he stiffened she realised how stupid her action had been. Thanos now had irrefutable proof that she had not been his brother-in-law's mistress, but she was sure he still blamed her for Melina's accident. She expected him to reject her sympathy, and she made to snatch her hand back. But to her shock he curled his tanned fingers around her paler ones and held her prisoner.

'How is your mother now?'

'Completely recovered—thankfully. Actually, her recovery is a miracle—even her consultant says so,' Tahlia said with a ghost of a smile. 'Dad was overjoyed when we heard the news.' She swallowed the lump in her throat as she recalled how her father had wept tears of relief when he had phoned her with the news. 'That's why it seemed so...so *cruel* that on the same day Mum was given the all-clear Dad learned that Carlton House was in danger of being repossessed by the bank. He took out a mortgage on the house to finance Reynolds Gems,' she explained when Thanos frowned. 'My mother has no idea of the situation. She thinks they are going to enjoy a wonderful retirement in the house that has been in her family for generations. And that's exactly what's going to happen,' she added fiercely. 'My parents have been through two years of hell, and now they deserve to be happy. Dad was so relieved when he heard that Vantage Investments were prepared to buy Reynolds because it meant that he could pay back the bank loan and the mortgage, and Carlton would be safe...'

'And that is why—after you learned that Vantage is a subsidiary of Savakis Holdings, and I made it clear that I had no intention of saving Reynolds Gems—you agreed to sell yourself to me?' Thanos suggested grimly.

Tahlia bit her lip, sensing his renewed anger. 'Yes.'

'*Theos!*' he exploded, aware of a curious hollow sensation in his stomach. 'Why didn't you tell me your parents were in danger of losing their home?

Tahlia gave him a puzzled look. 'Why would you have

cared? You made it clear that you would never help my father. Time was running out, and I knew I would never find another buyer for Reynolds before the bank seized Carlton. The only thing I had to trade was my body,' she finished huskily.

The silence that fell between them simmered with tension. Thanos could not bring himself to look at Tahlia as guilt at the way he had misjudged her surged through him. Far from being an immoral slut, like his father's mistress, it seemed that she was a devoted daughter who had been desperate to help her parents. Her motivation in agreeing to be his mistress had not been to ensure her own financial security but to prevent her parents from being evicted from their home. And she had made the ultimate sacrifice, he thought bleakly. She had given him her virginity, aware that his motivation for taking her to bed was to seek revenge for a crime she had not committed.

He closed his eyes, shutting out the image of her pale, tear-stained face. In the name of heaven, what had he done?

'How did you meet James Hamilton?' he asked abruptly.

Tahlia shot him a startled glance. 'A friend of mine was starring in a play, and James was a member of the cast. We got chatting when I went backstage after the performance, and he…swept me off my feet.' She shook her head, remembering the buzz she had felt when James had singled her out. 'He was handsome, charming, funny… My mother was desperately ill, and I was sick with worry about her, but when I was with James he made me forget my fears for a few hours. I hadn't dated anyone in the years since Michael died,' she explained quietly. 'I was devastated by his death. He was so young and vibrant. We weren't lovers, but our friendship had been developing into something deeper, and I was heartbroken to lose him. For a long time after he died I blamed myself. I had thought he was suffering from the flu virus that was going around the university campus, and by the time I realised that it was something much more serious it was too late. Michael died a few hours after being admitted to hospital.' Her eyes darkened with pain as she remembered the horror of that day.

'When I met James, he was so energetic and full of life—just as Michael had been—and I felt that nothing bad could happen while I was with him.' She bit her lip. 'It never crossed my mind that he could be married. He even took me back to his flat a few times, and it was a typical bachelor pad—there was no sign that Melina lived there.'

'She didn't,' Thanos said heavily. 'I bought her and James an apartment in Athens for a wedding present, and she remained in Greece while he went to England for two months to star in that play. When his contract was extended Melina flew to London to join him. She was immediately suspicious that he was being unfaithful, but instead of confiding in me she read the text messages he'd sent you on his mobile phone, discovered that James had arranged to spend the weekend with you at a hotel, and decided to confront you.'

In her mind Tahlia saw Thanos's sister, standing in the doorway of the hotel suite, the look of shock on her face mirrored in James Hamilton's eyes. But where Melina's expression had been one of utter devastation, James had simply looked annoyed that he had been caught out.

'Poor Melina,' she whispered. 'She must have been distraught. I understand why you blamed me. I *would* have become James's lover that night,' she told Thanos, forcing herself to meet his gaze. 'He'd told me that he loved me, and I thought I loved him. Mum's illness had cast a shadow over everything, and James was the one person who could make me smile. I needed him, and I overlooked things like the fact that he always wanted to borrow money from me.' She swallowed. 'I was a fool, and because of my naïveté Melina almost lost her life. No wonder you hate me,' she said thickly. 'I will always feel guilty that I didn't go after her.'

No one could fake the level of emotion evident in Tahlia's voice, Thanos brooded. The pain she felt at James's treachery was as genuine as her sympathy for Melina. Shame burned like acid in his gut at the way he had treated her. He should not have brought her to Mykonos and forced her to share his bed, and now that he knew what a terrible mistake he had made he should send her back to England immediately. But hard on the heels of that thought came the unsettling realisation that he did not want to let her go.

Guilt filled him with a sudden restlessness, and he stood up and strode over to the window, staring out at the black sky and the silver moonlight dancing on the sea.

'You have nothing to feel guilty about,' he said gruffly. 'James duped you and Melina, and clearly he broke your heart as well as hers.'

Tahlia's heartbeat quickened. 'You believe me?' she asked shakily, shocked by how much his answer mattered.

He swung round from the window, the glow from the bedside lamp casting shadows over his hard-boned face, making his expression unfathomable.

'Yes, I believe you,' he said heavily. 'I'm sorry I misjudged you so badly. But when I first saw Melina in the hospital and learned the extent of her injuries I wanted to kill the two people I believed were responsible for her accident. Now I know you were not to blame, and I bitterly regret forcing you into this damnable deal.'

He walked back over to the bed, his mouth twisting when he saw Tahlia stiffen. *Theos*, he must have terrified her, he thought bleakly, remorse tearing at his insides when he recalled the demands he had made on her untutored body. Her hesitancy should have warned him of her innocence, but she had responded to him with such intense passion that he had believed she was as sexually experienced as the newspaper stories about her had suggested.

As Thanos came closer Tahlia was startled by the almost haggard expression in his eyes, and she felt a pang of compassion for him. How awful it must have been for him to come so close to losing his sister, who was his only living relative. He had cared for Melina since she was a small child, and she could understand how angry he must have felt that she had been hurt. It was understandable that his anger had turned into a quest for revenge.

'You didn't force me into anything,' she said softly. 'You simply offered me the opportunity to ensure my parents can keep their home and I took it. I knew what I was getting into.'

Thanos gave her a level look. 'Patently you did not,' he murmured, and a feeling he could not define stirred deep inside him when her cheeks flooded with colour. 'I deeply regret that I did not know I was your first lover. My impatience to take you to bed made me brutal, and I probably scared the life out of you.' He paused, and then said in a low tone, 'But, in all honesty, I cannot say I am sorry for making love to you. The sexual alchemy between us was obvious from the moment we met at the art gallery, and despite knowing who you were, the role I thought you had played in my sister's accident, I desired you more than I have ever wanted any woman.

'I still do,' he said harshly. 'The deal we made still stands. I am prepared to buy out Reynolds Gems and save your father from financial ruin in return for your agreement to remain here on Mykonos as my mistress until the end of the month.'

He wanted her to stay with him. Tahlia was shocked by the heady relief that swept through her, but it was quickly followed by a hollow feeling of despair. Making love with Thanos had been an incredible experience that she would never forget; not simply because it had been her first time, but because the feel of his satiny skin beneath her fingertips and the exquisite brush of his mouth caressing every inch of her body were imprinted on her brain for all time. One night was all it had taken for her to be utterly captivated by him. What would she be like after a month as his mistress—when he dismissed her from his life?

Surely it would be better for her to leave him now? To walk away with her pride restored and forget the deal that had turned her into the wanton creature she had become in his arms? But her father's financial problems still remained, and until the buy-out of Reynolds Gems was completed Carlton House was still at risk of repossession. Nothing had changed—except that Thanos was no longer looking at her with contempt in his eyes.

He sat back down on the bed and trailed his finger lightly over her cheek, the sudden warmth in his eyes making Tahlia's heart lurch. 'The passion we shared tonight was beyond anything I have ever known with any other woman. I was blinded by my anger, and determined to take revenge for the heartbreak I believed you had caused Melina, but I was wrong about you. Can we start over?' he asked quietly. 'Whatever this is between us, it is nowhere close to burning out—not for either of us, is it?'

She wanted to deny it—wished she could coolly thank him for initiating her into the pleasures of sex before she caught the first flight home. But the words would not come, and her breath snagged in her throat as he slowly lowered his head until his mouth was a whisper away from hers.

'Stay with me, Tahlia? Please?'

She must have taken leave of her senses, but she could not resist him. That had been her trouble right from the start, she acknowledged as she sagged against him and parted her lips beneath the gentle pressure of his. The slow, sweet kiss was like nothing she had ever experienced before, and the element of gentleness tugged at her heart. When he curved his arms around her she slid her hands up to his nape, and the familiar melting warmth started low in her pelvis as he deepened the kiss to another level and desire swiftly built to a crescendo of need.

She was sure he would ease her down onto the pillows, and she slid her fingers into his hair to guide him down on top of her. But to her disbelief he lifted his head, his eyes darkening a fraction as he saw the confusion in hers.

'Wait here.' He dropped a light kiss on her still parted lips and strode into the *en suite* bathroom.

Had he been playing with her? she wondered sickly, clutching the sheet to her. Did he want to demonstrate that *he* would call the shots in any relationship they might have? She must have been out of her mind to have agreed to stay with him, she thought wildly.

But while she was debating whether to get up and pack her suitcase before she informed him that she wanted to leave after all, he re-entered the bedroom.

'What are you doing?' she gasped when he flicked the sheet out of her grasp and leaned over to scoop her into his arms.

'I've run you a bath. I have a feeling you ache in places you didn't know existed,' he murmured, chuckling when she blushed scarlet.

'I can take care of myself,' she muttered, when he shouldered open the door to the bathroom and carried her over to the huge marble bath filled to the brim with fragrant bubbles.

'Humour me, hmm…?' There was a hint of steel beneath his soft tone, and before she had time to argue the point he lowered her into the water.

It felt blissful, Tahlia acknowledged as she leaned her head back against the padded neck support and closed her eyes.

Thanos had been right; she had discovered muscles that were previously unused. But the memory of how he had driven into her over and over again until she had reached the pinnacle of pleasure caused molten heat to unfurl deep in her pelvis. Shocked by the erotic imagery, she let her eyes fly open to discover that he had shrugged out of his robe and was standing naked and unashamedly aroused by the side of the bath. The flickering light from the dozens of candles around the room gave his body a satin sheen, and her gaze moved down, following the path of crisp dark hairs that covered his chest and arrowed over his flat stomach. He was a work of art, she thought shakily, as she dropped her eyes lower still and absorbed the awesome power of his masculinity.

'Look at me like that for much longer and I won't be responsible for my actions,' he warned softly, his slow smile stealing her breath.

How could she ever have thought that his eyes were cold? she wondered, her heartbeat quickening when he stepped into the bath and sat opposite her, drawing her towards him so that she was aware of the muscular strength of his thighs holding her prisoner. Not that she wanted to escape, she acknowledged ruefully, giving a little gasp when he skimmed his hands over her ribs and cupped her breasts in his hands, the delicate brush of his thumb pads across her nipples sending exquisite shafts of sensation spiralling through her.

'How can I wash when you're doing that?' she mumbled, her eyes locked on the sensual curve of his mouth as he slowly lowered his head and claimed her lips in a long, drugging kiss that stoked the fire inside her to an inferno.

'Allow me to help you.' He picked up a bar of soap and smoothed it over her shoulders, breasts, stomach and thighs, with such dedication to detail that she made a muffled sound in her throat.

'I'm sure I'm clean. You can stop now,' she said huskily, her eyes widening in shock when he discarded the soap and slipped his hand between her legs, parting her with gentle skill and sliding a finger deep inside her. Moist heat flooded through her as he stretched her wider and slipped another digit into her, his fingers moving in an erotic dance that drove her higher and higher towards an orgasm.

'Do you want me to stop, *agape*?' he queried gently as he brushed his thumb pad delicately over the tight nub of her clitoris. Sensation speared her and she arched her hips, nothing in her mind now but desperation for him to give her the release she craved.

'No. Don't stop…please…' She groaned when he withdrew his fingers, and clutched his shoulders when he stood and swung her into his arms before climbing out of the bath. Water streamed from their bodies and dripped onto the carpet as he strode into the bedroom, but he seemed unconcerned that her wet hair soaked through the bedspread as he placed her on the bed and stretched out next to her, his mouth capturing hers in a kiss of pure possession.

'This time we'll take it slowly,' he promised, pausing to swiftly don protection before he nudged her legs apart and moved over her.

Tahlia appreciated the care and consideration he showed as he eased the solid length of his erection into her, but as he filled her, inch by tantalising inch, she discovered that she did not want him to be gentle. Her desire for him was as fierce as a forest fire blazing out of control, and she wanted him to make love to her with the same savage passion that had overwhelmed them both the first time he had possessed her.

She was too shy to voice her need for him, but instead she moved with him, arching her hips to meet each powerful thrust and digging her fingers into his shoulders to urge him to take her faster, harder…

'*Theos*, Tahlia, I don't want to hurt you,' he growled, fighting to retain his self-control.

'You won't. I want you.' Words could not express the depths of her passion, the throbbing ache of her need for him to take her to the heights, but when his lips claimed hers she kissed him hungrily, sliding her tongue into his mouth so that he groaned and tensed before increasing the power of each thrust into her eager body.

Thalia clung to his damp shoulders and tossed her head from side to side, feeling the first spasms building inside her growing, growing until they were an unstoppable force, and she gave a thin, animal cry as her body arched with the explosive force of her climax.

Thanos felt the delicious tightening of her muscles around his shaft and gritted his teeth, determined that this time he would remain in control. He slid his hands beneath her buttocks and tilted her hips, driving into her with deep, steady strokes, taking her higher again, until she sobbed his name and raked her fingers on the silk bedspread. Only when she had climaxed for the third time did his restraint slip, and he paused, savouring the anticipation of the pleasure to come, before he gave one last powerful thrust and experienced the shattering ecstasy of release.

Long moments passed before his breathing returned to normal. He rolled off her and immediately drew her into his arms, frowning when he caught the glimmer of tears on her lashes. 'Forgive me,' he said deeply. 'I was afraid I would hurt you. It was too much, too soon. I should have curbed my impatience.'

Tahlia shook her head, blinking back the tears she had hoped he would not see and giving him a brilliant smile that evoked a peculiar feeling in his chest. 'I was impatient too,' she assured him, and then to her surprise could not prevent herself from yawning so widely that Thanos chuckled, the sound echoing beneath her ear as he curved his arm around her and settled her against him.

'And now you are tired. Go to sleep, *agape*,' he bade her softly, when she opened her mouth to deny it. Her lashes were already drifting down, and Thanos was shaken by the unexpected surge of protectiveness that swept through him as he watched her fall asleep.

# CHAPTER SEVEN

TAHLIA was awoken by the bright sunlight filtering through the blinds. She turned her head and found that she was alone, the faint indentation on the pillow beside her the only indication that Thanos had slept in the bed last night. That and the slight tenderness of her breasts, the ache of muscles never previously used…

She blushed as she recalled in vivid detail the passion they had shared. Sex with Thanos had been a revelation, and in all honesty she did not regret that he was her first lover. The incredible sensuality of their lovemaking was proof that it was possible to enjoy physical intimacy without emotional involvement—because of course her emotions were *not* involved, she assured herself. Sexual chemistry was a powerful force and she had been unable to resist its pull. Yet she was conscious of a dull ache around her heart that had nothing to do with the pleasurable excesses of the previous night.

The most important thing was that Carlton House was safe and her parents would be able to spend their retirement free from financial worries, she told herself firmly as she threw back the sheets and headed for the *en suite* bathroom. It was ridiculous to wonder what would have happened if she and Thanos had simply been two strangers who had met one evening and been instantly attracted to one another. Perhaps he would have invited her out to dinner or the theatre? Would they have gone the conventional route of dating for a while before their relationship progressed to the bedroom?

It would not have been long before their mutual sexual awareness had exploded into passion, she thought with a rueful smile. But she wished they'd had the chance to get to know one another, to become friends before they became lovers. Instead their relationship was a business arrangement, and although Thanos no longer seemed to despise her, there was no escaping the fact that he was paying for her to share his bed.

The sun was already hot when she stepped onto the terrace, and she was glad of the shade cast by the large parasol as she sat down to breakfast. A note propped up against the coffee pot informed her that Thanos would be in meetings until late afternoon, and, recalling his scathing comments about her lack of clothes, she decided to go shopping in Mykonos Town.

'Yes, there is a bus,' the maid told her, looking puzzled when Tahlia asked her for directions to the town. 'But Mr Savakis would not expect you to take a bus. His chauffeur will drive you wherever you want to go.'

'The bus will be fine,' Tahlia replied cheerfully. She could not rationalise why she did not want to make use of Thanos's personal staff. It was simply important that she retained her independence as much as possible.

Using public transport also meant that she had an excellent tour of the island, she discovered an hour later, as the bus sped along the road. She stared at the rocky hilltops where goats were grazing, and then turned her head to admire the stunning view of the sea. On the horizon she could see the famous windmills, standing like sentinels on the hills above the port, and as the bus wound down into the town centre she was entranced by the myriad square white, flat-roofed houses, jumbled together in impossibly narrow streets.

Even this early in the season the town was bustling with tourists who strolled along the rows of souvenir shops and sat beneath brightly coloured parasols outside the cafés and tavernas. Mykonos was one of the most cosmopolitan of the Greek Islands, and unfortunately this was reflected in the price tags inside the fashionable boutiques. Determined not to allow Thanos to buy her clothes, Tahlia spent the last of her savings, earmarked to pay her electricity bill, on two evening dresses which she did not particularly like but were the cheapest she could find.

She spent another enjoyable hour window-shopping, had lunch in a charming little restaurant in an area of the town called Little Venice, where the buildings were so close to the sea that the balconies overhung the water, and finally caught the bus back to the Artemis, feeling hot and weary, but satisfied that she had two suitable outfits to replace the blouse that Thanos had ruined.

She was surprised to see him standing by the French doors when she walked into the suite, and his grim expression as he swung round to face her made Tahlia's heart sink.

'Where have you been for the past five hours?' he queried tersely. 'The maid said you went out at eleven this morning,' he added, when Tahlia frowned and checked her watch.

'I can't believe I was out for so long. I went into the town, and there was so much to see. Time just flew,' she said defensively.

'Particularly as you travelled by bus,' Thanos said disapprovingly. 'The maid told me she had explained to you that I have assigned a driver to act as your personal chauffeur. Yianis would have given you a tour of the island—and carried your shopping,' he added, his eyes dropping to the bags she was holding. 'I was beginning to worry that something had happened to you,' he said tensely. 'You are a stranger to Mykonos, and some of the bars are not good places for you to go on your own.'

Tahlia's temper prickled at the note of censure in his voice. 'I'm a big girl now, and I can take care of myself.'

Did she have any idea how young she looked, with her face bare of make-up and her hair caught up in a ponytail? Thanos mused. He could imagine the interest she had aroused among the male population of Mykonos in her faded denim shorts and a white strap top, beneath which she was clearly not wearing a bra, and he felt a caveman instinct to lock her away in the highest tower.

'During my student days I spent two summers backpacking around Europe. I know the kind of seedy places to avoid. I worked in many of them,' she admitted ruefully.

'Doing what?' Thanos asked curiously.

'Waitressing, mainly—although I did try a brief stint cooking pancakes in a crêperie in Spain. Until I set light to the kitchen and the manager sacked me,' Tahlia told him cheerfully. 'I was better at bar-work, or cleaning. Often I worked seventy hours a week, and saved the money I earned to see me through my next term at university.'

Thanos frowned. 'Didn't your parents support you financially while you were studying?'

'They couldn't afford to. Carlton House suffered serious structural damage in a storm a few years ago, and the cost of the repairs was astronomical. But I was happy to pay my own way. I never expected hand-outs.'

The Tahlia he was getting to know was nothing like the image fostered in the tabloids of a spoilt party-girl, Thanos brooded, trying to picture her waiting on tables. He remembered the exhaustion of working ridiculously long hours as a labourer, struggling to earn enough to pay the bills and feed and clothe Melina. Memories of those years of poverty were the reason why he now made regular donations to charities supporting the under-privileged, and they had made him appreciate all that he had. Until now he had never met any woman, apart from his sister, who respected the value of money.

'But presumably your parents paid for your flat? You could not have afforded to buy a property in such an affluent area of London on the money you earned as a waitress.'

'Oh, the flat isn't mine, it belongs to George. My aunt Georgina,' Tahlia explained hastily, when Thanos's brows drew together. 'I moved in with her after I left university. She's elderly, and had had several falls. I wanted to take care of her, but sadly she developed dementia and it got to the point where I was terrified of leaving her to go to work because she had so many accidents. After she left a plastic jug on the electric hotplate and the kitchen caught fire my parents and I decided that it would be better for her to move into a residential home where she could have full-time care. I visit her twice a week—' Tahlia broke off at the realisation that she would be unable to visit her aunt for the next month. 'I don't suppose she'll miss me,' she said quietly. 'She doesn't recognise me any more.'

'Yet you still visit her regularly?' Thanos murmured.

'Of course.' Tahlia shrugged. 'Dementia is a cruel illness, but it doesn't define Aunt George. She's still a wonderful person.'

Far from being heartless, as he had once believed, Tahlia clearly possessed a depth of compassion and kindness that he had never found in any other woman, Thanos acknowledged. He did not want to dwell on how he had misjudged her and he strolled towards her, glancing curiously at her shopping bags.

'So, what did you buy?'

'Clothes—as ordered,' she replied brightly. 'Two evening

dresses, to be precise.' She pulled a garish pink gown from one of the bags and held it up for his inspection. 'What do you think?'

'I think you had better show me the other one,' he said flatly.

'If you don't like the pink, I thought I couldn't go wrong with classic black.' Tahlia held the plain black dress against her and gave an impatient sigh when he shook his head. 'What's wrong with it?'

'It's cheap, badly made, and it drains the colour from your face,' Thanos told her bluntly. He lifted his hand and ran his finger lightly down her cheek, watching the soft flush of rose-pink stain her skin. 'If they are the only two choices, then I have to say that I definitely prefer you wearing no clothes at all, *agape*.'

The sultry gleam in his eyes caused a delicious little shiver to run through Tahlia, and her breath snagged in her throat when he slid the strap of her cotton top over her shoulder. It would be so easy to close the few inches between them and tilt her head in readiness for his kiss, but she was suddenly gripped with shyness. She was here with him to fulfil her side of a business arrangement, she reminded herself fiercely. She had not expected to be so utterly captivated by him—or to feel this lingering regret that their relationship would never be more than sex.

'I think I'll hit the shower,' she mumbled. 'It was hot and dusty in town.'

She quickly made her escape, crossing the lounge to the bedroom and carrying on into the *en suite* bathroom. A long, tepid shower cooled her heated skin and went some way to restoring her equilibrium. When she'd finished she wound a towel sarong-like around her body and blasted her hair with the hairdrier, wondering if Thanos had returned to work.

The sight of him propped up in bed halted her in her tracks, and her heart missed a beat as her eyes travelled down from his bare muscular chest, covered with whorls of dark hair, to the sheet draped low over his hips. The word handsome did not do justice to his stunning looks and simmering virility. One look at him was all it took for her to melt, she thought despairingly, unable to tear her eyes from the sensual promise of his mouth. The feral heat in his gaze was both an invitation and a demand, and when he wordlessly flicked back the sheet to reveal the awesome strength of his arousal, she swallowed, her eyes locked with his as she walked slowly towards the bed.

Heart pounding so hard she was sure he must hear it, she stretched out beside him, her faint sigh muffled as he lowered his head and claimed her mouth in a slow, drugging kiss that sparked a flame inside her. His tongue probed between her lips, demanding access as he deepened the kiss, and she responded mindlessly, her body quivering with delight. He unwrapped her towel and stroked his hand over her breasts, teasing her nipples into hard peaks before he replaced his fingers with his mouth and laved each dusky tip until she gasped with pleasure.

Passion built swiftly, and when he slipped his hand between her thighs she spread her legs wider, heard his low groan of approval as he parted her and discovered the slick wetness of her arousal.

'You can touch me too,' Thanos murmured, smiling when colour stained her cheeks.

After a moment's hesitation she complied, and tested his restraint to its limit when she stroked her fingers lightly along his swollen length and then grew bolder and encircled him. Her innocence was indisputable, but she was an apt pupil, he acknowledged, his heart racing as he reached for a protective sheath and then positioned himself over her. He entered her with slow deliberation, watching her eyes widen as she fel him slide deeper, filling her to the hilt before he withdrew almost fully and thrust again, establishing a rhythm that drove them both to the edge and over, as their passion exploded in the glory of mutual climax.

It was just good sex, he reminded himself when he finally withdrew and rolled onto his back, taking her with him and tangling his hand in her hair. He guided her mouth down on his and kissed her with lazy appreciation. Physical compatibility at its best—which left him with a feeling of contentment that he had never experienced with any other woman.

'I need to work for another couple of hours,' he told her as he pulled on his trousers. 'This evening we're attending a reception. The shipping magnate Christos Petrelis is hosting a party on his private island.'

'Which dress shall I wear?' Tahlia mused. 'The black or the pink?'

He gave her a level look. 'Neither.'

'You think I should go nude?' she teased him, her impish smile tugging faintly on his heart.

'It would certainly be an attention-stealer, but I admit I like the fact that I am the only man who has ever seen your naked body,' he told her, frowning slightly as he acknowledged a degree of possessiveness that was unexpected. He reached for his phone and spoke rapidly in Greek before cutting the call. 'Fortunately, I am a much better shopper than you. Come and see.'

Puzzled, Tahlia pulled on her robe and followed him into the lounge. He strode over to the door and opened it, to admit three porters laded with bags and boxes emblazoned with the names of famous design houses.

'What…?' She lifted her eyes to his face and waited for his explanation.

'You need new clothes,' Thanos murmured coolly. 'So I phoned a friend in Paris who is a personal stylist, gave her your measurements and a description of your colouring, and asked her to send over a selection of suitable outfits.'

'Well, you can just send them straight back.' Tahlia stared around at the dozens of boxes and bags, from Chanel, Gucci, Prada, and felt sick with misery. The laughter she had shared with Thanos a few moments earlier had been replaced with a tangible tension. 'I won't wear clothes paid for by you. I told you—I pay my own way and I won't accept hand-outs. Even though they are haute couture,' she added grimly.

Thanos's smile had faded and his expression was unreadable, although Tahlia sensed that she had angered him. 'You will wear them,' he told her, with a note of implacability in his voice that warned her she would have a fight on her hands if she refused. 'As we discussed before, your sole purpose for the next month is to please me, and I expect you to dress appropriately.'

'I don't need reminding that you are paying for me to act the role of your mistress,' she said stiffly, hurt pride churning in her stomach. In a battle of wills he would be a clear winner, and a dignified retreat was her only option. 'Very well, I'll wear the clothes while I am here on Mykonos. But I shall regard them as a uniform, and I will leave them behind when our contract is over.'

Thanos restrained himself from pulling her into his arms and shaking some sense into her, and ignored the stronger urge to kiss her into submission. 'Suit yourself,' he said laconically, snatching up his jacket from the back of the chair and heading for the door. 'I believe Monique included a Valentino evening gown in the collection. Wear that tonight,' he ordered, and he stepped into the corridor and slammed the door behind him without giving her the chance to argue further.

Tahlia worked off her fury at Thanos's high-handedness by swimming thirty lengths in the private pool. When she re-

turned to the bedroom she discovered that the maid had unpacked the clothes and hung them in the wardrobe: beautiful
classical evening dresses, elegant trousers, skirts and tops, all
with matching shoes and accessories, and a variety of exquisite nightgowns and sets of lacy underwear which were
nothing like the plain cotton bras and knickers she usually
wore.

Presumably Thanos believed that as he was paying for her
he could indulge in a typical male fantasy of seeing her in
flimsy scraps of silk and lace, she thought dully as she held up
a low-cut black basque complete with silk ribbons which laced
up at the front. In different circumstances she would have
taken huge delight in a cupboard full of designer outfits, but
the knowledge that Thanos had bought them emphasised the
fact that she was—as he had pointed out—here to please him.

The Valentino dress *was* stunning, she was forced to admit
later, after she had taken a leisurely bath and smoothed
fragrant body lotion onto her skin before dressing for the
party. The heather-coloured silk gown left her shoulders bare
and clung lovingly to her waist and hips, the side-split in the
skirt reaching to mid-thigh. It was the most daring dress she
had ever worn, and as she stared at her reflection in the mirror
she barely recognised the sultry seductress looking back at her
as sensible Tahlia Reynolds.

Thanos walked into the bedroom as she was spraying
perfume to her pulse points. She guessed he must have used the
spare bedroom as a dressing room, because he had changed into
a black dinner suit which emphasised his lean length and the
formidable width of his shoulders. She hated the way her heart
jerked as her gaze skittered over the chiselled beauty of his face.

Her heart thudded as his eyes swept over her.

'You look beautiful.' His voice was as deep and sensuous
as crushed velvet, and her senses flared as she caught the drift

of his cologne when he strolled over to her. 'I bought this for you to wear tonight.'

Tahlia caught her breath when he held up a large peardrop-shaped amethyst, surrounded by diamonds and suspended on a fine white-gold chain. Before she had time to argue Thanos fastened the pendant around her neck and stood back to admire the sight of the violet-coloured gem sitting in the V between her creamy breasts.

'Perfect,' he murmured, his eyes gleaming with feral hunger as he traced his finger over the pendant and then slipped it lower and settled it between her breasts. 'It matches the colour of your dress exactly. But whenever I look at you this evening I will be imagining you wearing nothing but the necklace,' he added thickly.

The pendant felt heavy on Tahlia's skin, and she was tempted to tear it off. She felt as though he had branded her—as if every time he looked at her he would be reminded that he had paid for her.

'You think you can buy everything, don't you?' she snapped. 'You have so little understanding of the value of money that the cost of a valuable piece of jewellery is irrelevant to you. I suppose that's what comes of being born into wealth,' she finished scathingly.

Thanos's face had darkened at her outburst, and now he gave a mirthless laugh. 'I wasn't born into wealth,' he said harshly. 'There was no grand mansion house in *my* family to pass down through generations. I didn't enjoy a privileged childhood or have the advantage of a private education. I was born on a small island called Agistri, and I grew up in a tiny stone-built house with no running water,' he explained flatly. 'As a youth I assumed that I would spend my life as a goatherd. I had no expectations of ever moving away from the island where my family had lived for generations.'

'What made you decide to leave?' Tahlia asked, stunned by his revelation that he had not inherited his vast fortune.

'An English woman called Wendy Jones.' Thanos could not disguise the bitterness in his voice. 'She was my father's mistress—and after he walked out on his family and divorced my mother she subsequently became his new wife. Wendy had already been married and divorced twice when she bought a villa on Agistri. She employed my father to carry out renovation work on her house, but it soon became apparent that she wanted him for more than his building skills. A few months after he began working for her he dropped the bombshell to my mother that their marriage was over.

He continued harshly, 'My mother was distraught, especially when my father stopped all financial support. I was fifteen, and Melina was just three years old. I dropped out of school, lied about my age, and managed to pick up some labouring work, using the skills my father had taught me. My mother wept about the disruption to my education, but I had no choice—I couldn't allow her and my sister to starve, and my father was too besotted with his tart to spare a thought for his wife and children. I lost all the respect I had felt for my father,' Thanos said savagely. 'He made a complete fool of himself. Wendy flirted with him outrageously. She knew he was married, but that little fact didn't seem to matter to her. She'd decided that she wanted him for herself and she deliberately pursued him, uncaring that she had ripped my family apart—'

He broke off abruptly, and in the tense silence Tahlia could feel his barely leashed anger. No wonder Thanos had been so ready to believe that she had stolen James Hamilton from his sister, she brooded. His family had been blown apart by his father's mistress. It must have seemed as though history was repeating itself when his sister had discovered that her husband was having an affair.

'I never spoke to my father after he married again,' he continued grimly. 'Eighteen months after the wedding he was killed in a horrific accident. Wendy had insisted on having a swimming pool, and he was crushed when the mechanical digger he was driving overturned.' He ignored Tahlia's shocked gasp and continued. 'My father had not made a will, and everything he owned—namely the house where my mother, Melina and I still lived—passed to his wife. Within a week of his funeral Wendy demanded that we leave her property. It was the final blow to my mother, to be evicted from the home where she had lived for her entire married life by my father's whore. She died of pneumonia six months later, leaving me to care for Melina, who was then just five years old.'

Tahlia tried to imagine Thanos at seventeen—a boy who overnight had had to become a man and take responsibility for his young sister while he was grieving for both his parents. 'You must feel very protective of Melina,' she murmured.

He turned his head and stared at her, his dark eyes blazing. 'I would give my life for her,' he vowed fiercely. 'I promised my mother as she lay dying that I would always take care of Melina. When I first saw her after the accident and I was told she had less than a fifty percent chance of surviving…' His throat moved convulsively. 'I was haunted by the knowledge that I had failed to protect her.'

Tahlia was shocked by the raw emotion in his eyes. There was no doubt that Thanos adored his sister, and she realised that far from being the hard, ruthless man she had once believed his feelings ran deep. If he ever fell in love he would give his heart utterly, she brooded, aware of a faint tug of envy for the woman who might one day win his devotion.

He had fallen silent, seemingly lost in his thoughts, but after a moment he picked up her stole and placed it around her shoulders. 'Are you ready to leave?'

When she nodded, he escorted her out of the suite. To her surprise the lift carried them upwards, and when the doors opened she stepped out onto the roof of the hotel where a helicopter was waiting.

'The chopper is the quickest way to travel between the islands,' he explained as he assisted her into the cockpit. 'I've held a private pilot's licence for ten years. You'll be quite safe.'

Tahlia had always been nervous in the air, but as they took off she had no qualms about Thanos's ability to fly the chopper. Was there nothing this man could not do? she wondered as she watched him manoeuvre the joystick and the helicopter responded smoothly to his control. She glanced out of the window and watched the streaks of pink and gold which flared from a fiery sun as it slipped below the horizon.

Twenty minutes later they landed on the lawn in front of a huge white-walled villa and were escorted inside by a uniformed member of staff.

There was serious money here, Tahlia mused, glancing around at the stunning array of diamonds and designer gowns worn by the predominantly young and blonde women who were being paraded on the arms of their significantly older male companions. Fortunately she was practised in the art of making small-talk with people she had never met before—or was likely to meet again, and she moved around the room with Thanos, sipping champagne and forcing herself to smile until her jaw ached.

She was aware of the envious glances she received from other women, the thinly veiled speculation in their eyes that she would not remain his mistress for long. Thanos Savakis's relationships were notoriously short-lived, but tonight he only had eyes for her, and he kept his arm around her waist, as if he shared her reluctance for them to be apart for even a moment—although that was surely just wishful thinking, Tahlia told herself firmly.

He dominated her mind: a tall, dark and brooding presence at her side. A man who, in a few hours, would take her to bed and make love to her until he had sated his hunger for her. She would not offer any resistance, she thought wearily as his eyes fused with hers and the flare of heat in their depths sent a jolt of awareness down her spine. He had taken her innocence and awoken her sensuality, and she could not deny the desire that he alone aroused in her.

'Dance with me.' His eyes seemed to scorch her soul, and without waiting for her to reply he drew her onto the dance floor and into his arms.

He swamped her senses, the warmth of his body and the sensual musk of his cologne drifting around her so that she relaxed against him and rested her head on his chest, the ache inside her soothed by the steady beat of his heart. When he lowered his head and claimed her mouth she parted her lips and kissed him back with a fervency that caused him to tighten his hold and pull her closer, so that she could feel the throbbing force of his arousal press impatiently into her pelvis.

At last he lifted his mouth from hers and stared down at her quizzically. 'Ready to go?' he queried softly.

The champagne was flooding through her veins, sweeping away her doubts and inhibitions and leaving her weak and boneless and the slow drumbeat of desire was thudding irresistibly deep inside her.

'Yes.'

His eyes darkened, his mouth twisting in a self-derisive grimace as he slid his hand down to her bottom and pulled her up hard against the swollen shaft straining beneath his trousers. 'You are like a fever in my blood, *agape*,' he muttered thickly. 'I am burning up with wanting you.'

The short flight back to Mykonos seemed interminable. The silence grew ever more intense as the lift carried them down a floor to Thanos's suite. The moment they stepped through the door Thanos swept her into his arms and strode into the master bedroom, the purpose in his eyes causing anticipation to coil low in Tahlia's stomach.

She helped him remove her clothes and then his, her heart thudding as she ran her hands through the mass of wiry black hairs that covered his chest and felt the erratic beat of his life-force beneath her fingertips. The solid length of his arousal pushed insistently against her thigh, and she felt the familiar melting warmth between her legs as her body grew impatient for him. She wanted him so desperately that her limbs trembled, and when she tentatively stroked her fingers along his swollen shaft and heard his swiftly indrawn breath she expected him to lift her onto the bed, to possess her with the same raw passion of their previous encounters.

Instead he stroked his hands through her hair, before trailing his fingertips in a butterfly caress along her collarbone and then down to cup her breasts in his palms. His slow smile told her that he understood her impatience, but his movements were unhurried as his mouth claimed hers in a deep, drugging kiss that seared her soul.

It was just good sex, she reminded herself. It meant nothing to him, and she would be a fool to open her heart to him. But when he sank down onto the bed and lifted her over him, guiding her gently down so that she absorbed the full strength of his erection, she looked into his dark eyes and acknowledged on a wave of sheer panic that her heart was in serious danger.

# CHAPTER EIGHT

THE prickling sensation on Tahlia's shoulders warned her that she would be wise to move out of the sun. It was almost four p.m., she noted, her stomach tightening as she glanced at her watch. Soon Thanos would come back to the suite, and she would go inside, to the cool, shaded bedroom, where he would make love to her as he had done every day of the past week since they had arrived on Mykonos.

She moved her sunbed beneath the parasol and picked up her book—the third paperback novel she'd read this week—but she could not concentrate on the story, and after a few moments she set it down again, looking towards the French doors. Her heart-rate accelerated when she discovered that he had stepped onto the terrace and was watching her, his expression hidden behind his sunglasses. He dipped his head in silent greeting before walking back inside, and, like a puppet controlled by invisible strings, she stood up and followed him.

When she reached the master bedroom she found him naked, stretched out on the silk sheets like a sultan waiting for his favourite concubine. That was all she was to him, she reminded herself despairingly. But he had treated her with respect and consideration since he had made her his mistress, and day by day she had fallen deeper under his spell.

It was ridiculous to still feel shy when he had explored every inch of her body with his hands and mouth, but she could not bring herself to strip off her bikini, and stood watching him, her eyes unconsciously wary, until he held out his hand and murmured, 'Come here,' in the deep, velvet-soft voice that sent a quiver of longing down her spine.

In the sensual feast that followed he aroused her to a fever-pitch of desire, peeling her bikini from her breasts and hips and probing the moist heat of her femininity with his tongue before he moved over her and possessed her with fierce, powerful thrusts that drove them both to the ecstasy of simultaneous release. Afterwards she lay limply beside him, knowing that he would soon stroll into the shower, before dressing and returning to another of his interminable meetings. But to her surprise he propped himself up on one elbow and stared down at her.

'So, what did you do today?'

She shrugged, puzzled by his unexpected interest. 'Sat in the sun before it got too hot, swam, read a book—the same as I've done every day,' she added, unable to disguise the faint note of frustration in her voice.'

Thanos's eyes narrowed. 'You could go shopping. There are some excellent designer boutiques in the town, and I've told you to use the money I left for you.'

'And I've told you I don't want your money,' Tahlia said fiercely. 'Besides, you've already provided me with more than enough clothes. I don't need to go shopping.'

'Most women I know do not shop out of necessity,' Thanos murmured dryly.

'Well, clearly I'm different to your other women.'

Tahlia's tart comment filled Thanos with a mixture of amusement and frustration. He had made love to her every night—and most afternoons—he acknowledged wryly, and he knew every secret dip and curve of her body. But her mind remained stubbornly closed to him. He was no nearer to understanding what made Tahlia Reynolds tick than he had been a week ago.

He trailed his hand lazily down her body, feeling a spurt of triumph at the sharp catch of her breath as he pushed her legs apart. 'If you are bored, I will have to spend more time…entertaining you,' he drawled.

'It's not possible to have sex any more times than we do already,' she said ruefully. 'But if I spend many more hours sunbathing I'll turn into a crisp.' She pushed her hair out of her eyes and continued hurriedly, 'Isn't there any office work I could do? Filing, admin…? I don't care what it is, as long as I have something to do. I'm a working girl,' she told him seriously. 'I'm not used to sitting around all day doing nothing.'

Tahlia was so very different from the woman he had believed her to be when he had blamed her for his sister's accident, Thanos acknowledged. During the tense hours he'd spent waiting for Melina to regain consciousness his image of Tahlia had fused with his memories of his father's English mistress, and his hatred of her had grown as intense as the hatred he felt towards the woman who had destroyed his family. But over the past week he had discovered that Tahlia was nothing like the callous, cold-hearted woman his father had married. True, she possessed an unexpectedly fiery temper beneath her gentle exterior, but she was unfailingly polite towards his staff, instinctively kind, and the most generous lover he had ever known.

He had not expected to like her, he conceded, but to his surprise he had found himself thinking about her when his mind should have been concentrating on profit margins, and for the first time in his life he resented the hours he spent in the office because he would rather have been with her.

He got up from the bed, retrieved his clothes from the floor where he had carelessly discarded them, and paused on his way to the *en suite* bathroom to look back at her. The sunlight filtering through the blinds turned her hair to pure gold, falling in a silken sheet around her shoulders, and her skin was still flushed from the passion they had just shared. He must be mad to be considering working with her when she was such a serious distraction to his thought process, he thought wryly, but his logical brain insisted that she could be extremely useful to him.

'I've a meeting scheduled for the next hour. Come to my office after that and we'll discuss an idea I've had which I'm certain will alleviate your boredom,' he murmured, smiling at her look of surprise and striding on into the bathroom before she could question him.

Thanos was standing by a window which afforded a spectacular view of the sea when Tahlia entered his office. 'Take a seat,' he invited, the warmth of his smile doing strange things to her insides.

She quickly sat down in the chair in front of his desk, her eyes drawn to his hard profile, and her composure wavered as she studied his chiselled features, the slashing line of his cheekbone and his square chin. An hour ago, that sensual mouth had traced every inch of her body and lingered in her most secret places to wreak havoc. The memory caused liquid heat to flood through her veins, and she knew from the sudden flare of heat in his eyes that he had read her mind.

'You said you have an idea?' she said hastily, aware that she was blushing.

'I have several,' Thanos assured her throatily, conscious of the familiar tug of desire in his groin as he studied her. She had changed into an elegant cream linen skirt and a white blouse, and looked as chaste as a nun, with her hair drawn back from her face in a neat chignon. But somehow her wholesome, fresh-faced appearance was incredibly sexy. His eyes lingered on her lips, coated in a pale pink gloss, and his heart-rate quickened.

He ruthlessly suppressed the hunger that gnawed in his gut and picked up the folder on his desk. 'However, I think we had better concentrate on the idea I asked you here to discuss. The Artemis is due to open in three weeks' time,' he said abruptly.

Tahlia nodded. 'I'm sure it will be a great success,' she murmured, not sure what the opening date of his new hotel had to do with her.

'I hope so. We're fully booked for the whole of the summer, but it's vital we make an excellent first impression. To that end I have invited tour operators and travel writers to come and enjoy all that the Artemis has to offer, in the hope that they will give a glowing report. If they don't, many of those bookings could be cancelled,' Thanos added tersely. 'I hired a PR company to organise a party for the opening night. Three hundred guests have been invited, including several world-renowned celebrities. I learned yesterday that the PR company has failed to fulfil its promise that the party will be the most spectacular event ever held on Mykonos. In fact I seriously doubt they could organise a kindergarten party,' he added, his irritation palpable. 'And so this morning I fired them.'

Thanos was not a man who gave second chances, Tahlia surmised as she stared at the rigid set of his jaw, and she felt a pang of sympathy for the head of the PR company who must have borne the brunt of his fury.

'Ordinarily my PA would have alerted me to the fact that Cosmo Communications were useless,' Thanos continued. 'But Stephanie is on leave—visiting her family in South

Africa—and I have spent much of the past six months in America with Melina.'

Tahlia felt a pang of guilt for the unwitting part she had played in his sister's accident. 'What will you do? Can you find another PR consultant at such short notice?'

'I've already found one.' He leaned back in his chair and gave her a level look. 'I'm impressed by the work you did for Reynolds Gems, and I want *you* to organise the party.'

For a few seconds Tahlia was lost for words. 'That's an enormous responsibility,' she said slowly. 'Do you really trust that I can meet your expectations?'

'I trust you implicitly, Tahlia, which is why I am awarding you the contract for the Artemis party.'

The words hovered in the air between them, and for some reason Tahlia felt a lump form in her throat. 'Well, that's good to hear,' she said huskily, shocked by how much his opinion of her mattered. 'I'd be honoured to do it.' Panic kicked in as she contemplated the prestigious event he had asked her to organise at short notice. 'But how can I make arrangements for the party when I don't speak Greek?'

'A member of my staff will assist you. Ana speaks English fluently, and she can translate for you when necessary. Your job is to come up with ideas for a party that will be unforgettable and will put the Artemis on the list of the world's most exclusive hotels.'

Thanos handed her a folder.

'This is the guest list. You'll see that many of the celebrities have specific requirements on everything from the size of room they want to the colour of the towels in their bathrooms. It will be your job to ensure that they cannot find fault with the Artemis.'

Tahlia scanned through the file and noted that a well-known actress had given instructions that she was only to be served foods from those listed on her strict macrobiotic diet sheet. She would have liked six months to organise an event of this magnitude instead of three weeks, and her doubts must have shown on her face.

'I have every faith that you can do this, Tahlia,' Thanos murmured. 'And I will, of course, pay you a salary for your professional expertise,' he added in a tone that brooked no argument. 'Your work for Reynolds has proved that you have talent and a wealth of innovative ideas, which are exactly the qualities I'm looking for.'

After all the misunderstandings between them, and the contempt he had shown her when he had believed she had been his brother-in-law's mistress, the note of respect in his voice was balm to her battered self-respect. She was ashamed that she had agreed to be his mistress in return for him helping her father, but there had been no other way. Now, in offering her the party contract, she felt as though Thanos considered her an equal, and there was a new confidence in her voice when she stood up and smiled at him.

'I'd better make a start,' she said briskly. 'Three weeks will fly past.'

She refused to dwell on the knowledge that at the end of that time Thanos would no longer need her in any capacity, and that she would go home and probably never see him again. Enjoy the here and now, she bade herself as she followed him into Ana's office. She could no longer kid herself that being with him was a hardship. She was drawn to him in a way she did not understand, and she could only pray that her fascination with him would have faded by the time he ended their relationship.

'Why the frown?' Thanos queried, regarding Tahlia across the restaurant table. 'Don't you like the *baklava*?'

'Unfortunately I like it too much,' she replied ruefully, popping the last piece of the delicious pastry made with ground nuts and honey into her mouth. 'I adore Greek food— but it's not doing my waistline any good.'

'You look gorgeous to me, *agape*.' Thanos watched the flush of rosy colour stain Tahlia's cheeks and felt the same curious ache in his gut that had assailed that morning, when he had woken before her and studied her while she slept.

Three weeks in the Mediterranean sunshine had given her skin a light golden tan and added streaks of blonde to her pale red hair, making her eyes appear an even denser shade of sapphire-blue. He felt the familiar flood of heat course through his veins, but he had given up trying to fight his desire for her and instead savoured the anticipation that very soon they would return to the hotel and he would make love to her.

'So, what's troubling you?'

Tahlia gave him an incredulous look. 'The Artemis party— what else? You do realise it's a week from now? I was just thinking that I must phone the pyrotechnic company tomorrow, to check the arrangements for the firework display they're giving as a finale.'

It was one of several dozen items on her 'to do' list, she brooded anxiously. To celebrate the fact that Thanos owned hotels around the world she had decided on an international theme, and she had booked entertainers and chefs from the Caribbean, South America and the Far East to fly out to Mykonos. But, as she had feared, it was proving difficult to make the arrangements at such short notice, and her long days in the office were fraught with problems. Despite being involved in intense negotiations to buy the Ambassador Hotel in London, Thanos was taking a close interest in the party. She just hoped it would live up to his expectations.

'Ana can phone them,' Thanos told her. 'We're going to

Santorini tomorrow. I have another hotel there—the Astraea. It opened a year ago, and has already gained an excellent reputation. I thought it might be useful for you to see a hotel similar to the Artemis in operation.'

That made sense, Tahlia acknowledged. She had planned the various entertainments for the Artemis party while the hotel was empty, and she was having trouble visualising the reception rooms packed with people. 'How long do you think the trip will take? If we're going in the morning I should be able to go into the office in the afternoon.'

'Uh-uh.' Thanos shook his head, and his smile stole her breath. 'We'll be out all day—maybe all night too,' he added, a devilish gleam in his eyes. 'You've worked ten-hour days for the past two weeks and you need a break.'

He did not add that he had planned the trip so that he could spend some time alone with her away from the office, where the predominant topic of conversation between them was the forthcoming party. He could use some relaxation time too, he conceded, running his hand around the back of his neck and feeling the tight knot of tension. In the weeks after Melina's accident his usual coping strategy of suppressing his emotions had kicked in and he had functioned on auto-pilot as he'd combined running a billion-pound company with helping to nurse her. Now Melina was recovering so well that her doctors predicted she would soon be walking unaided. His relief was indescribable, but in the last six months he felt as though he had aged ten years.

He settled the bill for their meal and followed Tahlia out of the restaurant, slipping his hand into hers as they strolled along by the harbour, where fishing boats rocked gently on the calm sea. 'We're travelling to Santorini on my boat. I've a meeting scheduled with the manager of the Astraea, but it shouldn't take too long. After that we'll have the day to ourselves.'

Don't read too much into it, Tahlia told herself firmly. It was true she had worked hard these past couple of weeks. Thanos was simply being kind in offering to take her out for the day. But she could not deny her excitement at the prospect of sharing a whole day with him. Usually they only spent a few hours in the evenings together, when they ate dinner at the Artemis, or walked into Mykonos Town and found a little restaurant, before strolling back to the hotel to make love until they were both sated.

'Would you like to go to a club or head back to the Artemis?' he murmured as they passed the doors of one of the island's many nightclubs.

Would she seem too eager if she said she would prefer to return to the privacy of their suite? The gleam in his dark eyes told her he had read her mind, and she gave him an impish smile. 'I'd like to go back to the hotel.'

His brows lifted quizzically. 'You're tired?'

'Not at all.'

'Ah.' His deep laughter rumbled in his chest. 'Then an early night is definitely in order, *agape mou*. Come on—we'll walk back along the beach.'

They walked down the steps, onto the sand, and kicked off their shoes. Thanos rolled up the hems of his trousers and led her down to the shore, slipping his arm around her waist as they wandered slowly along the water's edge.

She would not be seduced by the moonlit beach, or the myriad stars that studded the velvet sky above them, Tahlia assured herself. Thanos was a charming companion, and they had enjoyed some wonderful dinners together—and of course the sex was amazing—but he meant nothing to her. But when he halted and turned her to face him she felt the familiar weakness invade her bones and knew she was kidding herself. They had become friends as well as lovers over the past weeks, and had discovered a shared interest in films and authors as well as a mutual love of travel. His dry sense of humour made her laugh, and his desire for her, which showed no sign of lessening, equalled her passion for him.

'Come back,' he murmured, his deep, gravelly voice tugging her from her thoughts. 'You keep leaving me tonight. What are you thinking about?'

About how empty my life is going to be without you, she thought silently. About how afraid I am that I'm falling in love with you.

'I was thinking about Melina,' she told him. It was not completely untrue—his sister had been on her conscience since Melina had discovered her in bed with James. She felt him stiffen, but he said nothing so she continued huskily. 'I would like to write to her and explain…that I never meant to hurt her…that I didn't know about her, and that if I had I would never have dated James. He fooled both of us,' she said sadly. 'I would do anything to change the events of that night, and I would like to tell her how sorry I am about everything.'

No sound disturbed the still air and the darkness seemed to press in on them.

'Have I made you angry?' she whispered, when she could bear his silence no longer.

'No. I'm not angry with you.' His anger was solely with himself, for the way he had misjudged her, Thanos acknowledged bleakly. He had believed the press stories about her and assumed she was a callous bitch. He had given Tahlia every reason to hate him, but during the past weeks he had come to know her, and he seriously doubted that she possessed the capacity for hatred. She had neither judged nor condemned him for the way he had treated her when he had first brought her to Mykonos, and he felt humbled by her generosity of spirit. Somehow she had slipped beneath his guard, and he wasn't sure what he was going to do about it.

'I have already explained the situation to Melina, but I think she would like to hear from you. She has moved to the convalescent wing of the hospital now. I'll give you the address.'

'Thank you.' Tahlia breathed the words against his lips as he claimed her mouth in a slow, sweet kiss that drew her urgent response. Don't fall for him, her head whispered. But her heart knew that the warning came too late.

The *Leandros* was a ninety-foot luxury yacht, so lavishly fitted out that Tahlia lapsed into stunned silence while Thanos gave her a guided tour.

'Besides the master bedroom there are four additional guest cabins, as well as staff quarters,' he told her as he led the way back through the sumptuous lounge and dining room up the stairs to the main deck. She followed him over to the seating area beneath a white canopy which billowed gently in the breeze. As she sat down a uniformed deck-hand immediately stepped forward and served them flutes of Buck's Fizz.

'It's an amazing boat,' she murmured, taking a sip of her drink and then blinking hard. 'The bubbles have gone up my nose,' she giggled self-consciously. 'I hope there's a higher ratio of orange juice than champagne. I don't usually drink alcohol at ten o'clock in the morning. It'll probably send me to sleep.'

'I will do my best to ensure you stay awake,' Thanos murmured, his eyes gleaming with amusement when she blushed.

He looked more relaxed than she had ever seen him, and utterly gorgeous in close-fitting sun-bleached jeans and a black tee shirt which was stretched tight over the powerful muscles of his chest and abdomen. His black hair was brushed back from his brow, and he looked lean and fit and so incredibly sexy that Tahlia almost melted on the spot.

His smile made her heart flip, and she grinned back at him. 'Do you take the *Leandros* out often?'

'Not as often as I'd like. Work tends to dominate my life. Melina and I used to invite a crowd of friends and cruise around the islands for a few weeks in the summer, but that stopped once she married. James's idea of fun was to go clubbing every night, and he moaned that the pace of life on the boat was too quiet,' he said grimly.

He had known from the outset that James Hamilton and Melina were not suited, he thought heavily. Given the chance, he would have done his best to dissuade his sister from marrying the brash American actor, but he'd had no opportunity to voice his doubts. Melina had arrived at his house in Athens with a cocky Hamilton in tow and revealed that they had married on the spur of the moment in Las Vegas.

'Don't be angry,' she'd pleaded, when Thanos had muttered his disapproval. 'I know James is the right man for me, and we're going to spend the rest of our lives together.'

But James had quickly grown bored with married life. He had never trusted his brother-in-law, Thanos conceded. In all honesty he had expected Melina's marriage to fail. He had known of James's reputation as a playboy, but in his fury over Melina's accident he had blamed Tahlia and refused to believe her claim that she was innocent.

At his mention of Melina and James, Thanos had fallen into a brooding silence that stretched Tahlia's nerves. 'How long will it take us to reach Santorini?' she murmured, keen to change the subject.

'We'll be there in about half an hour.' He stretched his long legs out in front of him and regarded her from behind his designer shades. 'Have you visited the Greek islands before?'

She shook her head. 'No. I backpacked around France and Spain, but other than that I've always spent my holidays with my parents in Cornwall.'

'You're close to your parents, aren't you?'

'I adore them,' Tahlia agreed. 'I'm their only child, and I guess there was a danger they could have spoiled me rotten, but they brought me up to appreciate the value of love and friendship rather than money, and they encouraged me to work hard at school so that I would have good career prospects. They would have liked more children, but Mum miscarried two babies after me and said she couldn't face the heartbreak of it happening again, so they decided to be thankful that they had one child. They're great people,' she added softly. 'I'd do anything for them—'

She broke off abruptly, wondering if Thanos would make some scathing remark about how she had sold herself to him to help her parents, but he remained silent and she quickly changed the subject again.

'Do you own hotels on any other Greek islands?'

'The Alkimini on Agistri was my first hotel, followed by the Athena on Poros, and my latest project, the Aphrodite, is currently being built on Rhodes and should be ready to open next spring. My aim is to build hotels on all the most popular islands.'

Thanos was not joking, Tahlia realised as she heard the determined note in his voice. 'How did you start your business?' she asked him curiously. 'I mean, what made you decide to build hotels?'

He was silent for a moment, considering the question, and then he said grimly, 'Desperation is probably the best answer. Desperation to keep the promise I had made my mother that I would look after Melina. I had nothing, you see. No money and little education. The only thing I had was some land on Agistri. My mother had inherited it from her family, but I did not know about it until after her death. I learned that I owned six acres of land and a spectacular view of the sea.' He laughed. 'To be honest I was not overly impressed. The ground was too rocky to farm, and its only use was as grazing land for goats. Meanwhile I was travelling to the nearby island of Aegina every day, to work as a labourer on the dozens of hotels being built there. One evening back on Agistri I watched the sun setting over the sea, and it struck me that if I could build a hotel on my land the view would be a major attraction for tourists.

'It wasn't easy,' he admitted. 'But I managed to talk the local bank manager into giving me a loan for building materials, and I convinced the island's councillors that a hotel would help Agistri's economy. For the next two years I worked on construction sites on Aegina during the day and in the evening I paid a group of labourers to help me build my hotel. The Alkimini is named after my mother. Agistri's close proximity to the mainland and Athens meant that many Greek families came for holidays, and the hotel was soon so successful that I was soon able to repay the loan and buy a prime site on the island of Poros.'

Thanos made light of his route to success, but Tahlia was sure that his life had been incredibly tough, and she felt a surge of admiration for him. 'How did you manage to take care of Melina while you were working all those hours?'

He shrugged. 'She was at school during the day, and then she would sit in the site office and do her homework. On Poros we actually lived in a Portakabin on the site while the Athena was being built, and as she grew older she often cooked for the workers. It wasn't an ideal childhood,' he said heavily. 'In the early days all the money I earned went into the business, and I often felt guilty that she missed out on the things her friends took for granted, like new clothes and school trips. But she never complained,' he said, his face softening. 'Although she did go through a stage of pestering me to get married. I think her reasoning was that if I had a wife she would no longer have to do the cooking.'

'Did you never consider it?' Tahlia murmured.

He was silent for so long that she thought he was not going to answer, but then he shrugged laconically. 'I was engaged briefly. Yalena came from my village and we grew up together. I suppose I was about fifteen when I first fell in love with her. When my parents' marriage ended, and then they both died, Yalena was the one person I could confide in. I worshipped her,' he admitted, his face hardening, 'and I believed that she loved me. I was overjoyed when she agreed to marry me. She seemed fond of Melina, and I thought we would live together as a family. But a month before our wedding Yalena admitted that she had secretly been seeing one of my closest friends.

'Takis came from one of the wealthiest families on Agistri. His father owned a fishing fleet and Takis had a secure future—whereas I had a scrubby patch of land, a crazy idea, huge debts and an orphaned kid sister.' He gave a harsh laugh. 'Hell, if I'd been in Yalena's shoes, I'd have picked the richer guy too.'

Tahlia caught the note of bitterness in his voice and her heart turned over as she imagined Thanos as a young man, struggling to make a living and care for a young child. 'What did you do when she told you?' she asked curiously.

He gave another shrug. 'What could I do? Takis was the better choice, and I loved Yalena enough that I wanted what was best for her. I released her from our engagement, gave them my blessing, and drowned my sorrows in ouzo on their wedding day,' he finished, with a self-derisive laugh that did not quite disguise the pain he had felt. At twenty he had worn his heart on his sleeve; now he was determined that no other woman would have the power to touch his emotions.

'I'm not surprised you got drunk,' Tahlia said softly. 'You had been deceived by the girl you loved, and your best friend. You must have been hurt.'

Thanos frowned. He had never spoken about his relationship with Yalena to anyone, and he did not understand why he had shared such a personal confidence with Tahlia. Maybe it was because she actually listened—unlike the self-centred women he usually dated, who only wanted to talk about themselves.

'To be honest, I had put Yalena on a pedestal,' he said grimly. 'But six months ago I discovered her true nature. She contacted me out of the blue and suggested we meet up to talk about old times. I assumed Takis would be with her, but she came to my hotel alone and made it clear that, since I was now far wealthier than her husband, she regretted dumping me all those years ago. She offered to divorce Takis, and seemed to think I would jump at the chance to marry her. She was rather put out when I turned her down,' he added sardonically. 'But I was glad I had met her again. It made me realise what a lucky escape I'd had all those years ago, and confirmed my belief that love is an illusion and marriage is an outdated institution.'

'I don't believe that,' Tahlia said quietly. 'My parents have been happily married for thirty years.'

'I guess there are always a few exceptions,' Thanos conceded. 'But my parents' marriage was destroyed by my father's infidelity, and Melina was devastated when she discovered that James was having an affair.'

Tahlia bit her lip. Thanos had told her he accepted that she had been deceived by James Hamilton, but she still felt guilty for the part she had played in ending Melina's marriage. She did not know what to say, and after a few moments she stood up and walked across the deck, leaning against the boat rail as she absorbed the beauty of the crystal-clear Aegean shimmering in the sunshine.

The *Leandros* was heading towards a land mass which rose steeply out of the sea, and as they drew nearer Tahlia saw that the reddish-brown cliffs were topped with hundreds of white houses, which from a distance looked like icing on top of a cake.

'Santorini is on the site of a volcano,' Thanos explained as he came to stand next to her. 'The cliff-sides are volcanic rock and the island forms a bay around the caldera.'

'The cliffs are so high,' Tahlia murmured, staring up at the rugged rocks towering above them.

'I believe the capital, Fira, is over two hundred metres above sea level. The views from the cable-car that you can see running up the side of the mountain are spectacular, but today we are sailing further up the coast. The Astraea is close to the village of Oia, which is reputed to have the most fantastic sunsets in the world.'

'You like your sunsets, don't you?' Tahlia teased him, remembering how he had said that watching the sun setting on Agistri had given him the idea to build a hotel there.

Thanos's mood seemed to have lightened, and he laughed. 'Sunsets and spectacular views attract tourists. We can travel up to the Astraea by car, or climb the three hundred or so steps up the cliff-side,' he told her, when the *Leandros* had sailed into the tiny port and dropped anchor.

Tahlia lifted her face to the sun and breathed in the salt tang of the sea. 'I'm game for the steps,' she assured him, her pulse racing when he caught hold of her hand. The breeze ruffled his dark hair, and his sudden grin made her heart contract.

'Okay—but don't say I didn't warn you.'

She was panting by the time they reached the top of the cliff, but her lack of breath was not only because of the steep climb, she acknowledged ruefully. Thanos kept hold of her hand as they strolled through the narrow streets of Oia, and waited patiently while she paused to admire the stunning architecture of the blue-domed church and the jumble of sugar-cube white houses with their window boxes full of scarlet pelargoniums.

The Astraea was perched on the edge of the cliff, and as Thanos had promised, offered wonderful views over the bay and nearby islands.

'There are one or two problems that need my attention, but I should be finished in an hour,' he told her, after he had given her a guided tour of the hotel. 'Ask one of the reception staff to give you directions to the beach, and I'll meet you there later.'

She had found paradise, Tahlia decided some while later, when she had scrambled down a steep path from the hotel and arrived at a tiny picturesque cove. The *Leandros* was moored out in the bay, and she guessed that one of the deck hands had brought the parasol and picnic rug, which were now arranged on the beach, from the boat. The cove was deserted, hidden from view by the rugged cliffs, and she stripped down to her bikini and stretched out on the rug, wriggling her shoulders in pleasure as the sun warmed her skin. Her eyelids felt heavy. She hadn't had much sleep the previous night, she thought wryly, recalling how Thanos had made love to her with all his considerable skill, so that she had climaxed three times before he had finally lost control and experienced his own shattering release…

'I hope you applied plenty of sunscreen.'

Thanos's deep voice roused her from a shockingly erotic dream in which he was stroking his hands over her naked body. She glanced at her watch and saw that she had been asleep for almost an hour, and then let out a yelp as she felt something cold on her back.

'You don't want to burn,' he murmured, as he began to smooth lotion over her shoulders.

Tahlia's eyes flew open to see him lying on the rug beside

her, propped up on one elbow, while he continued to smooth the cream onto her skin. He had stripped off his jeans and tee shirt and looked devastatingly sexy in a pair of navy swim-shorts, his skin gleaming like polished bronze in the sunshine. The rhythmic stroking of his hands on her back was wickedly sensuous, but she resisted the urge to turn over and pull him down on top of her.

'That should do,' she said in a strained voice, blushing furiously when she sat up and saw that her nipples had hardened and were straining beneath her Lycra bikini top. She felt his eyes slide down her body, and when she glanced at his face she was startled by the feral hunger blazing in his eyes.

'We'll spend an hour or so on the beach, and then return to the *Leandros* for a late lunch,' he said idly, brushing her hair over her shoulder and trailing his mouth up her neck.

'Good plan…' Tahlia drew a sharp breath when his teeth nipped her earlobe, sending a quiver of delicious sensation through her. 'How did your meeting go? Did you resolve the problems?'

'Concerning the Astraea, yes. But a new set of problems has arisen in the Caribbean. My hotel on St Lucia was damaged in a tropical storm that hit the island at the weekend. I'm flying out there immediately after the Artemis party.'

That meant that this time next week he would be on the other side of the world—and she would be back in England. Sudden tears blurred her vision, and she turned her head, pretending to stare at the sea while she fought to control her emotions. She had always known that their relationship was a temporary affair. The deal they had struck had been for her to spend one month with him as his mistress and soon their contract would be finished, leaving him free to continue with his own life.

Did he have a lover on St Lucia? Probably, she acknowledged bleakly. Ana, the Greek girl who had been helping her with the party arrangements, had said that Thanos had various mistresses around the world. A week from now he would most likely have forgotten her.

He moved his hands to her shoulders and gently tugged her towards him, but she stiffened, unable to bear the thought of making love with him while she was breaking up inside.

'I've been sunbathing for too long. I'm going to have a swim,' she choked. Tears were falling unchecked down her face, and with a muffled sob she jumped up and raced down the beach.

# CHAPTER NINE

THE sea was shockingly cold on Tahlia's sun-warmed skin, but she tore through the shallows and dived beneath a wave so that her tears mingled with the spray. She struck out away from the shore, wanting to put as much distance as possible between her and Thanos, who was watching her broodingly from the beach. She swam until she was out of breath, and then flipped onto her back and allowed the waves to carry her. He was no longer sitting on the sand. She squinted against the sun, trying to spot him, and then gasped when strong arms suddenly closed around her.

'You frightened the life out of me,' she snapped, and she pushed against his chest, trying to force him to release her. But he merely tightened his grip and dragged her closer, so that she was trapped against his hard thighs. 'Let me go,' she cried frantically, hating her treacherous body as molten heat coursed through her veins, undermining her determination to resist him.

'I can't,' he growled savagely, tangling his fingers in her hair and lowering his head.

He captured her lips in a kiss of pure possession, thrusting his tongue deep into her mouth and exploring her with such erotic skill that she instantly melted. She was out of her depth in more ways than one, she acknowledged, as she tried to stand and realised that the ocean floor was far beneath her. She had no choice but to cling to Thanos for support. And as she curled her arms around his neck she knew she had lost the battle. She wanted him, *needed* him to make love to her. And when she kissed him back with feverish passion and heard the low groan torn from his throat nothing mattered except her desperation for him to possess her.

He waded back to the shallows and lowered her onto the damp sand, not lifting his mouth from hers as he came down on top of her. She was a drug in his veins, and like an addict he could not resist her lure. His hunger for her consumed him utterly, Thanos acknowledged as he stared into her eyes, as blue and crystal-clear as the Aegean.

What was it about this woman that made him wish for something more than simply sexual satisfaction? He had been a fool once before, he reminded himself savagely. Yalena had ripped his heart out, and he had sworn never to open himself up to such pain ever again. He had thought that if he made Tahlia his mistress his obsession with her would eventually fade, leaving him free to continue with a life dominated by work and occasionally enlivened by meaningless affairs with women who meant nothing to him. But as he stared down at her and saw the shimmer of tears in her eyes it struck him that he was tired of his old life.

He kissed her throat, the fragile line of her collarbone, the creamy swell of her breast. Her nipples were jutting provocatively through the wet Lycra of her bikini top, and with a muffled oath he unfastened the strings around her neck and peeled the tiny triangles down, his body tautening as he revealed her breasts in all their naked beauty.

'You are exquisite,' he said hoarsely, and he lowered his head and took first one dusky tip and then its twin into his mouth, smiling against her skin when she cried out and arched her hips in unmistakable invitation. 'I want you.' The admission was torn from him. His hands were clumsy as he dragged her bikini pants down her legs, and he struggled out of his shorts with an equal lack of finesse, his powerful erection nudging impatiently between her thighs. 'You want me too, don't you, Tahlia? We are both prisoners of the desire that thunders through our veins, and *this* is the only truth between us.'

He entered her with one savage thrust—then instantly stilled and cursed beneath his breath. 'Did I hurt you?' he demanded, his voice rasping with self-disgust at his brutality. But Tahlia's body was aroused and eagerly receptive, and she wrapped her legs around his back to prevent him from withdrawing.

'You couldn't hurt me,' she assured him softly, knowing that physically at least it was the truth. Her body had been designed for him, and she gloried in his wildfire passion that matched her own. She kissed him, telling him with her lips what she could not say out loud: that she was his for all time, and he was the keeper of her heart.

She felt him relax momentarily, but almost immediately his body was gripped with a different kind of tension as he moved, slowly at first, and then with increasing pace and strength, claiming her with a primitive hunger as he drove her higher and higher towards the climax her body craved. The sea lapped gently around them, and overhead the sun blazed in the dense blue sky. The haunting cry of a gull broke the still air, but Tahlia only was aware of Thanos's powerful body, driving into her with deep, steady strokes. She could feel his heart thudding in unison with her own, and she dug her heels into the sand, her body arching as the first spasms of exquisite pleasure ripped through her. Still he thrust, faster and faster, his breathing coming in ragged groans as he took her to the edge, kept her poised there for timeless seconds and then with one final hard stroke sent them both into freefall.

*I love you.* She moved her lips over his sweat-slicked chest and breathed the words she could not utter. Soon he would dismiss her from his life, and somehow she would have to live without him. It would be a colourless existence, she thought, her heart contracting painfully. The lonely days and nights ahead would seem unbearable. But he was with her now, and she clung to him as if she could somehow imprint the feel of his body on hers for all time.

'Are you all right?' he asked roughly, lifting his head from her neck and smoothing her hair back from her face with a hand that shook slightly. 'As you may have noticed, you have a disastrous effect on my self-control.' His jaw tightened, and he added in a raw tone laced with self-disgust, 'I regret that with you I become a barbarian.'

Tenderness overflowed Tahlia's heart, and she stroked her hand down his cheek. 'I don't regret your passion. I love the way you make love to me,' she whispered shyly.

He stared down at her, the expression in his dark eyes unfathomable, and she was afraid she had revealed too much. When he rolled away from her and stood up she tensed, waiting for him to make some scornful remark, but he reached his hand out to help her to her feet and drew her into his arms.

'Come to St Lucia with me?'

She must have misheard him. A gull mewed in the sky above her, and her heart hammered in her chest as she stared at him wordlessly, searching for signs that he had been joking. But the expression in his eyes was deadly serious, and her heart beat faster. Why? She wanted to ask him. For how long? A week, a month? Did it matter when her whole being was crying out to agree? she thought shakily. Nothing in life came with guarantees—losing Michael had taught her that. Why not live for the here and now, and enjoy an affair with him for however long it lasted? Was she brave enough?

'I can't,' she whispered. 'I need to go home, start looking for another job…'

'There would be no need for you to work while you are with me.'

Colour flared in her cheeks. 'I would *never* allow you to keep me. I pay my own way. It was only for my parents' sake that I…' She stumbled to a halt, shame sweeping over her at the memory of how she had sold herself to him.

'The reasons why I brought you to Mykonos are in the past,' Thanos told her fiercely. 'I want us to have a future—to enjoy our relationship for as long as either of us wants it to last.' He could not envisage a time when he would not desire her. She had captivated him like no other woman ever had. But the clichéd happy-ever-after? He'd seen too many relationships fail to contemplate commitment.

What would he say if she revealed that she wanted to be with him for ever? She stared up at his hard-boned face and acknowledged that he was as untameable as she had first thought, when she had looked across the art gallery in London and seen him. His early years had been tough, and had made him into a resolute, independent man who relied on no one, who forged his own destiny, and she doubted he would allow any woman to breach his defences.

'After St Lucia I was planning to take a break for a couple of weeks at my villa in Antigua. It's beautiful there, and we could spend some time away from everyday pressures—chill out and enjoy each other's company,' he murmured persuasively.

His mouth was a whisper away from hers, an unbearable temptation she did not have the strength to resist. 'That sounds good.' Her breath feathered his lips. 'You work too hard. Maybe I can help you to relax?'

Laugher rumbled deep in his chest. 'The last thing I feel when I am with you, *agape*, is relaxed.' His smile faded and his eyes focused intently on her face. 'You'll come?'

She ignored the feeling that she was about to cast herself off a cliff without the assurance that a safety net would catch her, and nodded. 'Yes.'

The inherent tenderness of his kiss pierced her soul, and she kissed him back with all the emotion she could not reveal in words. When he swung her into his arms she clung to his shoulders and gave him a questioning look.

'You are very lovely, *agape mou*, but also very sandy.' He grinned, looking suddenly like the boy he had been many years ago, before he had been weighed down with responsibility. 'We need to swim.' He carried her into the sea, laughing as he lowered her into the waves, and splashed her until she dived into the crystal depths. The cool water felt sensuous on her naked body, and when Thanos caught her and held her against his chest she curled her arms around his neck, her laughter fading as he captured her mouth in a hungry kiss that revealed the urgency of his need to possess her.

Thanos propped himself up on one elbow and watched the early-morning sunlight dance across Tahlia's hair, turning it into a golden halo on the pillows. Her long lashes fanned her cheeks and her face was serene. His sleeping angel, he brooded, feeling a curious tugging sensation in his chest. But the feelings she evoked in him were far from pious, and he could not resist drawing back the sheet so that the sunlight gilded her slender limbs and her small, firm breasts. Her skin felt like satin beneath his fingertips as he trailed a path over her flat stomach, then moved lower to the triangle of tight gold curls that hid her femininity. She was unutterably beautiful, and he hardened instantly as he slid his hand between her pale thighs and very gently parted her.

'Thanos?' Her lashes drifted upwards, her eyes still dazed with sleep.

'Who else were you expecting?' he demanded arrogantly.

Her smile stole his breath. 'You,' she whispered softly. 'Only you.'

She opened her mouth beneath his, welcoming the bold thrust of his tongue, and kissed him back with drowsy passion until he eased the pressure of his lips so that the kiss became a slow, sensual tasting, with an underlying tenderness that brought tears to Tahlia's eyes. Her breath hitched in her throat when he trailed his mouth down to her breast and teased her swollen nipple with his tongue, before administering the same delicious torture to its twin.

The feather-light brush of his lips on her inner thigh demolished her thought process—but something was niggling in her brain.

'Thanos! The party!'

'It's not until tonight, *agape*. I promise I'll let you up by then.'

'But there are things to do…'

She caught her breath as he lowered his head and his tongue probed delicately between her velvet folds. Moist heat pooled between her thighs and she instinctively spread her legs wider, gasping when he closed his lips around the sensitive nub of her clitoris. Sensation scorched her, and she whimpered with pleasure, desperate for him to continue his sorcery but unable to dismiss the voice in her head which pointed out that this was the day of the Artemis opening party, and she had planned to get up at dawn.

Frantically she dug her fingers into his luxuriant black hair and tugged. 'But, Thanos, I should…'

He lifted his head briefly and murmured, 'You want me to stop?'

'Yes.' She lifted her hips in mute supplication, groaning when his wickedly invasive tongue dipped between her silken folds. 'No… Don't stop—don't ever stop.'

She was trembling by the time he moved over her, and she sobbed his name as he penetrated her with deep, thrusting strokes, his movements slow and deliberate, demonstrating his complete control.

'This is all that matters, Tahlia *mou,*' he said roughly, his heart pounding so hard beneath his ribs that he felt as though he had run a marathon.

He was shocked to realise that he had spoken the truth. His need to make love to her was a driving force inside him: more important than his business, more important than the forthcoming party to celebrate the opening of his new hotel—even, he acknowledged grimly, more important than his sister. *Theos*, what was he thinking? But his powers of reasoning were slipping away, and he was conscious of nothing but the desperate clamouring of his body as he strove for the release he craved.

He slipped his hands beneath her bottom and lifted her hips, driving into her with faster and deeper strokes until she cried out. The exquisite sensation of her muscles contracting around him threatened to shatter his restraint.

'*Tahlia.*' He threw his head back, the cords on his neck straining as he fought for control. Sex had never been this good with any of his previous lovers. Only with Tahlia did he feel a sense of utter abandonment. With a harsh groan his control splintered and he shuddered, wave after wave of pleasure ripping through him until he collapsed onto her and closed his eyes, wondering why his heart ached every time he made her his.

In the aftermath he held her close, stroking his fingers

through her hair. She could stay here all day, Tahlia thought dreamily. But the Artemis party was important to him, and she wanted it to be perfect.

'Now I'll let you go to work,' he said with a grin, dropping a stinging kiss on her mouth as she gave a languorous stretch.

'Thank you, kind sir,' she teased with an impish smile before she walked unselfconsciously across the room to the *en suite* bathroom, aware of the heat in his dark eyes as he focused on her naked body.

'Have you decided what you're going to wear tonight?'

She paused in the doorway and glanced back at him, feeling the familiar dip in her stomach at the sight of his bronzed, muscular body stretched out indolently on the rumpled sheets. 'I'm not going to the party. I can't,' she continued quickly, when his brows lowered in a slashing frown. 'There will be huge media coverage tonight, and I don't want to risk being photographed with you. How would you explain my presence to Melina? It would be…awkward.' She bit her lip, rattled by his ominous silence. 'I'll ensure that all the preparations are in place, and tonight Ana will be on hand to deal with any last-minute problems.'

Thanos regarded her for a few moments, his expression unfathomable. 'Melina is my responsibility,' he said quietly. 'You don't have to worry about her. You *will* attend the party as my partner. That's an order, Tahlia,' he added forcefully, when she opened her mouth to argue. 'You've put in all the work, and tonight is your night as much as mine.' He jumped up from the bed and strode out of the room, reappearing seconds later, holding a flat box. 'I bought this for you to wear tonight.'

She gave him a startled glance, and then lifted the lid from the box and pushed aside the layers of filmy white tissue paper to reveal an ivory silk gown. With shaking fingers she took it from the box and caught her breath as she held it against her.

'Oh, Thanos…it's beautiful.' Her throat did not seem to want to work and her voice sounded distinctly rusty. The dress was exquisite: a floor-length silk sheath, covered in layers of fragile chiffon and embellished with tiny crystals and pearls on its narrow shoulder-straps and around a sweetheart neckline. 'It's a fairytale dress,' she whispered, dropping her gaze from him so that he would not see her sudden rush of tears.

He slid his hand beneath her chin and tilted her face to his. 'Tonight you will be my princess, *agape mou*.'

Her smile tugged at his insides, and the ache in his gut intensified when she reached up and brushed her lips over his in a feather-light caress that pierced him with its poignant sweetness. They needed to talk, he acknowledged as she walked into the bathroom. There were things he needed to say, to tell her. But he could not forget the original terms of the bargain they had made, and he wondered if he was a fool to hope that his money was not the only reason she gave her body to him every night with a tender passion that stirred his soul.

Tahlia was confident that all the preparations she had made over the past three weeks would ensure that the Artemis opening night party would be a success, but as she had feared there were still unexpected problems which required her attention. She spent the day making last-minute calls, organising media coverage, and attempting to meet the demands of the celebrity guests. It was early evening by the time she returned to the suite, and after a quick shower she blowdried her hair and applied minimal make-up—mascara on her lashes to emphasise the deep blue of her eyes, and a pearly pink gloss on her lips—before she stepped into the dress Thanos had chosen for her.

It was from a well-known design house and must have cost a fortune. She felt uncomfortable that he had spent so much money on her when he was already paying a huge sum for Reynolds Gems—but he had been adamant that he wanted her to wear it tonight, and she would have worn a wetsuit and flippers if it had pleased him, she acknowledged ruefully.

The door opened and he stepped into the bedroom, halting abruptly when she spun round to face him. 'You take my breath away, *agape*,' he said at length, sweeping his eyes over her in a lingering appraisal which encompassed her amber-gold hair, falling in a silky curtain around her shoulders, and the ivory dress that skimmed her slender figure.

He walked over to her and withdrew a slim velvet box from his jacket pocket. 'This will complement the dress perfectly,' he murmured, lifting out a necklace of creamy pearls inter-linked with glittering diamonds. 'It is a gift in thanks for the hours of hard work you have spent organising the party.'

'Thanos, I can't accept it,' Tahlia said faintly when he turned her to face the mirror. She stared at their twin reflec-tions: the tall, impossibly handsome man in a black dinner jacket, and the woman at his side wearing a couture gown and an exquisite necklace around her throat. 'You don't need to give me presents. I've enjoyed working at the Artemis.'

'Even so, you deserve a break. I will have to spend some time dealing with the problems at my hotel on St Lucia, but our trip to Antigua is purely for pleasure—or impurely,' he murmured wickedly, his eyes gleaming with sensual promise. 'I admit I am impatient to have you to myself, without other distractions, *agape mou*.'

His smile tugged at her heart, and when he lowered his mouth to hers, tears pricked her eyes at the sweetness of his kiss. She'd thought she had imagined the feeling of unity between them every time they made love, and had told herself she was a fool to hope that the Greek words he murmured in the aftermath of their passion meant that she was special to him.

He had once stated that love was an illusion, but the erratic thud of his heart beneath her fingertips was excitingly real.

'We need to talk,' he said quietly, when at last he broke the kiss and stared down at her flushed face. His heart turned over when her lashes swept down a fraction too late to disguise the emotion blazing in her eyes.

'But there's no time now.'

As if on cue, someone knocked on the door of the suite and his mouth tightened.

'That's probably Ana,' Tahlia said huskily. 'I'll just get my purse.'

The phone on the bedside table rang and she picked it up, frowning as the receptionist relayed a message.

'I have a call from my mother,' she told Thanos in a puzzled tone. When she had first arrived on Mykonos she had contacted her parents to explain that she was staying in Greece with a friend for a few weeks, and had given the phone number of the Artemis. An inexplicable feeling of dread coiled in her stomach. 'I hope she's okay.'

'I'll go down with Ana while you take the call,' he said, striding towards the door. 'We're not due to greet our guests for another twenty minutes.'

Tahlia watched him walk out of the room and heard him speak to Ana, followed by the snick of the door as he left the suite. 'Mum?' she gripped the phone as the sound of sobbing met her ears. 'What's wrong?'

'Oh, Tahlia, I don't understand anything,' Vivienne choked incoherently. 'Your father and I arrived back from Cornwall today to find a letter from the bank saying that Carlton House is to be repossessed. Your father admitted that he hadn't paid off the mortgage he took out to finance Reynolds Gems, and we're behind with the payments. He phoned some people—Vantage something or other…'

Vivienne paused and took a shuddering breath. 'He assured me that Vantage had agreed to buy Reynolds, and we would have the money for the house. But when he finished speaking to the CEO he was as pale as a ghost. It seems that Vantage was never interested in Reynolds. The parent company—whatever that is—refused permission for the buy-out. Dad had already assured the bank that Vantage were going to purchase Reynolds Gems, and that he would immediately clear the mortgage. But the bank checked with Vantage, and when they discovered the sale wasn't going ahead they called in the loan on Carlton.' Vivienne's voice broke. 'When your father heard that he collapsed.'

'What do you mean, he collapsed?' Tahlia demanded shakily. 'Mum…?'

'He's all right,' her mother assured her. 'Hobson called an ambulance, and the hospital did lots of checks on his heart, but all the results were fine. They say he's just suffering from extreme stress. Tahlia, I don't know what to do.'

Her mother wept, and the fear in her voice tore at Tahlia's heart.

'The bailiffs are coming at midday tomorrow to evict us, and they will seize any of our possessions that are still in the house. I don't know where to begin with the packing.' Her voice was shrill with panic. 'Our whole life is in this house.'

'Mum, you don't need to pack,' Tahlia assured her mother swiftly. 'There's been some sort of mistake. Vantage Investments definitely agreed to buy Reynolds. I'm in contact with someone at the parent company—Savakis Enterprises.' She paused and closed her eyes briefly, wondering what her mother would say if she revealed just how closely her body had been in contact with Thanos's muscular frame every night for the past month. 'Don't cry. I'll sort everything out—okay?' she said softly. 'And then I'll come home.'

It must be a mistake, she told herself frantically as she dragged out her suitcase and started to fling her belongings into it. A misunderstanding between the bank and Vantage seemed the most likely explanation. She took a deep breath, forcing herself to calm down. She would explain the situation to Thanos, and he would resolve the problem—whatever it was.

Unless *he* was the problem? a little voice whispered in her head. No, of course he wasn't. They had made a deal, and he had promised that the buy-out of Reynolds Gems would go ahead. Her relationship with Thanos was no longer based on his desire for revenge, and there was no reason why he should have reneged on his promise. She trusted him, she assured herself as she snatched up her purse, desperate to hurry down to the lobby where he was waiting for her.

But she could not dismiss the heavy sense of foreboding in the pit of her stomach, and after a moment's hesitation she turned back into the room. The likelihood that Vantage's CEO, Steven Holt, would still be in his office late on a Friday evening was remote, but if she could just speak to him first…

The phone rang several times, and she was just about to cut the call when a woman answered. 'Mr Holt is unavailable,' she said tersely. 'I'll put you through to Mark Lloyd.'

Five minutes later an impatient-sounding male voice interrupted Tahlia's frantic explanation of the reason for her call. 'Miss Reynolds, I am an executive director at Vantage Investments and I assure you I am not mistaken. It is true that we were briefly interested in buying your company, but the idea was vetoed by our parent company on the direct orders of the head of Savakis Enterprises.'

'But Mr Savakis promised me…' Tahlia insisted desperately, gripping the phone so hard that her knuckles whitened. 'You *must* be mistaken…'

'I think you'll find that it is *you* who have made a mistake,' the voice on the other end of the line said coldly. 'There is not, and never was, any deal to buy Reynolds Gems. Now, it is late, Miss Reynolds, and I would like to go home. So unless there is anything else…?'

'No…nothing else.' Tahlia's throat felt as though she had swallowed glass, and she had to force the words out. 'Thank you for clarifying the situation, Mr Lloyd.'

She replaced the receiver and sank down onto the bed. The room spun alarmingly. Surely she was not going to do something as melodramatic as faint? Bile rose in her throat and she hunched forward so that the blood rushed to her head. She couldn't faint; she had to get back to Carlton House and her parents before the bailiffs threw them onto the street.

Footsteps sounded on the marble floor, and she jerked her head round as the bedroom door opened.

'What's going on?' Thanos demanded, his eyes narrowing on her white face. 'Why haven't you come down? The guests are gathering in the lobby, waiting for the party to begin, and I want you at my side. Damn it, Tahlia,' he said explosively, when she stared at him with dull eyes. 'What's the matter with you?' He could not forget the anguished moan he'd heard as he had entered the suite. 'Are you ill?'

The pain in her heart was sheer agony—but there could still be a simple explanation for the news she had just heard, Tahlia reminded herself. Slowly she got up from the bed and faced him, her eyes locked on his face.

'Tell me, Thanos, did you ever intend to buy Reynolds Gems? Or did you bring me to Greece and make me your mistress—allow me to believe my father's problems would be solved—while all along you *knew* you had told Vantage Investments not to proceed with the buy-out?'

For a split second something indefinable flared in his eyes, before the mask fell and his expression became unfathomable.

But that tiny hesitation had told Tahlia everything—and her heart splintered.

*Fool*, a voice in her head taunted. Seven months ago she had believed James Hamilton when he had told her that he loved her. She had trusted him implicitly. But he had deceived her as cruelly as he had deceived his wife, and she had vowed never to give her love or trust as easily again. But here she was, with another man, in another hotel bedroom, utterly destroyed by the realisation that Thanos had lied to her. When would she learn that men either abandoned you, or lied and cheated for their own ends, and that they were not worth the heartbreak they caused? she wondered bitterly.

## CHAPTER TEN

'MY MOTHER phoned to tell me that the bank has taken possession of Carlton House,' Tahlia told Thanos tensely. 'The bailiffs are due to arrive tomorrow to evict them.'

He frowned. 'Banks do not usually issue a repossession order unless there are serious mortgage arrears on a property.'

'Dad hasn't kept up with the payments on Carlton for months,' Tahlia said heavily. 'All his money has been tied up in the company. I *told* you all this,' she flung at him bitterly. 'You *knew* my parents were in danger of losing their home.'

'I had not realised that it was quite so imminent.'

'No—I suppose you thought you could string me along for a while longer before you revealed what a lying bastard you are.' Tahlia felt a curious sense of detachment as she watched his mouth tighten with anger. 'My father informed the bank that Vantage was buying Reynolds Gems, and that as soon as the sale went through he would pay off the mortgage on Carlton House. But when the bank checked with Vantage they were told that no sale had ever been agreed. Ten minutes ago I spoke to Mark Lloyd at Vantage, who verified that the buyout had been vetoed by none other than the head of Vantage Investments' parent company, Savakis Enterprises—in other words, by *you*.'

In the simmering silence following her accusation, his lack of denial felt like a knife through her heart.

Tears scalded her throat, but she forced herself to swallow them. 'You've destroyed my parents' lives, and I will *never* forgive you,' she told him, her voice shaking with emotion.

Thanos moved towards her, but halted abruptly when she flinched away from him. 'You're jumping to conclusions,' he said tersely. 'If you would give me a chance to explain—'

'In the same way that you allowed me to defend myself against your accusations that I had deliberately stolen James Hamilton from your sister, you mean?' she interrupted in a brittle voice. 'You refused to listen to me, and in your misguided quest for revenge you demanded that I became your mistress. But worst of all,' she said brokenly, tears slipping down her cheeks, 'you lied to me.'

'Listen to me,' he said urgently. 'I admit that when I first brought you to Greece I had no intention of bailing your father out of his financial mess. My sister had suffered appalling injuries, and as you know I believed you were partly responsible for her accident. The newspapers were full of reports about your wild partying, and your penchant for stealing other women's husbands, and I wanted to hurt you as I believed you had hurt Melina—' His mobile rang. With a muttered curse he answered it, and snapped impatiently, 'I'll be five minutes. Tell the bar staff to serve more champagne to the guests.'

He raked his hand through his hair and stared at Tahlia, frustration etched on his face when she glared at him. 'All that changed when I took you to bed. Sex with you was an incredible experience. I had never known such intense pleasure before,' he admitted harshly. 'And when I discovered that you were a virgin, that I had completely misjudged you…' His voice deepened with an emotion Tahlia could not define. 'I immediately phoned Steven Holt to tell him that I had changed my mind and wanted Vantage to proceed with the buy-out of Reynolds Gems.'

Tahlia recalled the phone call she'd made before Thanos had come back to the suite, and shook her head. 'I don't believe you,' she said dully. 'Mark Lloyd was adamant that Vantage have no plans to buy Reynolds Gems. One of you must be lying—and I don't think it's him.'

'You're calling me a liar?' Thanos snapped icily, his eyes darkening with anger.

His outrage, after he had refused to believe she was telling the truth about James, was almost funny—but Tahlia doubted she would ever smile again.

'I'm not sure why Mark Lloyd is involved. I left instructions with Steven Holt,' he said tersely. 'There has obviously been a misunderstanding somewhere along the line.'

Tahlia closed her suitcase and reached up to unfasten the pearl necklace that he had placed around her neck earlier. 'Mr Lloyd said that *I* had made a mistake, and he's right,' she said quietly. 'I mistakenly thought you were a man of honour, but you are a liar and a cheat, and I hope I never see you again for as long as I live.'

'*Theos*, Tahlia. You don't really mean that.' Sharp knives were ripping his insides to shreds, and he gripped her arm and swung her round to face him. 'Tell me the truth. Is the deal we made when you came to my hotel in London a month ago the only reason you have given yourself to me so passionately night after night?'

In the silence that trembled between them, Mark Lloyd's voice echoed inside Tahlia's head. *'There is not, and never was, any deal to buy Reynolds Gems.'*

How could her heart still ache for Thanos after the way he had tricked her? Tahlia wondered desperately. She must be the biggest fool on the planet. But at least she retained sufficient pride to hide her stupidity from him.

'What other reason could there have been?' she demanded coolly. 'I believed you were paying me to be your mistress.'

His eyes were so hard and cold that she took a hasty step backwards.

'I must congratulate you on your exemplary performance every night,' he said, in a dangerously soft voice that sent a trickle of ice down her spine. 'Perhaps you should consider whoring as a new career.'

She closed her eyes briefly as pain tore through her. 'I have to go,' she muttered, grabbing her case and heading for the door. 'I need to get back to my parents.'

Thanos strolled towards her, reminding her of a sleek, dark panther stalking its prey. 'Aren't you forgetting something?'

'I put the necklace on the bedside table. You saw me.'

He smiled pleasantly, like a wolf before it sprang for the kill. 'Not the necklace—the dress.'

'Oh.' She shook her head, feeling an idiot. The old skirt and top she'd left out to travel in—*her* clothes, not the ones he had bought her—were on the bed. 'I'll get changed in the bathroom.'

'I'd like it back *now*.'

The gleam in his eyes warned her that he would have no compunction in stripping the dress from her body. She was breaking up inside, but she would not let him see it. 'What is this, Thanos? Last-minute titillation?' she demanded scornfully, and she reached behind her and slid the zip down her spine. He must have known the dress did not require her to wear a bra, but she refused to drop her gaze from his as she allowed the silk gown to slither to the floor.

Dull colour scorched his cheekbones. 'We both know I could take you right now and you would do nothing to stop me,' he said roughly.

There was little point in denying it when her nipples were jutting eagerly towards him, begging for the tender ministrations of his hands and mouth. But she tore her eyes from him and managed a nonchalant shrug. 'So you press all the right buttons. You're a fantastic stud, Thanos.'

She swung away from him and clumsily dragged on her skirt and tee shirt, hating the way her breasts were tingling in anticipation. She would *never* allow him to touch her again, would *never* make love with him again and know the indescribable pleasure that she had only ever experienced with him. Her eyes ached with tears as she stumbled to the door, but there was one last thing she needed to know.

'How long had you anticipated our relationship lasting after the trip to Antigua?'

Thanos stared at the streaks of tears and mascara running down her face and felt an overwhelming urge to pull her into his arms and kiss her, until she acknowledged that what they had shared this past month was too good to throw away. But obviously she did not think so, he brooded bitterly. She had come to him in London because she'd needed his money to help her father, and no doubt she had agreed to go to the Caribbean with him because she enjoyed the benefits associated with being the mistress of a millionaire. She was no better than Yalena, and the countless other women who saw dollar signs when they looked at him. He was better off without her.

'I hadn't planned on it lasting at all. I'm not a fan of commitment,' he drawled sardonically. 'A few weeks of sun, sea and sex are all I have ever wanted from any woman, and you are no different.'

'I see.' The tiny flame of hope inside her died, but she could not drag her eyes from him as she committed to memory his sculpted features and his hard body sheathed in the superbly cut black dinner suit—before she turned and walked out of his life.

By the time Tahlia reached the airport she had missed the last plane to London, but she was so desperate to leave Mykonos that she caught the next flight to Athens and, after spending a sleepless night in the terminal there, managed to book a seat on the first flight to Gatwick the following morning. As the taxi turned through the gates of Carlton House she half expected to see the bailiffs waiting on the drive, but to her relief there was just her father's car parked by the front steps.

'They're not here yet, then?' she murmured, when her mother opened the door and immediately burst into tears at the sight of her. 'Where's Hobson?'

'Unpacking,' Vivienne mumbled, wiping her eyes.

'*Unpacking?* But…I thought you had to be ready to leave by midday?'

'No.' Vivienne shook her head, looking as dazed as Tahlia felt. 'We can stay. Apparently the money for Reynolds Gems was paid into our bank account late last night, and first thing this morning your father cleared the mortgage. I don't pretend to understand what's going on, but Dad says that everything has been sorted out. Isn't it wonderful, darling?' She gave Tahlia a watery smile. 'The last twenty-four hours have been a rollercoaster.'

'It's brilliant news,' Tahlia said slowly.

Why had Thanos done it? she wondered. Had she damaged his pride when she had proved him to be a liar? She longed to send the money straight back to him, but Carlton House was saved, and her mother was smiling again, and that was really all that mattered, she told herself wearily.

'How's Dad?'

'Relieved—as you can imagine—and resting. He's admitted he hasn't slept properly for months.' Vivienne sighed. 'I wish he had told me about our financial problems rather than going through all that worry on his own.'

'He was trying to protect you,' Tahlia said softly. Her parents' love for each other was as strong as it had been on the day they had married. Some marriages lasted. But Thanos thought that marriage was an outdated institution, and she could not believe she had been so stupid as to hope that he might have begun to care for her a little.

'I have another piece of news,' her mother said gently. 'Aunt George passed away in her sleep two days ago. She was ninety-two, you know. Dear Georgie—she told everyone she was five years younger.'

Charlie stalked into the room, his tail held high, and sprang onto Tahlia's lap, purring loudly when she buried her face in his ginger fur.

Vivienne patted her shoulder and reached for the box of tissues. 'I'm sorry, darling. I know how fond of her you were,' she murmured, unaware that Tahlia's tears were not just for her aunt, but for an enigmatic Greek man who had stolen her heart.

A week later, Tahlia stared at the cheque on the desk in front of her. Then she lifted her gaze to the family's elderly solicitor, Harold Wimbourne, her eyes wide with shock. 'I had no idea Aunt George was so wealthy,' she said faintly.

'Miss Prentice was a shrewd investor on the stockmarket,' the solicitor explained. He cleared his throat and added conspiratorially, 'I believe she also made a fortune from betting on the horses. Your aunt bequeathed to you her flat in Pimlico, and various other assets detailed in her will. She also set up a trust fund which was to mature on your twenty-fifth birthday or on her death—whichever happened first. As trustee of the fund, I have the happy task of handing you that cheque.' He chuckled. 'I can see it has come as a bit of a shock. I don't suppose you have any idea yet about what you'd like to do with the money?'

'A bit of a shock' was an understatement, Tahlia thought numbly as the row of noughts swam in front of her. She gave Harold a faint smile and said steadily, 'Actually, I know exactly what I'm going to do with it. I assume I can spend it straight away?'

'Oh, yes. It's yours to spend in whichever way you choose, my dear. I can advise you on secure investments, and so on, but I'm sure Georgina wanted you to have fun with it.'

Tahlia could not imagine a time when she would ever have fun again, but she was grateful to her aunt for giving her the means to restore a little of her pride. Immediately she sent Thanos a cheque for half the amount he had paid for Reynolds Gems, and an assurance that she would send him the remainder once she had sold the flat.

*You paid for my body and treated me as your whore, but now I am buying back my self-respect,* she scribbled furiously. *I wonder if you will ever be able to regain yours, Thanos?*

But he had not really treated her like a whore, she acknowledged honestly, as the week dragged into the next and the pain of missing him grew worse with every day. He'd accepted that she had not known James Hamilton was married to his sister, and, with his reason for wanting revenge no longer valid, it did not make sense that he had double-crossed her—especially as the day after she had walked out on him he had paid her father for Reynolds Gems.

Doubt gnawed at her as she recalled his insistence that he *had* instructed the CEO of Vantage Investments to buy Reynolds. Maybe she had been too hasty when she'd refused to listen to him? But she had been so afraid that he had deceived her, as James had done, and so unbearably hurt at the idea that he had tricked her. And then he had revealed that he had only invited her to his villa in Antigua to be his convenient sex partner. She had been kidding herself that their relationship might develop into something deeper, she acknowledged miserably. She'd known of his reputation as a commitment-phobic playboy, and it was her own fault that her heart was shattered beyond repair.

Thanos watched the rain bounce off the windscreen, and wondered how much longer he would have to sit outside Tahlia's flat waiting for her to return. He would sit here for the rest of his life if necessary, he thought grimly, but when he glanced at his watch and saw that barely five minutes had crawled past since he had last checked his frustration escalated.

He had received her cheque a week ago, and since then it had been burning a hole in his pocket—along with her terse note questioning whether he would ever be able to regain his self-respect. Anger surged through him, but he fought to control it. He had been angry on the night of the Artemis party, when she had accused him of tricking her about buying Reynolds Gems. Fury had burned in his gut that she did not trust him. But later, when his temper had cooled, he'd conceded that he had done little to earn her trust. He had believed every damnable lie the tabloid press had written about her, and forced her to become his mistress without giving her a chance to defend herself. His treatment of her had been unforgivable, he thought wearily. He was probably wasting his time sitting here, but he had discovered over the past two weeks that, as he could neither work nor sleep, he had a lot of time to waste.

A figure came into view, head bowed against the rain, the pale red hair instantly recognizable. The dejected slump of her shoulders tugged at Thanos's insides. She'd lost weight, he noted, his mouth tightening. She looked achingly fragile, and even more beautiful than the woman who had haunted him night and day for the past two weeks. He longed to snatch her into his arms and simply hold her, but as his eyes lingered on her breasts, clearly outlined beneath her damp top, he acknowledged that holding her would not be enough. His body stirred, but he ruthlessly ignored the sharp clamour of desire. There were things he must say, and this time he was determined she would listen to him.

Tahlia dumped the bag of groceries on the kitchen table and pushed her wet hair impatiently out of her eyes as she unpacked a week's worth of cat food. 'At least one of us still has an appetite,' she muttered, when Charlie wound around her ankles.

The doorbell pealed and she groaned, tempted to ignore it. Although she had not confided the full details of her relationship with Thanos to her friends, they had guessed that she was suffering from 'man trouble' and were running a campaign to drag her out of the depression that some days seemed to swamp her. She knew they meant well, but she seriously doubted she would ever get over him, and she preferred to be on her own.

The bell rang again and, cursing beneath her breath, she walked down the hall and opened the door.

'Hello, Tahlia.'

The gravelly, accented voice was so poignantly evocative that tears stung her eyes. She had experienced the same peculiar rushing noise in her ears on the night she had discovered his deception, but this time she could not control the feeling that she was on a carousel, spinning faster and faster. It was a relief when blackness claimed her.

She opened her eyes to find herself lying on the sofa, Thanos's furious face inches from hers as he crouched beside her. '*Theos*, why haven't you been eating?' he demanded roughly.

'I do eat,' she lied, forcing herself to sit up, relieved that the walls were no longer revolving.

'You're too thin,' he insisted harshly, 'and too pale; there are shadows beneath your eyes.

'So? I haven't been sleeping too well.' She would rather die than have him guess that she was pining away for him. 'I've been having bad dreams,' she told him pointedly, tilting her chin. 'Why are you here, Thanos?'

He stood up, but to her dismay settled himself next to her on the sofa—so close that she was conscious of his hard thigh muscle pressing against her jeans. 'Firstly, I want an answer,' he said coolly. 'Are you pregnant? I did not use protection when I made love to you on the beach on Santorini,' he said, when she gave him a startled look.

She made her decision in a split second. 'No,' she said quickly, praying he had not heard the faint tremor in her voice.

When he made no reply she risked another glance, but his face was expressionless. 'I see,' he murmured at last. 'Then that leads us to the second reason for my visit—which is to return this.' He withdrew the cheque she had sent him from his jacket pocket and held it out to her.

'Keep it,' she said sharply. 'I know you transferred the money for Reynolds Gems into my father's account the day after I left Mykonos, but now I'm repaying every penny. My family are no longer indebted to you.'

He tore the cheque into pieces with tightly leashed savagery and said harshly, 'When I first met you I believed you had seduced my sister's husband as callously as my father's mistress had wrecked my parents' marriage. I could see little to differentiate you from Wendy, and I transferred the hatred I had felt for her onto you.'

She almost preferred his lies to his brutal honesty, Tahlia thought numbly.

A tremor of sheer misery ran through her, causing Thanos to frown. 'You should change out of your wet clothes,' he said abruptly. When she shook her head he gave an impatient sigh and shrugged out of his jacket, draping it around her shoulders. The leather collar was as soft as butter against her cheek, and the silk lining carried the lingering scent of his cologne. His compassion, when seconds before he had been comparing her to his father's mistress, twisted the knife in Tahlia's heart. She wished he would just say what he had come to say and leave—before she broke down in front of him.

'While we were on Mykonos I was heavily involved with the negotiations to buy the Ambassador Hotel in London,' he said quietly. 'And of course the Artemis party was looming. Vantage Investments *is* a subsidiary company of Savakis Enterprises, but it functions as an independent company. After I had instructed Steven Holt to proceed with buying Reynolds Gems I had no reason to contact him again. I was unaware until the night you left Mykonos that Steven's wife had gone into premature labour the day after I had spoken to him. Their son was born twelve weeks early, and Steven has barely left the hospital since the birth. I understand that the baby is still in the special care unit, but he is now thriving,' he murmured, when Tahlia looked horrified.

'Perhaps understandably, Steven forgot to pass on the message to Mark Lloyd about my change of decision over the purchase of Reynolds Gems. Once I discovered what had happened I immediately transferred money from my personal account to your father's bank.'

Without Thanos's swift intervention her parents would have lost their home, Tahlia acknowledged, guilt sweeping through her when she recalled how she had accused him of being a liar.

He stood up and walked over to the window, staring at the rain lashing against the glass. 'If I am honest, I knew almost from the start that you were nothing like Wendy—or the vacuous bimbo portrayed by certain tabloids,' Thanos continued tensely. 'You were gentle and kind.' He glanced disparagingly at Charlie, who was curled up in an armchair like a fluffy ginger cushion. 'You rescued stray animals. I wanted to hate you,' he said roughly, 'but you got under my skin and I discovered that I enjoyed being with you. I wanted to come after you the night you left, but I couldn't leave Ana to cope alone at the party—and I was furious that, although the month that we had been lovers had been the happiest of my life, you clearly did not feel the same way. You did not trust me. The next morning I learned that the damage to my hotel on St Lucia was more serious than I had first realised, and that several of my staff had been injured in the storm. I had no choice but to fly immediately to the Caribbean.'

Tahlia could think of nothing to say as she absorbed his words, and a tense silence quivered between them before Thanos finally spoke again.

'I'm sorry for the way I treated you when we first met. I blamed you for hurting my sister, and in my damnable desire for revenge I stole your innocence.'

The bleakness in his eyes tore at Tahlia's heart, and even in the midst of her misery she wanted to absolve him. 'Neither of us could deny the sexual chemistry between us,' she said softly. 'I wanted you to make love to me.'

She got to her feet and held out his jacket, praying he would take the hint and go, but he strode towards her, his eyes blazing, and threw the jacket carelessly onto the sofa.

'I dishonoured you,' he said harshly. 'And the only way I can try to make amends is to marry you.'

'*What?*' Tahlia's jaw dropped, and as the room tilted alarmingly she was afraid she was going to faint again.

Thanos was deadly serious, she realised as she stared at his taut face, his skin stretched tightly over the razor-sharp edges of his cheekbones. He was impossibly beautiful, and equally impossible to understand—although in a way she did understand his reasoning. At heart he was a traditional Greek male and an honourable man. His self-respect had been badly damaged by what he perceived as the wrong he had done to her. But *marriage*! That was taking contrition a step too far.

'I don't want to marry you,' she said quietly.

Thanos felt as though he had received a hammer-blow to his heart. It was the same pain he had experienced when Yalena had broken their engagement and revealed that she had been sleeping with Takis; the same pain that had ripped through him when he had seen Melina for the first time after the accident, when she had looked so tiny amid all the wires and tubes which had been keeping her alive.

'You must know I would never do anything to hurt you,' he said roughly. 'And I am a wealthy man—you would not want for anything.'

Dear heaven, this was torture. Didn't he realise that her resolve was perilously close to crumbling? That she longed to snatch this chance of happiness even though she knew she would never be truly happy when he did not love her?

'But I would want something that you cannot give me, Thanos,' she whispered, forcing the words past the constriction in her throat. 'I would want love. I don't care about your wealth or the material things you can give me. I would marry you if you were a goat-herd on Agistri if you loved me as much I love you.'

Tears blurred her vision, so she felt rather than saw him move, but she guessed that her admission would have him striding out of the door without a backward glance. She was unprepared for the strong arms that closed around her, and she gave a startled cry when the walls revolved again as he lifted her and carried her down the hall.

'Thanos, what are you doing?' she choked, unable to stem the tears that had been gathering since he had first appeared on her doorstep.

He kicked open her bedroom door and lowered her gently onto the bed. Her heart turned over when she saw that his thick eyelashes were spiked with moisture.

'Thanos?' She raised a trembling hand to his cheek, her eyes widening at the unguarded expression in his eyes as he knelt over her.

'You love me?' he said in a strained tone, all his arrogance stripped away, leaving him achingly vulnerable.

It was small wonder that he sounded disbelieving, Tahlia thought gently. Years ago he had been so cruelly rejected by the woman he had loved. Since then he had shouldered the responsibility of bringing up his sister and building a hugely successful company, and she guessed that deep down he had never come to terms with being abandoned by his both his parents. For most of his life he had felt alone.

Her pride suddenly seemed unimportant—especially when he was staring at her as if her answer mattered desperately to him. 'I love you with all my heart,' she assured him quietly.

He closed his eyes briefly and drew a ragged breath. 'You are my world, Tahlia *mou*,' he said simply, his voice shaking with emotion. 'And I will love you and cherish you until I die. You stole my heart, and now it is yours for ever.' He kissed away the tears slipping down her face. 'Does knowing that I love you make you cry?' he murmured, and the shadow of uncertainty in his eyes tugged at her heart.

'Only because I have wanted you to love me for so long and I can't believe it has happened,' she said shakily.

'Believe it,' he bade her urgently, taking her hand and holding it over his heart, so she could feel its thunderous beat pass through her fingertips into her veins. 'The month we spent together on Mykonos was the happiest I have ever known, and day by day my feelings for you grew more intense. Now you know that I love you with my heart and soul and everything I am, will you do me the honour of marrying me, *agape mou*?'

She saw the love that blazed in his eyes, and finally began to hope that everything really would be all right.

'Melina…?' she queried anxiously.

'Melina knows how I feel about you and she gives us her blessing. In fact, she says if you don't agree to be my wife she'll catch the next plane to England and try to persuade you herself,' he quipped lightly, his smile not disguising the fierce tension that still gripped him. 'She's looking forward to meeting you and getting to know you properly.'

That left one last doubt, Tahlia acknowledged, catching her lower lip with her teeth. 'I love you, and I would love to marry you.' She pressed her finger to his mouth when he bent his head to kiss her. 'But I have a confession. I lied to you, Thanos.' He held her gaze steadily, and she took a deep breath. 'When you asked if I was pregnant I denied it. I didn't want you to come back to me out of duty.'

She suddenly felt ridiculously shy, and the look of dawning comprehension in his eyes gave no clue to how he felt.

*'Tahlia?'*

'I going to have your baby,' she said softly. 'Are you…are you pleased?' She watched his smile widen to a grin that made him look almost boyish, and her heart overflowed with her love for him.

'*Pleased* is such an inadequate word to express how I feel, *agape*,' he said deeply, his voice cracking with the emotion. 'Overjoyed is better—and thankful, humbled that I have found you, *pedhaki mou*. And most of all determined that you will never have reason to doubt my love for you and our child.'

He bent his head again and claimed her mouth in a kiss that spoke of passion and desire and a powerful, abiding love that would last a lifetime.

Tahlia responded to him with everything that was in her heart, so that the kiss became a sensual feast that fanned the flames of their mutual hunger. Their clothes were a barrier he swiftly removed, and she cried his name as he cupped her breasts and teased each rosy tip with his tongue. He groaned when she traced her fingers over his body, and fought for control when she encircled him and caressed him until he could not wait a second longer.

'I love you,' he whispered as he gently parted her and discovered the drenching sweetness of her arousal.

She was the love of his life, and he told her so as he entered her and joined their bodies as one, moving with exquisite care until passion overwhelmed them both and they reached the heights together before tumbling back to earth to lie replete in each other's arms, their hearts beating in unison.

# EPILOGUE

THEY were married six weeks later, in the village church where Tahlia had been christened, and they held a reception for family and friends in a huge marquee on the lawn at Carlton House.

Melina was well enough to fly over from America, accompanied by a tall, handsome doctor. She revealed that Daniel Sanders had asked her to marry him.

'We've both fallen in love with the right man this time,' she murmured to Tahlia as the guests gathered on the driveway to watch the bride and groom depart for their honeymoon in Antigua.

Tahlia had felt nervous about meeting Thanos's sister, but Melina had quickly assured her that she did not blame anyone but her ex-husband for the collapse of her marriage.

'Do you think Thanos approves of Daniel?' Melina asked anxiously, as Tahlia was about to climb into the limousine next to her new husband.

'He likes him very much,' Tahlia reassured her. 'But I can't believe you want me to be your bridesmaid. My obstetrician has already said that the baby is bigger than average. I'm going to look like a whale in six months' time.'

'What was your whispered conversation with Melina about?' Thanos murmured when the car finally sped away.

Tahlia gave her parents one last wave and turned back to smile at him. 'She wanted to know if you approve of Daniel— I told her that you did.'

'I think he'll make her happy.' Thanos lifted Tahlia's hand to his mouth and pressed his lips to the plain gold wedding band that he had slipped onto her finger, next to her diamond solitaire engagement ring, during the ceremony. 'And I will spend the rest of my life making *you* happy, Tahlia *mou*,' he told her seriously. '*S'agapo*. I love you.'

The raw emotion evident in his dark eyes brought a lump to her throat, and her mouth trembled slightly as she kissed him. 'And I love you. Always and for ever.'

They spent a blissful month in Antigua, before returning to Thanos's stunning villa in a leafy suburb of Athens. Tahlia's parents were frequent visitors, and Thanos refused to be away from home for more than one night, ruthlessly delegating business trips to his executives.

By the end of her pregnancy Tahlia was as big as she had predicted. 'You don't look like a whale. You are my beautiful and very pregnant wife,' Thanos told her softly when she bemoaned her expanding waistline, 'and I love you more than words can say.'

He said those words over and over when she went into labour a week early, and said them again in a voice choked with emotion when she gave birth to their son. They called him Petros. And as Tahlia held her newborn son to her breast, and stroked his shock of dark hair, Thanos claimed her mouth in a lingering kiss.

'You are never going through that again,' he muttered rawly, unable to forget the sight of her pain-ravaged face as she delivered their baby. 'I would have given everything I own if I could have suffered in your place.'

'It wasn't so bad,' Tahlia assured him, her labour pains

already forgotten as she stared in wonder at the precious new life in her arms. 'I always wanted a brother or sister when I was growing up, and I don't want Petros to be an only child. Three children is a nice-sized family, don't you think?'

Thanos stroked a lock of damp hair from her face, and closed his eyes briefly as emotion swept through him. 'I think you are incredible, *kardia mou*, and there are not the words to say how much I love you. You know I'd agree to half a dozen children if it's what you want. But for now we have Petros, and we share a love that will last a lifetime. I could not ask for more, my love, because you are everything.'

# CASTELLANO'S MISTRESS OF REVENGE

**MELANIE MILBURNE**

To my beautiful friend, Louise Gordon. You are such a giving soul, so gentle and understanding and so non-judgmental. You have supported me through some very dark times and I dedicate this book to you in honor of our friendship.

# CHAPTER ONE

'OF COURSE, Madame Cole, you get to keep the jewellery and any other personal gifts Mr Cole gave to you during your marriage,' the lawyer said as he closed the thick document folder in front of him. 'But the Monte Carlo villa and the yacht, as well as Mr Cole's entire business portfolio, now belong to Signor Marcelo Castellano.'

Ava sat very still and composed in her chair. She had trained herself over the years to keep her emotions under strict control. No flicker of fear showed in her eyes, and no tremble of her neatly manicured hands as they lay elegantly on her lap betrayed her. But, deep inside her chest, her heart felt as if a large hand had closed over it and begun to squeeze it with a brutal strength. 'I understand,' she said in a coolly detached tone. 'I am in the process of making arrangements for my things to be moved from the villa as soon as possible.'

'Signor Castellano has insisted you do not leave the villa until he meets with you there,' the lawyer said. 'Apparently there are things he wishes to discuss with you to do with the handover of the property.'

This time it was almost impossible to control the widening of her eyes as she looked across the wide desk at Monsieur Letourneur. 'I am sure the household staff will be perfectly capable of giving him a guided tour,' she said, tying her hands together to stop them from fidgeting with her bag.

'Nevertheless he insisted on seeing you in person, at 8:00 p.m. this evening,' Monsieur Letourneur said. 'I believe he wants to move in immediately.'

Ava stared at the lawyer, her heart starting to flap in panic. 'Is that legal?' she asked. 'The short-term lease on an apartment I had lined up fell through and I haven't had time to search for an alternative. There's been so much to do and I—'

'It is perfectly legal,' Monsieur Letourneur said with a hint of impatience. 'He has owned the villa for several months now, even before your husband passed away. In any case, a letter was sent to you a few weeks ago to inform you of Signor Castellano's intention to take possession.'

Ava felt her insides turn somersaults, not smoothly executed ones, but jerky and uncoordinated tumbles that left her feeling dizzy. She stared at the lawyer, unable to speak, barely able to think. What was she to do? Where was she to go at such short notice? She had money in her account, but certainly not enough to pay for a hotel for days, perhaps even weeks on end whilst searching for a place to live.

Right from the start Douglas had insisted on every-thing being in his name. That had been part of the deal he had made when insisting she become his wife. Then upon his death there had been so many expenses with the funeral and the outstanding bills he had left unattended to in the last stages of his illness.

'But I received no such letter!' she finally said when she could get her thoughts into some sort of working order. 'Are you sure one was sent?'

The lawyer opened the file in front of him and passed her a copy of a computer-written letter which confirmed her worst nightmare. Somehow the letter must have gone astray, for she had never received it. She stared at the words printed there, unable to believe this was happening to her.

'I believe you have a history with Signor Castellano, *oui*?' The lawyer's voice jolted her out of her anguished rumination.

*'Oui, monsieur,'* she said with a frown still pulling at her brow. 'Five years ago…' she swallowed tightly '…in London.'

'I am sorry things did not work out better for you, Madame Cole,' the lawyer said. 'Mr Cole's wishes were for you to be well provided for, but the global financial crisis hit him very hard, as indeed it did many investors and business people. It was fortunate Signor Castellano agreed to cover the remaining debts as part of the take-over package.'

Ava's stomach suddenly dropped like a faulty elevator. 'D-debts?' The word came out of her parched mouth like a ghostly whisper. 'But I thought everything had been seen to. Douglas assured me everything was sorted out, that there would be nothing to worry about.' Even as she said the words she realised how stupid and naïve she sounded. She sounded exactly like the empty-headed trophy wife the Press had always made her out to be. But then didn't she deserve the slight? After all, she had been a naïve fool to take Douglas at his word five years ago, only to find out within hours of marrying him his word was not to be trusted.

Monsieur Letourneur looked at her gravely. 'Perhaps he did not wish to distress you with how bad things were towards the end. But let me tell you, without Signor Castellano's generous offer you would be in very deep water indeed. Every financial institution in the world is jumpy these days. Margin calls are happening almost daily. Signor Castellano has agreed to cover all future requests for payment.'

Ava quickly ran the tip of her tongue across what remained of her lip gloss, tasting a sweet and sour cocktail of strawberries and fear. 'That seems rather generous of him,' she said, keeping her shoulders straight and her spine even straighter.

'Yes, but then he is one of the richest men in Europe,' the lawyer said. 'His construction company has grown phenomenally over the last few years. He has branches all over the world, even in your country of birth, I understand. Do you intend to return to Australia now?'

Ava thought longingly of returning to her land of birth, but with her younger sister now married and based in London, she felt it was too far to relocate, especially now. Serena wasn't back on her feet after suffering from a devastating miscarriage after yet another failed IVF attempt. Ava had not long returned from visiting Serena and had promised to come back as soon as she could to help her through such a harrowing time. But going there now was out of the question. Serena would immediately sense something was up and it would not do her recovery any good to find out about the mess Ava was in. 'No,' she said. 'I have a friend I would like to visit in Scotland. I thought I might try and find a job while I am there.'

Ava could see the cynicism in the lawyer's eyes as he got to his feet. She supposed from his perspective she deserved it; after all, she had to all intents and purposes been a kept woman for the last five years. No doubt he thought finding a regular job with the sort of perks she had been used to was not going to be easy.

Ava was well aware of the precarious position she was in. It *wasn't* going to be easy, but she needed a regular flow of income to help her sister have the baby she so desperately wanted. Her husband, Richard Holt, earned a reasonable income as an academic, but nowhere near enough to cover the expense of repeated IVF treatments.

Ava glanced at her watch as she left the lawyer's building. She had less than three hours until she saw Marc Castellano for the first time in five years. Her stomach fluttered with feathered wings of fear as her footsteps click-clacked along the pavement.

Fear, or was it excitement?

It was perhaps a perverse bit of both, Ava acceded. She had more or less been expecting him to contact her. She knew he would relish in the opportunity to gloat over the way things had turned out for her. The news of Douglas's death six weeks ago had gone around the world. Why Marc had waited this long to see her she supposed was all part of his plan to make the most of her very public fall.

The villa was cool after the heat of the summer sun and she released her sticky hair from the back of her collar, rolling her neck and shoulders to try and ease some of the tension that had gathered there.

The housekeeper, an older French woman called Celeste, came towards her from the main reception room at the foot of the grand staircase. *'Excusez-moi, madame, mais vous avez un visiteur,'* she said and, changing to English, continued, 'Signor Marcelo Castellano. He said you were expecting him.'

Ava felt a scuttle-like sensation pass across her scalp, like tiny panicked feet tripping through her hair. *'Merci, Celeste,'* she said, placing her bag on the nearest surface with a hand that was almost but not quite steady, 'but I was led to understand he was coming much later.'

The housekeeper raised her hands in a what-would-I-know? gesture. 'He is here now, in there.' She pointed to the formal reception room that overlooked the gardens and the port and sea beyond.

Ava set her mouth, although her heart gave another flip-flop-like beat. 'You can leave now,' she said. 'I will see you in the morning. *Bonsoir.'*

The housekeeper gave a respectful nod of her salt-and-pepper head and backed away. Ava drew in a breath, held it for a beat or two before releasing it in a jagged stream.

The door of the reception room was closed, but she could sense Marc standing the other side of it. He wouldn't be sitting. He wouldn't be pacing impatiently either. He would be standing.

Waiting.

For her.

Putting one high-heeled foot in front of the other, Ava moved to the door and, opening it, walked into the room.

The first thing she noticed was his smell: citrus and sharp with an undertone of masculine body heat, it played about her nostrils, teasing them into an involuntary flare.

The next thing she noticed was his eyes. They locked on hers within a heartbeat, deep and dark as blackened coal, inscrutable and yet dangerously sexy. Fringed with thick black lashes beneath equally dark brows, his gaze was both intelligent and astute and intensely, unmistakably male. After holding hers for what seemed an eternity, his gaze then went on to sweep over her lazily, leaving a trail of blistering heat in its wake. Flames erupted beneath her skin, licking along her veins, lighting a fire of need deep and low inside her that she had thought had long ago turned to ashes.

He was wearing a dark charcoal-grey finely pin-striped suit, which showcased the breadth of his shoulders and the taut leanness of his frame. His ink-black hair was longer than he had worn it in the past, but Ava thought the slightly tousled just-out-of-bed look suited him perfectly. His crisply white shirt and silver-embossed tie emphasised his olive skin, the shiny cuff-links at his strongly boned wrists a touch of class that reminded her of how incredibly successful he had become over the last five years.

'So, we finally meet again,' Marc said in that deep, husky male tone that had always made her spine feel watery and unstable. 'I am sorry I didn't make it to the funeral or send you a card with my condolences.' He gave a small movement of his lips which belied the sincerity of his statement. 'Under the circumstances I didn't think either would be appropriate.'

Ava pulled her shoulders back to counteract his effect on her. 'I suppose you are only here now to gloat over your prize,' she said with an attempt at haughtiness.

His dark eyes glittered meaningfully. 'That depends on which prize you are referring to, *ma petite*.'

Ava felt her skin burn as his eyes ran over her again. It had always made her heart skip when he used French endearments in that sexy Italian accent of his.

She wondered if he knew how much it hurt to see him again. Not just emotionally, but physically. It was like an ache deep in her bones; they creaked with the memory of him holding her, kissing her, making her body explode with passion time and time again. She felt the sharp twinge of response even now by being in the same room as him. It was like strings being tugged deep inside of her, reminding her of all the heat and fire of his desire for her, and hers for him.

She had hoped he would have stopped hating her by now, but she could see the fire of it in his eyes, she could even feel it in the stance of his six-foot-four frame, the tension in his sculptured muscles, and the clenching and unclenching of his long-fingered hands as if he didn't trust himself not to reach out and shake her for how she had betrayed him. If only he knew the truth, but how could she explain it now, after all this time?

Ava raised her chin with a bravado she was nowhere near feeling. 'Let's not speak in riddles, Marc. Say what you came here to say.'

He stepped closer. It was only one step, but it halted the breath in her throat. She swallowed, but it only made the restriction tighter. She had to crane her neck, for even in her heels he towered over her. His eyes bored into hers, dark and deep pools of simmering anger.

'I am here to take possession of this villa,' he said, 'and to offer you a job for which we both know you are highly qualified.'

She frowned at him, her stomach curdling with unease, her skin tightening all over with apprehension. 'D-doing what?'

His top lip lifted, his eyes glittering with icy disdain. 'Servicing a rich man's needs. You are well known for it, are you not?'

Ava felt a tremor in her spine as his hatred smashed over her in soundless waves. 'You know nothing of my relationship with Douglas,' she said, trying to keep her voice steady and controlled.

'Your meal ticket is dead,' Marc said bluntly. 'He's left you with nothing, not even a roof over your beautiful blonde head.'

'Only because you took it all off him,' she shot back. 'You did it deliberately, didn't you? There were hundreds if not thousands of companies going for the asking, but you hunted him down and took everything off him to get at me.'

He smiled a victor's smile, but there was a hint of cruelty about it. 'I will give you a minute or two to think it over,' he said. 'I am sure you will come to see it as the most sensible course of action at this point in your life.'

'I don't need even a second to think it over,' Ava said through tight lips. 'I don't want your rubbish job.'

A lightning flash of fury lit his gaze from behind. 'Did your lawyer not explain to you how things are?'

'I would rather live on the streets than work in any capacity for you,' she said. 'I know what you're trying to do, Marc, but it won't work. I know you think I deliberately betrayed you, but that's not the way it was. I knew nothing of Douglas's business interests. He didn't tell me he was bidding for the same contract as you.'

His mouth was a thin, flat line of tension. 'You double-crossing liar,' he ground out venomously. 'You did everything in your power to ruin me and you damned near got away with it. I lost nearly everything. *Everything*, do you hear me?'

Ava closed her eyes in distress. The vibration of his anger in the air was like pummelling blows to her flesh. She could not defend herself against her guilt at what she had inadvertently done to him by marrying Douglas Cole. But given her time again she would still have done it, for Serena's sake.

'Open your eyes,' Marc growled at her.

Her eyes sprang open, the nettle-like sting of tears blurring her vision. 'Don't do this, Marc,' she said, close to pleading. 'The past can't be changed by manipulating things now.'

His eyes blazed like twin black bowls of flame as he grasped her chin between two of his fingers, his touch like a blistering brand on her skin. His eyes drilled into hers, holding hers in a duel she could never hope to win. She lowered her lashes, but he countered it by pushing her chin even higher. 'I swore I would one day make you pay for what you did to me, Ava, and that day has come,' he said. 'This villa is mine and everything in it, including you.'

She swallowed convulsively as she tried to pull out of his hold. 'No...*no*!'

His fingers bit into her flesh. 'Yes and yes, *ma belle*,' he said. 'Do you not want to hear my terms?'

Ava fought for control of her emotions. She bit the inside of her lip, tasting blood and the bitterness of regret. 'Go on, then,' she said, dropping her shoulders slightly.

His fingers relaxed their hold, his thumb moving in a slow caress over the pillow of her bottom lip until every nerve-end was tingling. Ava was mesmerised by his touch. It was so achingly gentle after his flaying words. She felt herself melting, the stiffness going out of her limbs, her body remembering how it felt to press up against his hard, protective warmth.

After a moment he seemed to check himself. His hand dropped from her mouth and his eyes hardened to black coal again. 'You will be my mistress,' he said. 'I will pay you an allowance for as long as we are together. But I would like to make one thing very clear from the outset. Unlike the way you manipulated Cole into marrying you, I will not be offering the same deal. There will be no marriage between us. Ever.'

Ava felt her heart contract in pain at the bitterness in his tone. He had spoken the words like a business plan. But then, what had changed? Hadn't he said much the same five years ago? No marriage, no kids, no commitment. And she had been foolish enough to accept it...for a time.

Ava drew in a breath that scalded her throat. 'You seem very convinced I will accept your offer.'

'That is because I know you, Ava,' he said with a sardonic light in his gaze. 'You need money and a lot of it.'

'I can find work.' Pride pulled her shoulders back even farther. 'I've been thinking of returning to modelling.'

A determined look hardened his eyes to black ice. 'One word from me and there's not an agency the length and breadth of Europe who would take you on.'

Ava wished she had the courage to call his bluff. But after a five-year hiatus in her modelling career at Douglas's insistence she didn't like her chances of being picked up by her old agency, let alone anyone else.

'I can find other work,' she said with a defiant look.

'Not the sort of work that will pay you enough to regularly top up your sister's bank account.'

Ava felt her eyes widen. 'You *know* about that?'

He gave her an enigmatic look. 'You know the saying—keep your friends close but your enemies closer. I am making it my business to find out everything there is to find out about you, Ava.'

Ava felt as if he had pierced her heart with a long metal skewer. She felt the barb of it right to her backbone; it reverberated throughout her body, making her want to hug her arms around herself, to stop the pulse of pain. But somehow she stood firm, her eyes holding the black fire of his.

'Please keep Serena out of this,' she said hollowly.

'There will be no need for her to know anything other than we are together again,' he said.

Ava wondered how the news would affect her sister. Serena had out of fierce loyalty never mentioned Marc's name in her presence over the last five years. She had also kept the secret of Ava's real relationship with Douglas Cole quiet, so quiet her husband, Richard, was to this day unaware of it. Serena had been too terrified Richard's conservative family would be totally scandalised by her near-brush with a prison term that only Ava's actions had rescued her from experiencing.

But returning to Marc on the terms he had outlined was unthinkable to Ava. How would she bear his daily quest for revenge? How could she face that hatred day after day?

She looked up at him again, shocked at how cold and ruthlessly calculating he had become. He had certainly been no angel in the past—yes, he had been strong-willed and proud and had arrogantly insisted on his own way, but he had never been cruel. But what hurt most was that it was her choice to marry Douglas that had brought about the change in him. Of course Marc would think it had been deliberate, but then, unbeknown to her, Douglas had planned it that way.

She twisted her hands, unconsciously fingering the amethyst ring on her finger, a peace offering Douglas had given her during the last months of his illness. 'I need some time to think about this…'

Marc's eyes flashed like fast-drawn daggers. 'You've had six weeks.'

Ava blinked at the savage bite of his words. 'You surely don't expect me to accept this outrageous offer without some careful consideration, do you?'

His mouth was curled upwards in a sneer. 'It didn't

take you too long to consider moving on with another man after you walked out on me. Within a month you were living with Cole as his wife.'

'I am sure you moved on with your life just as quickly,' she said with a fiery flash of her eyes. 'In fact you are rarely out of the Press with a starlet on your arm.'

'I admit I do not live the life of a monk,' he said, 'which brings me to another condition of mine on the arrangement.'

'I haven't agreed to it yet.'

'You will.'

Ava ground her teeth at his imperious manner. 'Let me guess,' she said, glaring at him resentfully. 'You want me to be faithful to you while you get to do whatever you like with whomever you like.'

His dark eyes gleamed. 'You are well trained, I see. Perhaps your time with Cole has finally taught you how to behave.'

She tightened her lips until they went numb, anger bubbling inside her at his assumption of her as a gold-digger. It was so unfair. Why couldn't he leave the past alone? To come to her now, after all this time, was going to achieve nothing but more heartache for her. It had broken her heart to walk away from him the first time. It had taken every bit of willpower and self-respect to do so. Living as his mistress had been so bittersweet and in the end she had chosen the bitter over the sweet. He had flatly refused to promise her anything but a short-term affair. The concept of marriage was anathema to him; now it seemed more so than ever.

Marc took an envelope out of his jacket pocket and handed it to her. 'I have drawn up a legal document for you to sign,' he said. 'It states how much money I am willing to pay you to cohabit with me. By signing it you will be unable to claim support when our relationship is terminated.'

'A prenuptial?' she asked, frowning as her fingers took the envelope from him.

'Without the nuptials,' he said, his eyes diamond-hard. 'No marriage, no children.'

Ava felt her insides twist in pain. Watching her sister go through the agony of not being able to conceive had made her acutely aware of how much she longed to have a baby of her own. To hear Marc state so implacably that he wanted no children struck at the heart of her. She was twenty-seven years old, which was still young enough not to panic, but with her *younger* sister's fertility problems she couldn't quite quell the worry that she too might not be able to conceive naturally.

'I can assure you I would not for a moment think of bringing a child into such an arrangement as this,' she said, turning away from Marc to put the envelope to one side.

Ava heard him move behind her and froze. She silently prayed for him not to touch her in case she betrayed herself. The skin along her bare arms crawled with anticipation of his warm, gliding hands. How many times had he embraced her from behind in the past? His hands would move slowly from her hips to her breasts, cupping her, his mouth nuzzling on the sensitive skin of her neck until she would turn in his arms and offer herself to him.

Her mind exploded with images of them together. The passion he had ignited in her was something she had never experienced before even though she had not been a virgin when they had met.

When his hands came to rest on her hips she shuddered. 'You find my touch abhorrent, or is it that you are still hungry for it?' he asked, his warm hint-of-mint breath skating past her ear.

*If only he knew!* she thought as her heart rammed against her sternum like a giant pendulum inside the body of a too small clock. 'I told you…I…I want some time to think about this,' she said, trying to keep her voice even.

He turned her around to face him, his eyes boring into hers. 'You haven't got time to think about it, *cara*,' he said. 'You have debts up to your diamond-studded ears.' He fingered one glittering earlobe. 'Did he buy these for you?'

Ava's breath caught in her throat like a scrap of silk on a savage thorn. 'Y-yes…'

His hands fell to his sides as he commanded, 'Take them off.'

She frowned again, her stomach nosediving in alarm. 'What?'

His mouth was bracketed by lines of steel. 'Take them off and everything else he gave you. *Now.*'

Ava pressed her lips together to contain her pulsing panic. Was this really her Marc? The man she had fallen in love with so deeply and irrevocably? He was a stranger to her now, a terrifying stranger with not just revenge on his mind, but the total humiliation of her as well.

She would not give in to him.

*She would not.*

She tightened her hands into fists by her sides, holding his glacial glare with a feisty flash of her own. 'No.' Her voice came out too thready and soft, so she repeated it. 'No. Absolutely not.'

His pupils flared, his mouth flattening even further. 'I will give you one minute, Ava, otherwise the deal is off. Keep in mind the massive debts your husband left behind. At last count it was in the hundreds of thousands.' He set the timer on his watch, his dark gaze holding hers challengingly. 'Your minute starts now.'

She swallowed back her anguish, the determination in his eyes making the base of her spine rattle in fear. 'D-don't do this, Marc....'

A nerve flickered at the side of his mouth. 'If you will not do it then I will do it for you,' he warned.

Ava believed him well capable of it. Her hands began to tremble as she tried to remove the earrings, her fingers fumbling uselessly until she felt terrifyingly close to tears. She soldiered on, glaring at him bitterly, hating him with such intensity she could taste the acridity of it in her mouth. Finally she got the studs out and placed them on the coffee table to her right.

'Now the rest,' he said, standing with his feet apart, his arms folded across his chest in an authoritarian stance that boiled her blood.

Still glaring at him, she took each of her dress rings off and put them beside the earrings. 'There,' she said, arching one of her brows at him. 'Happy now?'

His black eyes stripped her mercilessly. 'Keep going.'

Ava's heart lurched against her chest wall. She sent the point of her tongue out over her lips, buying for time, wondering if he wanted her to crumble emotionally, to beg and to plead with him to stop.

She would *not* do it.

She would *not* bend or break, she would *not* cry, she would *not* beg.

She raised her chin and locked gazes with him. Blue-grey warred with black-brown for a pulsing moment. 'All right, then,' she said with a devil-may-care lift of one shoulder as she loosened the catch on her watch. She slipped it off her wrist and placed it beside the earrings and rings.

She straightened and, giving him a challenging look, slipped off her shoes, kicking them to one side before she reached for the zipper at the back of her skirt. She told herself she had stood undressed in front of hundreds of people before while she had been modelling. This would be no different; besides, he had seen it all before. Her body was no secret to him. He knew every curve and contour and every secret place.

The tension in the air was palpable.

Ava slid the zipper down, the metallic sound thunderous in the crackling silence. The fabric slipped to the floor and she stepped out of its circle, her fingers going to the hem of her pull-on top.

Marc's eyes followed her like a night-vision searchlight. She felt the heat of it scorch her flesh as her top joined her skirt on the floor. She stood before him in a black, French, lace push-up bra and knickers, her chin high, her right hip tilted in a model-like pose. 'I bought these myself,' she said with a defiant look.

His lips flickered, his dark eyes gleaming. 'Prove it.'

Ava clenched her teeth, fighting to keep her cool. He wanted her to fall apart, she had to remember that. He wanted her pride any way he could get it. 'I don't have the receipt any more, so I am afraid you will have to take my word for it,' she said, pushing up her chin to disguise its wobble.

'Your word?' His top lip lifted in a mocking curl. 'Since when should I take as gospel the word of a gold-digger?'

'I am not a gold-digger,' she said with quiet but steely dignity.

The timer on his watch beeped, informing her the minute was up.

Ava felt her stomach slip as Marc's gaze hit hers. 'Well?' he said.

She had never felt so naked and exposed in her life and yet she was still wearing more than most people wore on the French Riviera beaches she could see from the villa windows.

'How much are you going to pay me?' she asked, knowing it would be exactly the question a gold-digger would ask, but she was beyond caring. Serena was more important than her pride at this point. What her sister had suffered recently was far worse than anything Marc Castellano could do to her.

He named a sum that lifted her brows. 'Th-that much?' she asked in a croak.

He gave her an imperious smile, the black holes of his pupils flaring with passionate promise. 'I am going to make you earn every penny of it, Ava. I don't suppose you have forgotten how good we were together, hmm?'

Ava felt her cheeks flame with colour. She remembered everything: every touch, every kiss, every incendiary caress and every earth-shattering orgasm that had left her quaking in his arms time and time again. 'You want some sort of medal for being able to perform an act that humans, even the most base of animals, have been doing for centuries?' she asked with a cutting look.

He suddenly snagged one of her wrists and pulled her up against him, his chest to her pounding chest and his strong, immovable thighs to her weak, trembling ones. 'Don't push me too far, Ava,' he said in a low growl. 'I am this close,' he held up his index finger and thumb a pinch distance apart, 'to walking out of here and leaving you to face your sugar daddy's creditors.'

Again Ava desperately wanted to call his bluff. She would have if it hadn't been for Serena. A vision of her shattered sister, holding the ultrasound picture of the baby she had lost, was the only thing that stopped her. 'All right,' she said on an expelled breath. 'I'll do it.'

Marc's hold loosened, but he didn't release her. Instead his thumb found her thundering pulse, stroking over it in a rhythmic motion that was as powerful as a drug. 'I will release a Press statement for tomorrow's papers,' he said into the silence. 'We will begin living together as of now.'

Ava looked up at him in wide-eyed trepidation. 'So...so soon?'

His eyes went to her mouth before returning to hers. 'I have waited five years to have you where I want you,' he said.

She gave him an embittered look. 'Where might

that be?' she asked. 'In the palm of your hand, begging for mercy?'

He traced a long finger over each of the upper curves of her breasts before dipping into the valley of her cleavage, the nerves beneath her skin going off like miniature explosives. 'I think you know exactly where I want you,' he said in a tone that was rough and deep and sensually, sinfully dangerous.

Ava felt her body quiver at the thought of him plunging into her, claiming her as his.

Not in love.

Not in mutual attraction.

But in lustful, hate-filled revenge....

# CHAPTER TWO

IN SPITE of the warmth of the room Ava felt her skin rise
in goose pimples. She rubbed at her upper arms, trying
so hard to hold her ground. Her head was aching with
tension, her mind trying to stay clear and focused while
the earth seemed to be shifting beneath her feet. The air
was fizzing with Marc's hatred, high-voltage waves of
it zapping at her, making her skin pepper all the more.

'Are you cold?' Marc asked.

She kept her mouth rigid with anger. 'What is that
to you?'

He held her glare for a pulsing moment. 'Have you
had dinner?' he asked.

'No, and if you think I am going to dine with you
dressed like this you can think again,' she said with a
lift of her chin.

He smiled as his gaze raked over her again. 'Delightful as that sounds, no—I will not take you out in
public like that. As of this evening your body is for my
eyes and my eyes only.'

Ava found it hard to stand still for the rage that was
rumbling through her like seismic activity preceding a

massive earthquake. 'You know there are probably street workers who come much cheaper than me,' she said, goaded beyond caution.

'Yes, but I want you,' he said with a devilish gleam in his black-as-night gaze. 'We have unfinished business, do we not?'

Ava glared at him. 'Any business we had ended five years ago. I thought I had made that perfectly clear.'

His top lip lifted in disgust. 'Oh, yes, by moving out of the apartment I had set up for you without even telling me to my face. I came home to find the place empty apart from a note.'

Ava felt a twinge of guilt about not meeting him face-to-face back then, but she knew if she had he would have persuaded her to stay with him. A note had seemed safer, she'd had more control, the sort of control she had lost the moment she had met and fallen in love with him. She had been so weak where he was concerned, and, although she had put it down to her youth at the time, seeing him again frightened her that it might very well happen all over again. She had come full circle. The irony of it was beyond painful; it was like a razor blade stuck sideways in her throat. She felt as if she could taste the blood of its embedment, the bitter, metallic taste of regret and heartbreak at what she had lost by leaving him, and yet here she was, back in his life and under his command.

Ava lowered her gaze from the accusing glare of Marc's. 'I'm sorry,' she said, but it came out grudgingly and not at all convincing.

Marc watched as she stood before him with her bottom lip trembling, her heart-shaped face pale, and her grey-blue eyes like lakes of shimmering liquid.

He turned away, his anger making his movements stiff and jerky. He clenched and unclenched his hands, wanting to punch deep holes in the walls in frustration and fury. It sickened him that he had allowed her to drop his guard. For years he had sworn he would not do as his father had done: become totally captivated by a woman who couldn't be trusted.

His mother had slept her way through his childhood with an array of other men until she finally left the family home when Marc was seven years old. He could still recall the last time he saw her at the age of ten, getting into the top-of-the-range sports car of her latest rich toy-boy lover, waving at Marc as they drove off to their deaths three hours later on the Amalfi Coast. He had spent the next decade of his life trying to prop up the shattered shell of his father until death—with the aid of large amounts of alcohol—had finally claimed him.

Marc had waited for five years to avenge his bludgeoned pride against Ava McGuire. Five years of meticulously planning his revenge. Step by step he had rebuilt his empire, taking the greatest pleasure in finally bringing Douglas Cole to his knees, with a little help from the stock-market volatility.

Of all the people for her to marry, Ava could not have chosen a better way of ensuring Marc hated her for life. He loathed thinking about his arch enemy making love to her. His mind revolted at the thought of that bloated body heaving over her slim form. But then she was a gold-digger who would always sell herself to the highest bidder. She had just proved it by the way she had agreed to his terms. She had openly taunted him with her beautiful body, but he was not going to take what was on offer until he was good and ready. He wanted her, it was like a virulent fever in his blood, but he was not going to give in to it until she begged him to make love to her. But this time around it would not be making love; it would be sex, nothing but pure physical need that he would enjoy until he tired of her. She would not be the one to walk out on him the way his harlot of a mother had done to his father. This time around Marc would call an end to the relationship when he was satisfied he was over her.

He turned from the view at the windows and faced her. 'I want this placed stripped of everything that belonged to Cole,' he said. 'I have a removals van waiting outside to take everything away in order for my things to be brought in.'

Her slim throat rose and fell over a swallow. 'There's not much left of Douglas's things,' she said. 'Since the funeral I have sorted through it all and sent it to his ex-wife and children. The furniture came with the villa when he purchased it.'

'You have met his ex-wife and family?' Marc asked, his brows lifting in mild surprise.

She swept the point of her tongue across her lips, swallowing again. 'Yes, at the funeral. They came all the way from Perth in Australia. Mrs...' She hesitated for a fraction of a second before continuing, 'Renata Cole was very pleasant. Adam and Lucy, his adult children, too, were very gracious.'

'Considering their father had shacked up with a tart,' he said, watching as her cheeks bloomed with colour.

'Is this to be part of the deal between us?' she asked

with a defiant spark in her grey-blue eyes. 'For you to insult me at every available opportunity?'

He ignored her comment to say, 'You will no longer be using Cole's name. It is in the legal document I gave you. You are to revert to your maiden name even though you are anything but a maiden.'

She opened her mouth to protest, but he cut her off curtly. 'Go and get dressed. I have made a booking at a restaurant for dinner.'

Her eyes rounded. 'You were *that* sure I would agree to this preposterous plan?'

'But of course, *ma belle*,' he said with a mocking smile. He patted where his wallet was inside his suit jacket pocket. 'After all, money is the thing you most desire, is it not?'

Her eyes were like twin tornadoes, darkening with fury. 'Doesn't it make a difference to know I don't want it for myself?' she bit out through tight lips.

He gave a couldn't-care-less shrug. 'It is of no importance to me what or who you want it for. I understand the thickness of family blood even though I do not have a sibling. As it stands, I am happy to pay you to entertain me, but only until such time as I feel it is time to call it quits.'

The look she gave him would have sliced through steel. 'You mean when you've ground my pride into the dust.'

Marc moved his lips from side to side, reining in his temper. She had some nerve to lament the damage to her pride, considering what she had done to his. 'I have already told you to go and get dressed,' he said. 'I would advise you to do so and now, otherwise I may very well change my mind and take you dressed as you are.'

She turned with a swish of her shoulder-length blonde hair and padded up the sweeping staircase, the action of her endless legs and neat bottom making the blood surge to his groin.

He shoved his hands deep in his trouser pockets to stop himself from reaching for her as he so often had done in the past. He'd had lovers since, but no one made his blood heat the way Ava McGuire's did. All she had to do was look at him from those smoky grey-blue eyes of hers and he was rock-hard. He sucked in a harsh breath, fighting against the flood of memories, but it was impossible to mentally sandbag against such powerful sensual recollections. For five years they had tortured him, making him ache with the need to feel her again, to have her in his arms, to hold her and have his fill of her.

He ran a hand through the thickness of his hair as he paced the floor again. He would get her out of his system this time once and for all. Whatever it took, he would do it.

He *had* to in order to move on with his life. This was his last chance and he was going to make the most of every single minute.

Ava dressed in a slim-fitting black cocktail dress from her short-lived modelling days and, slipping her feet into heels, picked up a small evening bag.

She glanced at her reflection in the mirror, grimacing at the state of her hair. She put her bag down and quickly ran a brush through her tresses so they fell about her shoulders in casual waves. Apart from a dusting of mineral make-up and a quick dab of lip gloss she left the rest of her face alone. It wouldn't matter what she did to herself—she was never going to be good enough for Marc Castellano, she thought with aching sadness. He enjoyed the company of beautiful women all over the world, women who willingly grasped at the chance to hang off his arm or slip between the sheets of his bed. Ava's stomach hollowed in anguish at the thought of how many had been there since she had been his mistress. The thought of him touching others the way he had touched her made her feel as if her heart was being wrenched in two. She had tried over the years not to think of it; every time she saw a Press photo of him with yet another glamorous woman on his arm she had quickly turned the page, suppressing the wave of longing until it finally subsided.

When she came down the stairs, Marc was speaking to a man who was dressed in a removals company uniform, the first of some items already placed in the foyer in cardboard boxes.

Ava's stomach clenched at the thought of how quickly things had changed. Marc had wasted no time in taking possession of the villa; how soon would he insist on the other more intimate terms of the deal? In the past she had shared his bed with love, or at least on her part. But how could she possibly share it with the hatred that bubbled like volcanic mud between them now?

Marc dismissed the man and turned as she came down the last of the stairs, his dark gaze running over her in hot-blooded appraisal. 'Very nice,' he said. 'But then you have always had the amazing ability to look glamorous in whatever you are wearing—' his eyes glinted as he added '—or not wearing.'

Ava hoisted her chin at a haughty height. 'In case you are wondering, this dress is mine.'

'Yes, I know,' he said. 'I recognise it from our first meeting.'

She tried to hide her reaction to his statement, but it was almost impossible to control the flip and flop and flutter of her pulse. That he remembered such a minor detail made her wonder if he had cared more for her back then than he had let on at the time. He had always seemed so aloof and non-committal when it came to his feelings. She on the other hand had been effusive with stating hers, which had made her feel gauche and immature. She wished she had been a little more sophisticated back then. If only she had been able to look upon their affair as a casual fling she might not have had her hopes crushed so badly. But from the moment their eyes had met across a crowded bar she had felt something fall into place deep inside her. No one else had had that effect on her and after all this time she had come to the conclusion no one else ever would.

Ava followed him out of the villa to a waiting car outside. The driver held the door open for her and waited while she took her seat, with Marc joining her, his long, strong thighs brushing against hers.

He took one of her hands in his, holding her lightly, but with an undercurrent of strength that silently warned her not to try and pull away.

Ava thought of all the times they had dined together in the past. The romantic candlelit dinners where she had gazed into his eyes, his fingers lazily stroking hers, making her heart thud in anticipation of returning to the apartment to make love into the early hours of the morning.

She wondered if he was thinking of those times now. It was so hard to tell what was going on behind the hard mask of his face. He was just as heart-stoppingly gorgeous as before. The faint shadow of regrowth on his jaw made her fingers itch to touch him, to feel that sexy stubble under the soft pads of her fingertips. Her body trembled at the memory of how it had felt to feel his unshaven skin against her inner thighs as he pleasured her with his lips and tongue.

She crossed her legs, trying to quell the pulse of her body, but with him sitting so close it was like trying to stop ice melting under the flare of a blowtorch.

Marc lifted her hand to his mouth, the point of his tongue dipping between the sensitive web between her index and thumb. It was the merest touch, a hot, moist hint of what was to come. Ava shivered and closed her eyes tightly, calling upon every bit of willpower she possessed not to turn in her seat and place her mouth greedily against his.

He kept her hand in his, idly toying with her fingers, outlining the smoothly manicured shape of her nails. Ava was intensely aware of her forearm resting on his muscular thigh, her hand so close to the hot, hard heat of him she ached to explore him, to see if he was responding to her as she was to him. Her eyes glanced sideways, her heart nearly stopping when she saw the tenting of his trousers. She gulped and quickly looked out of the opposite window, but she heard his low deep chuckle, and felt his fingers tighten as they brought hers to his growing erection.

Her heart thumped as she felt his turgid length, her inner muscles contracting and the dew of desire anointing her in spite of every effort to curb her response to him.

'I can see—or rather, I can feel you haven't lost your touch, *cara*,' he said, keeping her hand against him. 'Tell me, did you ever service Cole in the back of his limousine?'

His crude question was like a slap across the face with an icy hand. She wrenched her hand out of his, wincing as her wrist caught on the metal band of his watch. She glared at him from her corner of the car, holding her wrist with her other hand, her emotions in turmoil as she struggled to keep control.

'Did you?' he asked, his expression hard with bitterness.

'Would you believe me if I said no?' she asked with a challenging look.

His eyes bored into hers as if he was deciding whether to believe her or not. 'You lived with him as his legal wife for five years,' he said. 'I can't imagine there would be much you didn't do with him, especially with the amount of money he spent on you. That's probably why he ended up close to bankruptcy, trying to keep your gold-digging hands full of designer goods.'

'I couldn't give a damn what you think,' she said, searching in her evening bag for a tissue. 'It's pointless discussing anything with you. You've made up your mind and you are never wrong, or so you like to believe.'

Marc frowned as he saw the scratch on the creamy skin of her blue-veined wrist. He took out his handkerchief from his inside pocket and, taking her arm, gently dabbed it. 'It was not my intention to hurt you,' he said.

Her grey-blue eyes glittered. 'That's the whole point of this, isn't it? To hurt me until I finally break.'

He frowned and released her arm, stuffing the used handkerchief in his trouser pocket. 'Perhaps there is a part of me that wants you to suffer the way I suffered,' he said, looking her in the eye. 'But I am not a violent man and you can be assured you will always be absolutely safe with me, Ava.'

*Safe?* Ava wondered if she could ever be safe from his effect on her. She had told herself over the years she no longer loved him. Denying what she felt for him had been a coping mechanism, a way of navigating herself through the heartbreak of having to leave him while she still could. But in the end it had blown up in her face, for men like Marc Castellano didn't forgive—they got revenge.

She chanced a glance at his brooding expression. He was looking straight ahead, his dark eyes narrowed in fierce concentration, his sensual mouth pulled into an almost straight line. A nerve ticked at the corner of his mouth, like a miniature fist punching beneath the skin.

As if he sensed her eyes on him, he turned and locked gazes. 'Tell me something,' he said, his eyes like steel as they pinned hers. 'Were you involved with Cole the whole time you were seeing me?'

'Of course not.' She bit down on her lip. 'How can you think I would—'

'A month,' he bit out the words as if they were bullets, his black eyes flashing with fury. 'Within a month you were married to that silver-tailed, silver-tongued creep.'

Ava closed her eyes, her head dropping into her hands. 'I can't do this…' Her voice was muffled as she struggled to hold back tears. 'Please take me back to the villa…'

'We are going out to dinner as planned,' he stated intractably.

She lifted her head and threw him a castigating glare. 'You never used to be such an unfeeling bastard, Marc.'

His eyes brewed with resentment. 'It's a bit late to be lamenting my lack of feeling. After all, you were the one who showed me how foolish it is to trust a woman who spouts words of love all the time. But that was your intention from the start, wasn't it? You lured me in and then once you had me dangling on the line you cast me off for a bigger, richer catch.'

Her brow creased in bewilderment. 'Is that what you really think?'

'I should have seen it coming,' he said, throwing his arm along the back of the seat. 'I've had enough gold-diggers try it on me in the past. You were good, I'll grant you that. Convincing and beguiling, and that little lie about only having one lover and it being an unpleasant experience was a nice touch. You really had me going there.'

Ava felt as if he had struck her. The pain she felt at his words was indescribable. He was one of the few people she had told of the night she lost her virginity at the age of nineteen. Even Serena, her sister, didn't know the full details, for Serena had suffered much worse at a much younger age, leaving her scarred and vulnerable for years until she had met Richard. For Marc to throw that confidence back in Ava's face as if it were a fiction to garner sympathy was beyond cruel.

She was glad the driver pulled up in front of the restaurant Marc had chosen, for she was beyond a reply. She got out of the car with stiff movements, not even flinching when Marc took her arm and looped it through his.

The restaurant was crowded, but the table the *maître d'* led them to was in a more secluded area. The lighting was low and intimate, the décor luxurious, the service attentive but not intrusive.

'Would you like an aperitif?' Marc asked after the waiter left them with a drinks menu.

'Soda with a twist of lime,' Ava answered, ignoring the extensive list of alcoholic drinks in front of her.

Marc raised his brows. 'Frightened you might lose your inhibitions and have your wicked way with me?'

She flicked her hair back behind her shoulders, sending him another caustic look. 'You can't make me sleep with you, Marc,' she said.

He leant back in his chair, his gaze running over her tauntingly. 'I don't think it would be too hard to get you begging for it. After all, your sugar daddy has been dead for some weeks now and there has been nothing in the Press about you having found a replacement. A woman like you is not made for celibacy.'

Ava buried her head in the menu rather than meet his sardonic gaze. It annoyed her to think how vulnerable she was to him. Her hand was still tingling from his touch earlier, and her body still smouldering. Every time she chanced a glance at him he seemed to be looking at her mouth, making her lips buzz and swell with anticipation of the passionate pressure of his. She wondered if he was stealthily planning his seduction, taking his time about it to make her feel on tenterhooks. If he was he was certainly succeeding. She could barely sit still in her chair at the thought of him possessing her again. Her inner muscles flickered with an on-off pulse that made it hard for her to concentrate. All she could think of was how it would feel to have him drive into her moist warmth the way he used to do. He was an adventurous lover and yet he could be surprisingly tender too. She had loved that about him, the way he made sure her needs were met before he sought his own release.

What would making love with him now be like? she wondered. Would his quest for revenge make him selfish and demanding instead of considerate and sensually satisfying? Would he treat her like the money-hungry woman he thought she was?

Ava put down the menu with a trembling hand. How had her dreams for a happy life turned into such a nightmare? All she had ever wanted was to find a man who would love her and protect her, to build a family, the sort of family she and Serena had missed out on by the early death of their mother and the rapid remarriage of their father to the woman who had been callously and rather too obviously waiting for her predecessor to die.

Ava had thought Marc was that special man of her dreams, but within a few weeks of living with him she had come to see a happy future would never be realised with him. He was too much of a playboy, a man who was used to having what he wanted, when he wanted. He was driven to succeed. She had never met a more driven man. He worked hard and he played hard. She had become a part of that play time, but only a very small part and she knew, just like all the other women he had been involved with, her days had been numbered. She had cut the countdown by leaving him, hoping it would protect her from further hurt, not realising how it had played right into the enemy's hands…

'Have you decided what you would like to eat?' Marc asked.

Ava placed her hands in her lap, twisting them together to stop them from shaking. 'I'm not all that hungry,' she said.

He lifted one of his brows. 'Dieting?'

She gave him a resentful look. 'No. I am angry at how you have orchestrated this…this situation.'

His eyes continued to tether hers. 'I am the one who has the right to be angry, Ava, not you. You betrayed me, remember?'

Ava's hands tightened in her lap. She hated thinking of how she had been manipulated into destroying him. How could she have not seen it? It had been a masterful set-up and she had stepped up to the noose without suspecting a thing until it was too late. How could she tell him how blind she had been? He would think she was trying to wriggle out of what she had done by playing the innocent victim. 'It wouldn't matter what I said. You're never going to believe me, are you?' she said.

His jaw ticked. 'I am not going to let you make a fool of me again,' he said. 'This time around I will have my eyes trained on you at all times and in all places.'

Ava stiffened. 'What does that mean? Are you're going to have me followed?'

His expression was inscrutable. 'Fool me once, shame on you, fool me twice, shame on me. Let's say

I am taking the necessary steps to keep what is mine exclusively mine this time around.'

She glared at him. 'Women are not possessions you can own, Marc, or at least not in this century.'

He gave a lift of one shoulder as if he couldn't care less what she thought. 'If you are not going to eat then you can watch me, as I am starving,' he said, signalling for the waiter.

'No doubt all the machinations you've been engineering have worked up quite some appetite,' she put in spitefully.

His eyes glinted as he laid the menu to one side. 'Not just for food, *ma belle*,' he said. 'I have other appetites that require satiation, but I am prepared to delay gratification, for a little while at least.'

Ava narrowed her eyes in wariness. 'What do you mean by that?'

He gave her an enigmatic slant of his lips that was almost a smile. 'You think I am such an animal that I would insist on you sleeping with me from day one?'

She pursed her mouth, thinking about it for a moment. 'You're paying me a lot of money,' she said at last. 'I am not sure why you would want to wait on your return on it unless you have a specific agenda in mind.'

'I have no agenda other than the one I stated earlier,' he said. 'I want you to be my temporary mistress. It's as simple as that.'

The waiter approached, which meant Ava had no chance to respond. She gave the man her simple order, while her mind shuffled through various scenarios.

Marc was a proud and bitter man who wanted revenge for the way she had supposedly betrayed him. He had gone to extraordinary lengths to get her back into his life, but it seemed he was not going to rush her into his bed.

Why?

She chewed at her lip as she heard him interact with the waiter, her eyes watching his mouth, the way it moved with each word he articulated. His lips were beautifully sculptured, the lower one fuller than the top one, hinting at the sensuality she had already experienced. Her mouth tingled at the memory of the pressure of his, the way his tongue had played with hers, teasing it, taming it and mating with it until she had melted in his arms.

Marc looked across the table and met her eyes, a hot spurt of lust shooting through his groin as he saw the way her small white teeth were playing with her soft lips. She released her lower lip and the blood flowed back into it, making him want to crush his mouth to hers to taste her beguiling sweetness. Her grey-blue gaze wavered for a moment under the scrutiny of his, her guilt no doubt making her lower it in shame.

His gut twisted with knots of tension as he thought of the photographs in the Press of her wedding to Cole. She had been a beautiful bride; he had never seen a more stunning one, which had somehow made it so much worse. He fisted his hands beneath the table, not trusting himself to hold his wine glass without breaking it. Hardly a day went past when those images didn't taunt him with her perfidy. What a fool he had been to trust her the way he had. He had thought she was playing a game when she left him. He had bided his time, waiting for her to come crawling back to him, begging him to take her back as his mistress. But instead she had humiliated him in the most devastating way possible.

But he was five years older now, five years wiser and five years more successful and powerful. This time things would be different. Ava McGuire had humiliated him before, but this time around he was going to have her right where he wanted her.

Not with his ring on her finger, not even in the palm of his hand, but in his bed for as long as he wanted her.

# CHAPTER THREE

ONCE their meals arrived, Ava picked at her salad, her stomach recoiling from every mouthful she tried to swallow. She was intensely aware of Marc's brooding gaze, the ruthless set to his mouth at times unnerved her far more than the sexual tension she could feel pulsing between them.

They had moved to the coffee stage when Ava became aware of a slight commotion behind her. She turned in her seat to see a photographer with his lens aimed at her sitting with Marc.

'Act as naturally as possible,' Marc said in an undertone as he reached for her hand across the table.

Ava felt the blood rush to her fingertips where his fingers touched hers, but she forced her stiff posture to relax, reminding herself all of this was for Serena's sake.

Several photos were taken and the young female journalist who had come in with the photographer asked Marc about his decision to reunite with his ex-mistress.

'Signor Castellano, earlier this evening you released

a Press statement citing your intention to resume your relationship with Ava McGuire, the woman who left you for the late property tycoon Douglas Cole five years ago. Do you have anything further to add to that statement?'

Marc gave his white slash of a smile. 'As you can see, we are back together and very happy,' he said. 'That is all I am prepared to say.'

The journalist scribbled madly before asking with a provocative smile, 'Is there any chance of wedding bells in the not too distant future?'

Marc's polite smile was still in place, but Ava could see the flint-like momentary flash in his gaze as it briefly met hers before returning to the journalist's. 'My stance on this subject has not changed. I have no intention of marrying anyone.'

The journalist turned to Ava. 'Mrs Cole, you have developed quite a reputation throughout Europe as a trophy wife. After all, your late husband was thirty-eight years older than you. Do you have any comment to make on that?'

Ava felt Marc's fingers subtly tighten around hers. 'Um…I am not prepared to comment on my private life,' she said, feeling her cheeks flame at the condescending look the journalist was giving her. 'It has always been, and will always remain, off limits.'

The journalist was undaunted. 'Do you have any intention of working for a living other than as Signor Castellano's mistress?'

Ava squared her shoulders. 'I am his…' she paused as she hunted for a word '…his—er—partner, not his mistress.'

The journalist lifted one finely plucked eyebrow. 'His lover, don't you mean?'

Ava felt another warning squeeze from Marc's strong fingers. 'I have already told you I am not prepared to discuss my private life,' she said.

Still with her hand encased in his, Marc rose to his feet, signalling to the journalist that the impromptu interview was now at an end. 'If you will excuse us,' he gave the young woman another smile, 'Miss McGuire and I have a lot of time to catch up on.'

'One last question, Signor Castellano,' the young woman said as she strategically blocked their exit. 'Does your reunion with Mrs...I mean, Miss McGuire mean you have forgiven her for marrying the man who won the bid for the Dubai hotel over yours? Word has it the contract was as good as yours until she shifted camps, so to speak.'

There was a stiff silence broken only by the clatter of plates and cutlery being cleared from the other tables in the restaurant.

Ava felt every slow-beating second like a hammer blow inside her chest. Her palm was moist and clammy within the cool, dry protection of Marc's hand, her stomach rolling like an out-of-control butter churn. Every breath she took was laboured, as if it had to travel the length of her body to inflate her lungs.

Marc's mouth tightened fractionally. 'But of course,' he said finally. 'The past is in the past. It is time to move on.'

This time the journalist had no choice but to step aside as Marc strode forward with Ava's hand still firmly gripped in his.

It was only once they were in the street outside that his hold loosened, but not enough to release her. The limousine purred to a halt in front of the restaurant entrance like a sleek black panther, its low growl as the driver opened the door for them making Ava feel as if she was stepping into the jaws of a predatory beast to be taken back to its lair and consumed at leisure.

She waited until they were on their way before she turned in her seat to face Marc. 'Did you mean what you said back there or was that just all part of the act for the sake of the public?'

His eyes held hers for a moment before he answered. 'What is done cannot be undone. I am prepared to drop it. It is of no significance to our relationship now.'

Ava screwed up her forehead in a frown. 'No significance?' she asked incredulously. 'How can you say that? Of course it's significant! You don't trust me. But then you never did, did you?'

His broad shoulders visibly stiffened as he held her look, although his expression remained coolly detached. 'I was in lust with you, Ava,' he said. 'From the moment I met you I wanted you. I foolishly let those feelings distract me. I will not make the same mistake again.'

Ava pressed her lips flat and turned to look out of the window at the twinkling lights of the port. His cold, cruel words were like poison darts in her skin, making her wince in pain as each one had hit its mark.

'Why didn't you and Cole have children?' Marc asked after another tense silence.

'It was not what I wanted from him.' Ava cringed as soon as she realised how it sounded, or at least how

Marc had interpreted it. She could see the disgust in his eyes, and the way his mouth thinned until it was almost bloodless. 'I mean…it was not on the agenda,' she quickly amended. 'It wasn't something either of us wanted. It wouldn't have suited our…our relationship.'

'What sort of relationship did you have?' Marc asked, using his fingers as quotation marks over the word *relationship*.

Ava felt cornered. She shifted on the leather seat, crossing and uncrossing her legs, her eyes darting away from the steely probe of his. It would be so easy to tell him the truth. That Serena, whilst working for Douglas in his accounts department, had made a series of errors that had meant thousands of pounds had gone missing. Just days after Ava had left Marc, Douglas had threatened Serena with legal action. He had mentioned prison and named a high-profile legal firm who would act for him to ensure Serena would not get away with it. Ava had gone and pleaded on her sister's behalf and a deal had been struck. As distasteful as it was, Ava had accepted the terms, and, although the Press had savaged her time and time again, she bore it with the assurance that she was doing the right thing for Serena—a marriage of convenience for her sister's freedom.

Ava had married a dying man who wanted a fake wife to fool his business associates that he still had it in him to attract a nubile mate. She had hated him for the first four years. She had loathed every minute, biding her time until the missing money was repaid through her role as his wife. But as his illness had finally taken hold she had come to see him not so much as a ruthless businessman, but as a lonely man who, as his life drew to a close, began to recognise the mistakes he had made, most particularly to do with his first wife and two children who no longer had anything to do with him.

Ava forced her gaze to meet Marc's. 'We were… friends.'

Marc threw back his head and laughed.

Ava scowled at him. 'Only someone with your sort of sex-obsessed mind would think like that.'

His arm stretched out on the back of the seat, his fingers so close to the nape of her neck Ava could feel her skin tingling in anticipation for his touch. 'Come now, Ava, don't take me for a fool,' he chided. 'You shared his villa for five years. Do you really expect me to believe you didn't share his bed during some, if not all of that time?'

She lifted her chin, her eyes glittering with hatred. 'I can't control what you think any more than I can control what the Press has reported from time to time. Yes, we shared the villa and, in time, a friendship that was very important to me as it was to him.'

'Were you in love with him?'

Ava eyeballed him. 'No, I was not in love with him, but that's exactly what you expected me to say, wasn't it? You have me pegged as a gold-digger and gold-diggers only love one thing—money, right?'

'You said it, baby,' he said as his fingers became entwined in her hair.

Ava felt a shiver cascade like a trickling fountain down her spine as he drew her closer, inch by inch, until she was almost on his lap. She pushed against his broad chest, straining to get away, but her hair had tethered her to him far more effectively than chains of steel. 'L-let me go,' she said, trying to keep the edge of desperation out of her voice.

'Is that what you really want?' he asked, his warm, coffee-scented breath skating over her lips.

Her eyelids lowered, her tongue coming out to brush over her lips to moisten them as her chest rose and fell in rising panic. 'Don't do this, Marc…not yet…I'm not ready…'

'Not quite ready to beg?' he asked, brushing the pad of his thumb where her tongue had just been.

She watched in a spellbound stasis as he ran his own tongue over the end of his thumb, tasting her. It was such an intimate act, it made her stomach hollow out and her legs weaken, the base of her spine melting into a pool, like honey poured from a hot jug. Her mouth prickled with the need to feel his hard mouth on hers, to feel the thrust and glide of his masterful tongue claiming hers, taming it into submission.

'It's all right,' he said, releasing her hair and moving back along the seat. 'I can wait until you are ready.'

Ava felt herself slump like a sack of wet washing without his support. She ran an agitated hand through her hair, hating him for being so in control when she was so undone by his very presence, let alone his touch. Every hair on her head seemed to be crying out for the sensual comb of his fingers. Her heart was still thumping inside her chest wall, the exquisite expectation of his kiss and then the sudden let-down was too much for her to have any chance of regulating her pulse.

It was a revelation to her that even after all this time and all the bitterness she had stored in her heart against him, he could still turn her into a helpless pool of need. She was ashamed of her weakness, knowing how it would please him no end to be aware of it as he surely must be, if not already, then as time went on as they shared the villa according to his arrangements.

*Think of the money, think of Serena*, she chanted to herself. She silently garnered her courage, steeling her resolve to keep her heart intact this time around. He could do what he liked, treat her like the wanton woman he thought she was, but this time he was not going to break her heart the way he had done before. She would be his mistress, she could act both in public and in private, but he was not going to have the one part of her that she had so freely given him before.

The driver pulled into the driveway of the villa, the gates swinging open via the remote security device as the car's wheels growled along the gravel to come to a halt outside the stately entrance.

Marc helped Ava from the car and escorted her up the stone steps to the massive foyer. The scent of the fresh roses Celeste had arranged on the marble hall table earlier filled the air, somehow giving the commodious residence a homely feel. Ava had done what she could over the last few months of Douglas's life to make the place as comfortable and peaceful as she could. She had always found the austere formality of the villa off-putting, and over the years she had lived there had made some subtle changes that had made her feel less intimidated.

The removal men had been busy while Ava and Marc were at dinner, for upon entering the formal sitting room she could see various works of art belonging to Marc already hanging on the walls. It was as if he was marking his territory. Even when she excused herself to use the bathroom upstairs she saw that he had taken over the master bedroom. Two well-travelled suitcases lay open on the bed as well as a black toiletries bag. Even the air smelled of him, that enticing aroma of citrus and male pheromones that never failed to make her toes curl.

'*Madame?*' Celeste appeared from the walk-in wardrobe. 'Did you want me for something?'

'*Non, Celeste,*' Ava said, blushing at being caught peering into Marc's domain. 'I was just…er…checking that Signor Castellano has everything he needs.'

'*Oui,*' Celeste said. 'I was given instructions to unpack for him.' She seemed to hesitate before asking, 'Shall I move your things in here too?'

Ava's eyes rounded, her heart banging against her breastbone like a church bell pulled too hard. 'Did he ask you to do that?'

Celeste gave a Gallic shrug. 'It is inevitable, *oui*?'

Ava pulled her shoulders back. 'What makes you say that?'

'He is a very handsome man,' Celeste said as if that explained everything.

Ava pursed her lips, wondering how to explain the situation. 'Look, Celeste,' she began, 'I don't want you to think the wrong thing, but—'

'It is all right, *madame*,' Celeste assured her with a knowing look. 'I was young once. You have a history with him, *oui*? It is hard to resist a man who has gone to such trouble to get you back in his life.'

Ava frowned. 'Celeste…I'm not sure you understand. Marc Castellano ruined Douglas. He took every-thing off him. His ex-wife was left with nothing, not to mention his children. Douglas wanted Adam and Lucy to have something to remember him by. It was his dying wish.'

Celeste glanced past Ava's shoulder, clearing her throat diplomatically. *'Excusez-moi, Signor Castellano,'* she said with a little bow. 'I am not quite finished un-packing your things.'

*'C'est bien, Celeste. Je vais me reposer,'* he said. *'Bonsoir.'*

*'Bonsoir,'* Celeste said and exchanging a conspira-torial raised-brow look with Ava on the way past, left to make her way downstairs.

'Do you have any objections to my taking over this room?' Marc asked.

'No objections at all,' Ava answered in an offhand, couldn't-care-less tone. 'The villa belongs to you. You can sleep where you like.'

His dark eyes contained a hint of amusement as they meshed with hers. 'Is that an invitation to join you in your bed?'

She crossed her arms, her mouth flattening with reproach. 'No, it is not.'

He lifted a hand to her face, trailing his fingertips down the curve of her cheek, his touch stirring every nerve to zinging life. He stopped just short of her mouth, his index finger touching the tiny crease at the corner that so rarely these days lifted upwards in a smile. Ava held her breath, feeling her whole body sway towards him. It was like a magnetic force pulling her towards him. She lowered her lashes to avoid his gaze, but he countered it by placing a fingertip beneath her chin, pinning her gaze with his.

'I was surprised to find you weren't occupying the master suite,' he said. 'When did you move out of your husband's bed?'

Ava felt her breath tighten in her throat. Should she tell him she had never occupied it? Would he believe her? No, of course not, she thought. Given the way Douglas had insisted they give every appearance of a normal relationship in public, it would take more than a few words from her to counter the many Press photographs that had been printed with Douglas's arm around her waist or gazing at her adoringly. It had sickened her to be complicit in the web of lies that surrounded their relationship, but it had saved Serena and that was all Ava really cared about. 'He was very ill towards the end,' she said. 'But in any case, we decided early on to have separate rooms. He wasn't a good sleeper. He…he had terrible insomnia.'

Marc moved away from her and, picking up a silver-framed photograph of Serena and Richard's wedding day, examined it for a moment or two before placing it back down. He turned back to face her, his expression mask-like. 'What did your sister have to say about your relationship with Cole?'

Ava tried to keep her expression as blank as possible. 'Serena was the one who introduced me to him in the first place,' she said. 'She worked in the accounts department in his London office.'

'So it was a whirlwind affair.' It was neither a statement nor a question, so Ava didn't respond. Silence seemed so much safer—fewer lies to tell that she might regret later.

He glanced at the wedding photograph again before returning his gaze to hers. 'Your sister lives a very different life from what you have chosen for yourself. And yet you are still very close, are you not?'

'We have our moments like any sisters do,' Ava answered. 'Since our mother died when I was nine, Serena, being two years younger, has always looked up to me as a mother. But you know all this. I told you about it when we met five years ago.'

He studied her for an endless pause, his eyes roving hers as if searching for something deep inside them. 'Yes, you did,' he finally said. 'I told you how I envied you, remember? Being an only child left me with many burdens to carry alone.'

Ava remembered well how deeply Marc's childhood had affected him. Whenever he had spoken of it, which was rarely, she got a sense of the acute loneliness of him as a young, bewildered little boy with no one to turn to for comfort. In the beginning she had hoped to be the one to heal him of his childhood wounds by loving him and cherishing him for the rest of their lives. Somehow it seemed all the more tragic now that he was likely to spend the rest of his life moving from one pointless relationship to the other, never trusting or loving someone long enough to build a lifetime together.

'I have to go to London early next week,' Marc said. 'I would like you to come with me. It will give you a chance to catch up with your sister.'

Ava's forehead creased again. Serena would take one look at her with Marc and realise something was up. 'But I've just come back from London,' she said. 'I've barely unpacked.'

'I am sure your sister will be delighted to see you again so soon,' he said.

Ava pressed her lips together, dropping her gaze from his. 'Serena hasn't been well just lately,' she said, twisting her hands together. 'I don't think now is the right time for her to have visitors.'

'I am sorry to hear that. Is it something serious?'

Ava lifted her gaze back to his. 'She has had several miscarriages over the last couple of years,' she said. 'The last one was at four months along, just ten days ago. It was very traumatic for her, as you can imagine.'

His dark eyes showed his compassion, which made it all the harder for Ava to summon up her ill feelings towards him. It reminded her of how tender he had been with her in the past whenever the slightest ailment had struck her. How she had longed for such tenderness over the last five years!

'I am very sorry,' he said deeply. 'The loss must be truly devastating for both your sister and her husband. But would not another visit from you be just what she needs to cheer her up?'

Ava crossed her arms over her chest again, hoping it would ease the tight ache of her heart. 'I am not sure... She was not up to visitors while I was there. I can call Richard and see what he thinks, but I don't think he'll be too happy about it. They both are suffering terribly. It's been a huge disappointment.'

'Ava, it is important that we are seen together as a couple, not just here in Monte Carlo, but also when I have to travel elsewhere for business,' Marc said in a serious tone.

She raised her brows at him cynically. 'What you mean is you want me under lock and key so you can control every move I make, don't you, Marc?'

He worked his jaw for a moment, as if trying to withhold a stinging retort. 'I am paying you to be my mistress, Ava,' he said after a small, tense pause. 'It is part of the job description. After all, you accompanied Douglas Cole whenever he travelled abroad, hanging off his arm like a limpet.'

'That was different,' Ava said without thinking.

He lifted one dark brow in a perfect arc. 'How so?'

She compressed her lips, lowering her eyes again. 'Douglas was very ill in the last few months of his life,' she said. 'He needed more and more support from me in order to travel for business.'

'I bet you hated every minute of tending to his needs,' Marc said. 'It is not quite the role you were expecting when you accepted the role as his bride, now, was it? But then the lure of the money would be enough to induce you to do anything, would it not?'

She gave him a cutting glare and turned her back to him. 'I hope you are not expecting me to mop your sweaty brow for you some time in the future, for I won't do it.'

Marc felt his hands tense and forced each of his fingers to unclench. Her defiance both irritated and aroused him. She was much feistier than she had been in the past, but then the sweet, loving woman he had thought he had known back then had all been an act, an artful, devious disguise to get him to take his focus off his business so she could undercut him with her partnership with Cole. This was the real Ava McGuire:

tough, combative and furious at him for having her under his thumb at last. He was going to enjoy every minute of taming her. They would be dynamite in bed together, perhaps even more so than they had been before. He could feel the electric tightness of the air whenever she came near him; her body gave off pulsing waves of attraction that ran over his skin, heating it to boiling point. It was all he could do not to push her up against the nearest wall and take her roughly any way he could, satisfying this aching, burning need that throbbed incessantly in his groin. He could feel it now, the burgeoning of his flesh, the rush of blood that made him swell with longing.

'I promise you I will not ask you to mop my brow, *cara*,' he said, watching as she shook the waves of her blonde hair back past her shoulders as if its length annoyed her. 'I have other places on my body I would much rather you pay close attention to.'

She swung back to face him, her grey-blue eyes flashing silver daggers at him. 'You think you can make me do anything you want, don't you?' she asked. 'But I am no man's plaything. I have never been and never will be.'

'Ah, but that is not true, now, is it, *ma petite*?' Marc asked as he came closer again, taking her by the shoulders this time. 'Cole got to play with you all he liked. Now it is my turn.'

Her slim throat moved up and down, the tension in her shoulders palpable under the gentle but firm pressure of his hands. 'I've changed my mind,' she said, eyeballing him determinedly. 'I want double the money.'

He lifted a single brow at her calculating behaviour. 'We agreed on a price, Ava. I am not paying you more than you are worth, especially since you are what one would call "used goods".'

Her mouth tightened, but to his surprise her chin gave a tiny wobble before she got it back under control. She blinked at him a couple of times, which made him wonder if she was close to tears.

A trick or a tactic? He couldn't quite make up his mind. Instead he did what he had longed to do from the moment he had turned up at the villa earlier that evening.

He bent his head and, before she could do anything to counteract it, he lowered his mouth to hers.

Ava had no time to prepare herself for his kiss, not that she could have even if she'd had a lifetime or two. The passion that roared between their mouths was like an inferno as soon as contact was made. Her lips throbbed and burned and blistered with longing as his ground against hers, roughly at first, angrily almost, as if he hated himself for still wanting her. She kissed him back with equal rage; annoyed at how she still wanted him, how she had wanted him to kiss her as if the last five years hadn't happened.

The pressure of his mouth on hers grew and grew until with just one stabbing thrust of his tongue she opened to him, her whole body melting in his rough hold, her spine almost collapsing, throwing her forward so his arms had to leave her shoulders to wrap around her body instead, holding her up against his rock-hard form. She felt every delicious arrantly male inch of him, the way his erection pounded against her belly, reminding her of how powerfully he was made, and how explosive he could be in the final moments of release.

His tongue explored her mouth in intimate detail, shockingly intimate: licking, sucking and stroking until she was whimpering in response. His teeth nipped at the fullness of her lower lip, fuelling her desire to an unmanageable, uncontrollable level. She gasped as he moved from her mouth to run his tongue over the sensitive skin of her neck before he used his teeth on her, pulling at her flesh teasingly, taunting her to play the same dangerous game with him.

Ava put her lips to the stubbly skin of his neck, shivering in response as his peppered skin rasped against the softness of her lips, relishing in that exquisite reminder of how male he was and how softly feminine she was in comparison. He tasted of citrus and salt and a hint of male sweat, a tantalising cocktail that had her head spinning faster than any triple-strength Cosmopolitan could ever do.

She used her tongue like a cat, licking him softly at first, tentatively, teasing him until he growled deep in his throat. She bit him then, a soft, playful little nip that tugged at his skin, making him press himself against her pelvis with throbbing urgency as his need for her grew thick and hard and insistent.

She rubbed against him wantonly as she went for his neck again, harder this time, her spine turning to molten wax as he swore roughly and returned to her mouth, covering it with his with almost bruising strength. Ava tasted blood, but she wasn't sure if it was hers or his. She didn't care, all she could think about was having this kiss go on and on, to be held like this, so firmly, so possessively and so passionately. It had been so long since she had felt this exhilarating sense of abandonment. Her body felt as if it had come to life again after being shut down for five lonely years. Every drop of her blood raced through her veins, every nerve-ending bloomed and buzzed with feeling and every pore of her skin ached to feel him touch her intimately.

She felt his hands glide over her breasts beneath her top, cupping them through her lacy bra, before he deftly released its clasp at the back to hold her skin on skin. The palms of his hands were warm and slightly rough, again a delicious reminder of how intensely male he was. She quivered as he gently pinched her nipples, rolling them between his finger and thumb until they were hard as pebbles and achingly sensitive.

Ava drew in a scratchy breath as he lowered his mouth to her right breast, taking her in his mouth, the hot moistness anointing her, ramping up her need for him until she was almost gibbering with desire.

'Please…oh, please…' she groaned as he moved to her other breast.

She felt him smile around her nipple, as if her reaction to him pleased him no end. She shuddered as he suckled on her hungrily, his mouth a sweet torture on her senses. She arched backwards, gasping for air, for release, for the pleasure only he could deliver.

'Marc…please…*please*…'

He lifted his mouth off her breast and met her feverish gaze. His eyes glinted with satisfaction, his mouth tilting in mocking amusement. 'Look at how easy you are for the taking,' he said. 'One kiss and I could have had you right here and right now.'

Ava had never slapped anyone in her life; she abhorred violence of any sort, but her hand went flying through the air towards his face before she could stop it. Luckily he did. He captured her wrist, halting its progress.

'Violence is not and will not be a part of this relationship,' he said with gravitas.

Ava raised her chin, not even bothering to blink back her tears. 'You started it.' She flung at him accusingly. 'You were too rough.'

His eyes went to her mouth. She saw the shock register in his gaze, the sudden flare of his eyes as they saw the tiny split she could feel on her lower lip. 'Forgive me. I was too rough with you. It will not happen again.'

Ava wanted it to happen again. She wanted him to lose control so she would not be the only one suffering this empty, unfulfilled ache deep inside. She also wanted him in this mood, this tender, concerned Marc she had once or twice caught a glimpse of in the past. Fresh tears came to her eyes, cascading down her cheeks unheeded as she stood before him, her heart contracting painfully for how she had loved and lost him.

Marc's brows drew together. 'Does it hurt *that* much, *cara*?' he asked gently.

Ava wrenched out of his hold with unnecessary force considering he was barely touching her, let alone restraining her in any way. 'It's not about my lip, damn you,' she threw at him, angry at herself for losing control in front of him.

He silently handed her a clean, neatly folded and pressed white handkerchief, his eyes intensely dark and watchful as they held hers.

Ava took the square of fabric with a hand that was a little unsteady, and gently dabbed at her mouth, conscious of him studying her every movement. She scrunched up the handkerchief after she had finished, but when he reached for it she held it behind her back. 'No,' she said. 'It'll need soaking. I'll see to it.'

'You don't need to do that,' he said with a wry look. 'You can throw it away or give it to the household staff to clean. I am not expecting you to do my laundry, Ava.'

Ava kept the handkerchief tightly clutched in her hand. She had smelled his clean male scent on it as she'd held it to her mouth. She wasn't going to give it back, she decided. If it was the only thing she had left of him when this was over then so be it.

'I would like to go to bed,' she said in a subdued tone as she felt the fight go out of her. 'I'm very tired.'

Marc stepped back and held the door open for her. 'I will bring you a nightcap once you are in bed. What about a little brandy in milk?'

She shook her head, the movement making her fragrant hair swing around her shoulders, making him ache to thread his fingers through the soft, silky strands. 'No, thank you,' she said a little stiffly as she moved past him.

'Ava?'

She froze mid-step; her slim back rigid, reminding him of a small ironing board standing upright. 'Please, Marc…not now. I just couldn't bear it.'

Marc drew in a breath that snagged at his throat as she continued on her way down the wide hall, disappearing into a suite several doors down.

Tears or a tactic? he asked himself again. But he was no closer to the truth. If anything, he thought he was even further away.

The following morning when Ava finally made it downstairs, Celeste handed her the phone. 'It is your sister, Serena,' she said, covering the mouthpiece with her hand.

Ava took the phone and wandered out to the terrace rather than have the housekeeper or indeed Marc overhear her conversation. 'Serena?' she said once she was out of earshot. 'How are you, sweetie?'

'Is it true?' Serena asked without preamble, her voice breathless with shock. 'Are you really living with Marc Castellano as his mistress?'

Ava took a deep but uneven breath. 'Serena…I was going to call you to explain, but it got late last night and I—'

'What's going on?' Serena asked. 'For all this time you've never mentioned his name. I thought you hated him. You told me it was over between you, that you would never go back to him.'

Ava knew she had to tread carefully with how much she told her sister. In accepting Douglas Cole's marriage proposal, she had pretended her feelings for Marc had been obliterated by his refusal to commit. She hadn't wanted Serena to feel any more guilt than she had at the time. To reveal Marc's motives for their reconciliation would cause unnecessary hurt to Serena when she already had enough pain to deal with over the loss of her baby. 'Serena, it's sort of complicated…' she began.

'Have you slept with him?'

Ava rolled her lips together, wincing as she felt the slight swelling of her lower lip. 'No,' she said on an expelled breath. 'Not yet.'

'So what's going on?' Serena asked again, her voice going an octave higher. 'It's in every paper over here. They all say the same thing—that you've reconciled with Marc. It even says here…' there was a rustling of pages being turned '…that he now owns Douglas's villa and his company. Everything! He owns the lot.'

'Yes, that's true,' Ava said, swallowing tightly.

'How long have you known about this?'

'Er—not long.'

'Ava?' Serena's voice cracked. 'This is all my fault, isn't it? If I hadn't been so stupid to make those mistakes in the books none of this would have happened. I feel so guilty. Don't think I don't realise you gave up five years of your life for me. I know you've always said you enjoyed being married to Douglas because of the money and the lifestyle but I never really believed it. You're not that type of person in spite of what the Press likes to think. Oh, God, I can't bear to think of Marc trying to get back at you for—'

'No,' Ava said firmly. 'None of this has anything to do with you and the past.' She mentally crossed her fingers at her little white lie and added, 'Marc still has—er—feelings for me. He's waited this long for the chance to come back into my life. We are both keen to have another go at our relationship. We were young and headstrong before. We've both moved on.'

'So…what about your feelings about him?' Serena

asked after a short silence. 'Are you saying you were in love with him all this time?'

Ava pinched the bridge of her nose. 'It's hard to know what I feel right now,' she said, carefully sidestepping her sister's question. 'I just want to enjoy getting to know him again. We're taking things slowly this time.'

'Has he changed his mind about marriage and kids?' Serena asked.

Ava felt a pain deep inside her heart, like a toothpick being twisted. 'It's a bit of a touchy subject.'

'Ava, don't waste any more years of your life, please, I beg you,' Serena said, starting to cry. 'You deserve a happy life. You've already sacrificed so much…'

There was the sound of someone in the background and then suddenly a male voice came on the line. 'Ava? Is that you?' Richard Holt said in his crisp Cambridge-educated voice.

'Yes,' Ava answered. 'Richard, I'm so sorry, I didn't mean to upset Serena but—'

'It's all right,' Richard sighed long-sufferingly. 'She's been through a bad patch just lately, poor little pet. The doctors say it's the hormones, you know…after… well…' he cleared his throat '…you know.'

Ava felt her own throat thicken with emotion for what they were both going through. 'I understand, Richard,' she said softly. 'I am *so* sorry for not breaking the news of my reunion with Marc to you both personally. It's just everything's been happening so quickly and I…well…I'm sorry. You and Serena should have been the first to know, not read about it in the Press as you did.'

'We are thrilled for you, really we are,' Richard said with genuine warmth. 'Don't pay any attention to Serena just now. She's not herself. Once she realises you are happy she'll be absolutely tickled pink for you.'

There was a tiny pause before he added, 'Erm…you are happy, aren't you, my dear?'

Ava forced her voice to sound light and carefree. 'I am happy, Richard. Marc and I are like different people now. It's a fresh start.'

'That's wonderful,' he said. 'Absolutely brilliant news. Bring him over to see us as soon as you can so we can toast your future.'

Ava grimaced. 'I'll do that.'

Ava hung up the phone a short time later just as Marc stepped out onto the terrace. She tucked a strand of her hair behind one ear with her free hand, feeling colour creep like a slow-moving tide along her cheeks.

'Your sister?' he asked, glancing at the phone in her other hand.

She nodded and, looking at the phone, put it down on the outdoor table, carefully avoiding his gaze. 'And my brother-in-law.' She gave a little sigh. 'They read about—er—us…in the papers.'

His steps sounded on the tiles of the terrace as he came to stand in a short distance in front of her. 'I should have suggested you call them last night.'

Ava glanced up at him. 'I should have thought of it myself.'

He came a step closer and gently lifted her chin with two of his fingers as his dark, fathomless gaze studied her mouth for an endless moment. 'Your lip is swollen,' he said with a gruffness she had not heard him use before. 'I should have brought you some ice to put on it last night.'

Ava stepped out of his hold, frightened she would betray herself by leaning into his solid warmth. 'I'm perfectly fine,' she said, injecting a tart quality into her voice. 'I need coffee, not first aid.'

'I have already instructed Celeste to bring it out to us here,' he said. 'You look like you could do with some sunshine. You look rather pale this morning.'

'I didn't sleep well,' Ava confessed, glancing up at him again as he pulled a chair out for her at the outdoor table setting.

'Not used to sleeping alone?' he asked with a wry lift of one dark brow.

She gave him a look that would have sliced through frozen butter. 'You just can't help yourself, can you, Marc?'

He pulled out a chair for himself and sat down, waiting until Celeste had brought out a tray with coffee and fresh croissants and preserve, and left them alone again, before he spoke. 'Why didn't you tell me you never shared a bed with Cole the whole time you were married?'

Ava stared at him for a moment, dumbstruck at the out-of-the-blue question. 'How…?' She swallowed and began again, 'How do you know?'

He nodded in the direction Celeste had gone. 'The housekeeper let it slip.'

Ava shifted in her chair. 'I'm surprised you believed her,' she said, throwing him a stinging look. 'If I had told you, I am sure you would have laughed in my face.'

A camera shutter-quick movement came and went in his gaze as it held hers. 'I guess I should take some comfort in the knowledge you married him solely for the money,' he said. 'After all, you never complained about our sex life while we were together.'

Ava felt her body quiver in remembrance and quickly shifted her gaze from the probe of his. Her shoulders went back until they met the sun-warmed wrought-iron lace of her chair, twin pools of heat burning in her cheeks.

She watched as he poured them both a coffee, his movements so steady and sure, while her body was trembling both inside and out. She swallowed a tight knot of tension in her throat, wondering how to fill the chasm of silence that had opened up between them.

Marc handed her a cup of steaming coffee, his eyes meeting hers across the small distance of the round table. 'I could have given you as much, if not more than Cole, so why did you do it?'

She took the cup from him, the slight rattle of it in its saucer betraying her outwardly cool composure. 'You refused to give me what I wanted,' she said. 'If I had stayed with you I would never have been a bride. Douglas at least allowed me to experience that.'

Marc felt the familiar punch of jealousy hit him in the midsection when he thought of her as a bride. Even knowing the marriage had not been consummated barely lessened its impact. For all he knew she could have taken any number of lovers during her marriage, after all, Cole had been very ill before he died. Perhaps his health had been impaired much longer than the public had been aware of. But when all was said and done, Ava had still ditched Marc to enter into a paper marriage to his enemy to bring about his ruin. What other reason could she have had?

He rested his right ankle over his left thigh, leaning back in his chair as he idly stirred his coffee with a silver-crested spoon that had been in his family for hundreds of years. It occurred to him then that once he died there would be no Castellano heir to inherit that and every other heirloom his father's family had collected over the years. Marc had fought so hard to keep every last object in his possession when his business had almost gone under. If he didn't have an heir when he died everything would have to go to another branch of the family, distant cousins Marc barely knew. He had never really thought about it until now. How it would feel to have no one to pass on the family name. The proud heritage he had built up almost from scratch when his father had toppled emotionally would be lost forever.

He pinned her gaze with his. 'Why is marriage such a big thing for you? It's little more than a piece of paper, or at least apparently it was in your case with Cole.'

'There were good reasons why that was the case,' she said, lowering her eyes. 'Douglas was unable to…to—'

'To get it up?' he offered.

Her eyes flicked back to his, irritation flashing in their grey-blue depths. 'Sex is not the only basis for a happy marriage,' she said. 'Illness or an accident can strike anyone at any time. That's the whole point of promising to love for better or worse, sickness and health and so on.'

'Were your parents happily married before your mother died?' he asked.

She averted her gaze once more. 'No, but that doesn't mean good marriages don't exist. Even people who are completely different can make a wonderful go of it. My sister and her husband are a perfect example. Serena is incredibly shy and Richard is at ease with people and very outgoing. They make a lovely couple in every way.'

Marc felt a frown pull at his brow as he sat watching her. The sunlight on her blonde hair highlighted its naturalness, the soft waves framing her face making her look like an angel. He had missed the sound of her voice. He hadn't realised until now how much. She had a softly spoken voice, her fluency with foreign languages giving her a cultured accent that was mesmerising to listen to. She could have read her way through the phone book and he would have gladly sat and listened for hours.

He gave himself a mental shake and took a deep sip of his coffee. 'Perhaps you are right,' he said. 'But then opposites attract. Like us, *sì*?'

'You seem more intent on attacking me than attracting me,' she put in with a testy look.

Marc put his cup back down, his mouth tightening at her jibe. The truth was he was deeply ashamed of how he had inadvertently hurt her by kissing her so savagely.

'I don't suppose people will take our reconciliation very seriously if we are forever sniping at each other,' he said, offering her a croissant.

She pushed the basket back towards him. 'No, thank you,' she said. 'I just want coffee for now.'

'You haven't even touched it.'

'I'm waiting for it to cool down.'

'You should eat something,' he said. 'You look thinner than when we were together five years ago.'

She gave him a flinty look. 'Yes, well, after the little strip show you insisted on last night you could probably calculate my weight to the nearest gram.'

Marc suppressed a smile at the memory which had kept him awake for hours last night. He had enjoyed every second of seeing her in just her bra and knickers and he couldn't wait to see her in even less. 'I know it is supposedly fashionable to be bone-thin, but personally I like a little flesh to hold on to,' he said.

She rolled her eyes in disdain. 'If you think I am going to stuff myself full of sugar and fat just to please you then you will be waiting a long time.'

'Are you on the Pill?'

Ava blinked at him, hastily trying to reorient herself before she answered. 'Yes, not that it's any of your business.'

He gave her a smouldering look. 'Soon will be, *cara*. We have a deal, remember?'

Ava crossed her legs and her arms, but even so her body still felt as if it had been set alight with longing. Just thinking about him making love to her made her skin tingle from the base of her spine to the roots of her hair. 'You can hardly force yourself on me,' she pointed out.

He gave her a knowing smile. 'I don't think there will be any chance of that being an issue for two reasons. The first is I do not believe in forcing a woman to have sex with me, and the second is you are just as attracted to me as I am to you. That is one thing that hasn't changed in the five years we have been apart.'

Ava shifted agitatedly in her chair. 'You're imagining it. I hate you. I detest every minute I have to spend with you.'

His mouth curved upwards into a lazy smile. 'Then perhaps the sooner we make love and get it over with the better, *sì*? Who knows? Perhaps I will be bored by you within a week or two.'

'I wish,' she muttered.

He reached across the table and took her wrist in his hand, his fingers overlapping her fragile form, reminding her yet again of how outclassed she was in trying to win a single battle with him, let alone the war. His eyes burned as they held hers, searing her to the core. 'I think it's time you stopped playing games with me, Ava,' he said. 'I know what you are doing. All those little secrets and lies are for a purpose, are they not?'

Ava gritted her teeth as she pulled out of his hold. 'I am not playing any games. If anyone is guilty of that it is you, blackmailing me back into your life the way you have.'

He gave her a contemptuous look as he rose from the table. 'You can leave any minute you wish, Ava,' he said. 'But if you go you will not be taking a penny or a single possession with you. All you will be taking is a folder full of bills your husband left unpaid. Do I make myself clear?'

She sat fuming at him, stubbornly refusing to

answer, hating him with such intensity she was practically shaking all over with it.

'I said, do I make myself clear?' he barked at her.

Ava rose to her feet in one stiff, angry movement which toppled her chair backwards onto the terrace tiles. 'Don't you dare raise your voice at me!' she said, glaring at him.

Celeste came running at the sound of the chair crashing to the ground, but Marc sent her away with a look that would have stopped an express train in its tracks.

He turned back to Ava once the housemaid had scuttled away, his eyes still flashing their ire. 'This is not how I wish our relationship to be conducted,' he said, lowering his voice with an obvious effort. 'You will learn respect if I have to spend every hour of every day teaching you.'

Ava curled her top lip at him, even though she knew it was likely to stoke his anger towards her. 'How is our relationship going to be conducted, then?' she asked. 'With you insulting me at every turn, calling me every vilifying name you can think of as if you've never put a foot wrong in your life. Your hypocrisy is nauseating. You've made plenty of mistakes, Marc. The difference is you won't admit to them.'

When she moved past him to leave the terrace Marc let her go without a word. He picked up the lukewarm coffee and took a sip, frowning heavily as he looked at the sparkling blue water of the ocean below.

# CHAPTER FOUR

AVA spent the rest of the morning in her room, filling in time by sorting through her wardrobe, a task that she could just as easily have assigned to Celeste, but she wanted the mental space of a menial activity to calm her restive mind.

When she came downstairs for a light lunch Celeste informed her Marc had left the villa and would not be back until dinner. Ava felt her tense shoulders and the tight band around her head instantly relax.

The heat of the day drove Ava out to the infinity pool Douglas had installed in the terraced gardens at the back of the villa. It was one of Ava's favourite spots, for the screen of the shrubs gave her a sense of privacy as she swam lap after lap. The sun was warm, but the water spilling over her with each stroke she took felt like cool silk, the sensual glide of her body through the water making her feel weightless and free.

She wasn't quite sure of when she first realised she was no longer alone. At first it was just a prickling-at-the-back-of-the-neck sensation that she was being watched, but when she stopped at the end of the pool she could see no sign of anyone about. However, it was on her last lap that she noticed Marc sitting on one of the sun loungers, looking magnificently male in nothing but his black close-fitting bathers. Every muscle of his abdomen looked as if it had been carved from dark marble. Not a gram of excess flesh was on him anywhere. She could see he was no stranger to the discipline of regular and hard exercise. If anything, he was looking even fitter and leaner than he had in the past.

'You swim well,' he said, lifting his sunglasses to prop them just above his hairline.

'Thank you,' she said and, using the steps at the side of the pool, came out of the water, trying not to feel self-conscious in her bikini.

She felt Marc's eyes on her as she went to the other sun lounger, where she had left her towel, the heat of his gaze warming her far more than the late-afternoon sun. She used her towel like a sarong around her body before she faced him. 'Celeste told me you weren't coming back to the villa until later this evening.'

He placed his hands behind his head as he stretched out on the lounger, the action making every carved contour of his biceps bulge with latent strength. 'I finished the business I had to see to earlier than expected,' he said.

Ava narrowed her gaze as she stalled in the process of wringing out her wet hair over her shoulder. 'Were you checking up on me by any chance?' she asked.

He crossed his ankles in an indolent manner, his dark eyes still roving her form so thoroughly she felt her skin prickle all over with sensory awareness. 'Were you thinking of an escape route?' he countered.

Ava pursed her lips, letting the damp rope of her hair go. 'Is there one I could use that would succeed?'

He smiled a confident smile. 'No.' He leaned back even farther in the lounger. 'I have thought of everything, *cara*. You have no choice but to stay with me or face the consequences of your late husband's debts.'

Ava tightened her towel around her body. 'If I am to be shackled to you indefinitely I would like something to do to fill my time,' she said. 'While I was...' she hesitated ever so briefly over her choice of word '...living with Douglas I helped him with some aspects of the business.'

Marc rose from the lounger, dropping his sunglasses back over his eyes. 'You can't have been keeping too close an eye on them, otherwise you would have seen the way things were and left him and his sinking ship long ago,' he remarked.

Ava felt her heart give a little flutter as he stepped closer. She had no way of escaping unless she stepped backwards into the pool. 'Th-that's because towards the end when he became ill I left things to his accountants and business manager and instead looked after him myself.'

'Why didn't you leave him while you had the chance, or didn't he give you a choice?'

'It might surprise you, but yes, he did give me a choice, but I felt I owed it to him to stay,' she said. 'He had no one else. He wasn't close to his children, which he regretted deeply. I felt sorry for him. He didn't want to die alone.'

Although Ava couldn't see Marc's eyes on account of his sunglasses, she could feel the cynicism of his gaze all the same. 'You expect me to believe you personally nursed him?' he asked.

Ava lifted her chin. 'It was the least I could do. After all, he had been very good to me.'

'Oh, yes,' he said with a lift of one side of his mouth. 'He was very good to you indeed. He apparently paid you a minor fortune, didn't he? Where is it now, Ava? Where is all the money he paid you over the years?'

Ava felt a footstep of unease press on the base of her spine. 'That is none of your business,' she said, instinctively stepping backwards, momentarily forgetting the body of water behind her.

She teetered for a nanosecond before Marc took her by the upper arms, his fingers warm and firm against her flesh. Her towel slipped to the pool deck, but Ava hardly noticed; she was far too aware of how close he was to her body and how hers was responding to him as if she had no choice in the matter. Her breasts pushed against her bikini top, the sensitive nipples tight with the ache to feel him touch her. Her hips were within touching distance of his, the temptation to press herself against him and feel his hardness was almost unbearable.

'Large amounts of money have been going from your account to your sister's in London,' Marc said. 'Do you want to tell me what that money was for or should I have someone investigate it for me at the risk of causing embarrassment to your sister or her husband or both?'

She glared up at him with stormy grey-blue eyes. 'How dare you invade my privacy, not to mention my sister's, like that?'

His fingers tightened as she tried to sidestep his hold. Anger was on her side, however, and somehow he misjudged his footwork. With a tangle of limbs Marc found himself falling, taking Ava with him into the open blue mouth of the pool.

She came up spluttering, her arms flailing at him in fury, knocking his sunglasses off in the process. 'You did that on purpose, you…you…beast!'

Marc captured her wrists and pulled her up against his body, his blood surging to his groin as soon as her pelvis rammed against his. Her body felt like silk against his, soft and sensual, her limbs curling around his to keep herself afloat. He took advantage of every sweet moment, relishing in the feel of her mound against the press of his erection. She was fighting herself rather than him, he realised with an inward smile of satisfaction. He could feel it in the way her body pressed and pushed against him simultaneously, as if she resented what she was feeling but wanted it anyway. In the end he made it easy for her—he bent his head and his mouth swooped down to cover hers, his tongue delving deeply to bring hers to submission.

Within seconds she melted with a sigh, her tongue dancing with his, her arms lacing around his neck as he nudged her to the edge of the pool where it was shallow enough to stand. He stood with his thighs apart, her slim form fitting perfectly against him, her mouth hot and wet and urgent under the heated pressure and exploration of his.

The blood roared in his veins, thundering in his ears until all he could think about was sinking into her slick velvet warmth. He had wanted to wait, to have her begging for him, not the other way around, but his body was on fire with flames of need so intense he could feel them licking at him with long tongues of blistering heat. His whole body throbbed with it, the powerful attraction he had always felt for her seemed to have intensified now he finally had her in his arms. He had never been so close to losing control, or at least not since he was a hormone-charged teenager. The thought of exploding within her, feeling her convulsing around him made his blood sizzle as it raced through him. He ached with the pressure, the need so great he moved against her softness, searching for her, his spine tingling as she responded by whimpering with desire.

Ava felt the tiled lip of the pool at her back as Marc's body pressed against her searchingly, the heady, probing thrust of his arousal turning her bones to liquid. Her mouth was still locked beneath the mind-blowing passion of his, her hands threading through the wet thickness of his hair, her legs no longer touching the bottom of the pool but curled around the hair-roughened length of his.

'I want you,' he growled against her mouth as he deftly untied the strings of her bikini top. 'Damn, it but I want you.'

Ava was vaguely aware of her top floating away as Marc's hands cupped her already peaking flesh. She gasped as his mouth covered hers again, her inner core beating with a pulse that was as strong as it was exigent. His tongue stroked and stabbed at hers simultaneously, making her breath catch with anticipation. Her heart raced with excitement, the sheer thrill of being in his arms again was beyond what she had imagined it would be. There was more heat, more urgency and more passion than ever before as kiss was exchanged for kiss, their teeth and tongues duelling until Ava had no idea who was in control any more.

Her hands left his hair and went to the cord of his bathers, untying it blindly as her mouth burned against his. She felt him spring into her hands as he stepped out of the bathers, the length of him heavy and hot with lust. She stroked him under the water, the rhythmic action as natural to her as breathing in spite of the five long years that had passed. She knew what he liked, how hard, how soft, how fast and how far she could go until he would check her movements before he lost control. She loved the feel of him; he was so strong and yet so vulnerable like this.

When he untied the strings of her bikini at her hips Ava drew in another little hitching breath of excitement. There would be no going back now. She could feel it in his body as it thrummed with need against hers. They had never made love in the water before. It was such a sensuous experience, the hint of the forbidden about it only adding to the allure.

She opened to him like a flower, gasping as he drove into her so thickly her back grazed the tiles of the pool. Her body clamped around him, waves of pleasure tingling through her with each deep thrust he gave. There was something so primal about his lovemaking; the pounding urgency of it made it her pulse soar. He was rough and fast, but she was with him all the way. Her body was humming with sensation as he drove harder and harder. She felt that delicious tight little ache start low and deep, the tight pearl of tension that needed just that little bit more friction for release to come.

She wriggled against him instinctively, wantonly, recklessly as she felt herself reach the summit of human sensation. She bit down on his shoulder to block her gasping cries of ecstasy, shuddering and convulsing as his body continued to pump within hers.

As she floated down from the heights of pleasure she heard him suck in a harsh breath before he gave a series of hard grunts as he spilled into her, his body tight as whipcord, his muscles clenched beneath her clinging fingers.

She felt him sag against her momentarily before he stepped back from her, raking a hand through his wet hair, his dark eyes briefly meeting hers before looking away.

'I'm sorry,' he said. 'That was not meant to happen, or at least not without protection.'

Ava gathered her pride, no easy feat when both pieces of her bikini were floating at the other end of the pool like an ill-formed octopus. How had she let herself be used by him? Where was her self-control? He had proved what her place in his life was going to be: as a sexual plaything he could access whenever he felt like it and she had given him every reason now to think she was more than willing to participate. She hadn't even had the presence of mind to insist he use protection. Didn't that prove how wanton he thought her to be? 'Wasn't it your intention to show me my place?' she asked with a flinty glare.

The space between his dark brows narrowed. 'Ava, this was always going to happen,' he said, brushing his wet hair back again, his chest still rising and falling as his breathing slowly returned to normal. 'Maybe it would have been wiser to have done it indoors and with less haste, but that's not something that can be changed. I will make it up to you right now. Let's go inside and I'll show you.'

She threw him a withering look before turning and climbing out of the pool. 'No, thank you,' she said, snatching up her towel off the deck and wrapping it around herself tightly.

Marc vaulted out of the water and stopped her with a hand on her arm. 'Wait, Ava,' he said crossly, although he was annoyed with himself more than her. He had caught sight of a graze on her back, a reddened patch that made him feel ashamed of himself for losing control. 'Let me see your back. It looks like it's sore.'

She tried to slap his hand away. 'Get away from me. It's obvious what I'm here for—your pleasure, in any way and any place and any time you like it. Douglas might have had his faults, but he never once made me feel the way you have just done.'

Marc felt each of her words hit him like lethally aimed arrows, but he kept his expression mask-like. 'You felt pleasure too, Ava, or are you going to deny it just to spite me, hmm?'

She threw him an icy glare. 'Think what you like. I might have been pretending for all you know.'

Marc chuckled at her spirited defiance. 'Then that was a pretty amazing performance, Ava.' He rubbed a hand over the indentation her teeth had made on his shoulder. 'But I know your body and I know an orgasm when I feel it, both yours and mine.'

Her eyes glittered with hatred, her body almost vibrating with the effort of containing her anger, but he wondered if she was furious with him or with herself for responding to him so unrestrainedly. Perhaps she had wanted to insult his pride by withholding her pleasure, but it had been such a powerfully explosive moment it had taken her by surprise, just as it had him. God knew, his body was still humming with the after-shocks of having her in his arms again. He couldn't wait to repeat the experience, time and time again.

But there were questions that required some answers first.

He reached for his towel on the sun lounger where he had left it earlier, and tied it roughly around his hips. 'You never did give me a straight answer to my question. Why did you give your sister the bulk of the money Cole gave you?'

She elevated her chin in a haughty manner. 'That is between Serena and me.'

Marc tightened his jaw as he held her fiery gaze. 'Has she got some sort of drug or gambling problem?'

She glared at him for suggesting such a thing. 'That is exactly the sort of thing you would think, isn't it, Marc?' she said. 'Think the worst before any other possibility comes to mind.'

'If there is nothing to hide then why not tell me what she has needed your financial help for?' he asked, fighting down his frustration. She was so wilful and defensive he couldn't get a straight answer out of her. He hated not knowing all the facts. It made him feel as if she had the power to tug the rug from under his feet. He was certainly not going to allow her the chance to do that again. Not in this lifetime.

She held his gaze for several taut seconds before

lowering hers, a whoosh of a sigh passing through her soft lips. 'Serena can't have children,' she said, 'or at least not naturally. I've been helping her and Richard pay for repeated IVF treatments.'

Marc absorbed the information for a moment. He wondered why Ava had been so determined to keep such a thing quiet. It was a wonderful gesture on her part and, given how she had been painted in the Press, he couldn't understand why she hadn't used her acts of goodwill to whitewash her reputation. Surely it would have gone a long way to turn the public's opinion around. But then her sister's privacy probably had a lot to do with it, if not Serena's husband, he thought. Marc had only met him once and only briefly at that, but Richard Holt had struck him as a rather conservative English gentleman who would no doubt be appalled at having such sensitive private issues hung out in public.

'Thank you for telling me,' he said. 'It will go no further than me if that is what you wish.'

Her grey-blue eyes came back to his, a shadow clouding them. 'My sister has suffered a lot over the years,' she said. 'Not just with the fertility issue, but long before that. Losing our mother was hard for both of us, but I think Serena, being that bit younger, felt it more, especially when our father remarried so quickly. I tried to protect her as much as I could but I didn't always succeed.'

Marc frowned as he took it all in. Ava seemed to be blaming herself for not doing a job she was far too young to be doing at that time. No one could replace someone's mother. He should know—the loss of his had deeply affected him, even though the circumstances were totally different. It made him wonder how far Ava would go to protect her sister, if in fact her marriage to Cole had been for exactly that purpose and no other. It was an uncomfortable thought that Marc himself had acted no less ruthlessly by forcing her into a loveless union for his own ends. Ava had sacrificed herself all over again in order to bring about her sister's happiness. Marc had always known Douglas Cole was a shady character who thought nothing of the odd dodgy deal, but what he couldn't stomach or even bear to think about was how Ava had been used as a pawn and he had added to her suffering by insisting on her becoming his mistress again. He was so used to looking upon her as the guilty one: the betrayer, the harlot who had stomped all over his pride by leaving him for another man, he hadn't stopped to think what other motive she might have for acting as she had. No wonder she hated him with such vehemence. She might have capitulated to primal desire as he had done, but it didn't mean she cared anything for him. Why would she? He had judged her without mercy, blackmailed her and virtually stripped her of her freedom for the sake of his pride. How he would ever make it up to her was beyond him at that point. He needed time to think. He was not used to being flooded by such a tidal wave of emotion, guilt being the primary one. It made him feel defensive, as if he needed to build a wall around himself until he could navigate his way through the mess he had made, to make some sense of where to go to from here.

He watched in silence as Ava gnawed at her lip and continued, 'I just want Serena to be happy. She had a terrible experience when she was a teenager. On her very first date she was sexually assaulted. It took years for her to get over it. I was worried she was going to…to…end it all, but thankfully I finally managed to get her the help she needed. Throughout the whole time, our father was next to useless and our stepmother even worse. They thought she was making it up to get attention.'

Marc felt a gnarled hand clutch at his insides. 'You are indeed a very devoted sister,' he said. 'I hadn't realised how much you had done for her over the years. I am sorry.'

She gave him a fleeting look before turning away. 'Serena wants a baby more than anything. She's finally found a man who absolutely adores her. Richard is so gentle and loving, so perfect for her. He would love her with or without having a family, but she is so very determined to give him a child.'

'I would imagine it would be a big thing for a woman,' Marc said. 'It's the sort of thing one takes for granted—fertility, I mean.'

She ran her tongue over her lips and glanced at him again before shifting her gaze. 'Yes…yes, I suppose it is…'

There was a three-beat silence.

'I know I asked you before, but in the light of what happened in the pool a few minutes ago…' Marc cleared his throat as he pushed back his hair with his fingers 'you *are* currently taking the Pill, are you not? If you weren't sleeping with Cole then you wouldn't need to be on it, unless, of course, you had other lovers.'

Her face coloured, but Marc wasn't sure if it was anger at being reminded of the reckless passion they had just shared, or whether she was embarrassed at discussing such personal issues. She had not exactly been prudish with him in the past, so he could only assume she was still furious with him for demonstrating she could still respond to him in spite of all her words to the contrary. He had to admit he was a little annoyed with himself for not holding back a little longer. It gave her power over him, the sort of power he didn't want her to have, to know she still had such an overwhelming effect on him. Given how he had treated her, what would stop her from using it against him? She could go to the Press and destroy him in a few choice paragraphs. Would she do it? Could he afford to trust her? Surely she had even more reason now to try and destroy him.

Marc set his mouth. 'I understand you are angry at me and I don't blame you. I have got a lot of things wrong, some by my own arrogance, but also from you keeping secrets that had no need to be kept. But while you may not have had a sexual relationship with Cole, how am I to know if you have had other lovers unless you tell me?'

'You have nothing to worry about as far as I am concerned,' she said in a self-righteous manner, pulling her towel tighter around her body. 'I have not been sleeping around, but then you might choose not to believe me, of course.'

Marc knew he deserved that little swipe of hers, but he could not have rested until he'd asked. It was going to take him some time to process all she had told him. She had said nothing of her sister's situation in the past, but then he hadn't told her half of his own background. Their relationship back then had been based on lust and very little else, or at least from his perspective. He knew Ava had wanted more from him, but he had sworn off marriage after seeing what happened to his father. It had been gut-wrenching to see a fully grown man totally shattered by the desertion of his wife. Marc had vowed from a young age he would never allow his heart to be engaged in any of his relationships with women. And he had been true to that vow. He had always kept things light and casual, or at least until Ava had come along. She was the first woman he had not been able to forget. It maddened and frustrated him that he had not been able to move on. If he had acted like a sensible adult none of this would have happened. He should have accepted her decision to end their relationship. The trouble was he had wanted her so much. He *still* wanted her. He wondered if there would ever be a time when he didn't.

'I will use condoms in future, just to be sure there are no accidents,' he said with perhaps a little less finesse than was called for. 'I don't want any nasty surprises.'

Ava stiffened in anger. 'You think I would do something like that?'

He bent down to scoop his bathers out of the pool, wringing them out in his hands and then stepping into them with no hint of self-consciousness. 'It has happened before,' he said. 'I know of several men who've suddenly had their lives turned upside down by a paternity case thrown at them by an ex-lover.'

Ava clutched at the knot of her towel. 'This is a totally hypothetical question, but if—and it's a big and very unlikely if—*if* I was to fall pregnant, what would you expect me to do?'

He finished retying the cord of his bathers before he answered. 'First of all I would expect to be told about it as soon as possible.'

'Why?' Ava shot back. 'So you could make the decision for me?'

'Don't put words in my mouth, Ava,' he said, frowning down at her. 'I merely said I would like to know as soon as it is humanly possible. As to what you decide… well, I have always believed it is a woman's choice, since ultimately it is her body that is involved.'

Ava met his gaze, her chin at a combative height. 'I wouldn't dream of having an abortion. I think you need to know that right from the start.'

'I would not ask it of you,' he returned. 'Especially given the trouble your sister is experiencing.'

Ava was surprised by the empathy in his voice as he spoke of her sister. She bit her lip and sank down to sit on the end of the sun lounger behind her. 'At least Serena has Richard by her side,' she said to fill the stretching silence.

'How many IVF attempts have they made?' Marc asked.

She shrugged. 'I've kind of lost count…six…maybe seven.' She looked at her hands resting on her thighs. 'The last miscarriage…the one she's just had has been the worst for her. Everything was going so well and then…' She bit down on her lip again, her eyes misting over.

Marc put a hand on her shoulder, his palm tingling at the contact with her soft, silky skin. 'It is not your fault your sister cannot have children. It seems to me you are going out of your way to see that she gets every chance to have a family.'

She looked up at him. 'Why have you always been so against having children?'

He dropped his hand from her shoulder and moved to the other side of the terrace, his gaze taking in the view without really seeing it. 'I have seen what happens when children are shunted back and forth between warring parents. I don't want to be responsible for that sort of emotional damage.'

After a lengthy silence he heard her rise from the sun lounger behind him. 'The sun is starting to burn me,' she said. 'Do you mind if I go inside and take a shower?'

Marc turned and looked at her. 'Ava, you don't have to ask my permission over every little thing.'

Her slim brows rose in twin arcs of cynicism. 'Don't I?'

He held her challenging gaze. 'You are not my slave, you are my current lover.'

'Is there a difference I should be made aware of?' she asked with that haughty look she had perfected that made Marc's hands itch to reach for her and kiss her senseless.

'What happened here a few minutes ago is not over,' he said. 'Rather it is just beginning. If you are not careful, *ma petite*, I will demonstrate it right here and now.'

She turned and stalked across the terrace and back into the villa, leaving Marc with nothing but the afternoon breeze to tease him with her lingering fragrance.

# CHAPTER FIVE

AVA was surprised when she came downstairs for dinner to find Celeste had set the large formal dining table for only one. 'Is—er—Signor Castellano not here for dinner this evening?' she asked the housekeeper.

Celeste smoothed a tiny crease out of the starched white tablecloth. 'He said he had some business to attend to at his office,' she said.

'I didn't realise he had an office in Monte Carlo,' Ava said, frowning as she took her seat.

Celeste gave her an unreadable look. 'He does not yet have an office here, although I believe he is in the process of setting one up,' she said. 'He flew to London an hour ago.'

Ava tried not to show how much the news affected her, but even so she felt as if she had been kicked in the stomach. Marc's passionate attention this afternoon out at the pool had stirred her senses into a frenzy from which they had yet to recover. To hear from someone else he had left for London hurt far more than it ought to have. Was he deliberately showing her what he expected her position in his life to be? She was nothing more than a chattel, a plaything he picked up and put down whenever he felt like it. Business came first, as it had in the past. She was a part-time lover, a position she had sworn she would never be in again.

He couldn't have chosen a more effective tool to make her uncertain of him, to stop her from feeling even the tiniest bit secure in his life: making mad, passionate love with her one minute, leaving her to fend for herself the next.

'Did Signor Castellano tell you when he is expecting to return?' Ava asked as Celeste brought in a tray with the first course.

'He said he would call you in a day or two,' Celeste answered. 'He left his contact details near the telephone in the library if you should need to reach him.'

Ava drummed her fingers on the table once the housekeeper had left. She was determined *not* to call him. She was going to carry on with her life as if he had not barged back into it, issuing his commands right, left and off-centre as if she had no will and mind of her own.

The following morning Ava left the villa, taking her time over browsing in the shops, stopping for a coffee and a pastry before making her way to a beauty spa, where she treated herself to a wash and blow-dry of her hair as well as a manicure and pedicure. She was on her way out of the spa when she ran into the wife of Douglas's business manager, a woman in her early thirties who dressed—and on far too many occasions acted—as if she were half that age.

'Ava!' Chantelle Watterson cooed as she air-kissed

Ava's cheeks. 'You look absolutely marvellous. And no wonder, eh?'

'Er—well, I just had my hair and nails done, so—'

Chantelle threw back her bottle-blonde head and laughed. 'Droll, darling, very droll. I'm talking about your new lover. He is *gorgeous* and much younger than Dougie too, you lucky thing. I read about it in the paper. I am *so* envious, I just can't tell you. Hugh is starting to show his age, not just in appearance, if you know what I mean. Not that I mind really—I keep myself occupied.' She gave a meaningful wink.

Ava ground her teeth behind her forced smile. 'Hugh always looks wonderful for his age.'

'If it wasn't for his money I wouldn't stay with him, you know,' Chantelle said in a conspiratorial tone as she slipped a too thin, too tanned arm through one of Ava's. 'But then, beggars can't be losers, right?' She cackled at her own joke before continuing, 'I think it's time we had a drink to celebrate your new life.'

'Actually, I have to get going,' Ava said, trying to extract herself from Chantelle's python-like hold. 'Marc will be expecting me.'

Chantelle's green eyes glinted. 'Liar,' she said. 'He's in London right now with Hugh. It's something to do with the takeover of Dougie's company. Hugh was quite worried about it. But I suppose Marc doesn't talk to you about business, eh?'

Ava pressed her lips together. 'There's hardly been time to talk about anything,' she said.

'Yes, well, Hugh told me Marc Castellano moves quickly when he wants something,' Chantelle said. 'But a word of advice, darling—men like Marc like things their way and their way only. If I were you I wouldn't make a fuss if he plays around behind your back or indeed right under your nose. I know for a fact Hugh's had a few flings, but what's the point in rocking the boat when it's sailing in the direction you want it to go?'

Ava couldn't wait to get away from the woman's gold-digging cynicism. She felt tainted by just being in her presence. 'Look, Chantelle, I really have to go,' she said, this time managing to get her arm out of the older woman's grip. 'Things are not what you think with Marc and me. We were together in the past. We are trying to make a go of it this time. I wouldn't want you or anyone to get the wrong impression or anything. You know how the Press has always had it in for me.'

Chantelle smiled a bleached-white smile that fell a little short of genuine. 'I understand perfectly, darling,' she purred. 'Marc Castellano is super-rich and super-sexy. You'd be a fool to let him slip through your fingers. Get a ring on your finger though and quickly. The Press can say what they like, but once you're legally his wife they'll leave you alone. That's what happened with me, in any case.'

'We have no intention of marrying at this point,' Ava said, even though for some reason it hurt to say it out loud.

Chantelle patted Ava's arm in a patronising manner. 'Then see if you can get him to change his mind,' she said, winking suggestively.

Ava made good her escape when another acquaintance of Chantelle's came out of the spa and diverted her attention.

As she made her way back to the villa Ava felt sick

at the thought of being associated with someone as shallow and selfish as Chantelle Watterson. She had always hated the thought of people assuming she had hooked up with Douglas Cole for the very same reasons Chantelle had married Hugh Watterson. But for Serena's sake she had put up with it, being—back then—reasonably confident it wouldn't be long before she would move to the other side of the globe and put it all behind her.

Douglas had told her from the start about his diagnosis of bladder cancer; however, he had wanted no one else to know for the sake of his business. He had said he was worried about investors pulling out if they knew he was terminally ill. He had said he had been given less than two years to live, but he had made it to five. Ava often wondered if he had lied to her about his prognosis but she had no way of finding out now. Although the five years at times had felt like a prison sentence, she felt she had done the right thing in staying with him that final year so at least he was not left to die alone.

Another three days passed without any contact from Marc and Ava began to hover around the villa phone as well as keeping her mobile switched on and with her all the time. It annoyed her that he was able to keep her on such tenterhooks in spite of her determination to carry on as normal. The trouble was the villa seemed to have breathed in the very essence of him. Everywhere she went she felt his presence. Even swimming in the pool made her feel every sensation he had evoked in her, unsettling her to the point where she came in after only a couple of laps. She felt him on her skin, she felt him in her body, even her inner muscles tweaked with the memory of him possessing her. The red patch on her back had almost faded, but she still found her fingers going to it, tracing over it as she pictured Marc thrusting into her so roughly, as if he couldn't contain his need of her. Her breasts, too, ached for the cup of his hands or the suck of his mouth. Day after lonely day she had to distract herself from thinking about him, holding her emotions in check in case they flooded out of control.

After giving up on a swim, Ava showered and changed and came downstairs to her favourite sitting room, which overlooked the port of Monte Carlo. She stood at the windows with her arms folded across her middle, and sighed with a combination of boredom and frustration.

'Don't tell me you are missing me after only four days.' Marc's voice sounded from behind her.

Ava spun around so quickly she felt the room tilt. She put a hand to her throat where it felt as if her heart was going to beat its way out. 'When did you get back?' she asked in a breathless gasp.

He reached up to loosen his tie. 'Just then,' he said, his face cast in an expressionless mask. 'Celeste told me on her way out that you were in here.'

Ava fixed him with an arch look, the anger she had felt at how he had left her dangling quickly replacing her shock at his sudden appearance. 'So how was your trip to London?' she asked. 'Was it business or pleasure or did you manage to squeeze in a bit of both?'

He closed the distance between them, stopping just in front of her, not touching her but close enough for her to feel his body heat. 'As my paid mistress, do you think you have got the right to question my movements when I am not with you?' he asked coolly and calmly.

Ava felt the anger swell in her veins until she thought she would explode with it. She raised her chin at him defiantly, her eyes throwing live wires of hatred at him. 'If I am to remain faithful to you I want you to do the same for me. In fact, I insist on it.'

'You sound rather adamant about it,' he said with that same mask-like expression. 'Has my absence made you feel unsure of your position in my life, *cara*?'

Ava was not going to admit to it even though it was painfully true. 'I am not going to share my body with you unless I am absolutely sure I am your only lover,' she said through lips pulled tight with determination.

He captured her chin, holding her gaze to his. 'You want exclusivity?'

'Yes. I won't settle for anything else.'

His eyes devoured hers as the silence beat like a tribal drum between them. Ava felt every one of her heartbeats; they seemed to be following a hectic syncopated rhythm instead of their usual slow and steady pace. Her breathing too was ragged and uneven, her lungs tight with the pressure of containing her spiralling emotions. She couldn't help dipping her gaze to his mouth, wondering if he was going to kiss her. If he did she would be lost. She could feel the pulse of need beating deep inside her. She had felt it the whole time he had been away and now he was here, touching her, she felt as if she would die without the pressure of his lips on hers.

'All right, but I have a few conditions of my own,'

Marc said. 'I forbid you to be seen with or speak to or make any contact whatsoever with Chantelle Watterson. Do I make myself clear?'

Ava frowned at the implacability of his tone. 'She is not a close associate of mine. I hardly know her.'

'You were seen talking to her for half an hour the day after I left.'

Her mouth dropped open. 'You really are having me watched, aren't you? My God, but you've got some nerve, Marc. I have a right to my privacy.'

He released her chin and stepped away to shrug himself out of his jacket, hanging it over the back of the chesterfield before facing her again. 'There are some things I am prepared to negotiate on in our relationship, but gossiping with that gold-digging cow of a woman Hugh Watterson was fool enough to marry is the very last thing I will allow.'

'I don't gossip and I only met her by chance,' Ava insisted. 'I had my hair done and ran into her as I came out of the salon.'

'That is not the way she told it to Hugh,' he said.

'So you'd rather believe what she said to him than what I am saying to you?' she asked bitterly.

His expression remained shuttered. 'I am just asking you to keep away from her, that is all. I don't want the Press to get the wrong idea about your association with her. I know you won't believe it, but I am trying to protect you.'

Ava rolled her eyes. 'You're right, I don't believe you. I thought the whole idea of this arrangement of yours was to cause as much damage to my reputation as you could.'

His brow darkened with a frown. 'Look, Ava, I'm still working through some issues. It's become more and more apparent to me that I have not always acted with the sort of propriety I should have, given the circumstances. It's taking me some time to see things from your perspective.'

'Take all the time you want,' she said with a scornful toss of her head. 'But given your cynical take on life, I reckon it will take a decade or two before you begin to trust any woman, let alone me.'

'I wasn't planning on continuing our affair quite that long.'

Ava felt as if he had just backhanded her. Her whole body stung with the aftershock of his clinically delivered statement, pain reverberating until she felt as if she was going to pass out.

'Is something wrong?' Marc asked, reaching for her as she swayed in front of him. 'You've gone completely white.'

'I—I'm fine…' She brushed off his hand, her eyes falling away from his. 'I haven't had much to eat today. It's been too hot.'

'Celeste told me you haven't been eating properly for some weeks now,' he said, still frowning as he took in her pallid features. 'Do you think you should see a doctor?'

'No. I'm just not quite over a stomach bug I picked up when I visited my sister a couple of weeks ago.'

Marc waited a moment before he asked, 'Are you missing him?'

She looked at him blankly. 'Missing whom?'

Marc had brooded over it the whole time he was

away, wondering if, in spite of her platonic relationship with Cole, deep down she had come to love him. After all, she had lived with him for five long years and nursed him through to his death. All the people he had spoken to in the London branch of Cole's business had confirmed how much Ava had done for him. How committed she had been to seeing that every one of his needs was met no matter what the time of day. Marc had gone away in order to gain perspective, to regroup and yet he had ended up even more confused about her motives. Ava McGuire had married a dying man—a very rich, old dying man. What better odds for her than that? She might not have slept with Cole, but that didn't mean she wasn't a gold-digger. She had banked on a big pay-out at the end, but now Marc was standing in the way of it. 'Your husband,' he said, jealousy rising like bile as he said those most hated of words.

Her throat rose and fell, the colour flowing back into her face as if someone had turned on a tap inside her. 'I would be a very cold person indeed if I could live with someone for five years and not miss them when they were gone,' she said. 'He deserves to be grieved. I know he was ruthless in business and he didn't always do the right thing by his family, but at least he tried to fix things before he died.'

Marc hated hearing her praise the man who had stolen so much from him. He hated thinking about the long hours he'd had to work to rebuild his business after Cole had won the bid over his. He had always believed Ava had been an active part of that betrayal, but based on the evidence he had gathered over the last few days it seemed more and more likely that Cole had worked alone. How much Ava knew of how she had been used was still open to investigation. There were still piles of papers to go through, but Marc was determined to uncover every motivation, both Cole's and Ava's. He had worked so hard for so long on exacting his revenge, he had hated Ava for five years; every thought he'd had was about having her back where he wanted her. The irony was he had her exactly where he had worked to get her, but she still wasn't his. He could see it in the way she looked at him. Hatred glittered in her grey-blue gaze, almost stinging him with its cold, hard intensity. She had used to look at him with such open adoration. He had found it claustrophobic at the time, but now he felt as if he would give anything to see her eyes soften and glisten with anything but the loathing he saw there now.

'Hugh Watterson told me how devoted Cole was to you,' Marc said. 'And yet you deny having been in love with him.'

Her eyes met his briefly before moving away again. 'There are many types of love,' she said. 'The love one feels for a parent, for instance, is quite different from that one feels for a friend or a lover.'

'So the love you felt for him was more parental than anything else?'

She gave him an irritated look. 'Could we please talk about something else?' she asked. 'Like why you felt you could just fly off to London without telling me when you were leaving or how long you would be away?'

'I had an issue to see to that cropped up without notice,' he said. 'I had to catch the first available flight.

There wasn't even time to pack a bag, let alone discuss my plans with you. I told Celeste on my way out to inform you of my absence.'

'I suppose you think it's amusing to make me look like a fool in front of the staff,' she tossed back crossly.

'It seems to me you have the full support of the staff,' Marc returned, 'Celeste in particular.'

'Celeste has been at this villa a long time,' she said. 'She was extremely fond of Douglas, for all of his faults. She of all people knows how much I did for him.'

Marc felt his insides twist all over again with jealousy. 'Yes, I have been hearing the same thing time and time again from Cole's London staff. It seemed you made quite an impression on everyone you met as the devoted, loving, self-sacrificing little wife, right to the very end.'

Her eyes threw flick-knives of disdain at him. 'Self-sacrifice is not something you are familiar with, is it, Marc? You have always put your interests first and, from what I've seen so far, nothing has changed.'

He blocked her with his arm as she made to leave. 'No, I have not finished talking to you,' he said.

Ava tightened her mouth and then, still holding his gaze, dug her fingernails into the flesh of his arm.

He swore and pulled his arm away, reaching for his handkerchief to dab where her nails had almost broken the skin. 'You have developed claws, *ma petite*,' he said calmly as he briefly touched her lips with his finger.

Ava felt her spine loosen at the gentleness of his touch. She felt herself drowning in the dark depths of his coal-black gaze, the silence growing, swelling, burgeoning with the erotic tension that buzzed like electricity between them. Her body responded to his closeness, her breasts feeling full and heavy, her belly quivering with flickers of longing, her inner core moistening at the promise of fulfilment she could see in his gaze just before it went to her mouth.

'Do not fight me, Ava,' he commanded softly, his breath feathering over the surface of her lips. 'Why not kiss me instead, hmm?'

Ava felt her eyelashes go down as her heels lifted off the floor to bring her mouth within touching distance of his. She pressed her lips softly to his, barely touching, breathing in his scent, his maleness, the heat and exhilarating potency of him.

He kissed her back equally softly, hardly any pressure, just a light, teasing touchdown of male lips on female, generating heat that was so combustible Ava could feel it like flames licking at her from deep inside her body.

His mouth slowly increased its pressure, his tongue stroking for entry, which she gave on a gasping sigh of pleasure. Her tongue caressed his, dancing with it, duelling with it until she finally allowed him to be the victor.

His hands cupped her face as he deepened the kiss, then his fingers were splayed in her hair, massaging, caressing her as his mouth worked its intoxicating magic on hers.

Ava pressed closer, wanting to feel the blood-thickened length of him where she needed him most. Her body felt so intensely alive, every part of her aching with need, fully charged to respond to him and him alone.

His mouth moved from hers down the side of her neck, searing kisses that burned her skin, his tongue a sexy rasp as it tasted each of her pleasure points. She threw her head back, delighting in the way he was taking his time, drawing out the pleasure to the point of torture.

By the time he got to her breasts she was close to begging. She whimpered breathlessly as he removed her clothing, piece by piece, in a reverse striptease that had her heart racing with excitement as each article hit the floor.

He was still fully clothed, which added to the daring sensuality of it. Ava reached for the zip on his trousers, but he pushed her hand away. 'Not yet, *cara*,' he said huskily. 'This is my chance to show you I have not forgotten how to take my time in pleasuring you.'

Ava shivered as he pressed her back against the leather-covered desk, her body splayed like a feast for him to devour. She was beyond shame; her need was too intense, far too out of control for her to think about how she might view this incredibly intimate act in the morning. Right now she wanted him to pleasure her; every nerve-ending was screaming for it, every cell of her body vibrating uncontrollably with the need for release.

She gasped as he stroked her first with his fingers, the slow-moving action arching her spine where it lay pressed against the desk. She felt her own moisture, the slickness of it making every glide of his fingers that much more thrilling and erotic.

'You are so beautiful,' he said in a deep, gravelly

tone. 'Like an exotic hot-house flower opening to the sun.'

Ava felt her sensitive nerves twitching in response to the waft of his warm breath as he brought his mouth to her. She drew in a sharp breath, holding it in her chest as he explored her with his tongue. The heart of her need gathered at that one pearl-like point; she felt the exquisite build-up, the growing wave-like tension taking over her completely. She couldn't think or feel anything other than what he was doing to her, the sensations he was evoking finally taking over. She felt herself shatter into a million pieces, each one a burst of bright, flashing colour, like fireworks exploding in a clear night sky. Her body rocked with the aftershocks, she was even vaguely aware of the ink well on the desk rattling as she convulsed with pleasure.

Almost as soon as the pleasure flowed out of her, the shame rolled in, great, giant waves of it, each one threatening to drown her. Ava propped herself up on her hands before sliding off the desk, bending to gather her clothes from the floor. She couldn't believe she had been so wanton again, let alone so foolish. By responding to him so feverishly she felt it had cheapened her, making her seem just like the pleasure-seeking gold-digger he thought her to be. She had acted like a sex-starved alley cat, opening her legs without hesitation every time he touched her. Did he have such power over her that she could act so recklessly with no thought to how it would make her feel or how he would look upon her?

'What are you doing?' Marc asked.

'What do you think I am doing?' she said, tugging at her bra, which was currently caught beneath his foot.

He bent down and picked it up for her. 'You seem in rather a hurry to leave.'

'The party is over, isn't it?' she asked, scrunching the bra into an odd-shaped ball. 'Or am I expected to service you?'

He frowned. 'Ava, there is no need for this petulance.'

She brushed her awry hair away from her face as she looked up at him. 'Aren't you going to make things a thousand times worse now by asking me whether I've done this, if not with Douglas, then with someone else?'

His jaw worked for a moment as if his mind was filling with the images of her writhing on the desk under someone else's caresses. 'No, actually I was not going to ask you that,' he said in a clipped tone. 'I know for a fact you did not sleep with Cole. That was another thing I found out from the ever-obliging Celeste. Cole was impotent and had been for many years as the result of surgery for his cancer.'

Ava pressed her lips together as she looked around for her shoes, privately marvelling at how Marc had managed to eke out so much information in so short a time from one of Douglas's most discreet and loyal staff members. It made her feel uneasy to think he had access to such intimate details. What if he found out the real reason behind her marriage to Douglas? As far as she knew Celeste knew nothing about it, unless Douglas had told her in the last stages of his illness as a deathbed confession. If Marc found out, how could she trust him not to expose Serena? What if he used Serena to get back at her?

'Answer me something,' Marc said. 'Did you know he was impotent when he asked you to marry him?'

Ava was still only partially dressed and a little too close to tears for her liking. 'I fail to see why that should be of any interest to you,' she said as she hunted about for her shoes. 'For God's sake,' she muttered in frustration. 'Where are my shoes?'

'They are over here,' he said, handing them to her. 'Answer the question, Ava. Did you know the full extent of Cole's condition when he asked you to be his wife?'

Ava clutched her pile of clothing close to her chest. 'He told me he was dying,' she said, not quite meeting his gaze. 'He told me he had two years at the most to live.'

'You must have been a much better wife than he bargained for,' Marc remarked wryly. 'You kept him alive for an extra three years.'

She gave him a cutting look. 'Are you finished with me now, Marc, or have you something else you require me to do as your paid mistress? I can get down on my knees if you like and return the favour, or would you rather a quick rough tumble on the floor?'

His eyes warred with hers for a stretching moment. 'I don't understand why you are being so testy about this deal between us, which as far as I can see is really no different from the deal you had with Cole, apart from a piece of paper, of course.'

Bitter tears burned at the backs of Ava's eyes, but she refused to allow them purchase. 'Everything is different about this deal between us,' she said. 'You have no idea how different.'

'Such as?'

'You hate me.' She said it like a challenge, willing him to deny it. When he said nothing in response Ava felt again as if he had slapped her.

One of her shoes thudded to the floor from the haphazardly gathered pile in her arms, but before she could retrieve it he bent down and picked it up and silently handed it back to her. 'Thank you,' she said tightly.

'If it is the amount I am paying you then all you have to do is say so,' Marc said after another taut silence.

Ava glared at him, knowing that if she didn't leave soon she would be howling like a child. 'It has *nothing* to do with the money.'

His brows lifted cynically. 'I beg to differ, *ma petite*, but it has everything to do with money,' he said. 'Are you forgetting the debts Cole left behind? That is why I had to go to London in such a rush. Hugh Watterson, your late husband's business manager-cum-accountant, has been skimming the books.'

Ava stared at him in open-mouthed shock. 'Are you sure Hugh is guilty? Have you any proof?'

The look in his eyes was like black stone. 'Of course I have proof. I have set my legal team to work to uncover every other discrepancy. I am sure I will find hundreds. Hugh is a very clever accountant. Over the last few months he has been busily stashing money in accounts where it was almost impossible to trace them.' He tipped up her chin, making her lock gazes with him. 'Was it a scheme you cooked up between you?'

Ava frowned until her forehead ached. 'What are you talking about? What scheme with whom?'

He kept his steely gaze on hers. 'You and Chantelle Watterson,' he said. 'When cornered Hugh said he did it for his young wife, to keep her in the manner to which she had become accustomed. You and she are very similar, are you not? You both hooked up with much older men, living a life of luxury in the hope that one day they would die and leave you their fortune. What a pity there was nothing left in the kitty for you when Cole conveniently obliged by dying while you were still young and attractive enough to start again.'

'That is a disgusting thing to say,' Ava said, stepping back in affront. 'I never wanted anything from Douglas.' *At least not for myself*, she thought.

'Now, that is not quite true, is it, Ava?' he asked. 'You would never have married him if he hadn't been filthy rich and terminally ill, now, would you?'

She raised her chin, meeting his gaze with fire in her own. 'He gave me an offer I felt compelled to accept. Anyway, it was more than you were ever going to offer me.'

The edges of his mouth flickered, as if anger was just beneath the surface, waiting to leap out and strike. 'I was always totally honest about what I was prepared to give you. I told you marriage was not an option for me.'

Ava continued to glare at him. 'It's not in your nature to compromise, is it, Marc? You just expect people to fall into your plans. Now, may I be excused, or do you want more bang for your buck?'

Marc unlocked his clenched hands, fighting every instinct to drag her into his arms and make love to her, to claim her in every way possible. His blood was thundering with the need to do so. But instead he gave a curt nod and stepped out of her way. 'I will see you in about a week's time,' he said. 'I have to fly to Zurich in the morning.'

He watched as she ran the point of her tongue out over her lips, a gesture of uncertainty or relief, he couldn't quite make up his mind which.

'I see,' she said. After a little pause she added, 'I take it you don't want me to come with you?'

He gave her an ironic look. 'Would you say yes if I asked you?'

The defiant glitter was back in her eyes like the flash of a silver sword. 'No, I would not.'

Marc smiled at her feistiness. He had plenty of time to tame her and tame her he would. 'Believe me, *cara*, if I wanted you with me you would not dare to say no,' he said, and before she could respond he strode out of the room, snipping the door shut behind him.

# CHAPTER SIX

AVA was intensely annoyed that during the week while Marc was in Switzerland he did not once call her. But then, he didn't need to speak to her to know what she was up to, she realised after the very day he left, for as soon as she prepared to leave the villa a man dressed in a chauffer's uniform, standing beside a luxury car, greeted her on the gravel driveway, informing her he was at her service during Signor Castellano's absence.

'But I have no need of a driver,' Ava insisted. 'I always walk whenever I can and I'm only going to the gym at the health club.'

The man, who had introduced himself as Carlos, was equally insistent, holding the door open for her with an intransigent set to his features. 'It is not worth losing my job, Miss McGuire,' he said. 'I have a wife and a young family to support.'

Ava frowned in irritation. 'I am sure Signor Castellano would not be so heartless as to fire you just because I chose to use my legs instead of your services.'

'I have been given strict instructions to escort you wherever you need to go,' Carlos said. 'I am to keep you protected from the Press. Signor Castellano does not want you to be annoyed by the intrusion of anyone without him being there to protect you.'

She rolled her eyes as she got in the car. 'This is utterly ridiculous. I do not need a babysitter.'

'Think of me as a bodyguard, then,' Carlos said.

Ava scowled as she was driven to the health club, knowing full well Marc had only engaged the driver to tail her in case she took it upon herself to give an exclusive interview to the Press of what it was like being Marc Castellano's mistress. If she was indeed the type of woman like Chantelle Watterson, that was quite possibly what would occur. Ava, on the other hand, had no intention of speaking to anyone about her relationship to Marc.

She took a covert glance at the driver who seemed vaguely familiar. No doubt Carlos had been the spy Marc had had following her during his last absence. He didn't trust her. That was the problem that just wouldn't go away. Marc believed her to have betrayed him and no matter what she did or said to the contrary he was never going to believe or trust her word ever again.

But then, did *she* trust him? He had said—or at least intimated—he would abide by her rule of exclusivity while they were together, but how could she be sure he would hold true to it? He had a reputation as an international playboy, women chased him daily—she had seen enough pictures in the Press over the years to realise he was in no shortage of female company. He could just be paying lip service to her demands and she would have no way of knowing for sure if he was being unfaithful.

Jealousy ate at her with primitive teeth, the sharp incisors savage as they gnawed at her relentlessly when she thought of Marc flying from one country to another, enjoying his glamorous bits on the side while she waited here, trapped by his demands.

There were compensations, however; she had only that morning checked the balance in her bank account via the Internet and her eyes had rounded to the size of saucers at the amount Marc had deposited there. It gave her at least the comfort of knowing she could continue to support Serena in her quest to have a baby.

Almost unconsciously Ava laid one of her hands across the taut plane of her belly. A child with her was the very last thing Marc wanted and yet she felt a yearning so great to have a baby of her own it was almost painful to harbour the thought of never being able to create that incredible bond with him. She could imagine a little boy just like Marc with coal-black eyes and springy black hair with tiny dimples either side of his mouth when he smiled, which Marc so rarely did these days, or at least not without a hint of mockery to it, she thought with another painful pang. But there was no possibility of her becoming pregnant even though he had not used a condom when he had made love to her in the pool; she had been taking a low-dose Pill for years to control a tendency for painful periods.

After she had finished her routine at the health club Ava returned to the villa, not sure what else she could do. There were numerous books she wanted to read and myriad tasks she could help Celeste with, as had become her habit, but she felt restless and bored. She wanted a real job, not modelling, as she had done before, but one where she could use her brain instead of her body.

It was a long-held dream of hers to go back to the university degree she had deferred the year she had come to London to model for the UK branch of the agency she had modelled part-time for, and in order to accompany Serena on her gap year. Ava had been studying history and languages and had looked forward to one day being able to teach. Living in a place like Monte Carlo was a history-lover's dream. The principality had a long and colourful past, the royal dynasty that had held state for so long all part of the glamour and intrigue.

In the last year of their marriage Douglas had encouraged her to pursue her studies online, but just as she was about to enrol his condition had deteriorated. After his slow and agonising death, with all the things she'd had to see to since in packing up his things and sending them on to his family, she had not had the time to think too far into the future. And then, of course, there was the cost to consider. Studying didn't come for free, or at least not these days. She could end up like so many others with huge debts and no guarantee of a permanent job at the end of it.

And then there was Marc. Marc Castellano—the man she had once loved with all her being now hated her with a passion that was almost as great as his continued desire for her. He had a ruthless agenda to have her as his plaything, no strings, no love, just plain and simple sex at his command. Reducing their relationship to one of physical convenience for him was a form of emotional torment for her. She had no idea how long he would want her in his life; he had given her no clue, other than to state quite clearly it was not going to be for the long term.

The evening before Ava expected Marc to return to the villa she was sitting in her bedroom, reading a book on the Second World War, when there was a tap at the door. Assuming it was Celeste to come to say *bonsoir* before leaving for the day, she gave permission for entry.

The book almost fell to the floor when Marc stepped into the room. Her heart gave a galloping lurch as she gaze took in his tall, commanding presence. He was dressed in dark casual trousers and an open-necked white shirt which emphasised his olive skin and ink-black hair.

'You look surprised to see me, *cara*,' he said, closing the door with a tiny but, all the same, heart-stopping click.

Suddenly her room, which had always seemed so commodious in the past, shrank to the size of a doll's house. Ava felt as if the walls were pressing in on her, the air sucked right out of the space, making it almost impossible to pull in a much needed breath.

'I—I was not expecting you until tomorrow,' she stammered, putting the book to one side and standing up on legs that were not quite steady. She ran her damp palms down the front of her thin and years-old-cotton-pyjama-clad thighs, wondering if he noticed she had no make-up on, not even a smear of lip gloss. Her hair was tied back in a high pony-tail, still partially damp from her recent shower. She wasn't even wearing a bra beneath her faded pink tank top and her feet had ballet-flat-like slippers on instead of heels. It made her feel at a huge disadvantage without a veneer of sophistication to hide behind. Without her usual armour she felt like a schoolgirl of thirteen instead of a mature woman three years off turning thirty.

'I cancelled the last meeting,' he said. 'In any case, I had achieved what I had set out to achieve, so I caught the next available flight.'

Ava tucked a strand of hair that had escaped from her pony-tail behind one ear. 'I am sure you always achieve what you set out to achieve,' she said archly, trying to regain the ground she felt she had lost in being caught off guard by his unexpected arrival.

He came up close, so close she could smell the hint of citrus in his aftershave, the combination of lime and lemongrass and something else she couldn't quite identify, but it was no less captivating. She breathed it in, unconsciously holding her breath, physically and mentally preparing herself for his touch.

His dark eyes meshed with hers, studying her with an intensity that was both unnerving and exciting. She felt each of her heartbeats pounding in her chest, wondering if he knew how deeply unsettled she was by his proximity.

When his warm, dry palm cupped her left cheek, she felt her heart give another crazy lurch, her breath coming out on a jagged sigh.

'Did you miss me, *ma petite*?' he asked in a low, sexy tone.

Ava fought to control her response to his caressing, lover-like touch. 'Not at all,' she said crisply.

He smiled a knowing smile, his palm still cradling her face, his thumb now stroking against the curve of her cheek in a back and forth motion that was totally mesmerising. 'Celeste told me just before she left for the evening that you have been moping about with a downcast set to your features all week.'

Ava gave him a petulant look. 'If I gave her that impression it is only because you have me practically imprisoned here with your bodyguard on permanent watch. I can't take a step outside the villa without him insisting on driving me wherever I want to go, even if it is only within walking distance.'

He placed his hands on the tops of her shoulders. 'Why haven't you moved your things into my room?' he asked.

Ava was momentarily thrown off course by his rapid change of subject, a tactic she was starting to see he used to his advantage time and time again. 'I…I didn't realise you wanted me on call twenty-four hours a day,' she said, hoping he couldn't hear the betraying wobble in her voice.

His eyes were like a force field as they held hers and his hands tightened on her shoulders. 'I want you in my bed,' he said. 'I want to know that when I come home you will be waiting for me.'

'You are living in the wrong century, Marc,' she said with a flash of defiance. 'Slavery was abolished long ago.'

His mouth curled up at the corners, not quite a smile, but close enough to make Ava's heart skip a beat. 'Are you annoyed with me for not taking you with me to Zurich?' he asked.

She rolled her eyes in a scathing manner. 'Why should I be annoyed? I would be bored to tears sitting around in hotel rooms waiting for you to return.'

'Like you were here, *si*?'

Ava marvelled at his perspicacity, but her expression—she hoped—gave nothing away. 'I am not used to being idle,' she said. 'I want to use my brain instead of filling in the day having my hair or nails done.' She took a little breath and announced, 'I want to go back to university and finish my degree. I've already made some enquiries about doing a course online.'

The silence was so long she wondered if Marc could hear the sound of her heart beating. She could feel it inside her chest, hammering away like a jackhammer on performance-enhancing supplements.

'Are you informing me of your intentions or asking for my permission?' he finally asked.

She moistened her dry lips with a dart of her tongue. 'Do I need to ask your permission?' she asked, keeping her eyes locked on his.

His hands dropped from her shoulders. 'No,' he said, his expression like a mask. 'Of course not. I have no problem with you wanting to finish your degree. I think it's a great idea. It is impossible to overeducate yourself, *si*?'

Ava looked up at him in astonishment. She had been so sure he would not agree to her plans she had been silently preparing herself for a showdown. Instead she felt strangely at sea, the wind suddenly too far away to inflate her self-righteous sails. 'Er—yes,' she said, running her tongue over her bare lips again. 'That's great, then. I can start straight away. I've already been reading some of the recommended texts. I will get some credit for the subjects I've already completed, not much, but enough to…' She stopped rambling when she saw the bottomless wells of his eyes studying her silently.

Her shoulders suddenly felt cold without the warm cup of his palms, her cheek still tingling from his earlier caress. Her heart was beating too hard and too fast, her stomach doing complicated little gymnastic routines that made her feel disoriented.

The silence stretched and stretched and stretched, like a rubber band being pulled by an invisible hand. Ava felt as if at any moment the air was going to snap with the incremental build-up of tension she could feel vibrating in the space between them.

'You look like a schoolgirl with your hair tied up like that,' Marc said in a gruffly masculine tone.

Ava felt a blush steal into her cheeks, which she knew was only adding credence to his words. 'I was getting ready for bed…' She blushed even further and stumbled on gauchely, 'Um…I mean, I'd just had a shower and was about to turn in when you…you…took me by surprise…'

One of his hands reached behind her head and began toying with her pony-tail, the sensation of him coiling it around his fingers making her scalp quiver in delight. His hold was loose, playful almost, but she felt the underlying tension, the daunting but delicious possibility of him tugging her towards his mouth and hard, powerful body making her heart beat all the faster. Her gaze wandered over his face, finally coming to rest on his mouth. He was in need of a shave, his jaw was peppered all over with dark shadow that she knew from experience would rasp sexily against her softer skin.

'You know, Ava, lovers usually kiss when they greet each other after an absence,' Marc said, glancing at her soft mouth before returning to her grey-blue gaze.

'Are you informing me of your intentions or asking for my permission?' she asked, throwing his words back at him in a pert tone.

His fingers coiled her hair like a rope, bringing her inexorably closer. He felt her breath on his face, the fresh mint and womanly essence of her making his groin instantly swell with blood. He rubbed up against her, letting her know how she was affecting him, gauging her reaction.

She looked up at him with widening pupils, her soft lips slightly apart, and her breathing rate gradually increasing. Her breasts were jammed against his chest, the tight buds of her nipples detectable through the fabric of his shirt. The feel of her feminine mound so close to his erection was mind-blowing. He ached to feel her slick, tight body enclose him, to take all of him inside her, each and every one of her inner muscles rippling and clenching as he thrust into her.

He slowly released the tie that bound her hair, letting it fall in a fragrant cloud around her shoulders. Without saying a word he lifted the bottom of her tank top. She put her arms up, her breasts full and rosy-peaked as he lifted the top over her head and tossed it to one side.

Her eyes meshed with his, the want, the need, the expectation he could see reflected there so like what he was feeling it momentarily stopped him in his tracks. It had always been like this from the first time they had met. Her eyes had fascinated him, their smoky-grey and blue-flame depths had captivated him, luring him into a sensual orbit he had never been able to escape. He wore the memory of her body on his skin. It was like a perfume he couldn't wash away. No one else before or since had affected him as she did. Her femininity, the dainty softness and yet athletic strength of her excited him.

The air of mystery about her now made her all the more irresistible. There were secrets in the moving shadows of her eyes, things he had not seen before but was now determined to uncover.

Marc ran his hands down Ava's slim waist to settle on her hips, holding her against his pulsing heat. He realised with a twinge of regret this was not the time for an inquisition. He knew enough about her to know if he pushed too hard she would clam up; her defiant streak would come to the fore, leaving him with a host of doubts to torture him into the long hours of the night.

Ava felt a sudden shift in mood and looked up at Marc with a mixture of wariness and uncertainty. She self-consciously crossed her arms over her breasts. 'Is something…wrong?'

The faraway look fell away from his gaze like heavy velvet curtains dropping in one quick movement over a stage. 'Nothing is wrong, *ma petite*,' he said and released his hold. He reached into his trouser pocket and handed her a long, thin jeweller's box. 'I bought something for you while I was away.'

Ava looked at the designer's name inscribed on the box and felt her heart give a little flutter. She had looked in that particular jeweller's many times, but it was the sort of place where price stickers were never placed in the shop front windows. She had no idea how much Marc had spent, but, putting her modesty aside for a moment, she opened the box to find an exquisitely beautiful diamond pendant, so fine and so delicate she knew the price would have been in at least six figures.

'I…I don't know what to say…' she faltered. 'It's beautiful…'

'Here,' he said, taking the box from her. 'Let me put it on you.'

She turned around, her skin shivering in reaction as his fingers brushed against her neck to fasten the pendant's clasp. He placed his hands on her shoulders again and turned her back to face him. The diamond rested just above her naked breasts, making her ache to feel his touch.

'Perfect,' he said, his eyes dark and intense as they held hers. 'The glitter of the diamond reminds me of your eyes when you are angry.'

Ava bit down on her bottom lip as she covered her breasts with her folded arms again. 'I guess it would look better if I was wearing something more glamorous than my oldest pyjamas.'

'I think it would look better if you were wearing nothing at all,' he said and untying her arms from across her body, scooped her into his arms as if she were a quarter of her weight.

'Marc, put me down. I'm—'

'At least five kilograms lighter than you were when we were together in the past,' he said, cutting her off mid-sentence. 'You are obviously not eating enough for all the activity you do.'

'You don't know anything about the activity I do,' Ava said, scowling, as he carried her through to the master suite.

His dark eyes lasered hers as he set her down in front of him, her body still pressed up against the warm sexiness of his. 'No, you are right, *tesora mia*,' he said with an inscrutable look. 'I know very little about your activities. Perhaps when there is an appropriate time you can tell me all about them, *sì*?'

Ava shifted her gaze from the laser beam of his to her hands, lying flat against his broad chest. She could feel the beating of his heart under her right palm, the *thump thump thump* so steady compared to her erratically skipping one.

Marc tipped up her face, making her look at him. 'I've missed you, *ma belle*. I have got used to you snapping at me. Tragic, isn't it?'

'Then why didn't you call me so I could snap at you on the phone?' Ava asked, looking into the black depths of his eyes, feeling herself melting as his lips curved upwards in a half-smile.

'I like to see you when I speak to you,' he said, bending down to press a light, brief kiss to her lips. 'I also like to feel you tremble beneath my touch.'

She pressed her lips together, tasting him, tasting the promise of passion that was brewing like a storm approaching. She felt it in his body, the surge of his flesh against her reminding her of how suddenly things could get out of hand. A kiss was never just a kiss with Marc; it was a prelude to a sensual onslaught that would leave her tingling for hours later. Her body was already preparing itself, the moisture of arousal hot and wet between her thighs, the persistent ache of her breasts for his touch and the heavy pulse of longing that made her feel hollow and empty inside.

He took her hands from his chest and, turning them over, kissed each open palm in turn, his eyes still holding hers. She shivered each time his tongue dabbed at the very centre of her palm, an erotic mimic of what was to come.

His hands released hers to undo the buttons of his shirt. Ava lifted her hands to explore his tanned chest as each part of it was revealed: the sculptured pectoral muscles, the tightly coiled ridges of his erectus abdominus, trailing her fingertips through the sprinkling of masculine hair that arrowed down to disappear beneath the waistband of his trousers.

'Touch me,' he commanded softly, urgently.

Ava's heart gave a sideways movement as she saw the naked need in his glinting eyes. She undid his waistband, rolling down his zip over the proud bulge of his manhood, her fingers impatient to feel him skin on skin.

He shrugged himself out of his shirt and, heeling off his shoes, stepped out of his trousers as they slid to the floor, leaving only his black underwear. Ava traced him through the tented fabric, teasing him, watching as he sucked in a breath to keep control. She became more daring, slowly peeling back the fabric, allowing him the freedom he craved, cupping him and then making a circle with her fingers, moving up and down his shaft in a rhythmic motion that she knew he would not be able to tolerate for long.

'*Mon Dio*, no more,' he groaned, dragging her hand away.

She lifted one of her fingers to her mouth, her eyes holding his, tasting him, watching as his throat moved up and down as he fought to contain himself. She loved seeing him like this, fighting the rampant flames of his desire for her while she slowly but surely burned in anticipation.

He snatched in another breath and reached for her pyjama bottoms, almost wrenching them down her legs in his impatience. 'You are the only woman on this planet who can do this to me, do you know that, *ma belle*?' he asked, nuzzling at the side of her neck where every nerve seemed to be calling out for his attention.

'How do you know that if you haven't been with every woman on the planet?' she asked, shivering as his tongue found the shell of her ear.

'Don't talk,' he said, sucking on her earlobe. 'I just want you to feel.'

Ava felt her spine slowly unhinge as he worked his way to her breasts, the moment when his mouth closed over her right nipple making her gasp out loud. He did the same to her other breast, sucking and circling her with his tongue until the flesh was achingly tight and pulsating with sensation.

He pushed her down on the bed, gently but in a primal alpha-male manner that made her skin tingle in delight. He opened the bedside drawer and took out a condom, ripping open the packet and applying it with a deftness she could only assume came from extensive practice, a thought that was as painful as it was unwelcome.

Marc looked at her questioningly, obviously picking up some nuance on her face she hadn't been able to disguise in time. 'As much as I would like to do this bareback, Ava, I don't want to have to deal with the consequences if an accident should occur.'

Ava felt her heart contract, as if it were suddenly jammed between two house bricks. 'It's quite all right,' she said, injecting her voice with just the right amount of nonchalance. 'I don't want any accidents either.'

His eyes stayed on hers a fraction longer than she was comfortable with. It felt as if he was peeling back her skin, looking at her innermost desires, one by one.

'Things are different now,' he said. 'You understand that, *si*?'

She nodded and reached for him again, stroking the sheathed length of him, watching as his face contorted with the effort of holding back his response.

He nudged her thighs apart, one of his legs going over one of hers in an erotic tangle of limbs that awakened every nerve in her body in feverish excitement. He plunged into her, so deeply she winced, her fingers digging into his flanks to anchor herself as the unexpected pain gradually subsided.

She felt him check himself, coming up on his elbows to look down at her, a frown narrowing the distance between his impossibly dark eyes. 'I should have used some lubricant,' he said. 'Did I hurt you?'

Ava felt it then, it took her completely by surprise, but then just about everything about Marc these days took her by surprise. She hadn't expected her love for him to survive how he had handled their break-up; she hadn't expected her love for him to survive his ruthless demands and conditions...she hadn't expected her love for him to come back with such intensity she could feel it fill the aching emptiness of her soul like water filling a dam after a flash flood.

'Ava?'

She gave herself a mental shake and gazed into his eyes. 'Make love to me, Marc,' she said, her voice barely above a whisper.

He hesitated, as if he was waiting for something.

She placed her hands around his neck and pulled his mouth down to just above hers. 'Please?' she said.

'It will be my pleasure,' he said huskily and covered her mouth with his.

# CHAPTER SEVEN

His kiss was like fire against Ava's lips, his tongue a sword of flame that burned her with each stab and thrust. She met his demands with feverish ones of her own, nipping at him with her teeth, sucking on his lower lip, pulling and releasing, teasing him, daring him to let his passion off the leash. She felt him straining to keep control, the tension building in his body as he re-entered her, slowly this time, waiting for her to stretch to accommodate him, her own silky moisture easing each of his movements within her.

His rhythm gradually picked up its pace, gently at first, but as she kept pace he moved on with increasing intensity, the friction against her sensitive nerves making her quiver in response. She could feel the way her body assembled all its feeling into one tightly budded point, the release she so desperately craved just out of her reach. She whimpered against his mouth as it kissed hers with tantalising thoroughness. She arched her spine, pushing her hips up to meet the downward thrust of his, but it seemed he was going to make her wait a little longer.

'Marc…' Her voice was a breathless whisper of sound. 'Please…oh, please…don't make me wait any longer…'

He increased his pace, his breathing hard as she urged him on with her hands and fingers pressed into his buttocks. The rocking of their bodies thrilled her, the way they fitted together so neatly. His hair-roughened limbs were such an erotic contrast to the creamy smoothness of hers, the strength of his taut muscles as they bunched beneath her touch making her breath catch in her throat. The pressure inside her was building up to a crescendo. She could feel every deep thrust of his send ripples of delight throughout her body. Her breasts were almost flattened beneath the pressure of his chest but she loved the scratchy feel of his masculine hair against her softness. It reminded her of how she used to trail her fingertips through it in the past, circling each of his hard flat nipples, kissing her way down to the throbbing heat of him until he exploded with passion.

Ava shifted restively beneath him, needing him to bring her to the ultimate moment, but too shy to ask. She felt him smile against her mouth as he reached down between their bodies, finding the core of her with heart-stopping accuracy, his fingers working at her, stroking slowly, gradually building his pace and pressure until she was gasping out loud. She was so close, agonisingly so, but suspended, hanging, dangling over a precipice so high it was terrifying.

'Let go, *cara*,' Marc coaxed gently. 'Come for me.'

'I can't,' she cried, writhing beneath him, her head thrashing about in frustration.

He stilled her with the cup of his palm against her cheek. 'Hey, look at me,' he commanded softly. 'It's me, Marc. You know how to do this—we've done this many, many times before, *sì*? Why should this time be any different?'

She opened her eyes and looked at him, her teeth biting into her lower lip, before she mumbled as her gaze fell away, 'I know…but it's…it's different now…'

'How is it different?' he said, slowly stroking her again. 'I have not forgotten a thing about your body. I don't think I ever will forget how you respond to me.'

She choked back a little gasp and he increased the pressure ever so slightly, watching as she rode the wave right to the top before finally free-falling. She cried out, a high, keening cry that sent shivers cascading down his spine. He felt her body spasm and convulse around him, sending him mad with the desire to let go, but he waited until her release had faded.

'There,' he said, smiling. 'I knew you could do it. You just needed to relax and to trust me.'

She looked at him in wonderment, her eyes still glazed with passion, her creamy chest a rosy hue, signalling how intense her release had been. She reached up and touched him on the face, her fingers a light caress that made Marc wonder if she had not experienced pleasure with anyone since him. Had she been celibate for five long years? Had no other lover touched her? It was a surreal feeling to think he had been the last person to bring her pleasure. That she had not sought it elsewhere, even whilst married to Cole, as so many women in her place would have done. It made him wonder all over again why she had agreed to such a marriage. If she was of such integrity why then had she been bought for a price like the gold-digging opportunist the Press had made her out to be? Was there something he *still* didn't know about her reasons for marrying Cole? He had searched and searched and yet he still felt as if a part of the puzzle was missing. It annoyed him, like a grass seed in his sock. He kept looking for it but no matter how much it pricked him he couldn't locate it.

'Marc?' Ava traced her fingers over the flattened line of his mouth. 'Is something wrong?'

He rolled away from her, lying on his back to stare blankly at the ceiling.

Ava felt her stomach cave in, wondering if she had disappointed him in some way. His erection had subsided and she knew it wasn't because he had come. She knew him well enough to know the signs and she had been waiting for them, waiting for that pressure-cooker-like tension, the way his body would go rigid before pumping his way through his release. She felt cheated, even though she'd had the best, most intense orgasm of her life. She reached out and touched his chest, her palm flat against his sternum. 'Did I do something wrong?' she asked.

He turned his head sideways to look at her, his dark eyes fathomless. 'No,' he said after what seemed a lifetime. He turned his head back and stared at the ceiling again, releasing a long and raspy-sounding sigh. 'It's not you, it's me.'

Ava pulled in a breath that felt as if it had barbs attached. She felt so unsure of herself. In the past if something like this had happened she would have seen to matters with her lips and tongue or even her hand and he would have been back in business within seconds.

She moved her hand experimentally, but as if he sensed her intentions, one of his came over it and stilled it.

'No,' he said, releasing her hand as he got off the bed. 'I'm not in the mood right now. Sorry.'

Ava felt assailed by doubts and insecurities. He had never spurned any of her advances in the past. Was he already tiring of her? She shrank back on the bed, pulling at the sheet to cover her nakedness. She watched as he silently dressed, each of his movements mechanical, as if his mind was elsewhere.

After he had disposed of the condom he turned and looked at her, his expression as unreadable as a blank sheet of paper. 'Maybe it is best if we keep to separate bedrooms,' he said, 'for the time being at least.'

Ava swallowed thickly, her heart feeling as if he had kicked it aside with one of his strongly boned feet. She moistened her lips, feeling vulnerable and perilously close to tears. 'If that's what you want,' she managed to say without a tremor in her voice.

He ran his hands through the thick pelt of his hair, leaving deep, finger-size trails. His jaw was moving beneath his skin, as if he was silently rehearsing the words before he got them out.

Ava held her breath, waiting for the words she dreaded. He was finished with her. He had set out what he hoped to achieve. He had extracted his revenge, he had made her beg. Well, she had well and truly done that, she thought with a scalding wave of shame. He couldn't have timed it better. Just when she realised she still loved him and would stay with him on any terms he was going to end it.

It was finished.

Over.

*Finito.*

The end.

'At the time of your marriage, or at any time leading up to it, did you know Cole was bidding for the same contract as me?' he asked, pinning her with his hawk-like gaze.

Ava moistened her lips, her mouth so dry she had to do it twice before she could speak. 'I know you will find this hard to believe, but I didn't know he was making a bid on the Dubai thing. I knew very little about that arm of his business at that point. I don't think he wanted me to know. I know that sounds terribly naïve of me, but it's the truth. By the time I found out about it I had already accepted his offer and signed a contract. I had no choice but to stick with it. I had already used some of the money.'

His expression revealed nothing to show he either believed or disbelieved her. 'So you married him and moved to Monte Carlo and lived as his wife, allowing everyone to think—including your sister—you were his wife in every sense of the word.'

Ava lowered her gaze. 'Serena knew the truth… about why I married Douglas…'

The room seemed to take a breath and hold it in the silence.

'And what was the reason, or am I to play twenty questions for the next hour or two?' Marc asked.

She pulled the sheet a little tighter around her body

as she got off the bed and slowly raised her eyes to his. 'Because…' Her tongue darted out to sweep over her lips. 'Because I did it for her.'

Marc felt as it something had just slipped into place, making him feel a heavy, clunking sensation somewhere in the middle of his chest. He stared at her for another stretching silence, mentally shuffling through possible scenarios, none of them making him feel particularly comfortable. 'Why?' he asked, surprised at how hoarse he sounded.

Ava felt under siege. His questioning technique would have put a professional interrogator to shame. She felt a river of perspiration roll drop by drop between her shoulder blades to pool at the base of her spine, which was currently doing a very poor job of keeping her legs upright and steady. *Forgive me, Serena*, she silently pleaded. *I had to tell him some time. How could I let this continue indefinitely, especially when I love him so?* The words were spinning around her head, making her feel dazed. She hoped he would keep it to himself. She had put her trust in him; maybe it was foolish to do so, but after making love with him she had felt so vulnerable, so desperate for him to understand and find it in himself to forgive her for the past.

'Answer the question, Ava,' he said.

Ava slowly raised her chin, even though her insides were quaking. 'She'd made a mistake in the books. It was because of her inexperience. It was her first real job. She was only eighteen and had never done any bookkeeping before. Douglas accused her of stealing. She panicked. I panicked. I went to see him on her behalf…' She bit her lip as if the memory upset her. 'I begged him not to press charges…'

Marc felt as if a giant hand had gripped his intestines. 'So he offered you a way to get your sister off the hook.'

She nodded, her features contorted in a grimace. 'It was the only way to pay back the money that had gone missing. I had no one else to turn to. Our father and stepmother wouldn't have helped either of us. I was so worried about Serena. She's not like me. She's fragile. I felt I had to protect her. I still feel I have to protect her.' She gave him a pleading look. 'Please, you mustn't tell anyone about this. Not even Richard knows.'

'Did you ever think to approach me for help?' Marc asked, not quite able to take the edge of bitterness out of his tone.

She gave a sigh that involved her whole body. 'I thought of it, but you hadn't contacted me since I had left the apartment. Then just as I was about to call you I read about you in one of the papers. You were dating again. I saw the photo of you with her. She was very beautiful.' She gave him a look that made his insides clench even more. 'Dark and exotic…nothing at all like me.'

Marc swore viciously in both Italian and French. 'You little fool,' he said roughly. 'I was only using her to make you jealous. Little did I know that less than a week or two later you would be married to someone else.'

She looked away, but he was almost certain he had seen the sheen of tears in her eyes. He took a steadying breath, trying to think, trying to clear the cloud of confusion and regret and recrimination inside his head.

'Our relationship,' he said after a moment. 'This thing we have going on between us…'

'What exactly is going on between us, Marc?' she asked. 'Blackmail, that's what. This is all wrong and you know it. It's been wrong from the start.'

'I can make it right,' he said, seriously wondering if he could. 'We could start afresh. We can forget about the past. We can pretend we've just met for the first time.'

She shook her head at him. 'Another game, Marc?' she said. 'Well, let me tell you something. I am tired of rich men's games.'

He frowned at her. 'This is not a game to me, Ava. I want you in my life. I thought I had made that clear.'

'Yes, you've made it very clear. The trouble is, I don't like the terms,' she said, and giving him an embittered look, marched past him to leave, her slim body encased like a small Egyptian mummy in the bed sheet. It heeded her progress, which was just as well, as his mind was working so slowly she might have got away before he could put his hand out to block her.

'Ava, wait,' he said, taking her hands in his. She had such tiny hands, he felt them fluttering inside the cage of his, like small, frightened sparrows.

He cleared his throat, trying to find the words to say what needed to be said. 'I didn't know all the facts before. What you've told me…well, it makes a world of difference. We can work it out, *cara*. Somehow we'll work it out.'

Her slim brows rose. 'Isn't it a bit late to right the wrongs of the past?' She clenched her teeth and added, 'One phone call from you and none of this would have happened. Do you realise that? One phone call. It's been *five* years, Marc. Five years of my life have gone and I can't have them back.'

'I know how long it has been,' he said heavily. God, he had felt every bitter second of them eating away at him. Why had he allowed his pride to do such damage? Why hadn't he gone to her? To think he might have prevented the last five years of hell, not just his, but hers, with just one phone call or a text or a simple e-mail was like mental torture. Why had he let his father's experience dominate his life to such a degree? And how could he ever turn things around? She hated him and had every right to for that and that alone. How could he expect her to ignore the past and move on? She had told him she had been friends with Cole, but what if that hadn't always been the case? What if she had suffered at his hands—maybe not physically, but what about emotionally? Marc knew all about the way people could destroy each other with emotional abuse. He had seen it happen before his very eyes; the stripping away of self-esteem and loss of power had devastated his father and flowed on to him, leaving him with wounds that still tugged at him deep inside like scar tissue.

'You've always been so vocal about your hatred of Douglas, but you exploited me just as he did,' she said. 'He used me to get what he wanted and you could have stopped it, but you didn't.'

Marc looked at her, for the first time in his life no words came to him. She was absolutely right: he was exactly like Cole. He had exploited her and ruined both of their lives in the process. The knowledge of it was like poison in his gut. He felt his insides churning with it. It was like spilt acid, eating its way through him, burning him with a pain like no other.

She pulled out of his hold with a strength he had no idea she possessed. 'I am going to have a shower,' she said, her eyes still flashing their daggers at him. 'I feel dirty all of a sudden.'

Marc let her go. Her words were like a slap—they stung long after she had left the room, echoing in the silence, like ghosts from the past coming back to haunt him....

It had taken hours for Ava to get to sleep that night. Once she had cooled down after her heated conversation with Marc, she had lain awake, vainly dreaming of him coming to her room and gathering her in his arms and pleading for her forgiveness for not begging her to come back to him after she had left that first time. If he had cared anything for her, wouldn't he have fought just a little bit for her? But then, she had always known Marc was a proud man. He wasn't the type to beg or plead. He hated being vulnerable and he hated being wrong. How he would deal with what she had told him was yet to be seen. But she had a feeling he would not be offering her anything permanent in the way of the future. He said he wanted her in his life, but those were the exact words he had used five years ago. They were temporary words, not forever words.

Marc was nowhere in sight during the following day and Celeste just shrugged distractedly when Ava asked if she knew where he was. 'I am not feeling well, *madame,*' Celeste said, putting a hand to her forehead. 'I think I am coming down with that virus you had.'

'Go home and rest,' Ava said. 'Take the rest of the week off. I am perfectly capable of cooking a meal or two.'

'Are you sure?' Celeste looked worried. 'Signor Castellano… Last time I saw him he seems…how you say…not quite himself?'

Ava forced a smile, but it felt more like a grimace. 'He'll get over it. You know what men are like—they like to brood over things for a bit.'

'He's a good man, *madame,*' Celeste said. 'You are much more suited to him than to Monsieur Cole. Signor Castellano will be a good husband and a wonderful father to your children, *oui*?'

Ava felt her heart tighten like a vice. 'Don't get your hopes up, Celeste,' she said. 'Marriage has always been a bit of a no-go subject with Marc.'

Celeste pursed her lips thoughtfully. 'Some men need more time to get there than others,' she said. 'Don't give up on him. He has come this far to have you back in his life.'

Ava sighed once the housekeeper had left. She resigned herself to another day of waiting and hoping for something to cling to, some sign that Marc was not going to end their relationship before it had even had a chance to start. It was the same as five years ago; the same anguished feelings of insecurity constantly plagued her. Would this be the day—or tomorrow, or the next day—she would see him for the last time? How could she live like that? She wanted so much more. She wanted forever.

When she came downstairs later that evening, Marc was standing near the drinks-preparation area, a drink of something amber-coloured in a tumbler. His expression was as difficult as ever to read, although Ava thought he looked tired about the eyes, as if he had not slept well the night before. There were lines of strain etched at the sides of his mouth as well, making her want to reach up and stroke them away with her fingers and to press her mouth to the flat line of his to ease away its tension.

'Can I get you a drink, Ava?' he asked. 'You look like you could do with one.'

She self-consciously tucked a wisp of hair back behind her ear. 'Do I?' she asked. 'Why do you say that?'

He lifted one shoulder. 'You look a little pale. Have you had anything to eat today? I'm not sure what arrangements have been made about dinner. I can't seem to find Celeste.'

'I gave her today and the next couple of days off,' Ava said. 'I hope you don't mind, but she wasn't feeling well. I think she's caught the same stomach virus I had before. It takes ages to shake off. I still don't feel one hundred per cent and it's been weeks.'

'How are you feeling now?' he asked, his eyes moving over her in concern.

She placed her hand over the queasy puddle of her stomach. 'I'm fine...I think...'

He set about pouring a drink for her, his movements measured and slow, as if he was rehearsing something in his head. 'I am sorry about last night,' he said as he finally faced her. 'I haven't handled this very well, have I?'

Ava was hard pressed to know if he was deliberately distancing himself preparatory to ending their short-lived affair. She took the glass he handed her, but she found her stomach turned at the taste of it as soon as she put it to her lips.

'What's wrong?' he asked. 'Would you like some water or some ice with it? From memory I thought you used to like it straight.'

She handed it back to him. 'Sorry, Marc, I'm not really in the mood for a drink.'

He put her glass to one side, meeting her gaze once more. 'I spent today working on some business,' he said. 'I thought you might be interested in hearing about some decisions I've made.'

Ava sat on the edge of the nearest sofa, even though with him still standing it made her feel at a disadvantage, but her legs felt unsteady and her stomach was still curdling. 'Oh? What sort of decisions?'

He looked down at the contents of his glass for a moment before returning his gaze to hers. 'I have set my legal team to work on drawing up a trust fund for Cole's children, Adam and Lucy. I have also organised some funds for his ex-wife. She won't have to work again unless she wants to.'

Ava stared at him, her heart beating so loudly she could hear a faint roaring like the ocean in her ears. 'That's…that's very generous of you, Marc,' she said. 'I am sure they will appreciate the gesture.'

He gave an indifferent lift of one shoulder as if he couldn't care either way what they thought. 'It seemed the right thing to do, and God knows I have not always done the right thing in the past.'

Ava pressed her hands between her knees, wondering if he was leading up to something.

There was a beat or two of silence before he asked, 'What does your sister know about us?'

She met his penetrating gaze even though it made her cheeks grow warm. 'I told her we were back together. I didn't want her to feel guilty about what had happened. She has enough on her plate to deal with.'

He studied her features for a moment. 'So you didn't tell her about our deal?'

Ava gave him an ironic look. '*Our* deal? Your deal, Marc, not mine. You know very well if it wasn't for the money I wouldn't be here for a moment longer than necessary.'

He twirled the last of his drink, his expression wry. 'Ah, yes,' he drawled. 'The money. It always comes back to the money.'

'What are you getting at?' she asked, feeling her hackles start to rise at his tone.

'It's pretty simple, isn't it?' he said. 'You needed money, I wanted a mistress. A fairly straightforward transaction, or so one would have thought.'

Ava decided to be straight down the line with him. 'If you are unhappy with the services so far then please say so. I would hate to be causing you any dissatisfaction. After all,' she injected her tone with reproach, 'you paid a fortune for me.'

He put his glass to one side and came up to her, lifting her face with one fingertip beneath her chin. 'I am very happy with the services, as you call them,' he said, looking deeply into her eyes. 'Very happy indeed.'

Ava wished she had the strength or wherewithal to

pull away, but with his light touch on her face, and his dark-as-night eyes locked on hers she felt ambushed by her feelings for him. This was the time to be putting some distance between them. She knew she should put her hands against his chest and push him away, but somehow she couldn't do it. She rehearsed each of the steps in her head, she even got as far as raising her hands, but instead of pushing him away, as soon as her hands felt the hard contours of his chest, she felt as if she had come home. She felt the strong, steady beat of his heart against her palm, and the blood in her own veins began to race. Her tongue flicked out over her lips in nervous anticipation, her heart hammering inside her chest, her legs feeling as if they were not bones and ligaments and muscles and tendons, but two pipe-cleaners without their wires. She felt the rest of her body sway towards his, her mouth opening on a breathless little sigh as his warm breath caressed the surface of her lips, her heart coming to a screeching standstill when his mouth came inexorably closer, closer and closer until finally sealing hers.

# CHAPTER EIGHT

AVA wound her arms around Marc's neck, giving herself to his kiss with a sigh of deep, shuddering pleasure. His tongue stroked for entry and then roved the moist cave of her mouth, finding all the sensitive nerve-endings that made her cling to him all the more.

His hands skimmed her breasts, his light touch sending off shooting sparks of awareness as her nipples sprang to attention. His kiss deepened, one of his hands going to the back of her head, cupping the nape of her neck as his lips and tongue drove her crazy with longing.

His other hand worked on her clothes, lifting her top, unclasping her bra so he could cup her breast in the warmth of his hand. She pressed against him, her nipple rock-hard, the feel of him exploring her making her flesh pepper all over with goose pimples.

Ava stroked her hands down his back, pulling his shirt from his trousers so she could feel the warm silk of his skin beneath her fingers. He groaned into her mouth as she moved to his buttocks, her hands cupping him tightly, holding him against the heart of her need.

She felt the hard ridge of his erection, and quickly released the waistband of his trousers, desperate to hold him, to caress and stroke the satin and steely length of him.

He sucked in a sharp breath as she finally freed him. She ran her fingertip over him, teasing him with circular motions until he pulled her hand away with a growl that sounded primeval and intensely male.

He pressed her to the rug on the floor, dispensing with clothes and shoes with breathtaking haste, pausing only to retrieve a condom from his wallet in the back pocket of his discarded trousers.

Ava shivered as he came over her, his weight pinning her, his arousal probing for entry, but gently this time, holding back until he was sure she was ready to receive him. She relaxed her pelvis, opening to him, drawing him in with a hitching sigh as he filled her, his thickness smooth and sure as it finally and fully claimed her.

She felt every thrust against her sensitive inner muscles, each one rippling over him as he drove a little harder and faster. His mouth covered hers with a searing kiss, his tongue mimicking the thrusts of his lower body, sending her senses into a spinning vortex of feeling. She felt the tension build and build inside her, like climbing a high mountain in anticipation for the spectacular view at the top. Step by step she was getting there; each movement of his body in hers made the journey all the more exhilarating. She heard his deep groans, each one as it rumbled through his chest against hers making her pleasure all the more intense. She hovered at the pinnacle, her body desperately seeking that final plunge into paradise.

Marc sensed her need and used his fingers to coax her over the edge. He loved the feel of her in full arousal, the soft silk of her, the swollen heart of her pulsing against his fingertips as she finally let go. He felt each of her spasms, heard each of her startled gasping cries as her orgasm swept her away. She shuddered and shook and thrashed beneath him until he could hold on no longer. With a grunt he surged into her, losing all thought, all he could do was feel. The sensations flowed through him, the hot wave of release that left him lying in the blissful shallows of lassitude.

'Am I too heavy for you?' he asked into the silence of the aftermath.

'No,' she said softly, her fingertips tracing a feathery pathway up and down his spine that made every hair on his head stand on end in pleasure.

Ava sat up and hugged her knees to her chest, affording herself a small measure of dignity, considering she was in the middle of the sitting room with not a stitch on. 'You really are dead set against having a child, aren't you?' The words were out of her mouth almost before she had realised she had been thinking them, let alone about to say them. It was too late to take them back.

His eyes cut to hers, dark and inscrutable. 'I realise this must be a sensitive issue with you given what your sister is going through, but yes, I am not interested in having a child.'

Ava felt annoyed at his dismissal. It was so easy for men; they could put fatherhood on hold indefinitely. She on the other hand had felt her biological clock ticking like Big Ben ever since she had turned twenty-five. Nearly three years had passed since then and she was rapidly approaching thirty. She had read the statistics: female fertility dropped alarmingly after the age of thirty-five. The thought of ending up alone and childless was unbearable to her. For as long as she could remember Serena and she had shared a deep longing for true love and a little family to call their own.

Ava gathered her clothes and struggled back into them, suddenly desperate to get some time alone, to think about what she should do. She was back right where she had started with Marc. He was unwilling to compromise in any way. She would always be the one to make the sacrifices. She had made so many already, how could she continue to give up her hopes and dreams indefinitely?

'I would like us to dine together this evening,' Marc said. 'Take your time getting ready. The restaurant at the casino will not mind how late we are.'

'I'm not hungry.'

'Then you can watch me eat because I am.'

'There is plenty of food in the kitchen,' she said. 'Help yourself.'

'I want you to come with me, Ava. I've told you before, it is important that we are seen together.'

Her top lip curled at him in contempt. 'So dining out is nothing more than a publicity stunt?'

'If you want to see it that way, but I would much rather view it as a chance to relax and get to know one another again over good food and good wine.'

Her eyes fell away from his, her bottom lip subjected to a savaging by her teeth that he was certain would draw blood.

He stepped towards her and brushed his thumb over her mouth. 'You must be hungry after all,' he said with a wry smile.

She gave him a fierce little scowl as she moved out of his reach. 'I don't feel like going out. I want to go to bed.'

He gave her a glinting smile as he reached for her again. 'Then that is where I will take you.'

Ava quickly stepped backwards but the sudden movement made her head spin crazily. Her stomach roiled with nausea, her whole body feeling clammy. A swirl of ghastly coloured patterns formed in front of her and she felt as if she was going to drop in a faint. She fought to hold on to consciousness, but her legs started to wobble.

'Are you all right?' Marc asked, steadying her with a hand on each of her forearms.

Ava swallowed back a mouthful of sickness. 'I...I think I've had too much sun...or something...'

Marc swept her up in his arms and carried her towards the staircase, ignoring her paltry pleas to put her down. 'No, I will not put you down,' he said. 'You can barely stand up as it is. I am going to call a doctor. You have obviously had a relapse of that stomach virus. You must have caught another bout of it from Celeste.'

Ava was suddenly too weak to fight him. Besides, there was something rather comforting about him taking charge. She felt the protective strength of his arms around her and wished she could stay like that forever.

Once he got to the bedroom he laid her down on his bed, and with gentle fingers smoothed her sticky hair off her face. 'Who is your regular physician?' he asked.

'I'm sure I'll be fine in a minute,' Ava said weakly. 'I just need to rest.'

He gave her an intractable look and picked up the handset from the bedside table, and in rapid-fire French had a medical service agreeing to a house call within the half hour. 'Now,' he said, replacing the phone in its cradle, 'I am going to get you a drink of water and something to eat.'

Ava felt her stomach heave. 'No food…please…no food…'

He looked down at her with a heavy frown. 'If you were feeling so unwell, why didn't you say so when I first came home?' he asked.

Ava plucked at the hem of the sheet he had covered her with. 'I was feeling all right then…'

He let out a deep breath as he sat on the edge of the bed. He picked up her hand and brought it up to his mouth, holding it against his lips while his eyes held hers. Ava wondered what he was thinking. He was studying her so intently; it made her feel on edge, as if any moment he was going to drop a bombshell on her.

The doorbell sounded and Marc released her hand. 'Stay put,' he commanded. 'I will bring the doctor up.'

Ava lay back on the pillows with a sigh. Her hand felt cold without the warm cradle of his, her heart empty without the promise of his love. Tears smarted at the backs of her eyes, but she fought them back, angry at herself for being so needy. Why couldn't she just let things take their natural course? He would no doubt tire of her within a month or two. She could move on with her life, maybe one day meet someone else. She choked back a sob, suddenly overcome with emotion. She didn't want anyone else. She had only ever wanted Marc. She blew her nose hurriedly as she heard footsteps approaching, and stuffed the tissue under the pillow as the door opened.

The doctor was in his mid-fifties and, after brief introductions, quickly and efficiently took a history. Ava felt self-conscious with Marc standing there listening to every word, but she answered the doctor's questions as best she could.

'What about your periods?' the doctor asked. 'Have you missed any lately?'

'Um…I'm on the sort of Pill that stops menstruation altogether…'

The doctor looked at her over the rim of his glasses, which were perched on the middle of his nose. 'Have you been taking it regularly?'

'Y-yes.'

The doctor tapped his pen against his lips in a thoughtful muse. 'Have you been ill recently? A stomach upset, vomiting or the like?'

Ava swallowed tightly. 'Yes…'

'Have you had unprotected sex recently?'

She felt her face heating and lowered her gaze back to the hem of the sheet, but before she could answer Marc had answered for her. 'Yes,' he said, 'just the once, about two weeks ago.'

The doctor pulled out a tourniquet and blood sample kit. 'I'll do a blood test to make sure,' he said. 'The results will be back in a couple of days.'

Marc spoke again. 'I would like to know the results as soon as possible.'

The doctor gave him an as-you-wish movement of his lips. 'I will mark it as a priority,' he said.

Marc saw the doctor out and while he was out of the room Ava got off the bed and went to the bathroom. She washed her face, pausing for a moment to examine her reflection. She was hollow-eyed and pale, but surely it was just the result of long weeks of nursing a terminally ill patient on top of a persistent virus. She dared not think of an alternative explanation, but even so one of her hands crept down to the flat plane of her belly and lingered there...

'Ava?'

She turned as the door opened. 'Do you mind?' she asked. 'Am I not allowed any privacy?'

'We need to talk.'

She pushed past him irritably. 'Too bad. I don't feel like talking.'

Marc took her by the arm and turned her to face him. 'Ava, this is a situation we have to face like two adults.'

Ava tugged herself out of his light grasp, pointedly rubbing at her arm as if he had hurt her. 'This is your fault,' she said, struggling against tears.

'I know it is,' he said in a low deep, tone.

She looked up at him in surprise.

He sent one of his hands through his hair, the only hint he was feeling out of his depth. 'I want you to know that if you are pregnant I will support you. You don't need to worry about the baby's future. I will make sure you and he or she are always well provided for.'

Ava ran her tongue over her dry lips. 'It's probably a false alarm...'

His dark eyes locked on hers. 'But what if it's not?'

She snagged her bottom lip with her teeth, her forehead crinkling in a frown of worry. 'If it's not, I don't know how on earth I am going to tell Serena.'

Marc studied her expression for a moment. 'You don't think she would be happy for you?' he asked.

She looked at him with her misty grey-blue gaze. 'It's seems so unfair,' she said in a whisper-soft voice. 'She's been trying to get pregnant for four years. How can I tell her I got pregnant by accident?'

Marc came over and placed his hands on her shoulders. He hated it when she flinched at his touch, but he knew he had only himself to blame. He had held her to ransom from day one. If she hadn't hated him before she surely did now. For a fleeting moment he had wondered if she had engineered this situation to her advantage, but one look at her tortured features made him realise he had once again misjudged her. She didn't want a permanent tie to him. She had told him outright. She was happy to take his money, but that was all she wanted from him.

Marc forced his thoughts back to the problem at hand. 'We don't know for sure if you are pregnant,' he said. 'But I am sure your sister will be happy for you in spite of her problems.'

She slipped out of his hold and crossed her arms over her chest, making him feel as if she was shutting him out. 'I can't believe this has happened...' She started to pace the floor. 'It's like a nightmare. I keep thinking someone is going to tap me on the shoulder and wake me up.'

'Ava, please stop pacing for a moment,' Marc said. 'You should be resting.'

She looked at him with antagonism in her gaze. 'You sound like a concerned father-to-be, but we both know this is not what you want. You've never wanted it. The last thing you want is a permanent tie to me, and you can't get much more permanent than a living, breathing child.'

He came over to her and, although she tried to resist, he soon had her hands in his. 'Listen to me, Ava. I know I have handled things badly. I know you are angry and upset and feeling uncertain. But I need you to forgive me for my part in how things turned out. I know it's asking a lot of you and I know I don't deserve it.'

Ava hovered in that dark place between uncertainty and hope. She looked into his unfathomable eyes and wondered if he was backing down because of the possibility of her being pregnant. He was an only child. He had no living heir. How convenient would it be for him to pretend to have feelings for a woman he had mistreated in the past just because she could be carrying his child? It seemed a little too coincidental that on the very day a pregnancy was suspected he came with apology in hand. 'I need some time to process this,' she said, once again pulling out of his hold.

His jaw worked for a moment as if he was fighting to keep in control. 'If you are pregnant I insist we marry immediately.'

Ava felt her mouth fall open. 'Pardon?'

He gave her a trenchant look. 'I do not want any child of mine to be called a bastard.'

'For your information it won't make much of a difference,' she shot back.

'I mean it, Ava,' he said. 'I will not be shut out of my child's life.'

'You said you never wanted a child.'

'That was before.'

She arched her brows. 'Oh? So what has changed?'

'Things are different now. Everything is different.'

Ava was not ready to capitulate so readily. 'I don't want to rush into anything. You weren't prepared to marry me before. Why should I accept a proposal that has been forced out of you by circumstances instead of out of genuine desire?'

'I will not be shunted to one side,' he said through gritted teeth. 'Don't mess with me, Ava. I will take the child off you if I need to. You wouldn't stand a chance in court, not with the way the Press has savaged your reputation over the years.'

Ava realised with a sickening jolt he was right. Taking on an opponent such as Marc was asking for a very public, very humiliating defeat. She had thought she still loved him, but right at that moment her hatred of him was immeasurable. It pulsed through her like a raging tide, sweeping away every poignant memory, every precious moment they had spent together.

It was war and he was determined to win, but she was not going down without a valiant fight.

She lifted her chin and aimed her knockdown punch where she knew it would hurt the most. 'You seem pretty convinced the baby I might be expecting is yours. Isn't that a little presumptuous of you under the circumstances?'

A lightning-fast zig-zag of anger lit his gaze as her words hit their target. It was a long moment before he spoke, the stretching silence so weighted Ava felt it pressing down on her chest like a concrete hand.

'I suppose I deserve that,' he said heavily. 'But I will not insult you by requesting a paternity test.'

Ava's mouth fell open again. 'You…you won't?'

He shook his head. 'Knowing what I know about you now, I have no reason to believe the child is anyone's but mine.'

Ava narrowed her eyes. 'Is that because you've had me tailed for weeks on end or because you genuinely believe I don't sleep around?'

His gaze remained steady on hers. 'Ava, this is not helping anything by bringing up the mistakes of the past. If we are to make a success of our relationship we will both have to let go of bitterness and blame.'

'I don't want to be railroaded into anything without first giving it careful thought,' she said, pulling on a wrap and tying it securely about her waist.

'I will not settle for anything but marriage,' he said with an intransigent set to his features.

She gave him a look of defiance. 'Then you have got a huge task ahead of you, Marc Castellano, because I am not marrying you.'

'Damn it, Ava, if you don't marry me I will ruin your family and your friends, every single one of them,' he said through white-tipped lips. 'Don't think I won't do it to get what I want.'

Ava felt the cold, hard determination of his words freeze her to the spot. Her heart beat sickeningly, each beat like a blow to her chest. He was ruthless enough to do anything. Hadn't he already proved it? He had forced her into his life as his mistress and now that the stakes had changed he wanted to rewrite the rules. He wanted control, absolute, total control. 'Blackmail is not the way to get a girl to agree to be your wife,' she said in a voice that was not quite steady. 'Anyway, aren't you jumping ahead a little? I might not even be pregnant.'

'It doesn't matter. We will be married regardless.'

'Why the sudden change of heart?' she asked, unable to keep the echo of suspicion out of her tone.

His dark eyes gave her no clue as to what he was thinking, although she could see a flickering nerve at the side of his mouth. 'There are some things I need to do in order to correct the mistakes of the past,' he said. 'Marrying you is one of them.'

Ava let out a breath of disdain. 'I can see why you failed the entrance exam to charm school. That has got to be the most appalling proposal I have ever heard.'

'What do you want me to say, God damn it?' he asked. 'I could wrap it up in flowery words and phrases but you wouldn't believe it for a second.'

'You're damn right I wouldn't,' she shot back.

He let out a harsh-sounding breath and, turning away from her, shoved a hand through his hair again. When he finally spoke his voice had lowered to a deep burr. 'I will make arrangements for us to marry in London later this month. It will save your sister from having to travel.'

'You can make all the arrangements you like, but it's not going to make me say yes,' Ava said with a furious scowl.

His eyes met hers across the room. 'You might want to have a rethink about that, *ma belle*,' he said. He came back to where she was standing and lifted her chin with two of his fingers, his voice lowering to a silky drawl. 'Don't fight battles you have no hope of winning.'

'You can't make me love you,' Ava bit out petulantly.

His gaze devoured hers as the silence lengthened, moment by moment, heartbeat by heartbeat. 'That is not a requirement of this arrangement,' he said, dropping his hand from her face.

'You're prepared to marry a woman who *hates* you?' she asked.

He gave her an inscrutable flicker of his lips that could have almost passed for a smile. 'If nothing else it will be a delightful challenge to make you change your mind.'

She pulled her shoulders back and sent him a flinty glare. 'Then you've got one hell of a task ahead of you.'

'I know.' He bent down and planted a hot, hard kiss to her tight mouth. 'I am looking forward to it.'

Ava watched in silence as he left the room, the soft click of the door as it closed, an ominous reminder of what he had promised and how determined he was to achieve it.

# CHAPTER NINE

WHEN Ava came downstairs the next morning Marc was on his way up carrying a tray with tea and toast, and a folded newspaper under his arm.

'Why are you out of bed?' he asked. 'It's only just seven.'

Ava eyed him suspiciously. 'I'm not an invalid and I always get up early.'

'I know, but you deserve breakfast in bed, surely?' he said.

She folded her arms. 'Why do I get the feeling this is all part of a scheme to get me to agree to your plans?'

'Why do I get the feeling you are fighting me just to prove a point?' he returned.

Ava blew out a breath and continued on her way downstairs. 'I'm not hungry.'

'You have to eat, Ava,' he insisted as he followed her down. 'You've got to think of the baby.'

She swung around at the foot of the stairs and glared at him. 'There probably isn't a baby. Then what will you do? Retract your proposal?'

He put the tray down on the hall table and handed

her the newspaper. 'It's a bit late for that,' he said. 'I've already released a Press statement.'

Ava stared down at the section he had folded the paper to. Her heart knocked against her rib cage as the words leapt off the page at her: *'Grieving widow to wed Italian construction tycoon.'*

She thrust the paper to his mid-section, taking some measure of satisfaction in the little grunt he gave as her hand connected with his abdomen. 'Then you'll have to retract it because I am not marrying you.'

'Damn it, Ava, you have to marry me.'

'Why?' she asked with a hand on one hip. 'Because otherwise you're going to ruin my family and every other person I know and love? I don't think so, Marc. You might be a bastard at times, but you're not that big a bastard. In any case, I am tired of being a pawn in rich men's games. If you want me to marry you then you will have to do it the old-fashioned way.'

Marc ground his teeth together in frustration. 'What would it take to get you to change your mind?'

She rolled her eyes at him. 'You shouldn't have to ask!'

He thrust his hand through his hair, leaving it messier than it had been before. 'Ava.' He cleared his throat and began again. 'I know I should have probably told you this before, but I had a miserable childhood. I know it's more or less fashionable these days to claim you've been stuffed up by your parents' behaviour, but in this case it's true.'

Ava felt her stiff stance ease as she watched the play of emotions on his face. She could see how hard it was for him, the bitterness he felt was written all over his face. She could see the pain in his dark eyes, the frown lines on his forehead bringing his brows almost together.

'My parents divorced when I was seven,' he said in a voice she barely recognised as his. 'But for the next three years I watched as my father was repeatedly and publicly humiliated by my mother's behaviour. She seemed to take some sort of perverse pleasure in dangling each of her toy-boy lovers in his face on every access pick-up. I was sickened by it. I was nothing but a pawn in her game. I don't think she had the capacity to love a child, or at least not the way a child deserves to be loved. She loved money and living in the fast lane much more. I was an inconvenience, a hindrance that she couldn't wait to get rid of.'

'Oh, Marc…'

He held up a hand. 'No, let me finish,' he said. He took a ragged breath and continued. 'From the age of ten, when I saw my father drown himself in alcohol after my mother's death, I swore I would not let any woman do to me what had been done to him. In the end he lost everything he had worked so hard for. The business that had been in our family for generations went bust, he owed money everywhere. I had to work three jobs while I was still at school and then four while I was at college to pay off the debt after he died.'

Ava bit her lip until she tasted blood. Her heart ached for the little boy he had been, for the pain and rejection he must have felt, for all he had suffered. How he must have hated her for marrying Douglas. It all made such perfect sense now. She had ruined him just as his mother had done to his father. No wonder he had come looking for revenge. 'Oh, Marc…' she said again.

'I know I should have told you this before,' he said. 'I should have told you before I set you up in that apartment in London. I know you wanted more and God knows you certainly deserved more. If I could rewrite the past I would do it, but I can't.'

'It's all right,' she said softly. 'I understand.'

He gave her a weary look. 'I'm not a good bet, Ava, but I can promise to take care of you and the baby. You have my word on that. You will not want for anything as long as I am alive.'

Ava didn't like to tell him that what she wanted most could not be bought with money. It was enough that he had shared this small part of his heart with her. He had revealed his past in a way he had never done before.

She stepped back to him and placed her arms around his waist. 'Thank you for telling me,' she said, looking up into his eyes. 'I am so sorry you had such a hard time as a child. No child deserves that sort of pain. No ex should hate their partner more than they love their child.'

His hands slipped around her back and pressed her closer. 'Are you still dead set against breakfast in bed?' he asked with a hint of a smile.

'I hope the toast hasn't gone soggy.'

He scooped her up in his arms. 'Let's go see, shall we?'

Ava woke from a blissful sleep an hour or so later. Marc was lying on his side, watching her. She reached out and touched him to make sure she wasn't dreaming. His flesh was warm and hard and her heart squeezed as she thought of how he had pleasured her earlier.

He touched her face lightly. 'You have a linen crease, right there,' he said.

Ava felt it with her fingers and grimaced. 'I must look a fright. I need a shower.'

His eyes darkened as he held her gaze. 'Why not join me?'

Ava felt the delicious thrill of anticipation trickle through her as he led her into the *en suite*. He set the water temperature and stepped in, taking her with him. His arms went around her, holding her against his growing erection. She relished the surge of his blood against her, her body quivering as he bent his head to hers.

The cascading water added a sensual element to the kiss. He cupped her face in his hands, his mouth exploring hers in exquisite detail, his tongue playing with hers, making it dance around his with excitement as her passion rose.

His hands moved down from her face to cup her breasts, his thumbs teasing each of her nipples before he bent his mouth to each one in turn. Ava leaned back against the marble wall, a river of delight running through her body as his lips and tongue worked on her sensitive flesh. Her feminine core pulsed with longing, her legs barely able to keep her upright as Marc's mouth slowly but surely travelled via her shoulders and neck before taking her mouth under his again. This time the kiss had more urgency in it. She felt the hard probe of his body nudging her and she opened her thighs, sighing with bliss as he teased her at her moist entrance.

She became brazen with him, reaching down and touching him, circling him with her hand, rubbing and stroking while she was swallowing each of his groans.

He pulled away from her mouth, looking down at her with glittering eyes so black with desire her insides twitched with heady excitement. 'Turn around,' he commanded.

Ava felt another thrilling wave of anticipation course through her as she turned her back to him. She shuddered when his hands gripped her by the waist, the feel of him behind her, so hard, so engorged, so powerful and so ready, made her shiver all over.

The difference in their heights was no barrier. Ava lifted herself on tiptoe as he bent his long strong legs, thrusting into her with such slick force she gasped out loud. 'Tell me if I'm going too fast for you,' he said in a gruff, passion-filled voice.

'You feel amazing,' she breathed.

'God, so do you,' he said, nuzzling at her neck. 'I love feeling you like this. I can feel every part of you holding on to me.'

Ava rocked back against him, anchoring herself against the marble wall of the shower, giving herself up to the powerful sensation of having him move within her. He upped his pace, the deep, thrusting motion making her flesh tingle all over. Her breathing became ragged as the tension grew inside her, her heart beating faster and faster. It was so incredibly intimate feeling him like this, her bottom pressed up against his lower abdomen, her feminine folds swollen and super-sensitive as he drove into her, time and time again. Every nerve-ending was screaming for release, every part of her seemed to be marshalling for that final plunge into paradise.

Marc seemed to be fighting his own battle to maintain control. Ava knew he was close to bursting, she could hear it in his breathing and she could feel it in the urgency of his thrusts as the water poured down over their rocking bodies.

Ava suddenly felt the trigger go on her control. It caught her by surprise, sending her into a cataclysmic roller-coaster ride of sensation. Her nerves felt as if they had exploded with feeling, each and every one of them vibrating like the strings of a violin played by a master. It went on and on, making her feel as if she had shattered into a thousand pieces and would never be the same again.

She was still breathless in the aftermath when she felt Marc prepare to come. He thrust harder and harder, his deep groans sounding so sexy she knew she would live with this erotic fantasy in her head for the rest of her life. She felt him burst with release, the pumping action of his body sending her flesh into a shiver of rapturous delight.

He held her against him as his breathing steadied, the water washing away his seed from her body. Ava wondered if he realised he hadn't used a condom, but thought against mentioning it. She didn't want to spoil the intimacy of the moment. She had never felt so close to him and yet he had still not mentioned anything about his feelings for her. She didn't want to repeat the mistakes of the past and hound him for assurances, even though she desperately wanted them.

He turned her around and kissed her mouth, softly

and lingeringly, his hands moving up and down her body in a caress that was as fluid as the water coursing down upon them.

After a while he reached past her and turned off the shower. He didn't speak; he just picked up a towel and began to dry her as one would do to a small child. Ava gave herself up to his ministrations, enjoying the tenderness after the mind-blowing passion they had shared.

Their eyes met.

Ava tried to keep her emotions in check. She didn't want to appear needy or clingy. That would be the ultimate turn-off for him. She affected a casual demeanour, keeping her voice light and carefree. 'What are your plans for the day? I thought I might go to the gym and then do some reading for the course I'm planning to do.'

He reached for another towel and roughly dried himself before tying it around his hips. 'I have some bookwork to pore over,' he said, watching her closely. 'And I have a wedding to plan. Why don't you give your sister a call and tell her the news before she reads about it in the papers?'

Ava kept her face impassive. 'I thought I'd wait until we hear from the doctor. No point rushing into things.'

He held her gaze for a throbbing pause. 'You are determined to make me beg, aren't you?'

'You don't strike me as the type to beg for anything, Marc,' she said, reaching for a bathrobe.

He blew out a breath as he followed her into the bedroom. 'What do you want from me? I've offered to marry you. That's what you always wanted, wasn't it?'

Ava rolled her eyes before she faced him. 'I am not

going to be browbeaten into a loveless marriage. I've already had one of those, remember?'

The phone rang at the bedside and Marc snatched it up impatiently. 'Marc Castellano,' he clipped out.

'It's your sister,' he said, handing it over.

Ava took the phone, watching as Marc grabbed at some clothes before he left. 'Serena...' she said. 'I...I was going to call you.'

'It's OK,' Serena said. 'I know things must be a little crazy for you right now. Marc sounded a bit curt just then. Is everything all right?'

Ava felt tears sting at her eyes, but valiantly fought them back. 'I suppose you read the news. He wants us to get married.'

'That's a good thing, isn't it?' Serena asked. 'I mean, you still love him, don't you?'

Ava bit her lip and took a deep breath before she answered. 'That's the problem. I love him but he doesn't love me.'

'How do you know he doesn't?' Serena asked. 'Has he said something to the contrary?'

'No, it's just our relationship has always been about... about other things,' Ava said, trying not to think about what had just happened in the shower. 'He's only offering to marry me now because...' She stopped, wondering how she could frame it to somehow lessen the blow.

'Is there a possibility you could be pregnant?' Serena got in first.

Ava let out a sigh that shook its way through her chest. 'I'm not sure... I've had a blood test.... I'm waiting for the doctor to call with the results.'

There was a little silence.

Ava could imagine how her sister was feeling. She could imagine the ambiguity of feeling joy and envy for someone you loved, wanting something so much that it hurt to hear of others succeeding where you had failed.

'Ava, I am so excited for you,' Serena said.

'You are?'

'But of course, silly,' Serena assured her. 'What, did you think that I would be upset or jealous or something?'

'Well, the thought had crossed my mind…'

'Ava, you've done so much for me, it's about time something went right for you for a change,' Serena said. She waited a beat before adding, 'Richard and I have decided to have a break from IVF. We are so grateful for all you've done to help us financially, but Richard feels uncomfortable taking any more money off you.'

'But darling, you can't stop trying,' Ava said. 'You'll get pregnant again. I'm sure of it.'

'I am hopeful of it, but right now I think Richard is right,' Serena said. 'We've spent our whole marriage focusing on me becoming pregnant. It's put us under enormous pressure, both emotionally and, of course, financially. We want to pay you back. I'm going to get a job and in a couple of years we're going to try again. I'm not like other women, who have their age against them.'

'Are you sure about this?' Ava asked. 'The money's not an issue. Marc has given me—'

'I don't want you to sacrifice yourself for me any longer,' Serena said adamantly. 'I feel worried that you might not be telling me the truth about your relationship with Marc. It's just the sort of thing you would do, like you did with Douglas. You made me believe you were happy about the arrangement and I guess because I wanted to believe it I went along with it. But no more, Ava. I want you to be genuinely happy. No one deserves it more than you.'

Ava blinked back tears. 'I don't know what to say…'

'How does Marc feel about the possibility of a baby?'

Ava gave another sigh. 'It's been a difficult time for both of us. It wasn't what either of us expected.'

'Is there anything I can do? What about coming over to stay for a while? If you are pregnant we could go shopping for baby things. It would be fun. It's just what I need to stop thinking about my own stuff.'

Ava chewed at her lip. Maybe some time with her sister would be a good idea right now. She couldn't think with Marc around her, tempting her into marrying him for all the wrong reasons. The more time she spent with him the harder it was to say no. 'It does sound nice…'

'I'm sure Marc will agree,' Serena said. 'Anyway, you have to buy a wedding dress. I can help you. It will be much more fun this time around.'

Ava didn't have the heart to tell her sister she couldn't bear the thought of another white wedding. Instead she promised to call as soon as she had heard from the doctor and rang off.

The phone had hardly been back on the cradle when it rang again. Ava stared at the number in the call-ID screen, recognising it as a local one. She picked it up and answered, her stomach folding over when she heard the doctor's voice.

'The results of your test were negative,' he said after

greeting her by name. 'But you do, however, have a slightly lower than normal blood count, which would account for the symptoms you are experiencing. I suggest you take an iron supplement for a few weeks, that way if you do plan a pregnancy you will be in much better health to carry it to term.'

Ava hung up the phone a short time later, her thoughts whirling. Disappointment sliced through her; she hadn't realised how much she had hoped for a positive result until now. She put her hand on her belly, an ache of longing filling her until she felt as if she wanted to curl up and howl.

The door opened and she looked up to see Marc standing there with a questioning look on his face. 'Was that the doctor?' he asked. 'I was outside and couldn't get to the phone in time.'

Ava fought back her emotions with an effort. 'Yes, it was.'

'And?'

She searched his face, wondering if he would be able to disguise his relief when she told him.

'Ava?' he prompted. 'What did he say?'

She took a little breath. 'He said I'm anaemic. I have to take a supplement.'

The air seemed to be sucked out of the room as the silence lengthened.

'So you're not pregnant?' he asked, his expression still giving nothing away.

She shook her head. 'No.'

'Could it be a mistake?' he asked. 'What if they got someone else's results? It happens sometimes. People's names and birthdates are similar, so—'

'Marc, I am not pregnant, OK? You're in the clear. There's not going to be a baby.'

He slowly let out the breath he had been holding. 'How do you feel about it?' he asked.

She frowned at him. 'How do you expect me to feel?'

'I don't know,' he said. 'I thought your greatest desire was to have a baby.'

'Under the right circumstances, yes—but not like this.' She turned away and began to leave the room.

'Where are you going?' he asked.

She turned and faced him with a challenging look. 'I'm going to pack.'

His brows snapped together. 'Pack for where?'

She lifted her chin. 'I'm going to stay with my sister. I want some time, Marc. You can't stop me from going.'

'Aren't you forgetting something?' A hard look came into his eyes.

Ava's hand gripped the doorknob. 'I don't need your money, Marc. Serena's not having any more IVF for a while.'

'What about the debts Cole left behind?'

She gave him stare for stare. 'I don't care about the debts. If you want to take me to court then fine, go right ahead. I'll find some way of dealing with it. I just want some time to think about my life, about where I go from here.'

Marc kept his hands clenched by his sides as he fought the desire to reach for her. He knew he had to tread carefully. So much was riding on how he responded. He had to fight every urge to force her to stay with him. Threats came to mind, horrible threats he would never, ever act on, but he left them unspoken. He didn't want her to hate him any more than she already did. Although for a time there he had wondered… He gave himself a get-a-grip shake. She only responded to him because sex was the language he had always spoken with her. He had to take it out of the equation, to see if there was anything else they could build a relationship on. It would be hard, it would be painful, it would tear him in two to let her go, but he would have to do it, to make sure if she came back it was what she wanted, not just something she had no choice in.

It was unfamiliar territory for him to feel so utterly, so helplessly vulnerable. 'I'll give you a month,' he said, stripping his voice of any hint of what he was feeling. 'But that is all. One month, no contact other than by phone or e-mail—then you can't accuse me of trying to coerce you into it.'

She seemed to consider it for a moment. 'A month…' Her tongue sneaked out to moisten her lips. 'O…K…and…and after that?'

'After that if you don't want to continue our relationship you will be free,' he said. 'I will not force you to marry me. You will never have to see or hear from me again.'

# CHAPTER TEN

'Ava, that's the third morning in a row you've been sick,' Serena said. 'Are those iron pills you've been taking disagreeing with you?'

Ava wiped her face with the hand towel her sister had handed her. 'God, I feel so ghastly.' She clutched at the basin as another wave of nausea hit her.

'You know, if it hadn't been for the fact you haven't been anywhere near Marc for the last month, I would swear you were pregnant,' Serena said, handing her a face cloth. 'Maybe you should do another test. Perhaps the blood test was wrong.'

'Blood tests are supposed to be far more reliable than any other test,' Ava said as she mopped her face and waited for the sickness to ease off.

How could she be ill on the very day she was supposed to meet Marc? She had wanted to look and feel her best. She had missed him so much; she had counted the hours until she would see him face to face again. He had phoned her a couple of times a week, but she had found it hard to talk to him. He seemed aloof, distant, as if he was already moving on without her. She had read every paper and gossip magazine, but there had been no sign of him out and about with anyone else. She took some measure of comfort in that, but it wasn't much. Maybe he was waiting until the month was up to get back to his playboy lifestyle.

'I know this is a very personal question, but did you happen to have unprotected sex with Marc since the blood test was taken?' Serena asked.

Ava met her sister's eyes in the mirror above the basin. She swallowed, and then, as if drawn there by a magnet, her eyes went to the shower stall. It was nothing like the luxurious one at the villa in Monte Carlo. For one thing there were tiles instead of Italian marble, and the water had a tendency to gush hot and cold unexpectedly, but each time she had stepped into the cubicle she had thought of Marc and that passionate interlude.

'Ava?'

Ava gave herself a mental shake and focused back on Serena's questioning gaze. 'Do you have any left-over pregnancy tests?' she asked.

Serena opened a cupboard with a flourish. 'Take your pick. I have eight different brands.'

Ava took the first one her hand touched. 'This is probably going to be negative. I'm on the Pill, for God's sake.'

'Yes, but only a low-dose one,' Serena reminded her, 'and they are not one hundred per cent reliable.'

Ava bit her lip. 'Give me a minute, OK?'

Serena smiled and, blowing her a kiss, closed the bathroom door.

* * *

Ava opened the bathroom door a few minutes later. 'You're not going to believe this…' she said, clutching the dipstick in her hand.

Serena squealed and began to jump up and down in excitement. 'Oh, my God!'

Ava bit her lip, torn between wanting to laugh and wanting to cry. 'I'm supposed to be meeting Marc tonight for dinner. Tonight's the big night. I'm supposed to give him my answer.'

'Honey, you didn't need to do a pregnancy test to confirm you're going to go back to him,' Serena said. 'I've known what your decision was from the moment you stepped in the door a month ago. Richard saw it too.'

Ava grimaced sheepishly. 'Was I that obvious?'

Serena smiled. 'Dreadfully, tragically, just like in the movies. It's a wonder Marc couldn't see it for himself.'

Ava sighed as she rested her hand on her belly. 'I miss him so much. I can't believe I went five years without seeing him. How on earth did I survive that?'

Serena wrapped her arms around Ava and hugged her tightly. 'I wish the last five years hadn't happened. I will always feel guilty about that. You gave up so much for me. I can never repay you.'

Ava returned her sister's embrace. In the four weeks she had been in London she had noticed a difference in Serena. Sometimes Ava felt like the younger sister. Serena had become protective of her, instead of the other way around. 'You don't owe me anything,' she said. 'Anyway, it's time to put it behind and move forwards. The past belonged to others, the future belongs to me.'

\* \* \*

The hotel they had arranged to meet at was where they had first met. Ava wondered if Marc had chosen it deliberately or whether it was just a coincidence, or even a matter of convenience. She knew he stayed at that particular hotel a great deal, as it was close to his office tower. He had been photographed numerous times over the years with other women in the same bar.

She took a deep breath and walked towards the bar, her heart beating way too hard and too fast as she searched for him amongst the other people gathered there. The pianist was playing a romantic melody, one that made Ava feel as if she was travelling back in time. But this time it was different. There was no tall figure leaning indolently against the bar, no dark, unreadable eyes meeting hers across the clot of other drinkers.

Ava felt her stomach sink in panic. He hadn't come. He had forgotten… No, he had decided he didn't want her any more. He had found someone else, a glamorous new lover who didn't want kids and commitment.

She glanced at her watch. She was late, not early. Was this his final revenge? To leave her dangling as she had done to him all that time ago?

Her teeth sank into her bottom lip, her eyes sweeping the bar again and again. Her panic turned to despair. She felt as if she was going to cry. Tears gathered and threatened to spill, and her chest ached with the effort of holding herself together.

'Ava.'

She spun around at the sound of that deep, unmistakable, mellifluous voice. 'Marc…' Her voice came out on a croak. 'I thought….' She blinked a couple of times. 'I thought…' She swallowed and just stood staring up at him.

Marc took her hands in his. 'Sorry I was late. I got stuck with a phone call.' He bent and pressed a light kiss to each of her cheeks. 'You look very beautiful.'

Her lips fluttered with a nervous-looking smile. 'So…how are you?'

He tried to smile back but it felt false. His chest was pounding and his skin had broken out in a sweat as if he were on his first date. 'I'm good, and you?'

'Er—fine…good…really good.' Her gaze fell away from his.

Marc felt a tight hand around his heart. He was losing her. She could barely look at him. 'So…you're not anaemic any more?' he asked.

'Er—no,' she said, blushing like a rose.

A silence swirled around them.

'Would you like to have a drink in the bar?' Marc asked, wishing the bar weren't so crowded, wishing he had thought to meet her somewhere else, somewhere more private. But he had hoped to recreate that moment when they had first met. It was a rather pathetic attempt to rewrite the past. There was no way either of them could do that, least of all him.

She shook her head and slowly raised her eyes to his. 'Could we go somewhere a little more private?'

'Sure.' He pulled out his room key, hoping she didn't notice how his hand was shaking. 'I have a permanent suite here, so we can go upstairs.'

Marc could see how uncomfortable she was with

him. He tried to compose himself, but it was so hard
with her within touching distance. He could smell her
perfume, that alluring fragrance of summer flowers that
had haunted him for the past month, let alone the past
five years.

He had found the last month unbearable. It had
brought home to him how much he needed her. He had
restricted his contact to twice-weekly phone calls to
keep from begging her to come back to him then and
there. The dreadful thought of never seeing her again,
or—worse—seeing her with someone else had eaten
away at him until he had nearly gone mad. He had barely
slept; he had barely been able to function in order to get
through each day. And then there was the disappointment about the pregnancy. He was still struggling to
overcome that blow. How had his feelings changed so
swiftly? Now all he could think about was a little baby,
a dark-haired boy who looked like him or an adorable
blonde little girl, the image of her mother. He looked at
Ava again, his heart contracting at the sight of her
standing there, chewing on her lip as if she couldn't wait
for this to be over.

The doors of the lift opened and Marc led her to his
penthouse. She moved past him in the doorway, her
slight frame brushing up against him, setting every
nerve on edge. 'Can I get you a drink?' he asked.

'Marc, there's something I have to tell you…' she
began.

'No,' he said, closing the door behind him. 'Let me
go first. Please, I need to say this. I've been rehearsing
it for the past month.'

She looked a little uncertain. 'O…K…'

He came over and took her hands in his again, his thumbs stroking the backs of her fingers gently. 'Firstly, I have to tell you something that I think will be quite upsetting to you.'

He saw the flicker of panic in her grey-blue eyes and the tip of her tongue as it darted out to sweep over her lips. 'Go on…'

'Your sister didn't make any mistakes in the book-work,' he said. 'That was a set-up by Cole and very cleverly hidden by Hugh Watterson. Cole wanted the Dubai account and he conjured up a scheme to make sure he got it. He knew about our relationship from various articles in the Press. Serena was on his staff, so it was too good an opportunity to miss. When you broke off our relationship he made his move. By blackmailing you into marriage he won over the vendor's confidence. He had the money to splash around on a young, beautiful wife who had chosen him over me. I didn't stand a chance in the vendor's eyes. I wasn't even in the same ball park.'

She closed her eyes as she took in the information. He could feel the tension in her hands as she held on to him. She opened her eyes again and looked at him. 'So…so I never needed to marry him?' she asked in a choked whisper.

Marc shook his head. 'I'm sorry. I know that's no-where near good enough to make up for what you went through, but I am so deeply sorry for not coming after you when you left. I will never forgive myself for that. I let you down in the most unforgivable way.'

She pulled out of his hold, hugging her arms around her middle, her expression contorted with bewilder-

ment as she began to pace the floor. 'I can't believe it…
How can people be so cruel? He never once told me.
He could have told me before he died. He *should* have
told me. Serena had a right to know. For God's sake, *I*
had a right to know.'

'Maybe he was frightened if he told you, you would
leave him to die alone,' Marc said. 'God knows, it was
what he deserved.'

'He set me up.' She looked at him again. 'He set you
up too and made you hate me.' Her face crumpled then,
tears sprouting in her eyes. 'That was the worst part.
Knowing you hated me so much.'

Marc felt emotion clog his throat. 'I don't hate you,
Ava.'

She blinked again as if his words hadn't quite registered. 'You…you don't?'

He shook his head. 'Why do you think I came after
you and forced you into a relationship with me?'

She pressed her lips together, thinking about it for a
moment. 'I thought you wanted revenge…'

He came over to where she was standing, unpeeling
her arms from around her waist so he could hold her in
the circle of his arms. 'I thought so too,' he said with a
rueful look. 'I convinced myself I was intent on making
you pay for what I thought you had done. But looking
back now, I realise what I was really doing was giving
myself another opportunity to start over with you. I
wanted to make you fall in love with me the way I had
fallen in love with you five years ago.'

Ava had to shake her head to make sure she wasn't

misinterpreting what she had just heard. 'You were in love with me? The whole time you were in love with me?'

'I know this sounds crazy, but I didn't realise how much I loved you until I thought I was going to lose you the second time,' he said. And, wincing, added, 'Go on, say it. Tell me it's too late, that you're well and truly over me. I can take it. I've been preparing myself for it for the last four weeks. It's no more than I deserve.'

Ava felt a smile slowly spread across her face. 'You think that's what I'm going to say?'

He made an effort to look as if it didn't matter, but this time she could see through it. She saw the way his throat constricted as he tried to disguise a swallow, and the way a little nerve pulsed at the side of his mouth. His eyes too had become dark and glistened with the suspicion of moisture. 'I can take it, Ava,' he said. 'You don't need to wrap it up to soften the blow. I didn't exactly treat you with any consideration for your feelings.'

'I love you, Marc,' she said, trying not to cry. 'I have never stopped loving you... Well, maybe for a week or two here and there.'

He tightened his hold, his eyes dark and intent upon hers. 'You're not just saying that, are you? I'm not going to do anything about the debts Cole left behind. I would never have held you to account for those. I just had to find a way to keep you with me.'

'Oh, Marc,' she said, hugging him tightly. 'Why have we wasted so much precious time?'

He buried his head in her hair. 'Don't let's waste

another minute. Let's get married as soon as we can and then we can start on trying for a baby. I was so disappointed when that test came back negative. Besides the fact it left me with no bargaining tool to keep you with me, I got to thinking about what it would be like to have a child. Everywhere I looked I saw young couples with a baby or a little child. It seemed so right all of a sudden.' He held her from him to look at her. 'What do you say? Do you feel ready to have a baby with me?'

Ava felt her heart swell inside her chest. 'You want a baby?'

He gripped her even tighter. 'Think about it, Ava, a baby who looks like both of us. A little person who will grow up with so much love they will have the best start in life possible. We won't make the mistakes our parents made. I will make sure of it.'

'Oh, Marc,' she said almost unable to speak for the wave of love that encompassed her. 'I have the best news for you. You won't believe it—I can barely believe it myself.'

'Try me.'

She nestled against him. 'Remember the shower?'

He gave her a smouldering look. 'How could I forget? I've relived that in my head every day for the past month.'

'Well, you did more than share a shower with me,' she said. 'You left a memento.'

A light came on in his eyes. 'Are you serious? You're pregnant? Really?'

She smiled. 'Are you pleased with yourself?'

He grinned back at her. 'Yeah, pretty much. So I guess this means you're not going to say no to marrying me.'

Ava threw her arms around his neck. 'I wouldn't dream of it,' she said and closed her eyes in bliss as his mouth met hers.

# LET'S TALK
## *Romance*

For exclusive extracts, competitions
and special offers, find us online:

**f** facebook.com/millsandboon

**𝕏** @MillsandBoon

**◎** @MillsandBoonUK

**Get in touch on 01413 063232**

For all the latest titles coming soon, visit
**millsandboon.co.uk/nextmonth**

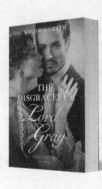

# MILLS & BOON

## THE HEART OF ROMANCE

## A ROMANCE FOR EVERY KIND OF READER

### MODERN

Prepare to be swept off your feet by sophisticated, sexy and seductive heroes, in some of the world's most glamourous and romantic locations, where power and passion collide.
**8 stories per month.**

### HISTORICAL

Escape with historical heroes from time gone by. Whether your passion is for wicked Regency Rakes, muscled Vikings or rugged Highlanders, awaken the romance of the past.
**6 stories per month.**

### MEDICAL

Set your pulse racing with dedicated, delectable doctors in the high-pressure world of medicine, where emotions run high and passion, comfort and love are the best medicine.
**6 stories per month.**

### True Love

Celebrate true love with tender stories of heartfelt romance, from the rush of falling in love to the joy a new baby can bring, and a focus on the emotional heart of a relationship.
**8 stories per month.**

### Desire

Indulge in secrets and scandal, intense drama and plenty of sizzling hot action with powerful and passionate heroes who have it all: wealth, status, good looks…everything but the right woman.
**6 stories per month.**

### HEROES

Experience all the excitement of a gripping thriller, with an intense romance at its heart. Resourceful, true-to-life women and strong, fearless men face danger and desire - a killer combination!
**8 stories per month.**

### DARE

Sensual love stories featuring smart, sassy heroines you'd want as a best friend, and compelling intense heroes who are worthy of them.
**4 stories per month.**

To see which titles are coming soon, please visit

## millsandboon.co.uk/nextmonth